SHAMELESS

Lust. Destruction. Love. Murder.

NEW YORK TIMES BESTSELLING AUTHOR

LISA RENEE JONES

Book 2 of the WHITE LIES Duet

ISBN: 9781635761610

www.lisareneejones.com

Dear Reader:

As always, thank you from the bottom of my heart for picking up a book of mine. But you're not here for me to wax poetic about what fantastic readers I have (it's true though!), you're here to see what happens between Faith and Tiger! So first off, I *think* this goes without saying, but if you haven't read book one in the White Lies Duet, PROVOCATIVE, stop here and go read it, because that's how this story begins. For those of you who have, I'm going to give a brief recap of book one for a refresher.

We met Nick "Tiger" Rogers, a badass attorney, as he was tracking down the woman he thought killed his father, and even her own mother. What Nick wasn't expecting to find when he cornered Faith Winter, the now owner and operator of her family's Reid Winter Winery, was a woman who would lay him out on his ass with her wit, charm, and his need to have her, fuck her, possess her. Then there's Faith, on the heels of her father's death two years ago she had to put a hold on her passion as an artist and come back to help her mother run the family winery, though her mother ran it into the ground, refusing to relinquish control to Faith so she could save it.

When Nick and Faith share one night of passion together, it's out of the ordinary for them both to let it go any further. Faith has been burned from a past relationship, an artist named Macom, who was a selfish and sabotaging asshole, those hang-ups of hers lead to hang-ups between her and Nick. She pushes him, he pushes back, alpha-style. And despite the secrets he's holding back, he continues to push, because he knows this woman is it for him. But his secrets are many: his father and her mother's murders, which he originally thought Faith to be the culprit of, but soon discounts that idea, and the sex club he owns, which he is sure will spook Faith based on her past reactions to his need for control, even though their bedroom time has gotten quite un-vanilla a time or two. Spanking scene, anyone? That one was an intense one to write! But while Nick battles with finding the truth, Faith finds her own truth. Amidst the monetary troubles at the winery, with the note past due, and the vendors unpaid from her mother's unknown antics, Nick has become the only person to inspire her to paint after a long drought. And those paintings, have made her eligible to delve back into the art world that she ran away from because of Macom. Though at the helm of pushing her back in the deep end in the most unhelpful ways is Josh, her agent, a sloppy one at that, who just so happens to also be Macom's agent. But she has been pulled right back into that world, just as Nick is pushing her to fall right into a relationship with him. It's overwhelming, exhilarating, and scary, but she takes the plunge. Her father never believed in her art, and wanted her to just take over the winery, but she is doing things for herself. But with every piece of herself she gives to Nick and her art again, Nick pushes for more of her. He wants to help her get the winery out of trouble, and spend more time with him.

Through this all Faith has been selected to be showcased at Chris and Sara Merit's gallery Allure, and also in the L.A. Art Forum. Two very high-profile opportunities, that she can credit to Nick's presence in helping her paint again. All the while Nick has people (his friend Abel, and he PI Beck) working his father's and her mother's murders and finding out why the winery was hemorrhaging money when it is a profitable business. To force the hand of the bank that holds the note on the winery, Nick pays the past due amount and six months ahead of schedule to take the pressure off of Faith and see if that alleviates the threat to them both, but that creates once more secret and one more push from him that may send Faith over the edge.

Provocative, comes to a conclusion right after the exclusive event at the gallery, where Sara and Faith hit it off as good friends, Chris sells 3 of Faith's paintings (proving she can make a living with her passion), and Chris and Nick having words over Nick's failure to mention the sex club to Faith. It's a tumultuous end to say the least, but then Nick's father seemingly reached out from his grave with a note he left in his belongings that reads: *Faith Winter is the problem. She's dangerous. Far more than her mother. She must be stopped.*

And after that ominous note is where we pick back up. Nick has his secrets. Faith has her doubts. But they have an intensely passionate affair going on that may shatter and break when all is revealed...

Enjoy!

xoxo,
Lisa Renee Jones

Characters

Faith Winter—30, blonde, green eyes. Heroine of the story. Owner of the Reid Winter Winery in Sonoma. Artist, paints black and white landscapes with bursts of red. Trying to help the winery recover from her mother pulling them under. Nick Rogers comes into the picture wanting her in a way no other an ever has, and making her want things she's never wanted.

Nick "Tiger" Rogers—36, long hair he ties back, navy blue eyes. Hero of the story. Attorney of his own firm. Deceased mother. Deceased father. He and he father had been at odds for years when he passes away. Though his death was suspicious which led Nick to Faith Winter. He thought she may have been a killer, but now she's the woman who possesses his heart and much more. Still keeps many secrets from Faith, but thinks he's doing it for the right reasons.

Meredith Winter—Faith's mother. Died two months ago. Left the winery in shambles. Cheated on her husband numerous times, including with his twin brother.

Reid Winter—Faith's father. Died two years ago. Always wanted Faith to run the winery, never believed in her art. Put up with his wife's wandering ways. Had a falling out with his twin brother when he learned his wife slept with him.

Bill Winter—Faith's uncle. CEO of Pier 111, a social media platform, that his wife founded. Slept with his brother's wife. Had a falling out with his brother right before Faith left for college.

Kasey—50, gray hair, tall. Long time operator and second-hand at the winery for twenty years.

Abel Baldwin—30's, buzzed blond hair. Nick's best friend. Criminal lawyer. Tries to help him find answers through his work connections concerning the autopsy for Nick's dad.

Beck—35, black spiky hair. Ex-CIA. The private investigator Nick hired to find the answers to this twisted web.

Rita—Older, married with children. Red hair. Nick's ever-so-efficient assistant.

Josh—30's, short hair, clean cut. Faith's agent for her art work. Macom's (Faith's ex) agent as well.

Macom Maloy—30's, spiky dark hair. Well-known artist. Faith's ex-boyfriend. All around jackass.

Shameless Playlist

"Black" by Dierks Bentley

"Every Little Thing" by Carly Pearce

"I'm Comin' Over" by Chris Young

"Moonlight Sonata" by Beethoven

"In My Head" by Brantley Gilbert

"Sober Saturday Night" by Chris Young

"Now or Never" by Halsey

"Bad Liar" by Selena Gomez

"Losing Sleep" by Chris Young

"Issues" by Julia Michaels

"Who I Am With You" by Chris Young

Chapter One

Nick

FAITH WINTER IS THE PROBLEM. SHE'S DANGEROUS. FAR *more than her mother. She must be stopped.*

Those are my dead father's words, scribbled on a piece of paper I'd found in his things only minutes ago. Words now burned in my mind, as I stand in the doorway of my bedroom, staring at Faith as she sleeps, moonlight from a nearby window casting her in a soft glow. Her blonde hair draped over my pillow. Her amber and vanilla scent a sweet whisper in the air on my skin. While the words *she's dangerous* repeat in my mind again and again, radiating through me like an electric charge, but not because I trusted my father's opinion about anything. But rather, there is no denying the fact that I did seek Faith out with the opinion that he was murdered, perhaps by her.

And he didn't say she's trouble or a problem or difficult. He said that she's dangerous.

And yet, as seconds tick by, I am riveted by the image of Faith *in my bed*, where I invited her to sleep, and holy fuck, I like her there. I *want* her there, when I never let anyone else in my house, let alone in my bed. I'm obsessed with this woman, and as Faith herself warned yesterday, obsession is dangerous. Some—most—would say fucking a woman you suspect killed her mother and your father is dangerous, but it doesn't seem to matter. I want her. I am crazy about this woman, and maybe that just makes me crazy.

Needing space to clear my head, I walk across the room toward the bathroom, my tie and jacket that I'd worn to tonight's event at the Merit gallery, gone, and I don't even remember removing them. I remember Faith. Her smile as she'd been praised for her art. The way she trembled with the news of her success, when she is not a woman that trembles. Not unless it's with pleasure. And these thoughts are exactly why I stop myself from turning back to her, because what I really want is to be in that bed with her. But, when I'm with her, touching her, kissing her, just fucking holding her, even looking at her in my bed, I am not objective. And yet, knowing this, I reach the doorway, about to escape into the quiet sanctuary of the next room, seconds from the space I need to rein in my thoughts, and fuck me, I find myself pausing in the doorway, facing the bed again.

She stirs suddenly, as if she senses me watching her, a soft, sexy sound slipping from her lips as she shifts from her side to her back, her hand settling on the pillow next to her. She instantly rolls over to where I should be, reaching for me, only to sit up, the sheet falling away, and even in the shadows, I am aware of her naked breasts, her naked body that I know feels so damn good against mine. "Nick?" she calls out, turning in my direction, sensing me here.

And the minute she says my name, her voice is like silk on the sandpaper of my nerves, and I know that if she's dangerous, I'm fucking high on the danger. And if that is what she is, I want that danger on my tongue, in my hands, in my bed.

I rotate and press my hand to the doorframe over my head, shutting my eyes. What the hell am I doing? Either I have a killer in my bed, which I reject as an option, or I have a woman I'm falling in love with who has to hate me for lying to her. *Love.* Damn it to hell, where did that come from? I don't do love. I don't do commitment, and once again, I have to remind myself that you don't prove guilt when you're looking for innocence. And yet, I know this woman is not a killer.

Dangerous, though. That word just won't let go of me. Why the fuck did my father use that word?

"I just finished up some work," I say, lifting my face to the ceiling, lashes lowered. "I'm going to shower and I'll be there in a few minutes." I've no sooner said the words before Faith is not only slipping between me and the wall, my gaze riveted to her moon-kissed naked skin, resting against the doorframe under my hand. My body arches in such a way that she can't easily touch me, and I don't touch her, but I want to, and I don't even remember in this moment, why I resisted doing so before now.

"What's wrong?" she asks.

Aside from the fact that my dead father called you dangerous, I think, or that your stunning, naked breasts should not be in my hands, I need time to think. But since she doesn't know about my father, *can't* know about my father, not yet, I offer her the expected answer of, "Nothing is wrong."

"Liar," she whispers.

"Work is on my mind," I supply, and that's not wholly untrue. I was working on the mystery of two murders when I found that note.

"Liar," she repeats, her tone sharp, some unidentifiable jagged-edged emotions radiating off of her, or maybe I'm wrong. Maybe it's my jagged-edged emotions that are crashing into her and then slamming right back into me.

"I've been watching you sleep," I say, embracing every honest word I can speak to Faith when so much, *too* much, has been lies.

Her eyes open, and even in the shroud of shadows, I feel the punch of her gaze colliding with mine. "That's not an answer," she says. "That's a deflection, and deflection doesn't suit you any more than fear." It's a reference to the night that she'd pulled a knife on me and used it to remove my shirt buttons, and I understand the message: We feel like we did then, uncertain, incomplete in some way.

"I wonder," she continues, pushing off the wall, her hands pressed to my chest, the slight but firm heft of her body weight knocking me backward, against the wall, "if I held a knife in my hand now, if you would trust me to cut the buttons off your shirt, or would you wonder if I would cut you instead?"

I'm not sure if she's daring me to trust her or pushing me to do the opposite. Pushing me away. Pulling me closer. It's all the same with her. With one always comes the other. "We aren't where we were then," I say, but I don't touch her. Once I touch her, I won't stop, though I'm really fucking trying to figure out why the fuck that feels important right now.

"And yet I feel the same now as then," she says, "and so do you. And don't lie again. You know I'm right."

"It's not the same."

"It is. And we are. And that leaves only one of the possibilities you had us proclaim earlier tonight. Me making us both forget all the rest. Whatever the rest actually is, since you won't tell me what's wrong."

Suddenly, she's peeling away her panties, the only garment she'd worn when she'd gone to bed. The next moment, she's kneeling, her hands on my knees, her head tilted down. I know exactly where this is going, and if I intend to keep my head clear, I should stop it now. Only the head on my shoulders isn't the one doing the thinking. Not when Faith's hand strokes the one between my legs that has been hard as a rock since her and all her naked curves slid in front of me. Hell, since practically the moment I met this woman. She tugs my shirt out of my pants and starts unbuttoning it, her gaze reaching mine as she says, "If I only had that knife."

I don't laugh. She doesn't laugh. The edge between us is as jagged as those emotions beating through me and obviously into her. I reach up and undo several buttons on my shirt, just enough to then pull it over my head, tossing it into the bedroom. It's not even hit the ground, and Faith has not only unbuckled my belt, she's pulling it free of my pants.

It hits the floor, and she reaches for my zipper, wasting no time freeing my cock. She grips it, her hold firm and confident. Her eyes boldly finding mine as she licks the end of my erection and then draws it into her mouth, her message clear: Right now, she demands control, a response I strongly believe to be a reaction, to the questions I've allowed to stir between us. She needs to own me right now. And while, I don't let anyone own me, even if they do have their mouth on my cock, I'm oddly at peace with this woman's power. There's a message in that regard, which I'll analyze when I'm not hyper-focused on the silk of her tongue and the sweet suction of her mouth.

And damn, if she's not licking every last inch of me.

And damn, if I'm not at her mercy.

Heat and adrenaline pulse through me, and my hand finds her head, fingers slipping into her hair, but I don't even need to guide her. She's exactly where I need her, *how* I need her. There is something about this woman's mouth, her tongue, that is quite possibly heaven on earth. It's a bliss that I welcome, and yet, suddenly I'm not in this heavenly moment. I'm flashing back to right before she fell asleep. To me helping her undress.

In my mind's eye, I see us standing next to the bed, her in the dress she wore to the Chris and Sara Merit gallery event, me in the same blue suit I have yet to fully remove. She'd just kicked off her shoes, finally coming down from the high of selling her art, her body calming. Me, I'd been reveling in her in my bed, and in our vow that "possibilities" were the new hard rule we'd follow. *"I'm completely wiped out,"* she'd confessed. *"I think you are going to wish I was someone else tonight."*

Those words had jolted me, and I cupped her head and pulled her to me. *"What did you say?"* I'd demanded, but I didn't give her time to reply. *"That came from someplace I'd most likely name as Macom,"* I'd said of her ex, whom I already knew used sex as a weapon against her. *"I'm not him,"* I'd continued. *"And we are more than the sum of how many times we manage to fuck each other. And for the record. To repeat what I've already said. I don't want anyone else."*

Her lashes lowered. *"I think that was possibly the most perfect thing you could say to me right now."*

And in that moment, I'd remembered her comment about Macom competing with her, and I'd decided that Faith thinks her success comes with punishment. A problem I needed to fix. I *need* to fix. I had intentionally put her to bed without touching her. I come back to the present, to her mouth on my cock, pleasure with every stroke, pump, and lick, and I am so damn hard and close to release. I want it. Holy hell, I want it so fucking badly, and I have no doubt that she would take me to absolute completion and rock my world. But this, what we are doing right now, and why we are doing it, is exactly what I *didn't* want tonight to be for her or us.

Suddenly, my orgasm doesn't matter, no matter how close I am to heaven, or sweet Jesus, how damn good it would be. "Faith," I say, and despite my determination and intention to end this, her name comes out a pained near-growl. "Stop." I slip my fingers from her hair, and cup the sides of her head. "Stop, Faith. Sweetheart. Stop." She stills, as if the words and my touch finally penetrate her brain, and pulls her mouth slowly back until it's no longer on my cock. But her hand still grips my erection, and I swear just the idea of removing it is torture.

Confusion flits across her beautiful, desire-laden expression, and I pull her to her feet and to me, my hand at the back of her head. "I've decided that your mouth on my cock is the best thing in this world, outside of my mouth on you while you come for me, and because of me."

"Then why did you stop me?"

"Because you were on your knees for all the wrong reasons, sweetheart. I don't need this to be with you, and that's what you thought, wasn't it?"

"You needed something. You were watching me."

"And wondering how the hell it felt so fucking good just to watch you," I say, relieved to speak the truth, and it is the truth. "Like I said. We are not the sum of how many times or ways we fuck, and that's new territory for me. I'm trying to figure it out."

"I'm trying to figure all this out, too," she confesses.

"Does that mean you like being in my bed?"

"I like many things about you, Nick Rogers, that I didn't expect to like, but yes. I do."

"We'll figure it out together," I promise, scooping her up in my arms, her gorgeous, naked body pressed to mine. She is so tiny, and yet she's seized my world in gigantic proportions, in ways I never thought any woman capable.

I stop at the side of the bed, setting her down on the mattress, and to ensure my control stays firmly intact, I adjust my cock back inside my pants. And I did so, just in time considering, she's now scooted across the bed, and rolled to her side, to prop up on one elbow. Her breasts displayed, the curve of her waist, the rise of her hip, sexy as hell, and I'm hard as nails all over again. I toe-off my shoes and slide into bed with her, pulling the covers over us, and before she can protest, I'm turning her back to my front and pulling her close. And just the feel of her next to me, the sweet amber scent of her, consumes my senses, in every right way. The truth is this woman is everything I've known right in this world.

"Nick," she says softly.

"Yes Faith?"

"Why are you not naked with me?"

"If I do that I'll end up inside you."

"And that's bad why?"

"Because," I say. "Tonight, I really want you to know that I see the beautiful, talented part of you, not just your body."

She gives an insistent tug and twist, rotating to face me, her fingers curling on my chest. "If there is anyone in my life that I believe sees beyond the surface, it's you."

"And yet you thought I was upset because we didn't fuck tonight," I say. "Which means you don't trust me, or us, yet."

"It's not about you," she says, "or us. It's about my own baggage that I wish didn't exist." She touches my cheek. "But whatever the case. I told you. I don't need a knight in shining armor."

"And I told you," I say, "I know that, but the more evident that becomes, the more I seem to want to be that for you. And I don't do the knight routine."

"Well then, if you are going in that direction, and it appears that you are, then you should know that my knight, should I want one, would be inside me right now." She leans in, her lips a breath from mine, her fingers tearing away the tie holding my hair in place, before her fingers are diving into the loose strands. "Be inside me right now, Nick."

She presses her lips to mine, and the minute her tongue touches mine, I need her. I just plain need this woman, and I don't hold back. I kiss her, and touch her, and it is not long before my pants are gone, and I give her what she wants, what I want. I press inside the wet heat of her body, my hand sliding up her back, fingers splayed between her shoulder blades, molding all her soft perfection to every hard part of me.

"Now I'm inside you," I murmur, my lips closing down on hers, my tongue licking against hers, in what becomes a drugging kiss that has nothing to do with fucking, and everything to do with how much this woman is inside me. And I still don't taste murder. I don't taste lies. There is just hunger. Hers. Mine. Ours. And we savor it, and each other, with slow kisses, our bodies moving in a gentle dance. My lips on her shoulder, her nipple, her neck. My hand everywhere I can find skin. But it's when she whispers my name, when she says, "Nick," in that same way she kisses me, like I'm the only way she can take her next breath, that I know *I can't breathe without her.*

I tangle fingers in the silk of her blonde hair and pull her closer, her mouth lingering one of those breaths from mine. "What are you doing to me, woman?" I demand, but I don't give her time to respond. I kiss her, and the instant our tongues collide, there is a shift between us, the hunger turning darker and more demanding, and I drive into her, pulling her against me, her face buried in my neck until she trembles into release. I quickly follow with shuddered finality, but there is nothing final about my desire for this woman.

I hold her close but force myself to release her and walk to the bathroom, returning with a towel I offer her. She's barely slipped it between her legs before I'm behind her, pulling her back into my arms, wrapping my body around hers. Neither of us speak, but I can almost hear her thinking as hard as I'm thinking. I want to clear my conscience and tell her everything, but tonight is about her art. Tonight is about us sharing her life, a life.

Fuck. That's what I want.

I could tell her the truth now, about why I sought her out, with the hope that together we can solve the mystery of our parents' deaths. But not only is this night her night to celebrate her art, and I would never strip that well-deserved joy from her, but she'd push me away before I solve this mystery and save her winery. Before I am certain that she is not in danger, and more exposed without me than with me. And the moment I opened us up to possibilities, I knew, even if she did not, that I wanted her in my life, not just my bed. And the minute I decided she wasn't a killer, I became a liar who needs her to trust me, when her reaction to me tonight says she does not. Not fully, not yet. And somehow, while she exposes herself, while she gives me that trust, and before I reveal the truth, as I must, I have to convince her that just as we are not the sum of how many times or ways we fuck, neither are we the sum of my lies.

Chapter Two

Faith

I WAKE TO THE SOFT GLOW OF A NEW DAY, A BARELY REALIZED sunbeam splaying through the bedroom windows, and the woodsy, wonderful scent of Nick surrounding me, his hard body wrapped around mine, and I don't want to wake up. I shut my eyes again, reliving this weekend in random little pieces, starting with our arrival at his house. His expensive cars in the garage. Me calling him a "rich guy," which he claimed with pride and a declaration of hard work. Boldly himself, and it had stirred both envy and arousal in me.

"*Let's go inside, Faith,*" he'd said.

"*Yes,*" I'd replied. "*Let's go see what a man like you calls home.*"

"*A man like me,*" he'd repeated. "*You can explain that later. Naked.*"

I'd hurried into the house, and once there, I'd took in the stunningly gorgeous house, the pale wooden floors, the high ceilings, layers of beautiful décor and fixtures as complex as the man and all he made me feel. I'd turned to face him. "It's a beautiful house, Nick. It smells like you."

"And how do I smell, Faith?"

"Like control. Like sex. Woodsy and sexy."

"And you, sweetheart, smell like—"

"Amber and vanilla," I'd said, before he could say roses. Or flowers. Because the last thing I wanted to be reminded of that night was the garden at the winery, my mother's garden.

"Yes," he'd confirmed, "you do. And I'm obsessed with your scent. I'm obsessed with you."

"Obsessed," I'd said. "That sounds dangerous."

"It is dangerous."

Dangerous.

I blink with that word, and in contrast to the reaction you'd think that word would evoke, I snuggle a little closer to Nick, my hand on his where it rests on my belly. And yet as I shut my eyes again, that word echoes in my mind, and I don't know why.

Dangerous.

Dangerous.

Dangerous.

Sex is safe. It's just sex. It's just fucking. Or it was with Macom. It was supposed to be with Nick. But now there is a new hard rule: possibilities, and possibilities are dangerous. They expose me in ways I don't know if I want to be exposed. And yet I crave every one I might have with Nick. In other words: *Nick is dangerous.*

Letting him get too close is *dangerous.* Maybe that's what I've been trying to capture in my paintings of him. Nick Rogers is dangerous. He has secrets. He'll discover *my secrets.* He once told me that he wanted to see the woman behind the wall. The real me, stripped bare and not just exposed. *Willingly* exposed. Will I ever be willingly exposed?

Do I dare?

My lashes open, and this time there is a beam of bright sunlight in my eyes, and I no longer feel Nick behind me. Rolling over, I find the space next to me empty. I glance at the clock that reads ten o'clock and suck in air. Oh no. I fell back to sleep and stayed asleep a long time. I sit up, frustrated with myself. I'm supposed to fly home today and I've wasted the little time I have with Nick in bed without him. Tossing aside the covers, I assume he's up, dressed, and busy by now.

I start to get up, and my gaze lands on that card from my father, a knot forming in my chest. What does it say that I want to open it *with Nick* and have him spank me, to deal with the emotional explosion to follow? I wouldn't even tell Macom about that card. Never. Ever. In a million years. And I would not invite him to spank me to deal with it. Sex with Macom was the wall Nick talked about me putting up, a big, thick emotional wall I didn't even recognize until near the end of our relationship. Macom never knew it existed. And yet Nick knew from the moment he met me. And sex with Nick is raw and real. So damn raw and real that it is terrifyingly addictive.

I throw away the blankets and stand, feeling naked and exposed beyond the physical with Nick, and in some ways, I'm not sure I have ever felt naked and exposed with anyone. And I've been in some pretty intense, naked positions with Macom, that's for sure. I'm halfway across the room when footfalls sound on the steps, and I react to that emotion, darting forward and into the bathroom, where I grab my robe and pull it on, swiping at the wild mess on my head. And oh God. Why do I look like that *Ring* horror chick again, with mascara under my eyes? I need new makeup.

It's in that moment that Nick steps into the doorway, his broad shoulders consuming its width, his fierce masculinity consuming me. And while last night he was the picture of corporate power in a blue suit, refined with that hard, alpha edge of his, today, in black jeans, a black t-shirt, and biker boots, a light stubble on his jaw, his longish hair barely contained in a tie at his nape, he personifies that raw, real feeling of every touch and kiss that we share. Most definitely the ones we shared last night. I swear even the coffee cup in his hand somehow makes him sexier. I really, really think I need to lick him all over after watching him undress.

"Hi," I say, not even sure why that's what comes out of my mouth.

"Hi," he says, his eyes lighting. "You're looking bright-eyed this morning."

I laugh and shake my head, pointing at my cheeks and then turning to the mirror, hands pressed to the counter. "This is your fault," I say, looking at myself and then him. "I'm always naked and in bed before I get my makeup off."

He saunters toward me, setting the cup on the counter. "I'd apologize," he says, "but I just can't be sorry." His hands find my waist, and he turns me to face him, his touch somehow more electric than ever before, the collision of our eyes, which is always intense, now downright combustible. "I like you naked and in my bed too much," he adds, a rough quality to his voice that is somehow both silk and sandpaper at the same time. And as we look at each other, there is something I cannot name expanding between us. Something happening between us. Something rich with those possibilities we've vowed to explore.

And suddenly, I can't seem to catch my breath. "I…uh…" I swallow hard. "It turns out I sleep really well in your bed, when I haven't been sleeping well really ever." That confession is out before I can stop it, exposed all over again, and in turn, I change the subject, "Why didn't you wake me up? My flight—"

"Your flight leaves when I say it leaves, and I didn't wake you up because I like you in my bed." He reaches for the coffee cup. "I made this special for you, and there are chocolate croissants on the nightstand that I had delivered from the bakery on the corner."

"Thank you," I say. "For an arrogant bastard, you're very considerate."

"Let's keep that as our secret," he says. "I don't want anyone but you believing I've grown a heart." I'd ask if he has, but he quickly, almost too quickly, moves on, offering me the cup. "Try it."

I accept the cup, my gaze lowering as the brush of our fingers sends a rush of sizzling heat rushing up my arm, and I wonder if Nick feels what I feel. This crazy, fierce magnetic pull that wants me to just melt into him. I take a sip, the secret rich beverage surprising my taste buds, my gaze lifting to his. "Is that Baileys I taste?"

"You know your whiskey," he says.

"Only the sweet-tasting, wonderful stuff, like Irish cream," I say. "And are you trying to get me drunk? Because you know I'm a lightweight. Or if you don't know, you're about to if I finish this."

"Nothing wrong with a little buzz," he says, stroking my cheek, his tone sobering. "We need to talk, sweetheart, and I thought I'd help you relax a little in advance."

My defenses prickle, and the fear that I've read him wrong, *us* wrong, comes at me hard and fast. "Nick, if you regret last night and that talk of a new hard rule—"

"I don't," he says, taking the cup from me and setting it

down. "We need to talk about the winery, and I need to be your attorney for a few hours. And I know that's not easy territory for you. It's not going to be easy territory for us."

"Oh."

"Oh," he says, cupping my face. "Sweetheart, I *am* an arrogant bastard. A ruthless, arrogant bastard."

"Your point?"

His lips curve. "Your point," he says, at my obvious agreement. "My point," he says, softening his voice, "is that all the good that is in me is here with you—hell, maybe because of you. So, I don't just want those possibilities. I'm pretty damn sure that I need them, which means you. Stop looking for the bad. Unless you—"

"I don't want to back out," I say, realizing only then how much I mean that statement. "Hard rule: possibilities."

"Good," he says, his hands settling back on my waist. "Drink your coffee. Take a hot bath if you want, and relax. No one uses that tub, so you should. There's no rush. I'll be in the kitchen at the bar working when you're ready. Okay?"

"Okay," I say, and then he's releasing me and walking to the door, gone before I can stop him, though I'm not sure why I want to. I just do. I want to pull him back, but he disappears. I inhale as he departs and face the counter, staring at my mascara-stained face, which he actually seems to find acceptable. Macom would not have thought this was acceptable, and I think back to all the times I thought I was raw and *real* with Macom. I was never real with Macom, and as for raw, well, perhaps, but in a cutting, harsh way, not like what I have with Nick, which I can't even name or truly describe.

But if that is what Nick wants, raw and real, then raw and real means he's willing to let me see all those hidden pieces of himself I try to paint. And if he lets me see his, I'll need, even

16

want, to show him mine. But I'm not sure I can take that risk, even with him. Even if I want to. And I do. I want to trust Nick. Maybe I can. Maybe he can handle all of me. Maybe I need to know before I get any further in this. Or maybe not. Maybe I just need to enjoy him while I can.

Chapter Three

Faith

MAYBE I WILL ENJOY HIM WHILE I CAN.

Or maybe I can't enjoy him past today.

Because I have secrets that I hold close to my chest, the ones I try not to think about, to deny even to myself, and at least one of them, the one that stirs guilt in me, leads to the winery. And Nick Rogers is not the kind of man, or attorney, to leave a stone unturned. That man will wade into the muddy, crocodile-infested waters of my family secrets, and kill the crocodile. Which is good and bad. Good because I need that kind of attorney. Bad because I really care about this man and I haven't been honest with him about who and what I am. But how could I be? We were two strangers who crossed paths and chose to stay on one.

I down the whiskey-laden coffee like it's a shot, because

Nick's right. I need it, and the fact that he knows that I need it suggests that he's already been diving into those muddy waters. But he hasn't found the crocodiles or he wouldn't be offering me hot baths. Then again, he gave me whiskey. I glance at the tub and walk to the shower, eager to just get dressed and pack, so I'm ready to leave if things go south. Moving quickly, I step under a spray of warm water in no time, when the buzz of the Baileys hits me, numbing my brain. Numb feels pretty darn good right now, too, just like the water, and while I am in a rush to get downstairs, I am not in a rush to say goodbye, and I find myself lavishing in Nick's shampoo, conditioner, and body wash, rather than my own.

Soon after, I stand at *Nick's* sink, in *Nick's* house, feeling incredibly comfortable in the alpha domain, of a man who might have his head in the mouth of my crocodiles. I apply my makeup and dry and flat-iron my hair, while, of course, stuffing my face with croissants. Because why wouldn't you stuff your face with loads of calories when you're pretty certain the alpha man of the house won't be seeing you naked again after this talk? Once I've packed on five pounds, I spray on Nick's cologne, because he smells better than me, and I'm obviously feeling a bit more clearheaded, because I'm not vowing to eat carrot sticks, rice cakes, and nothing else tomorrow. Which is me lying to myself, the way I feel like I lie to the world. And I really hate carrot sticks and lies, I think, and part of me just wants to confess all to Nick, and see if he can handle it.

I think I will. I'll confess all.

Or not.

I make my way to Nick's large walk-in closet, where I've hung my clothes, the neat, organized way his clothes are lined up exactly as I expect of a dominant control freak. Exactly as Macom's always were. There are similarities in the two men that

I only just now am acknowledging, though on some level I've known they existed. But Nick is not Macom. Not even close to Macom, and it's an insult to him that I even think of them in the same box. And damn it, all I'm doing is justifying reasons to walk away when I get downstairs, and I know it. I shove my own nonsense away and get dressed, choosing black jeans and a lacy top, I pair with knee highs, and lace up black boots. And when I'm done, I don't let myself pack my bag. Instead, I retrieve my coffee mug and after a quick path through the bedroom, I'm traveling down Nick's glass and steel stairwell, toward the lower level of his home. The high ceilings and long, clean lines of the entire structure, as well as the pale hardwood floors, as sleek and sexy as the man—everything in this house screams sex and power, like the man who owns it. I'm quite certain everything about my demeanor right now screams of guilt.

I step into the living area, a white rectangular island dividing the two rooms. And the man who is power and sex sits at one of the four gray leather barstools on either side of it, paperwork and a MacBook sitting in front of him. His eyes meet mine, his keen and intelligent, too intelligent for my own good, and I remind myself: I have attorney-client privilege. I'm protected, and Nick just told me himself that he's no saint. If he knows what I've done, he didn't exactly go cold and brutal on me. If anyone can handle the truth, he can. If anyone can protect me, he can. Of course, if anyone can destroy me, he can as well. And so, I have to decide, right here and now: Can I trust Nick Rogers?

Chapter Four

Nick

FAITH ROUNDS THE CORNER LOOKING SO DAMN GOOD IN A pair of snug jeans, with some sort of lace top that hugs her breasts, and that makes me wish my hands were hugging them instead. And for just a moment, I contemplate marching her back upstairs, stripping her naked and fucking her one, two, or maybe ten times while having this conversation. Or perhaps before and after. But the problem with fucking is that it makes everything better while you're doing it, even lies, and I don't want to feel better about my lies, or invite her to spin any of her own. Not that I think Faith lies. I came looking for a liar and a killer, and all I found was a liar: me. But today is not about lies. It's about the facts as I laid them out in my head while she slept last night.

"How was the coffee?" I ask, as she steps to the opposite

side of the island and sets her cup down, my gaze finding her delicate little hands—talented, gifted hands, her nude nails somehow simple, yet elegant. I don't notice women's hands. But then, other women are not her, nor are they talented with a paintbrush, and Faith most definitely is talented.

She turns her cup upside down. "It's empty and dry. And as for how it was. It was strong enough to make me stuff my face with croissants and weak enough to have to devour three thousand calories worth of croissants to return me to sanity."

"Well then," I say. "Let's make you another cup."

I start to move away and she catches my hand, and I don't remember ever feeling a woman's touch like I do Faith's. Like a punch in the chest, I feel it go straight to my balls, which, to a man, might just be the perfect contradiction. "I don't want to be impaired when we talk," she says, her pale, pink-painted lips tightening, as she adds, "*Tiger,*" my legal nickname. "You'll rip out your opponent's throat, right?"

I turn my hand over and close it around hers. "Your Tiger, sweetheart," I say, sensing the apprehension in her. "And the only throats I'm going to rip out are those of your enemies. You know that, right?"

"I do, actually," she says, her eyes meeting mine. "I know, and I needed someone on my side, and suddenly you were just there. Fate, I guess, if you believe in that kind of thing, and I'm not sure I've told you how lucky that feels."

"Then why are your nails digging into my hand?" I ask, while guilt over the fate that I created jabs at me like a blunt, rusty blade, trying to bleed me dry.

"I'm sorry," she says, softening her grip on my palm. "Your 'we need to talk' clearly has me uptight. Maybe I do need that Baileys."

"And there's nothing wrong with that," I say. "I keep a bottle of scotch in my office. Sometimes you need to take the edge off."

"But you're Tiger," she says. "Confident. Arrogant and—"

"Sexy as fuck?" I supply, trying to get her to ease up a little.

And my feisty, amazing woman doesn't disappoint, smacking me down with, "Are you?" she quips back, making a soft sexy sound that has my cock twitching, before she adds, "I hadn't noticed, but surely someone as confident—scratch that—as cocky as you doesn't need a drink to take the edge off."

"Sweetheart, I prefer my moves, even the ones that require teeth, to be calculated, which is why taking the edge off serves me, and my clients, well. So, what do you say? One more cup?"

"I don't hold my tongue when I drink," she warns.

"Hold your tongue with the rest of the world," I say, "not with me." I grab the pot of coffee from the counter behind me, fill both of our mugs halfway, and then top them off with Baileys. "Let's go to the living room."

She nods, and we both pick up our mugs and head in that direction, and yes, I watch the sway of her heart-shaped ass, because she has a fucking amazing ass in those jeans. It, like her breasts, would be even more amazing in my hands. "What's that saying?" she asks, as we sit down on the couch and angle toward each other. "Loose lips—something?"

"Sink ships," I supply, and fuck, I need to get my head back in this conversation where it belongs. "And so does letting your attorney, and the man you're spending every naked moment possible with, get sideswiped," I add.

"Because being naked with you comes with rules?"

"Yes," I say. "Like I don't want you to fuck anyone else but me, but that's another conversation. For now, we stay on topic, which is your business and legal affairs. And I can't protect you, or help you get what you really want, if you don't speak frankly with me."

"The same goes for you," she says. "I don't want you to fuck anyone but me, and be frank with me. Treat me like your other clients. Don't talk around things, because that makes me uptight. And I'm not some delicate flower."

"First, no other woman could get my attention, and as for you not being a delicate flower, believe me, sweetheart. You've made me well aware of that fact."

"And yet I got softened up with Baileys and croissants. Is that a service you're providing your other clients?"

"Sweetheart, I have clients I'd pour a bottle of whiskey down to either shut them up or get them talking. The croissants, however, and the fuck after this conversation, I reserve for you."

"You're still not getting to the point," she says. "Thus all the bedroom talk. It's a distraction."

"Actually, it's not."

"So I'll just get to the point for you," she continues as if I haven't spoken, before sipping the coffee and setting the cup down on the granite coffee table in front of us.

"Okay then," I say, taking a drink before setting my cup down as well. "What's the point?"

"I need to write the bank a check for the sixty thousand dollars I got paid for my art last night. And yes, that sucks in some ways, but in another it doesn't. My art allows me to get out of this mess."

I move to sit on the coffee table in front of her, not quite ready to spark the anger sure to follow once she learns that I've paid off that note. "That money won't save the winery."

She pales instantly. "Oh God. Did I already lose the winery? Did the bank already take it?"

"Of course not," I say, my hands settling on her knees. "I'm your attorney, remember?"

"I know that, but you weren't until a few days ago."

26

"I'm your attorney," I repeat, "and I'm not going to let that happen."

"But why would you even have to fight the bank at all at this point? The money should be the end of the bank's involvement in my affairs. They can't hold up probate if the debt is up to date. Right?"

"Correct," I say. "Based on the documents that you've shown me."

"Implying there's something I haven't shown you?"

"Easy, sweetheart," I say softly. "Implying there's more that you don't have."

"Wouldn't they have to give that to my attorney?"

"Yes. But your attorney has to be smart enough to ask for everything, rather than assume he has it. And since I've talked to the bank and they're playing hardball, they could be bluffing, but they didn't back off when they heard my name. Thus why I'm of the strong opinion that your father, or your mother, signed documents that gives the bank rights that I don't know they have. Any idea what that document might be?"

"None. No idea. That would have required trust and communication from my mother I simply never had." Bitterness etches her tone, cold in that way that tells me the chill didn't happen overnight, but then, I knew that already. "But regardless of what legal document was signed," she adds, "what's the end game here? If I sold the winery, the net after that note, and all debt, would be seven to eight million. I know that's a lot of money, but enough for the bank to go to this much trouble?"

"It's not a lot of trouble to intimidate you into handing it over, and when you have a limp-dicked attorney allowing it to happen."

"Nick!"

"I tell it like it is, sweetheart. If you haven't gotten that by now, it's time to wake up and see the Tiger roaring in your face."

"Frank is not a limp-dicked attorney. He's just old."

I arch a brow. "And your point? Or was that my point you were making?"

"I assume your point is you're not him."

"No one knows that better than you, sweetheart," I say, handing her the coffee and preparing her for what comes next. "Drink."

She holds up a hand. "No. I need to know what's happening here. If the bank takes us to court, then you just do your Tiger routine, rip their throat out, and it's over, right?"

"They want to have the property evaluated."

"What? Why? Can they do that, and again, *why*?"

"That crop destruction you had last year could lead them to believe the value is now below that of the note."

"That's simply not the case," she says. "I don't believe that. I hope not. But let's just say it is—then what? Does that allow them to call the note due in full?"

"Not according to the documents I've seen and read."

"But we think there are other documents," she supplies, following where I've been leading.

"Exactly," I say. "And again. They could very well be bluffing, but we just won't know until they choose to show their hand or until we get to court. But the good news here is that my involvement alone tells them that they can't push you into a rash decision."

"And the bad?"

"It may take me getting in front of a judge to find out what we're up against."

"Which will be when?"

"If the bank has a leg to stand on, they won't be afraid of a judge, which means—"

"Right away," she says. "And if they don't, they'll stall. How long can they do that?"

"A few weeks at most, and that's if everything works against me, and I won't let that happen. But they're in this deep. They will try to force you to crack under the pressure. In the meantime, we'll prepare to hit back, and hard."

"What about me paying down the debt? Why wouldn't I do that?"

I steel myself for her reaction, and set down her mug that I'm still holding. "Because I paid the past-due amount and six months in advance."

She blanches and holds her hands up. "I think I misheard you. I need to pay six months in advance? That's double what I have in the bank."

"I paid it, Faith."

"No," she says.

"Yes."

"No."

"Yes."

"Get it back," she says fiercely. "Tell them you want it back. I'm not taking your money."

"They will and they did. It's done, and by cashier's check."

"I'm not taking your money, Nick," she says, her tone absolute. "Thank you. I mean that and those words feel too small for what you've done, but you don't know me well enough to do this. And even if you did, I don't want charity."

"It's not charity. It's a gift that I want nothing in exchange for. And as I've asked before, when do I know *enough*, Faith? I can fuck you all I want, but I can't give a damn? Because I give a damn. I get it. It's early. It's new. But it is what it is, and I can't change that."

She presses her hands to her face, and I can see them

tremble, as they did last night when she found out that she'd earned sixty thousand dollars on her art. And I don't know how it's possible, but I know this woman in a way that defies the time we've been together. I reach for her hands and pull them between us. "I'm alone in this world too. You know that, right?"

"You don't seem alone."

"Why? Because I'm foul-mouthed, cocky as you say, and sexy as fuck?"

"Nick," she whispers, no laugh this time.

"I know that we are new to each other. I know it feels like you could count on me and then I'll be gone, but I'm not going to be. Even if you decide you don't want to be *us* anymore, I'm your friend. I will remain your friend. And I don't have a lot of friends, but the ones I have, I take care of. Okay?"

"The money—"

"Is not a big deal to me. I know that feels big to you, but it's not a lot to me. I've done well for myself, but my bastard of a father was rich as fuck and now I have his money. And I'd like to do more than a few good things with it."

"How much was the check you wrote?"

"A hundred and twenty thousand."

"Nick," she breathes out. "You can't—"

"I already did."

"It's a lot of money."

"I just told you. I have a lot of money."

"It's a lot of money," she repeats.

I grab the notepad on the table, write down my bank balance, and show it to her. "That's how much I have in the bank."

Her lips part in shock. "That isn't even comprehensible to real people. Did you—Are there too many zeroes on that number?"

"No, there are not."

"Okay. I… Okay. But even if you took two or three zeroes off that, I'm not taking advantage of you."

"No," I say. "You're not. Because it's a gift." I release her hands and settle mine back on her knees. "But let's talk about why I did it and what it does for us. I have documents for you that state this is a gift. You do not owe me anything in return. But I have a plan to make this go away, and we need it to go away. But it means you're going to have to trust me, and Faith, I mean *really* trust me."

"I trust you, Nick," she says. "Why do you think I slept so well in your bed?"

"You sure about that? Because you seem to have a calendar and a timeline for when we're allowed to do certain things."

"This is new to me, too," she says. "It wasn't like this with…I trust you."

"Macom," I supply. "It wasn't like this with Macom. You lived with him, Faith."

"I did."

"You trusted him."

"I'm actually not sure I did."

I study her for several beats, wanting to unwrap that package she just handed me, but knowing now is not the time. I show her that bank balance again. "That kind of money is power that we can use to end this, and I'm not talking about me spending more money, though that is not off the table."

"By disclosing your involvement," she assumes. "And therefore giving yourself a vested interest in the case."

"We have to go further than that. I drew up a separate set of dummy documents which give me an interest in the winery. But again, you'll have documents that cover all of this and protect you."

She doesn't even blink. "I trust you. What else?"

31

"I have a number of tools in the chest, but among them, I'll offer to move some of my money to your bank, which will have influence. But not until we have our day in court. I want to see their hand before I play ours."

"Ours," she repeats.

I reach up, and brush a strand of the pale blonde silk of her hair from her beautiful green eyes, the many shades of torment in their depths accented by flecks of yellow. "Ours," I say. "I told you. I'm in this with you until the end."

Her hands come down on my forearms and lifts the right to stare down at the black and orange tiger etched into my skin, but her gaze shifts to my left, her fingers tracing the words there. "An eye for an eye," she says, reading them as she did once before. "I don't believe in an eye for an eye."

I believe her. She is a kinder, gentler soul than me, the moonlight on the water when I'm the sun bringing it to a boil. And I like that about her, about us. The contrast, the good and the bad. And I don't mind being the bad. "Only one of us has to go for the throat," I say. "I'll be the killer. You be the artist. And maybe you'll tame the beast along the way. But I wouldn't count on it."

"You'll be the killer," she whispers, letting out a choked laugh. "Right." She reaches for the coffee and gulps it down like water, then sets down the cup. "I need air." She scoots around me, stands up, and walks away.

I'm on my feet standing almost immediately, watching her track across the room to exit the open patio doors onto the terrace. Aware that I've thrown a lot at her, but also that she's rattled when she doesn't rattle easily, and I don't like the word that had that impact: killer. Fuck. What is happening here? I pursue her and I find her at the railing, her back to me, her attention on the city, the ocean, and the Golden Gate Bridge before her. I close the space between us, stepping to her side, close, but not touching her, my hands also resting on the railing. And while there are times when I push people to talk, there are others when silence leads them to reveal what is there but not yet spoken. With Faith, I don't speak. I wait, giving her the opportunity to speak when she's ready. Confident that she needs to say whatever it is she hasn't spoken yet.

"When I went to L.A.," she says without looking at me, "it hurt my father. He didn't want me to chase a hopeless dream."

"Was hopeless his word or yours?"

"His," she says. "But I couldn't give up my dream for his."

"And his was for you to run the winery."

"Yes. Exactly. And yet, I almost stayed. I was going to stay, because I was worried about my father. But then the night of my college graduation happened. That disaster changed my mind."

"What kind of disaster?"

She looks at me. "You know the details on that already. It was when my mother got mad at my uncle. To get back at him, she told my father that she slept with my him."

"Holy fuck," I breathe out. "I still can't believe she slept with his brother and he forgave her."

"Yes. And the truth is, that I hated my father a little afterwards, too. I mean, he never spoke to his brother again, but he forgave my mother. I couldn't look at him in the face, and see the same man anymore." She cuts her gaze, staring out at the city. "I wasn't as angry at my mother at that point as I was at him. I mean, he was the one who'd become the fool."

"And then he died."

"Yes. On the same night I had an explosion with Macom that was the end of us—in my book, anyway. So, leaving felt right. It had for a long time. But I didn't think it meant leaving my art. But my mother was a train wreck, and I wasn't without a head for business. I wanted to protect my father's pride and joy, but also, one day that winery would be mine. And with a management team, I knew it would be an asset and an income that supported, not destroyed, my painting." She glances over at me. "I hated to think like that. It meant thinking beyond my mother."

"It's business. It's smart business."

"Yes. Well, I took it a step further. She refused to tell me what was going on, and the vines were lost and bill collectors were calling. I'd lost any hope of painting. I was consumed by her screw-ups and I couldn't take it. I hired an attorney, Nick. I tried to take it from her. It was brutal." Her hands clutch the railing. "She threatened suicide. She cried. She yelled. She made scenes at the winery, and I was losing my mind. I wanted her to go away. I *needed* her to go away. And then…she was gone. Then she was dead. And Nick…" She looks down, her grip tightening on the railing. "I *killed* her."

Chapter Five

Nick

"I KILLED HER."

Faith's words, her tormented confession, roar through me like a tiger trying to rip *my* throat out. I didn't, I don't, believe she is guilty of killing her mother or my father, but my father's warning is burned into my mind: *Faith Winter is the problem. She is dangerous.* And mixed with her own statement, I need an explanation, peace of mind. I need to know what happened, and therefore, what I'm protecting her, and myself, from and I need to know now.

Still standing at the balcony, she has yet to look at me, like she doesn't want to see what might be in my face. Or maybe she doesn't want me to see what is in hers. Or both. Both, most likely. But I read people. It's what I do. It's who I am, and I glance down at her hands where they grip the railing, and her knuckles are white, telling the tale of dread and guilt. Urgency and need boil inside me, and not in the way they normally do for this woman. I step behind her, turn her to face me, and press her back to the railing, my big body pinning hers to it, my hands on the railing at her shoulders. "What the fuck does that mean, Faith?" I demand.

She looks up at me, her green eyes flashing with anger. "I shouldn't have told you. Get off me."

Her withdrawal stirs a spike of anger in me I can't seem to control, when I control everything around me—but this woman, it seems. It's a claw opening a wound I don't even understand, and I don't like anything I don't understand. My hands go to her waist, my tone hardening. "I'll let you when you explain yourself."

Her hands go to my hands. "Let go of me, Nick," she warns, her voice tight, icy. She tries to move.

My legs close around hers. "*Not until you explain yourself.*"

"I *shouldn't* have told you," she says again. "I shouldn't have trusted you."

"Attorney-client privilege, Faith."

This time, it's her anger that is hard and fast. "Are you serious right now, Nick?" The question rasps from her throat. "Is that what we are now? Or I guess we always were? Is that why you think I told you everything I just told you? Because I have attorney-client privilege?" Her fingers press into my chest, the prelude to the shove I steel myself for, as she adds, "I don't know why I thought we could be more than that," and then throws her body into pushing me away.

I don't budge under her impact, not physically, but I feel the emotional jab of those words. "I'm trying to give you the room to say whatever you need to say. I'm *trying* to protect you."

"Are you? Because that's not what I feel right now. Not

36

when you're demanding what, a few minutes ago, I didn't need you to demand. I *wanted* to talk to you." Her voice lowers, but it's not less biting as she adds, "Get off me, or I swear to you, Nick-asshole-fucking-Rogers, I will make you. And don't think I can't, though maybe I should add: Don't worry. I won't kill you. I'm not quite as skilled in that area as you might think."

My grip on her legs and waist tighten. "I was not implying that you were a cold-blooded killer."

"Just a killer."

"Stop."

"Gladly. Let me go."

"Damn it," I bite out, feeling that urgency and need again. "Talk to me, Faith."

"Not anymore," she says. "Not ever again."

"Don't do this."

"*You* did this."

"I'm trying to protect you," I repeat.

"By acting like I *really am* a killer? Because that's not what I needed from you, but then, that's the problem. I know better than to need anything from anyone. Mistake noted. Lesson learned. Again."

That wall she slams down between us is far more brutal than any tone or word spoken, and I don't even think about what comes next. My mouth closes over hers, my tongue stroking against hers and at first, she doesn't kiss me back. I mold her close, deepening the kiss, demanding she give me what I want, and finally, her fingers curl around my shirt, and that tongue of hers licks against mine. And there it is, exactly what I want, need, know to be this woman. Desire, hunger, sweetness. And damn it, I know what she meant now, and I am such a fucking asshole. I tear my mouth from hers, my hands cupping her face. "I know who you are. I know how you taste. And you are not a killer. And yes, I know that I'm a fucking asshole."

"You don't know me. We are too new, and you—"

"Know you like I know my own smell. Know you like I haven't known people I've known for years. I can't explain it, but you really are nothing I expected and everything I wanted. And needed."

"You came at me like—"

"I'm sorry," I say. "And I never say I'm sorry, but I'm fucking sorry. I go at things, Faith. I know you know this about me. I push. I want answers the minute something threatens what matters to me. And *you*, Faith Winter, matter to me." I lean back to look at her. "And no matter what you tell me right now, or when you're ready, I meant what I said. I'm in this with you until the end. I am not leaving. I'm not turning on you. I am not letting you go."

"And yet you thought the worst of me."

"Not you. But the worst, yes. Things happen that are sometimes out of our control." *Like everything I feel for this woman*, I add silently before I continue, "I always go to the worst place, because then I get ahead of what I'm facing. What *we're* facing, Faith. I pushed because—"

"Like I pushed *her*," she breathes out. "I pushed her, Nick. I pushed her until she was dead like my father." She buries her face in my shoulder and sobs, but in another instant, she's pushing away and swiping at her cheeks. "I think I'm going to keep crying. I need to go…"

"No," I say, cupping her face. "No. You do not." I thumb the tears from her cheeks. "You're right where you belong, Faith. *With me.*"

Her lashes lower. "You don't understand."

"Make me understand."

"Not now or I'll cry and that is weak and confusing." Her

lashes lower and her fingers curl around my shirt.

"Why is it confusing or wrong to cry?" I ask, my hands moving to her shoulders.

Her lashes open, her eyes meeting mine. "You haven't cried for your father."

"I didn't see my father for years before he died, sweetheart. It's different."

"I was with her. When she died. We were fighting, and then she just dropped dead. And the guilt—Oh God." Her hand goes to her forehead. "I told you. I can't keep talking now." Tears pool in her eyes again. "I can't keep talking...now." She leans into me and buries her face in my chest, her body quaking with silent tears that she clearly struggles to control. I don't want her to stop crying, to hide anything from me, and bastard that I am, I all but created that need in her.

I scoop her up, carry her to the sitting area to our left, and set her down on the couch, framed by a table and two chairs, her legs over my lap. But she doesn't let go of my shirt, her face still buried in my shoulder. And she hasn't stopped trembling, trying to pull herself into check, and still she says, "I'm okay." She pushes away from me, swiping her cheeks and sitting up. "I'm fine."

Guilt, and my intense need to control every damn thing around me, is now my enemy. I went at her. I pushed when she didn't need to be pushed. But saying that to her won't make her believe me now. I have to show her she can trust me again. I cup her head and pull her to me, giving her a quick kiss and saying it anyway. "It's okay to not be okay with me, Faith. I'm an asshole, but this asshole is crazy about you and on your side." I don't force her to reply. She doesn't need to do that. "I'll be right back." I kiss her again and release her, standing up and walking into the house.

I cross the living room, kicking myself for my reaction to Faith's confession. She baited me, and I let her, though I'm not certain she even realizes she did it. She's punishing herself. Maybe testing me at the same time. Trying to decide if she really can trust me. Fuck. I need her to know she can. And I failed whatever that was. Worse, I failed because I let that note of my father's mess with my head when I meant what I said to Faith. I know her in ways I'm not sure I've ever known another human being. I know she is not a killer, and yet I reacted as if I thought she was just that: A killer.

Entering the kitchen, I stop at the corner built-in bar, pressing my hand to the edge of the counter. "You're an asshole," I murmur. "Such a fucking asshole, just like she said." And why, I think? Because I felt, for just a moment, like control was lost, and I had to grab it and hold onto it.

I push off the counter, and grab a glass, needing the drink I came in here to get for Faith. Scanning my many choices, I opt for my most expensive Macallan, pour three fingers, and down it. Smooth. Rich. Almost sweet in its perfection. I open the mini freezer under the counter, add ice to the glass, and refill it. Then, with the bottle in hand, I return to the balcony, where I find Faith standing at the railing again. Seeming to hear, or sense my approach, she rotates and meets me back on the couch, her tears gone. Her hands steady. She sits down and I go down on a knee in front of her. "Drink this," I order, offering her the glass.

"I'd argue," she says, accepting the whiskey, "but I never allow myself to be numb like I was a bit ago, and as it turns out, I'd like to feel that again." She sips, testing it, and then downs it before handing me back the glass. "Thank you. That was smooth and, I suspect, quite expensive."

"You're worth it, and I vote we sit here and down the entire bottle." I move to the cushion beside her and refill the glass, down the contents and refill it again, offering it to Faith. "I know you didn't kill her."

She studies me a moment, takes the glass, downs the whiskey, and sets the glass on the table. "Do you? Because I don't. I think that's why your reaction got to me so much."

"I told you—"

"It's okay," she says, grabbing my leg. "In fact, I should apologize, because when you walked into the house, I realized something. I set you up. Not on purpose. But come on, Nick. I dropped the 'I killed her' bomb."

I'm stunned that she's self-analytical enough to come to the same conclusion I did, and in the same timeline I did. "Why, Faith?"

"Some part of me feels so much guilt that I wanted you to come at me. I wanted you to punish me." She gives an uncomfortable laugh. "I think I'm pretty fucked up and you should run, Nick." She tries to pull her hand from my leg.

I cover it with mine, holding it in place. "I'm not going anywhere, Faith, and I'm not letting you either. Not without a fight. One hell of a fight. And as for being fucked up. We're all fucked up. Anyone who claims they aren't is lying."

"You don't seem fucked up at all. You're successful. You know yourself. You seem to know me."

"I do know you, but obviously you don't quite know me, yet, and I need to fix that. Starting with your current misconception of me. Of course, I'm fucked up. My mother left my father for slutting around and then died and left me with that man. I blame her. I blame him. I blame me. I fear the fuck out of being just like that man."

"You aren't."

"I am, Faith. I'm calculated. I'm cold with everyone but you, and yet I say that after the way I just treated you. I'm a bastard made by a bastard, and he was a damn good attorney. I drive myself to be better than he was. And I am."

"Your version of being a bastard is a man who demanded to know everything from me. Not a man who assumed he did. Once I came to the realization that I'd pushed your buttons, I realized that too, even if you did not."

"I pushed you."

"I pushed you, too. And for the record. It's pretty impressive that your version of 'fucked up' is to be amazing at your job."

"I've seen your art, Faith. Your version of fucked up makes you amazing at your job, too, and obviously, from your recent success, I'm not the only one who shares that opinion. But there's a difference between the two of us. I know I'm amazing at my job. You don't."

"I'm working on that," she says. "You've helped. Last night helped. But right now, in this moment, I'm consumed with the same demon I've been consumed with since my mother died. I go back and forth between anger and gut-wrenching guilt. But never grief, and that starts the guilt all over again."

I hand her another glass of whiskey. "I shouldn't drink this," she says.

"Why not? Are you driving?"

"Right," she says. "Why? I'll just go slower."

"And as for your current demon," I say when she sips from the glass, "I predict that once we get the chaos your mother created under control, you'll find the grief. Or not. Maybe you'll find out things about her that make that grief impossible."

"Is that what happened with your father?"

"Yes," I say. "It is, but I feel like I should remind you of what I just said. I came to terms with what I felt for my father many years before he died. And he wasn't in my life, therefore there wasn't anything to change those terms."

"And you really feel no grief?"

"I really feel no grief," I say without hesitation. "But you asked me if I feel alone now."

"You said that you don't."

"And I don't," I confirm, and when I would offer nothing more to anyone else, I do with Faith. "But, on some level, I have moments where I'm aware that I have no blood ties left in this world, and that stirs an empty sensation inside me. Maybe that is feeling alone. I just don't name it that."

"You have no family at all?"

"My mother's family has been gone for many years. My uncle on my father's side died a few years back, but I hadn't seen the man in a decade and as far as I know, neither had my father."

"We live odd parallels," she says. "My father and my uncle hadn't spoken for about that long when my father died either." She sinks back against the cushion. "And I'm feeling all the alcohol now." She shifts to her side to face me. "I'm not drunk," she adds. "Just kind of numb again, which is a good thing. It's better than guilt."

"How many employees do you have?"

"Is this a sobriety test?"

"If it is, will you pass?"

"Yes," she says. "I told you. I'm numb, not drunk. And I have fifty employees, at least part of the year."

"And your mother's mishandling put all of those jobs on the line. You had to protect the winery."

"I know. Especially Kasey's job, and another ten or so key people who have been with the winery for their entire careers."

"And yet you still feel guilt for fighting for them?"

"I feel guilt for not finding a way to fight for my mother and them."

"Your mother didn't want help."

"But she needed it," she argues. "She was clearly an addict, both with alcohol and sex."

"You said you hired an attorney?"

"Yes. An expensive one, too. That's what happened to part of my inheritance."

"Who?"

"Cameron Lemon. Do you know him?"

"In passing and by reputation. He's good. What happened with him?"

"One of my mother's many male friends was an attorney too, and he knew just how to nickel and dime me to death with Cameron. I ran out of money and with the winery in debt, I couldn't even promise him I'd pay him when we won ownership. I had to back off."

"Who was your mother's attorney?" I ask, steeling myself for the answer I am sure I will receive.

And as expected, she says, "Nathan Marks," her lashes, thankfully, lowering with my father's name on her lips. "Do you know *him*?" she asks, looking at me.

"Yes," I say, telling her every truth I can at this point. "I do. And your mother chose her friends wisely. He would have been a formidable opponent."

"She got naked with my uncle. She didn't choose wisely. She just chose often." She downs the drink. "I can't believe this but the whiskey effect is wearing off. Maybe I wasn't really feeling it after all."

I fill her glass. "Try again."

"What if it hits me all of a sudden, and I wipe out on you?"

"I promise you that we won't fuck," I say, placing her hand on the glass. "Because I want you to remember every time we fuck."

Her teeth scrape her bottom lip. "You're really quite

memorable, *Mr. Rogers.*" She downs the drink. "I think my mother watched that program. I'm really glad that you don't wear button up sweaters and sing like the real Mr. Rogers on the show."

"Last I heard I was the real Mr. Rogers."

"Right," she whispers, giving a tiny laugh. "You are, but without a button up sweater. Or is it button down sweater?"

"I vow to never, ever wear a button up or button down sweater."

"It might be cute on you."

"I don't want to be cute," I assure her.

"What's wrong with cute? Women like cute."

"Only women who have been drinking really expensive, smooth whiskey or picking out a puppy."

"Or cat. I prefer cats. I really need to get a cat." Her hand goes to her face. "I was wrong. I'm feeling those drinks now and I just drank more." She sets the empty glass on the cushion between us, as if she can't quite sit up and get it to the table. "What have I done?"

I set the glass on the table, lower myself to the cushion beside her, and roll her to face me. "I'll catch you if you fall, sweetheart."

Her hand falls from her face. "Will you? Or will you fall with me?"

I stroke her cheek. "What does that mean, Faith?"

"It means that if we're both fucked up, then sometimes, two fucked up people fuck each other up more."

"We're all fucked up, remember? Which means that sometimes, two fucked up people make each other whole again."

"That's like a fairytale ending. We don't believe that."

"Now we have each other, don't we?"

"*Do* I have you, Nick?"

"Yes, Faith, you do."

She reaches up and strokes my cheek this time. "Ah Nick. I have to paint you again. You know that, right?" Her lashes lower and her hand falls from my face. I catch it, but she doesn't open her eyes. I count seconds. One. Five. Ten. She sighs and seems to fall asleep. I sit there, staring at her, searching every line of her face, and I swear she grows more beautiful by the second. Her full cheeks. Her fuller lips. The confession that says she wants to trust me, even if she doesn't quite yet.

"I don't want to leave," she murmurs, her eyes fluttering and closing again.

"Then don't," I say, pleased that the first confession came when she was sober, and this one comes when she's just drunk enough to make emotional confessions.

She doesn't respond. She's dozing off again, and I stand and scoop her up. She curls into me again, her body soft in my arms. "Kasey—"

"Can handle the winery," I say, already in the house and crossing to the stairs. "If he can't, he needs to be replaced." I start the upward climb. She's silent until we're almost to the top, and then she seems to remember the conversation.

"But the collectors," she says. "I need—"

"You don't," I say, entering the bedroom. "Debate me after you take a nap, preferably after Wednesday, when I can return with you."

"You're very convincing when you're holding me like this. Even with your clothes on."

I laugh. "I'll have to remember that."

"That's not the alcohol talking," she murmurs. "I mean it."

"Even better," I assure her, setting her on the bed, which remains unmade. She plops onto the pillow. "My head is spinning," she says, as I take her boots off. "I really hate being out of control."

I lean over her and press my hands to either side of her. "No. You don't. You hate always having to be in control."

"How could you possibly know that?"

"Because I know how to read people, you especially. And now you don't have to be in control all of the time. You have me. And you don't know it yet, or you don't trust me yet, but I'll take care of you."

"No one takes care of me but me," she says. "That's just how it is."

"Was," I amend. "That's how it was. Like I said. Now you have me."

"Ah, Nick," she whispers. "I don't."

"You don't what?"

"Have you. At least, not all of you." She traces my brow with her finger. "It's in your eyes right now. It's always in your eyes. The secrets I try to understand when I paint you...Things you don't want to tell me." Her lashes lower. "Maybe you will one day." She inhales again and her breathing slows, evens, while my heart is racing. She knows I'm telling her a lie. She senses it. Fuck. Fuck. Fuck. I stand up and shove fingers through my hair before walking to the door, and just as I would exit, she whispers, "Nick."

I face her, and she's looking at me as she says, "When you're ready," before shutting her eyes again. "I can wait."

And therein lies the problem. I'm never going to be able to tell her. I'm never going to be ready to lose her. Because I need this woman. I need her like I need my next breath.

Chapter Six

Nick

AFTER LEAVING FAITH IN MY BED, I END UP ON THE balcony, where I sit down, pour the last glass of whiskey in the bottle and down it. What the hell is this woman doing to me? No woman has ever consumed me the way Faith has, and does. No woman has ever made me not just want her, but need her, like I need Faith. As I, in turn, need her trust that I do not deserve. Forced lies are killing me and most likely will kill us, a likelihood that only gets worse with each day I continue to let them become a divide between us. She senses it. She knows it. She knows me in ways people who have known me for years do not. I need to fix this. I'm damn good at fixing things. This can't be the exception. I will make things right with Faith. I will make everything right in her world, including me.

Which is exactly why I left Faith sleeping this morning

and got to work doing just that, including a long conversation with Beck. Pulling my phone from my pocket, my finger hovers over the auto-dial with his number, but I remind myself that I didn't even send the man a copy of my father's note until early this morning. He's a damn good PI, but even he needs time to work. I punch Abel's number instead, who, as of a few hours ago, became more than my friend and personal attorney. He's now one of Faith's attorneys as well. She just doesn't know it yet. "Bring yourself and those documents I had you do up for me over here," I order, when he answers.

"Have that bottle ready for me," he replies.

He means the Glenlivet Winchester Collection: Vintage 1964 bottle valued at 25k that was gifted to me first by a client, and now by me to Abel for taking care of Faith. "It's ready and waiting," I say without hesitation, more than happy to give up a bottle of booze to ensure Faith knows she can trust me. Which is the role Abel is going to play in this web I'm weaving for her enemies.

"I might let you taste it when I open it," he taunts.

"I'll gladly share a drink of anything the day you finally get smart and stop fucking the wrong women, like your ex."

"She's not my only fuck these days, and even if she was, *I'm* fucking *her*. She's not fucking me. We're going to talk about how that plays out with you and Faith. I'll be there in fifteen." He hangs up and I stand up, taking the empty glass and bottle with me to the kitchen. I don't refill that glass. I make an old fashioned pot of coffee, because I like the insulated pot right next to me while I work, and on quick pour.

I then sit down at the island, my stacks of work in front of me, my briefcase locked and to my right. I punch in the combination and open it, pulling out my father's handwritten note to read it again, homing in on those poison words: *Faith is dangerous.* She was a threat. How? I grab a note pad and start writing down my thoughts:

—My father had to have been after the winery but why? Is it worth more than we think? It has to be. Actions needed:

—Get assessment done Monday.

—Beck needs to find out what might be beyond the obvious.

Moving on…next item:

—Why call Faith Dangerous? COVERED. He had to have felt she was dangerous to his plan.

—Seven to ten million wouldn't motivate a man who was damn near a billionaire at that stage in his life. Would it? No. COVERED.

—Why pay Meredith Winter one million dollars in staggered payments? Down payment on the winery? But she couldn't sell without Faith, is that why Faith was dangerous? She could stop the sale? Back to: Why is the winery more valuable than it appears?

—Autopsy results—WHEN?

—If someone killed my father and Faith's mother, doesn't that infer that my father and her mother were on the same side? Unless my father convinced Meredith Winter to be on his side. Or she convinced him to be on his side. Or they were both such players they were playing each other but either way they both ended up dead, by the same means. The same person had to have killed them. And that person was NOT Faith.

I move on to another key list, and one to discuss with Beck:

Suspects:

—Someone associated with the bank.

—Ask Faith for a meeting with Cameron Lemon, with her present so he will talk.

—Faith's present-day attorney when she met me—he's her father's friend but it appears her father's friends were usually her mother's friends as well and in Meredith Winter's case, that's a problem.

—Faith's uncle—enough said.

—Kasey, or another staff member at the winery, but Kasey would be the one who knows intimate details of the winery and family—sleeping with Meredith Winter?

—Any one of Meredith Winter's lovers, with a focus on the long-term boyfriend right before my father which Beck has found.

—An unknown I have yet to identify or see a link to connect them to Meredith and my father.

My coffee finishes brewing and I fill a cup, bring the pot to the island, and ready it for future pours before reviewing my new list several times over. My focus on why my father would pay Meredith Winter a million dollars and in installments. Somewhere in that act is an answer to every question I have and some I probably don't know to ask. Yet. I will.

The doorbell rings, which says the 25k bottle of booze has Abel showing some manners for once, and of course, he chooses now, while Faith is sleeping. Fully intending to soften his edges where she's concerned, and before he meets her, I make fast tracks for the door. Abel doesn't wait on my arrival. Clearly impatient, he's used my back-up key, and is opening the door as I arrive. He steps inside the foyer, his typical designer suit, replaced with his weekend faded, ripped jeans, and a t-shirt that sports the Harley logo, and supports the man's obsession with the brand and the bikes. "Take me to the wonderland of whiskey," he says, shutting the door, and sliding his key back into his pocket. "Because I do have something to celebrate." He runs his hand over his buzzed blond hair as he adds, "Remember that ex-Navy SEAL judge I buzzed my head to impress?" He doesn't wait for my confirmation. "He dismissed my case, and I landed a six-figure pay check."

I back up to give him space to pass down the hallway. "Not bad for a week's work."

"Not bad at *all*," he agrees, heading down the hallway.

I follow him, his destination the island, or rather, long-ass bar that serves as the island, but he doesn't stop there. He drops his briefcase on a seat, and heads to the bar. I walk back to my seat behind the island and face the living area, keeping the stairs that Faith would have to travel to join us, in view. While Abel's view is on my many whiskey choices. "Was the client guilty or innocent?" I ask, thrumming my pen on the shiny, white granite counter.

"He says he was innocent," he replies, walking toward me with a bottle of Scotch in hand, and two glasses. "I have to believe a client is innocent to take a case." He stops at the end cap by the chair his bag has now claimed and sets the bottle and glasses down. "I have to believe, man." He opens the bottle and fills one of the glasses. "You know that."

I narrow my gaze on him, not so sure we're celebrating after all. "But was he innocent?" I ask, waving off the pour he's about to give me. "I've had my share today." I lift my coffee cup. "I'll stick to this."

"Suit yourself," he says, his tone impartial. He really doesn't care. That's one of the things that I like about Abel. He is what he is and I am what I am. We are night and day in some ways, especially when it comes to women, who he tends to allow replays with that I do not. Not until Faith, I add silently and quickly refocus on Abel and our similarities. We like control. We like to win and we hit hard. And considering we've known each other since law school, I know he has some baggage, as Faith calls one's history, and like me, Abel trusts almost no one. Which means he won't be quick to trust Faith.

"And as for my client's guilt or innocence," he continues, snapping me back to the moment, as he downs the contents of his glass and refills it. "He was guilty as sin, but I didn't decide that until I got him off when he smirked and said: Who says only the innocent go free?"

"Ah shit, man."

"I know, right?" he says. "I thought I was good at reading people, but holy hell. I missed this one. But there wasn't even a semi-good case built against him, and I can't turn back time. Which is why I have to focus on the payday and celebrate that."

"What was the crime?"

"Murder," he says, his lips tightening. "And don't ask me who he killed. I don't want to talk about it." He scrubs the light stubble on his jaw. "I *really* don't want to talk about it." He refills his glass.

We're not celebrating. He's come to swim in the sea of guilt Faith is splashing around in, and I get it. Defending a killer sucks. Thankfully, Faith isn't a killer, but the guilt is killing her. I don't really understand guilt. I don't feel it. I do something. I did it for a reason. I own it. And so I only know one way to help with it. A good fuck, which Abel is on his own on that one. And a good drink. I stand up and round the counter, open a cabinet above the bar, and pull out that 25k bottle of booze before returning to the counter, and setting it down beside him. "This and a trip to the club and you'll forget the asshole you just banked on," I say. "But tell me again why you stick with criminal law?"

"Because the innocent ones need me and paydays like this one let me help people who don't have a bank account as big as the likes of that asshole I got off." He taps the bottle. "You really going to give me that?"

"You need it."

"I need a trip to the club to get fucked ten ways to next

Sunday, but I was never going to take that bottle, man. But hey. I'll work for the sentiment behind it." He opens his briefcase and pulls out a file. "The gift documents and the dummy documents," he says, setting the file on the counter. "But seriously, man. What the hell are you doing with this woman, Nick?"

"Protecting her."

"Protecting a woman who might be a killer."

"She's innocent."

"And you know this how?"

"Because I know and you know when I say I know, I know."

"Like I knew my client?"

"I know Faith personally now."

"Yeah well, you're fucking her and that tends to cloud a man's judgment."

"Not mine. You know that."

"And I've never known you to mix business and your personal life." He taps the file. "And these documents tell me you've either lost your fucking mind or you're brilliantly working a woman who doesn't know she's being worked. And you can tell me either way. I'm *cool*. You know that." He removes the lid from the scotch.

"She and I just downed a bottle of Macallan No.6 together and she's in my bed right now."

He's about to pour another drink and sets the bottle down, looking stunned. "You shared your No. 6 and she's in your bed?"

"Yes and yes."

"You don't share your No.6 or your bed. What happened to keeping your women confined to the club?"

"Faith isn't going to the club," I say, once again wishing I'd never bought the damn place. "Ever."

"So she's vanilla and you're chocolate, and that shit will get old."

"Faith is not fucking vanilla," I snap.

He arches a brow. "Got it. Not vanilla. Not going to play with you at the club. Does she at least know it exists and that you own it?"

"No," I say. "Now *focus.*" I slide the notepad I've been writing on in front of him. He scans it and his gaze rockets to me. "Faith is dangerous? When did your father say that Faith was dangerous?"

I open my briefcase and set the note in front of him. He studies it for several long beats before he glances at me, "You're sure Faith—"

"Faith is *not* a killer," I say tightly. "Assume I'm right on this because I am. Now. Where does that note lead you?"

"That your father wanted the winery, or something else, and she was in the way of him getting it."

"Exactly my thoughts," I concur. "But Meredith Winter. He was paying her. I can't make sense of that in my head."

"He clearly infers that Meredith was dangerous, as Faith was more dangerous but the tone also infers that he had Meredith under control."

"It's almost impossible for me to conceive of my father paying someone off. But the evidence supports just that."

He refills his glass. "What if he was getting something in exchange?"

"But what?"

"Ownership of the winery?"

"Faith would have had to sign off on that," I remind him.

"Thus why she was a problem," he says. "Or more dangerous to his plan than her mother. He had Meredith pinned down, but not Faith."

"But the bills were not being paid," I argue. "Meredith received a million dollars from my father and allowed a section of the vines to go untreated, and therefore become damaged."

He thrums fingers on the counter. "Could she have been trying to get Faith to sell? You know, making it seem that the winery wasn't worth owning?"

"Faith was working at the winery. She knew how well it was doing."

"And yet the bills weren't being paid?" he confirms.

"Correct," I say, "and finally, after trying to get her mother to come clean with her about what was happening, and failing, Faith took action. She hired an attorney and tried to take the winery from her mother."

"I can't say that I blame her. What was her mother's response?"

"She hired my father who nickel-and-dimed Faith into giving up."

"I'm not sure that disproves my theory about Meredith wanting her to sell. Did she ever directly ask Faith to sell?"

"My understanding," I say, "is yes. But all of this gets more interesting. I paid the bank off. You know that. And they still plan to hold up the execution of Meredith's will while they get the property appraised."

"Ouch. That's not good. They have to have a document that says if it's under the value of the note, they can take it," he agrees. "Which would make anyone who signed an agreement to that royally stupid, but it happens."

"Obviously I get my own appraisal, but why would the bank want a property that is under the value of the note anyway?"

"And why would your father want it?" He doesn't wait for a reply. "There's something about that property. Something that got your father and her mother killed."

"I agree wholeheartedly," I say, sticking the note back in my briefcase. "And I'd get my bank to buy out her note, but obviously, the bank isn't going to let that happen, if they feel they may own it outright, and with some back-end benefit we don't know about."

"You can try," he says. "But you'll have to disclose the bank's intent to have the property assessed."

"Agreed," I say, aware of the liability doing otherwise could represent.

"What does Faith think about all of this?"

"She doesn't have the luxury of knowing that my father and her mother are linked to truly evaluate the situation as we do."

"Tell her."

"If I tell her, she kicks me to the curb, and I can't protect her."

"What *does* she know at this point?"

"She knows that my father represented her mother and that her mother was involved with him."

"Well then. Both of them are dead and connected. Use that to convince her to exhume her mother's body."

"I'm not lying to her any more than I have to. And that plan would lead me to more lies."

"Then just talk about her mother. Someone wants the winery. Her mother is dead. Have her do an autopsy."

I shake my head and refill my coffee cup. "Negative again. I'm not putting her through that hell unless my father's autopsy is suspicious. If there's nothing to find in his reports, we won't find anything in her mother's."

"While I agree," he says. "Time is critical when a killer is on the loose, and when does that killer turn to Faith or even you?"

"That PI I hired has someone watching Faith."

"Does she know he's watching her?"

"No."

"Damn, man. I get it. All of it. I know why you can't tell her, but I don't envy you the moment she finds out. Especially the part where you sought her out and fucked her to prove she was a killer."

He left off the part where I wanted to ruin her. And I have to confess everything to her, in some brilliant way, that convinces her I'm not her enemy. In fact, I am the man, who's bed, and life, may never be the same again, without her.

Chapter Seven

Faith

I KILLED HER.

 I blink awake with my confession to Nick in my mind, the scent of him surrounding me, his bed cushioning me. The taste of the rich whiskey I'd drunk with him is still on my tongue, but it does nothing to erase the bitterness of those words or the way I feel them deep in my gut. I wait for the regret over telling Nick to follow, but it doesn't exist. I didn't plan to bare my soul to Nick, but I did, and the fact that I felt that I could, especially with my history with Macom, and my mother, brings one word to mind: *Possibilities.* Considering Nick and I started with a vow for one night, the place we've landed is pretty incredible. And scary. Because I really am naked and exposed with this man. That means vulnerability. That means he could hurt me.

 Oddly, my fear of him hurting me served as a mechanism

to push me to trust him more. The minute he'd told me he'd paid my debt, I'd panicked. I was feeling emotionally exposed, and then he claimed control over the winery situation that I had failed to control myself. He'd been generous, protective, a hero even, but unknowingly, he'd shifted the financial dynamic between us to resemble the one I'd shared with Macom. The next thing I knew I was throwing out the: I killed her statement, and in hindsight, wanting Nick to prove he wasn't worthy of my trust. Wanting Nick to judge me the way I was judging me.

And it had not only been a beautiful failure, that lead me to share more of myself with Nick. He understood my choices, and I think believed them to be more right than I do. Even approving of my decision to try to take the winery from my mother, and unbidden, that thought has my mind trying to skip over Nick and go back to that night when my mother died. It is not a gentle memory and I reject it, throwing off the blanket, and sitting up, swinging my legs to the floor, feet settling on the ground. I really need my feet on the ground, but it's not enough to keep the past at bay.

I'm there, living it, my fingers curling on the edge of Nick's mattress, my eyes shutting as I return to the winery and that brutal night. I'd just finished being humiliated by a bill collector in front of several staff members. Furious, I'd sought out my mother, and found her in her gardens on her knees, fussing over the ground around a cluster of some sort of white flowers. And the past is so vivid right now that I can almost smell the flowers, bitter and sweet in the same inhaled breath.

"Where is the money, Mother?" I demand.

Of course, she knows what I'm talking about but choses to play dumb, glancing up at me and saying, "What are we talking about, dear?" which only serves to infuriate me more.

"Where is all the money we're making?"

She pushes to her feet, pulling off her gloves, her hands set-tling on her slender blue jean-clad hips. "You need to go back to L.A. and let Macom take care of you, because you clearly cannot handle the pressure here. And this is my winery anyway."

"It will be mine one day and I'll inherit the debt and prob-lems you're creating."

"Oh, so that's it?" she demands. "This is all about protecting your money. Wouldn't your father be proud? You finally give a damn about the winery and it's about money."

"I have no choice but to care about the debts I will inherit."

"Like I said," she bites out. "Go back to your rich artist boy-friend and let him take care of you. This is my world, not yours. I bet your father turned over in his grave when you sued me."

"He's in his grave because you fucked my uncle and everyone else that would have you."

She laughs. "You didn't even know your father," she says. "He liked watching me with other men."

"He did not," I spit back. "He did not."

"He did," she insists, turning away from me and she seems to take a step forward before she falls face first into all of those dozens of white flowers.

My thoughts shift at that point to the place they always go after that memory: The funeral, and as expected, the grave site, and the final goodbye. *There are rows of filled seats surround-ing me, people lined up beside and behind me while rain splat-ters down atop a sea of umbrellas. Appropriate actually, since my mother loved the rain. It also saves me when I didn't save her, because no one knows that I'm not crying. But I know. I know so many things I don't want anyone else to know. Like the fact that as the preacher speaks, I'm wondering how many of the random men here that I don't know slept with my mother. And how many did my father know, too? Did he like to watch? God. Is that why* he tolerated her?

I shiver, wishing I had a jacket, my thin black dress doing little to offer me shelter. There just isn't shelter I can find anywhere. My grip tightens on the umbrella I'm holding, which someone gave me. I don't know who. I don't even remember how it got into my hand. I just keep remembering the moments before my mother had died. The speech and time ticks on for what feels like an eternity, while time has now ended for my mother and my father. I'm alone in this world, and as the rain begins to fall with a fierceness rarely rivaled, the crowd scatters, a few people try to speak to me, but soon, I am alone here now, too.

Everyone is gone, and I walk to the casket and just stare at it. I go back to then, to those moments in time, reliving the fight with my mother, the moment she'd tumbled forward. My knees are weak and so is my arm and I can't seem to hold onto it. I don't want to hold it anymore so I don't. I just can't. I drop to the ground and let the force of the rain hit me, my black dress instantly wet, my hair...

"Faith."

At the sound of my name I turn and Josh stands there. "Josh? How are you here?"

"I wanted to be here for you."

"Where's Macom?"

"I'm sorry, Faith. He's not coming."

"Good," I say, "I told him not to come. I don't want him here." And knowing how he operates all too well, I add, "Being my agent doesn't require that you do funeral duty. I don't like that kind of plastic friendship and I don't want it in my life or career."

"Faith—"

"Go home, Josh," I say and needing to escape the obligatory sympathy from him and everyone else, I start to run toward my car.

My cellphone rings, jerking me back to the present, and I grab it to ironically discover Macom's number on caller ID, feeling as if I've willed a ghost of my past into the present. I hit decline, noting this as his third call and I really want to block the number. I'm about to do just that when my cell rings in my hand and this time it's Josh's number. I answer immediately, "Why is my agent calling me on a Sunday?"

"To tell you not to answer Macom's call."

"You're a little late since he's called three times."

"Holy hell. Please tell me he didn't get in your head about the L.A. Forum show."

"I didn't talk to him," I say, well aware of why he is concerned, since Macom pretty much declared my work an embarrassment the last time I wanted to submit. To protect me, of course. "And even if I had, I'm in the show."

"And I'd prefer you get there feeling confident."

"Why exactly is Macom calling me?"

"To give you advice you don't need."

My mind goes back two years, to me standing in my workspace, in the home I'd shared with Macom, while I'd proudly revealed new paintings. Certain that my work on the three pieces would finally capture the L.A. Forum's attention.

"Stunning," Josh had said, motioning to a Sonoma mountain shot I'd so loved. "This one," he'd said. "It's one of your best yet."

"Absolutely not," Macom had said, shoving his hand through his spiky dark brown hair before motioning to the three paintings. "These are not what they're looking for. None of them. You'll look like a fool."

The words had been like knives in my heart, and I'd instantly doubted myself, questioning why I was even picking up a paintbrush any longer.

"I respectfully disagree," Josh had argued, daring to go against

his moneymaker Macom.

Macom's gray eyes had flashed. "Who is the star of that show for the second year running? Not my fucking agent, I'll tell you that. I'll help Faith pick her submission."

"Faith?"

At the sound of Josh's voice, I snap back to the present. "He doesn't get to shove me back down a rabbit hole, Josh," I say vehemently. "I'm not that girl anymore. I was never that girl. I was simply lost in Macom's translation."

"Yet you let him choose your show submissions over and over, and you received a rejection in response over and over."

I think back to every rejection I'd gotten and Macom's replayed response: *It doesn't matter, baby. Paint for you, not them. I pay the bills. You don't need them. You have me.* Like I didn't need my own success because I had his.

"That man shuts you down," Josh adds. "You didn't paint after you left him. Not until a few days ago."

"Because I wasn't going to paint until it was for me again," I say.

"And if he gets in your head again, how long will it be before you get there again?"

"I'm past him. And this show is for me."

"And what about Nick Rogers?"

I frown. "What about him?"

"Is he still distracting you?"

"You mean, inspiring me?"

"I take that as a yes. And I thought you were painting for you?"

"I am."

"And yet, one man convinced you to stop painting. Another convinced you to paint again."

That assessment hits me hard. "That's not—"

"I need to know that you're a painter no matter who is in your life or what is going on in your life." His line beeps and he curses. "Macom's calling me. I'll handle him. You avoid him. And paint. Fuck the winery, Faith. Be a damn painter." He ends the call and I grimace. Fuck the winery. He knows I can't do that, not with the money connected to it, but it doesn't matter to him. It's not his money. My art could be. It's a thought that reminds me that Nick understands why I can't walk away from the winery, and yet, he pushes me to embrace my art.

Glancing at the time on my phone, I suddenly realize I've been sleeping for two hours when I'm supposed to fly home today. I grab my boots and my head spins, while my stomach growls. I'm not drunk, but I'm not myself, and I don't like it. There is enough spinning out of control in my life without me drinking myself there, too. But then, doesn't the fact that I let this happen here with Nick, say trust? On a core level, I didn't even recognize until today that I trust Nick. I'm not sure who I said that about last.

Finishing the task of pulling on my boots, I stand up, testing my footing, and decide that I'm light-headed, but otherwise, really okay. I walk to the bathroom to pee and fix my face, frustrated as my conversation with Josh replays in my mind, as does the memory of Macom that Josh had brought forth. And suddenly, I need to see Nick. I need to feel the connection I have with him, the trust. And the minute he touches me or kisses me or simply looks at me, I will.

Chapter Eight

Faith

O N MY QUEST TO FIND NICK, I QUICKLY MAKE MY WAY
through the bedroom to the hallway. I head down the
stairs, only to grab the railing with the queasy, dizzy
sensation called foolishly drinking syndrome, which I'm fairly
certain is a real medical term. Or perhaps it's the kind of college
kid I never was, and am not now, thus I should not be using it
in my life—ever. A thought that has me taking slow, cautious
steps, down to the first level of stairs to ensure I don't tumble
downward.

My feet are thankfully still on solid ground as I reach the
platform below and turn the corner to take the second level of
steps. Instead I find myself halting at the sight of Nick and another thirty-something man, with buzz cut blond hair, sitting
at the island bar, both men with files and computers in front of

them. Aware that I'm about to interrupt their obvious work session, I fully intend to sneak back up the steps, but instead, find myself staring at Nick. Something inherently sexy about the way his brown hair tied at his nape, his high cheek bones, and full mouth come together to accent his masculine beauty. The man literally oozes power and arrogance, reminding me that he is all about control. All qualities that remind me of Macom and my mother in different ways, and that I swore I never wanted in my life again. And yet, Nick might as well be a drug, and me an addict, because I am officially incapable of walking away. Some might even call my attraction to him a form of self-destruction, and yet, Nick is more than the sum of those descriptive words. He's become the wings in the wind of change for me. The one person in my life who has ever truly lifted me up.

Shaking myself, I take a step backward, but the stranger with Nick sits at the end cap of the island facing me, and suddenly, his gaze lifts and lands on me. Nick follows his visitor's lead, his attention immediately rocketing to me as well, and when his gaze meets mine, I forget leaving. I forget the stranger. There is just this man taking my life by storm in all the right ways, and that connection we share that I was looking for. The bond, I am now certain that we've shared in different incarnations since the moment we tangled words in my mother's gardens, our connection intense and fierce, even then.

"Faith," he says, pushing to his feet, his voice warm, welcoming, the look in his eyes, hot. "Join us."

"No," I say, holding up my hands. "Keep doing what you're doing. I just wanted you to know that I was going to do some painting." But he has already stuffed documents into his briefcase, shut the lid, and is now crossing the room toward me, his stride long, confident. Everything about this man is powerful, intense. Riveting.

"I'm going to go paint," I say again, hurrying to meet him at the bottom of the steps. "I can tell you're working and I didn't mean to—"

He pulls me to him and kisses me, his really wonderfully hard body absorbing the softer lines of mine. "Don't do that," he orders softly, a rough, intimate quality to his voice.

"Do what?"

"Act like you don't belong here, because you do. And since you obviously don't know that yet, I've got work to do. Abel's a close friend, of which I have few. I wanted you two to meet. And we ordered pizza with the intent of waking you up to join us."

"You did?"

"Yes," he confirms. "We did. How do you feel?"

"Unsteady," I admit, my hands on his upper arms. "I don't know what I was thinking drinking like that."

"I'd like to think that you trusted that you were here with me, and safe." He caresses my hair behind my ear. "If you fall, I promise I'll catch you."

"You already did," I say, my hand flattening on his chest, my mind reflecting on the secret I sense in him, and trying to understand when I pain him. "I'll catch you, too. You know that, right?"

His gaze sharpens and then darkens, a hint of that secret flickering in his eyes, here and gone in a few flashed seconds. "I'll hold you to that," he says softly, but I sense the wall he now throws up, even as he twines the fingers of one of his hands with mine. "Come sit down and meet Abel."

He attempts to put us in motion while I dig in my heels. "I'm not myself right now."

"I'm half a bottle in," Abel calls out, and Nick rotates to stand by my side, allowing us both to spy the bottle in Abel's hand. "We'll be speaking the same language, Faith," he assures me.

Nick glances at me. "He's an attorney," he explains. "And he just won a big case that he wishes he would have lost."

My brow furrows. "He wanted to lose a case?"

"I did not want to lose my damn case," Abel grumbles. "I win. That's what I do."

"All right then," Nick says dryly. "Pizza for you both and no more whiskey." And this time, he doesn't give me time to object. His arm slides around my shoulders as he sets us back in motion. While I can't help but think that Abel and I oddly have similar reasons for drinking. He had an obligation to save a client that perhaps didn't deserve to be saved, much the same as what I felt with my mother.

"How are you this clearheaded?" I ask, as we round the counter and Nicks pulls out the barstool for me that sits between his spot and Abel's. "Didn't you drink with both of us?"

"I drank a pot of coffee," he explains, indicating the thermal pot on the counter as we both claim our seats.

"He drank his No.6 with you," Abel comments, sounding less than pleased. "My bottle is beneath him, and for the record you better be damn special to score the No.6 over me."

"Perhaps he needed No.6 to deal with my version of crazy today," I rebuttal, with the full intention of dodging an awkward bullet.

He laughs and glances at Nick. "Quick-witted. I like that."

"Until she outwits you, and she will," Nick assures him.

"Game on," Abel says, glancing at me. "You know this now, but to make it official, I'm Abel. Especially when I'm not drinking."

I laugh, finding Abel, the official, or not so official version, easy to like. "You're pretty humorous, Abel, especially when you're not drinking."

"A perfectly acceptable assessment," he says, "unless it's next week when I'm in court."

"Ah well," I say. "You might not be funny at all. I'm pretty sure I'm easily amused right now considering my alcohol intolerance."

"That's a horrible condition, I hear," he says, refilling his glass. "Thank God, I don't have it."

"As you can see," Nick interjects. "He's a phone book of bad jokes, sadly, even when he's not drinking."

"My jokes amuse people with a sense of humor," Abel comments dryly, glancing at me. "In case you haven't noticed yet, Faith, Nick doesn't have one of those."

"You know what they say," Nick replies. "If you can't be the good looking one, be the funny one."

Abel snorts. "If you are inferring you're the good looking one, then you drank more than I realized."

Nick offers me his cup in response. "Drink this. None of us need to numb our brains to the kind of stupid Abel's attempting."

Smiling at the banter between these two, and also eager to put the whiskey behind me, I eagerly sip Nick's coffee, regretting it as the bitterness hits my tongue. "Oh God," I murmur, unable to control the intense grimace on my face. "That is horrible." Both men laugh fairly ferociously, and I shoot glowers between them. "It's not funny. That might be poison. I don't know how anyone drinks that."

"It's called lots of long work nights and building tolerance," Nick says. "You'd be surprised how good bad can taste when you need to stay awake and focused." His cellphone rings where it rests on the counter.

He grabs it and glances at the caller ID, his jaw setting hard as he stands back up. "I need to take this." Apparently, that translates to alone because he's already exiting the kitchen.

"And then there were two," Abel says dramatically, pattering fingers on the table, as if creating music. "Don't worry," he adds. "I do awkward small talk better than the average guy. For instance, I hear you're not only an artist but that you made a big sale last night. Congrats."

"Thank you," I say, feeling a bit taken aback and awkward that he knows about my payday. "I guess Nick has been talking."

"Bragging," he says.

A warm spot forms in my chest with the realization that Nick doesn't just support me when he's with me, but even when he is not. "That's nice to hear."

"Nice," he repeats. "Nice and Nick don't really want to compute for me, but maybe it's the whiskey. What are you going to do to celebrate your payday?"

Pay back Nick a chunk of the money he paid the bank, I think, but that's none of his business, so I settle on a generic, "Pay bills," I reply.

"Huh. A new car or even shoes would be a sexy celebration. Bills. Not so sexy."

"Sexy has never been on the top of my priority list," I say. "And paying bills is much sexier than not paying bills."

"That's true," he says. "And I'm sure Nick will help you celebrate anyway."

"He did that by being with me at the gallery last night."

He arches. "And gave you a gift, I assume? The man is rolling in money, which I'm sure you know."

A fizzle of unease slides through me. "I know he has money."

"A lot of money," Abel pushes. "You know that, right?"

"He told me," I say, my discomfort growing exponentially, as does my regret over the whiskey that still has me feeling less than sharp.

"Did he?" Abel asks, in what feels like feigned surprise. "Huh. He usually doesn't share details because, you know, everyone wants something from him." He stares me down, all signs of humor gone now, his green eyes cold, hard, as he adds, "Do you?"

Chapter Nine

Faith

I BLANCH AT ABEL'S QUESTION, AND OBVIOUS ACCUSATION, but recover quickly. "That's direct," I say, realizing what should have been obvious. He's sizing me up, looking for the vulture in a butterfly's clothing.

"Do you have a problem with direct?"

"Actually, I prefer it," I say. "Namely because I dislike secrets. So, to answer your question: Yes. I want *many* things from Nick, but none of those things include his money." I think of my fake friends back in L.A. that turned out to be all about Macom and his fame, which spurs me to add, "And for the record, I find the idea of a friend who wants to protect him, enviable."

Surprise flickers in his eyes and when I believe he's about to reply, Nick reappears. "What's enviable?" he asks, claiming the stool next to me again.

"My hot body," Abel says, holding out his hands to his sides. "Which is why I stay single. I need to spread the wealth." The doorbell rings and he is on his feet in an instant. "I'll get that," he announces, already walking toward the door.

"He's a piece of work," Nick says, and we face each other as he adds, "But I'm sure you figured that out."

"I did," I say. "But I think I might like him."

"Think?"

"I'll decide after I have more food than whiskey in me," I reply, appreciating Abel's loyalty to Nick, but not necessarily his approach in showing it. "Do you two work together?" I ask.

"No," he says, "but we run cases by each other with surprisingly good results, considering our fields of expertise."

"You trust him," I observe.

"I call no one a friend that I can't trust."

A comment that brings my little chat with Abel full circle. "Because everyone must want something from you."

His hand settles on my leg. "Where did that just come from, Faith?"

"The number that represents your bank account," I say. "It's rather sobering, quite literally."

"Most people would find it intriguing."

"I'm not most people, Nick."

"Of that," he says. "I would agree."

"Money changes people."

"I've had money all my life, sweetheart. Adding a few extra zeroes isn't a character-changing event for me."

"I get that," I say. "But just as money can make the holder less than genuine in many ways, it makes those around the money holder tend to be less than genuine. Nick, I don't want your money."

His eyes that are always so damn hard, soften. "I know that,

Faith," he says, seeming to understand that I'm speaking beyond the bank note.

"If anything, your money makes me nervous. It makes me—" I stop myself before I head down a path that leads to Macom, and is better traveled when we're alone. "You have to know that I can't—"

Nick's hand goes to my face, and suddenly his cheek is pressed to mine, his lips at my ear. "*We* can, Faith," he says softly, leaning back to look at me, our eyes lock and hold, I feel the deep pull between us. "Together, remember?"

"Yes, but—"

"No buts," he says.

"Nick—"

"Faith."

"We aren't done with this, Nick Rogers," I warn.

"You most certainly are for now," Abel says, setting the pizzas on the counter. "Eyes on the guest and the food people."

Nick lifts his brows at me, offering me the power of decision: Do I push for a talk I can't really have in front of Abel or cave to the scent of spicy cheese goodness currently teasing my nostrils? The spicy cheese goodness wins. I rotate to face Abel, who rewards my attention by opening a box top to display an impressive looking pepperoni pizza. My stomach growls again and I decide this delicious, calorie-laden lunch will either grow the brain cells I will need to negotiate a proper financial outcome with Nick "Tiger" Rogers or put me back to sleep, but the latter is a risk I will have to take.

Ten minutes later, we remain at the island, all with bottles of water and paper plates piled with slices of pizza, in front of us. "How do you two know each other?" I ask, and one slice into my meal, I'm already feeling sharper and far more present in the conversation.

"We met in law school," Nick offers, his answer seemingly simple, when I've come to know that there is nothing simple about Nick Rogers.

Or silent about Abel, I'm learning as he adds, "A long-ass time ago. Fourteen years ago?"

"I got my tattoos in July of 2003 and we met that week," Nick says. "So yes. That would be fourteen years ago." He glances at me. "Which I remember because he talked the entire damn time."

"Offering moral support when he almost backed out," Abel interjects. "You know the whole 'don't be a wuss' kind of support, though that wasn't the exact word I used."

"He's a big talker in every possible way," Nick says, holding out his bare forearms to display the black and orange tiger etched on one and the words 'An eye for an eye' on the other. A phrase that I hate, and that still isn't about him to me. I'm not sure it can ever be about him. "Two tattoos," Nick continues. "Ask Abel how many he got while talking big? None. He was afraid it would hurt."

"It's a good thing you two aren't competitive or anything," I say dryly. "Or else you might be enemies."

"Speaking of enemies," Nick says, shoving aside his plate. "Let's get serious and talk about the winery."

I stiffen instantly. "What are you doing, Nick?"

"Abel knows what's going on at the winery," he says, and before I can even register my shock at this announcement, he adds, "And he knows this because I've asked him to protect you from me."

I face Nick, my feet suddenly unsteady again, and I haven't even stood up yet. "What is this?"

"I promised you paperwork that protects you and the winery. And that needs to come from another attorney, who could be disbarred if he helped me deceive you."

His friend, who just not so subtly accused me of using him for his money. "I'm giving you my check from last night," I say. "That covers sixty thousand of the money I now owe you. After the L.A. Forum in a few weeks, I should be able to pay back the rest."

"You owe me nothing," Nick says, "which is exactly what Abel is going to guarantee."

"Abel doesn't decide this," I retort. "And neither do you. I'm paying you back."

"We can talk later," Nick states. "Let Abel do his part in this now."

"Abel's been drinking," I argue.

"Abel's had half a pizza," Abel says. "He's good. You can ask him, yourself, though, if you prefer."

I inhale and face him, shoving my plate aside as I do. "I appreciate your efforts, but—"

"But I'm Nick's friend," Abel supplies, wrongly assuming, at least partially, to know where my head is at right now. "Legally," he continues, "once you sign this document," he sets a piece of paper in front of me, "I'm your attorney before I'm his friend." He taps the document. "It's an offer of representation. And for the record, I might be a criminal attorney, but I had a few years of corporate experience right out of college, and I spend a hell of a lot of time with Nick Roger's cases. I know how to protect you."

"Nick's the one who needs to be protected," I argue. "He paid six figures on my behalf."

"That he doesn't want back," Abel replies, the simple statement contradicting his earlier tone and I don't like it.

"How," I challenge, "can you possibly back up that thought process when you just inferred that I want his money."

"He did what?" Nick demands. "What the fuck, Abel?"

"I didn't infer you want his money," Abel bites out, ignoring Nick. "I was reading you just like I do anyone who wants my representation."

"Except I didn't want your representation," I counter. "And I don't appreciate being read like a criminal using Nick for his money."

"And if I believed that now," Abel says, "I would have talked some sense into Nick, and declined to offer you representation."

"Let me get this straight," I say, my temper flaring, my tone controlled but biting. "A few minutes ago I was a low-down dirty user, and now I'm worthy of your services?" I don't give either man time to say anything else. "That's it. I need out of here." I slide off my barstool but Nick catches my arms.

"This is not the time to hold onto me, Nick," I warn, my gaze rocketing to his, the charge between us ever present, but this time the heat between us is my anger.

"This is exactly the time to hold onto you," he argues. "It's Sunday. We need these contracts signed by tomorrow morning."

My gaze rockets to his. "Then you give them to me."

"Abel's involvement not only protects you, it lawyers us up even further with the bank."

"You said my actions were enviable," Abel points out. "And I'm as good an attorney as I am a friend."

Angry all over again, I pull away from Nick and turn back to Abel. "It *was* enviable," I say. "But so is honesty and your behavior with me was not honest."

"You're right," Abel surprises me by admitting. "And first and foremost you need to know that my actions were mine and mine alone." He eyes Nick, who is now standing beside me. "Nick did not know what I was doing." He looks between us now. "But that said, I won't apologize to either of you. Considering our timeline, I had to make a decision on where I stood in my involvement now, not later. And I'm all in." He refocuses on me. "And that's the case for you as well, Faith, which is why I've prepared some guarantees for you."

He reaches in his briefcase and pulls out a folder, and sets one sheet of paper on top of the representation letter, and then creates two more stacks. "Start here," he says, indicating his offer letter. "I contacted your estate attorney, and without disclosing details, aside from my intent to aid Nick in your protection, I asked him to endorse the protection my agreement offers you. He not only read my representation offer, he scanned it back to me with a handwritten note to you that stamps it with his approval." He shuffles the papers and shows me the note which reads: *Faith – this agreement ensures Abel's legal obligation to protect your interests and privacy. It's a sound document.*

"Sign the agreement," Abel says, "and I'm now loyal to you first and Nick second."

"Questions?" Nick asks, his hands settling back on my leg.

"Not about this," I say, my hand waving over the rest of the paperwork. "What is the rest of this?"

Abel indicates the second stack of documents, which is actually not a stack, but one form. "Before I explain what this is," he says, "let me explain why it's important to you. When someone gives you a lump sum of money for a business interest, they could later claim it was with the promise of something in exchange."

"Even without a signed document?"

"Yes," Nick states. "Because a verbal agreement is binding and it would be my word against yours and I have the money to fight you on it."

"But that can't happen with this document in place," Abel interjects, "as it clearly states that the money he's given you is a gift, and it cannot be treated as leverage against you for any monetary gain. In other words, he can't claim it was a down payment on the winery, meant to kick in after you inherit. Additionally, the legal verbiage assures that this contract supersedes all others."

"Meaning," Nick says, "that nothing can be signed after the fact that voids its content."

"An important factor since this final document," Abel says, indicating the last stack of papers, "requires one hell of a thought of trust. This is the dummy document that will be shown to the bank and in court, which gives Nick half ownership of the winery once you inherit."

This isn't news to me. Nick warned me this was coming despite not warning me about Abel. I trust Nick. So why, right now, in this moment, are there warning bells going off in my head? Maybe it's Abel. I don't know him. Nick sideswiped me with his involvement. That has to be it, but as Nick's hand comes down on my shoulder and he softly says my name, I still find myself back at the art show, where Nick and I had first connected, replaying a conversation about secrets that I'd had with him there.

"People have secrets, Faith," Nick says. "It's part of being human."

"My mother sure did," I reply.

His hands find my waist, turning me to face him, intensity radiating off him. "What kind of secrets, Faith?"

"Her kind of secrets," I reply, not sure why he is suddenly so very intense. "Like you have secrets," I add, using his nickname, "Tiger."

"My enemies call me Tiger. You call me Nick."

"Why do I keep feeling like you're my enemy?"

"Why are you looking for an enemy?"

I return to the present and ask myself that very question: Why am I looking for an enemy? *Am I looking for an enemy?* And if so who is it that I don't trust? Nick? Abel? It has to be Abel. I've already established that I trust Nick. And he's earned that trust. He wouldn't lie to me. He wouldn't deceive me. And if he trusts Abel, I trust Abel.

So why am I still so uneasy?

Chapter Ten

Nick

ECONDS TICK BY AS FAITH STARES DOWN AT THE documents Abel has given her, no words, no action, but I sense that wall of hers slamming into place. "Let us have a few minutes," I order Abel.

"No," Faith says quickly. "I have questions."

"As you should," Abel says. "We can go through every line of the documents one by one."

"I'll read them myself," she says. "These questions are not questions that these documents can answer." She looks between us. "For starters, I want to verify that we're all on the same page that I believe us to be on. That being that the bank would not be ordering a property assessment if they didn't believe it would somehow allow them to stake a claim on the deed. Correct?"

"Correct," Abel confirms.

"That's the assumption we're operating under," I add. "And while my preferred method of operation is not to assume anything, winning is about being a step ahead of our opposition. Which is also why I called my personal banker today and have him on standby to buy out your note."

Her eyes go wide. "At what cost to you?"

"Nothing outside of paying for a rushed property assessment of our own."

"We can't use the current one?"

"If my bank finds out your bank is questioning the property value and we don't disclose that, we're looking at a fraud situation."

"Right," she says. "That makes sense." She moves on. "And if that assessment comes back under the value of the current note?" she asks. "Can we use the revenue the winery produces to justify the new note? I have that well documented."

"We not only can," I say, "we will. But set that aside and let's talk about the worst case scenario: My banker makes an offer and they decline."

Her brow furrows. "Why would they do that?"

"That's our question," Abel says. "What do they know that we don't beyond any piece of paper."

Faith gives him a puzzled look. "I don't follow where you're going with this."

"Where's the money?" I supply. "What makes the winery or something connected to it worth money outside the obvious? Do you have any idea?"

She shakes her head. "None. And by none I meant that I'm a complete zero on this entire premise. That said, if that were true, if there is some hidden treasure, be it literal or not, the bank will fight hard, and that doesn't bode well for the outcome we're after. Which brings me to another question." She picks up the dummy document and focuses on me. "If you present this, and the bank legally claims the winery, are you left with any liability?"

"No," I say. "I am not."

"Okay," she says. "Then can you use that dummy document to force them to pay you back the money you paid on not just my behalf, but that of the winery."

"I'd demand they compensate both myself and you," I reply. "and for all the monies paid on behalf of the rightful owner of the winery. And because under that treasure scenario, the bank would just want us to go away, I believe they'd settle with us. But we're a long way from that point."

"Nick's the expert here," Abel says, "I believe there would be a case to prove deceptive practices among other charges, and force the bank's hand into backing off. But we have to find the proverbial treasure."

"Which is why, among other things," I reply, "that we have a private investigator working on this."

"The private investigator that you're paying," Faith says, gathering up the documents and turning her attention to Abel. "I'll read these and let you know if I have questions."

"This is time sensitive," Abel says, before I have the chance. "Let's read through them together."

"Nick needs them by morning," she says. "It's afternoon. And I need two things from you. One is your fee agreement. I need to know how much you charge, so that I can budget to pay you."

"I've been paid," he states.

"By Nick."

"Not with cash," he clarifies.

"He's been paid, Faith," I reiterate.

She ignores me. "Please put together a bill," she states again.

"And additionally, I need a contract that states that I will pay Nick back any and all money he spends on my behalf with fifteen percent interest."

My jaw clenches. "Faith—"

"And," she continues, as if I have not spoken, "if I do not do so in a year, he receives thirty percent interest in the winery. There will need to be a financial ledger."

"He's not going to do that, Faith," I say.

She rotates to face me. "He is or he isn't my attorney, but yours, and I'm not protected at all."

"Don't be stubborn."

She looks at Abel. "I need those documents." She holds up the paperwork in her hand. "And I'm going upstairs to read these in detail."

"My cellphone number and email are on the offer letter," Abel says, drawing her attention again. "Email me and text me so that I have your contact information to get you those documents. And you can give Nick the signed documents, but if you have questions or concerns, text me, email me, call me. Whatever works for you, but do it this evening."

My cellphone rings, and I glance at the number to find Beck is calling for the second time in forty-five minutes, and just that fast, Faith has darted around me and is walking away. I hit the decline button, and take a step in Faith's direction. "Wait," Abel orders harshly, his tone insistent, his hands coming down on the counter. "Don't go after her yet."

"Now is not the time for whatever you plan to say," I say, taking another step, but he doesn't take "no" for an answer.

"Damn it, Nick," he growls. "*Wait.*"

With agitated reluctance, I halt, facing him, my gaze pinning his. "Now is not the time," I bite out again, "for whatever it is you want to say."

"Quite the contrary," he assures me. "It's the exact right time considering you're about to go upstairs and bulldoze Faith. Let her do what she feels she needs to do."

"You're supposed to be working for *her*. Do that. Protect her, not me."

"I am working for her," he says. "Which is why I repeat: Don't be a bull charging at her. If you—"

"I don't want her money."

"I know that," he says. "I get that. So does she." He grimaces. "Look, man. You don't deal with death with your job the way I do. I see how it impacts people. It steals your control. It makes you need to find it in other places, and finding it is part of healing."

"Death has nothing to do with this, Abel. Again. For the third time. Now is not—"

"Death *is a* part of this," he presses. "You both are dealing with its biting impact on your lives."

"There is no biting impact for me. I hated my father."

"And yet, despite hating your father, you had to solve the mystery of his death. Open your eyes and recognize how much you both need control right now. Because if you don't find a way to give Faith some of what you want to take, she will push back and perhaps even push you away."

I run a hand over my face, begrudgingly admitting that he's making sense. "Fuck," I grind out, stepping to the opposite end of the table from him and pressing my hands to the island. "Fuck. Fuck. Fuck."

"Go talk to her," he says. "But don't bulldoze her with your money, or even with good intentions. It will make her feel unsettled. It will push her away, and frankly, if she was willing to just take your money, I'd be concerned. I *was* concerned until I met her and she stepped up to do the right thing."

"I want—"

"Her," he supplies. "I see that. But money doesn't buy love or anyone worth having. Providing that paperwork to her proved to her that you're honorable. The fact that she didn't just accept the money proves she is as well. That's not a bad thing and neither is her having enough pride to want to pay her own way."

"I told you—"

"Even if," he continues, "you buy her a diamond the size of Texas and a wardrobe to match."

"Where *the fuck* did that come from?"

"You," he says. "It came from watching you with her and for years without her. And on a side note, you have an excuse for not telling her about most of this which is her safety. You don't have that excuse with the club. Obviously not now, but if you wait too long, that is going to bite you in the ass that is already in deep shit."

He starts walking toward the door and I don't move, his warnings radiating through me, as well as his comment about Faith and a ring. I have never considered myself a marrying man, and even if I did, the mountains I have to climb with Faith are many. The club matters. The truth about how I found her matters. Her safety comes first. And right now, I need to make sure that while I'm trying to destroy our enemies, I don't destroy us in the process.

Feeling the urgency of that need, I start walking, double-stepping the stairs, telling myself Faith trusts me. She told me about her mother's death, but did that come from a place of trust or guilt? Fuck. I need her to trust me. If she doesn't now, she damn sure won't when she hears about the club, let alone how I found her. Reaching the second level, I enter the bedroom and Faith isn't in sight. Continuing on to the bathroom, I find her suitcase open on the floor. She's exiting the closet with her clothes in hand. "I need to go home." Her announcement proves that the control I seek is not mine.

"We talked about this," I say. "You're staying and we're going back at the end of the week together."

"*You* talked about this," she says. "While I was drinking."

"The contracts—"

"I can read them on the plane and scan them back to you."

"I want you to stay, Faith."

She zips her suitcase and stands up. "I'm going to be honest with you, Nick, because you know: No one in my life has been honest with me and I really need honest things in my life right now."

Holy hell. She's killing me right now. I take a step toward her. She backs up and holds up a hand. "Stop. When you touch me I get more confused."

"Confused," I repeat. "That's what my touch makes you feel?"

"I can't think when you touch me, Nick."

"And that's a problem? Because I can promise you that if you can do a mathematical equation while a man is touching you, he's the wrong man. I'm not the wrong man."

"You can't just spend a hundred and twenty thousand dollars on me, Nick. Or more. You want to spend more." She presses her hand to her forehead. "I appreciate what you've done. You are acting like a hero, and I know in my heart that's your intent."

"And you don't want a hero."

"That's not it. I mean, no. I don't, but I'm not going to be foolish and not see that I'm pretty lucky to have one in you right now. But Nick. We decided on possibilities based on who we are together. And I like who we are together so far."

"But?" I prod.

"Money changes people."

"I told you. I've had money all my life."

"I'm not talking about you alone."

"You think it changes us," I supply.

"Of course it changes us."

My mind tracks back to the references she's made to her ex's fame and stature. "I'm not Macom."

"I know that," she says, folding her arms in front of her. "I do. But I'm still being honest. Once he paid all the bills and made a ton of money, I was subservient to him in ways I should never have allowed myself to be."

"Again. I'm not Macom, but I have money. I won't apologize for that any more than I will spending it on you."

"It's a six-figure bank note, Nick. It's not a dress."

"Whatever it is. I don't spend money on women, Faith. They aren't around long enough for me to even think about it. But you. You are different, and if there was a dress that cost six figures and you wanted it, I'd damn sure buy it for you. The money is nothing to me."

"But it is to me, Nick. I need—"

"What you need," I say, closing the space between us and before she can back away, my hands are on her waist, and I'm pulling her to me, "what *we* need, is to fuck, talk, and repeat." I cup her face. "Abel told me not to bulldoze you. That my money and the death of your mother had stolen your control, and I need to let you have some control. But what he, and you, don't seem to see, is that you have stolen my control."

"No one steals your control, Nick Rogers."

"You have Faith," I say, my voice low, a hint of rasp. "Because I can't think when I'm not touching you." I kiss her, a deep lick of my tongue against her tongue before I ask, "I once told you that I wanted you naked and willingly exposed. I still do. And we aren't there yet, which means you don't trust me."

Her fingers curl around my shirt. "I do trust you. I just want to trust in us. I want to trust that I know what is real. And I don't want money to get in the way of that."

"You want real, sweetheart. I'll show you real." I scoop her up into my arms and I start walking, heading into the bedroom. And as tempting as the idea is to strip her naked and show her my many different versions of real, I have another destination in mind. A place where I show her just how naked she's made me.

Chapter Eleven

Nick

I EXIT THE BEDROOM WITH FAITH IN MY ARMS, WHERE I want her to stay in every sense of the meaning.

"Where are we going?" she asks.

"Somewhere that apparently speaks louder than I do," I say, my stride long as I carry her down the hallway toward the room I designed for her, entering her new art studio. Her place to paint, to escape, to forget that damn winery she doesn't even want to own and yet, she can't walk away from without foolishly leaving behind a small fortune.

Entering the room, the glossy white flooring that I'd had installed for her painting process beneath my feet, I don't stop until I'm setting Faith down in front of her current work in progress. "You want real," I say. "This room is as real as it gets." My hands settle on her waist. "I didn't just invite you to stay with me, Faith. I invited you into my life. I want to be a part of yours. That's real. We're real. What I *feel* for you is real."

"Which is what?"

Words fly through my head: Protective. Aroused. Hungry. Connect. Quite possibly love. "Everything, Faith," I say. "Everything I can possibly feel. Stay with me this week." My fingers flex at her waist. "Paint. Prepare for your show, and by the time we go back to Sonoma *together* the bills will be paid, we'll know more about the bank, and we'll set up a plan to keep Kasey motivated."

"Kasey," she says. "Right." She inhales and exhales, and then abruptly twists away from me.

I go to touch her but she is just out of reach and before I can correct that wrong, she is standing in front of the canvas that is her current work in progress, where it sits on an easel. And that space, really like this one, is her space. A place I do not want her to feel I can invade, take, and control. Inhaling, I hold my ground, seconds ticking by and turning into a full minute as she studies the black and white Sonoma mountain-scape that has yet to find color, that one splash of red she always adds in completion.

"This room," I say, "is supposed to be the red you add to your works: the new life, the possibilities even before I asked you to consider the possibilities. *Talk to me*, Faith."

She turns to face me. "I've been asking myself that since I stood downstairs with you and Abel. I trust you and yet I was uneasy, and I really think it comes back to control. You have it. I don't. You create the red splash, not me. Not us."

"Because I want to help you with Kasey?"

"Because you're taking over my life, Nick. You have the control. All of it. I have none."

"Sweetheart, I told you. You have control. More than you

obviously realize."

"Really? Because I just walked downstairs and found out your friend that I had never met knew things about me I had only told you. You should have talked to me about him before he was here."

Guilt slices through me with the realization that I never even considered talking to her and for one massive reason: He already knew. And he knew because he was involved with my quest to prove she was a killer. I don't make excuses. There are none. "You're right. I fucked up. I'm sorry."

"You're sorry?"

"Yes. I am. Why does that surprise you?"

"Because you always surprise me, Nick. I feel like I shouldn't be upset at all. Abel is helping me. And I know you are trying to protect me. But the truth here is that you blasted into my life out of nowhere, and refused to be ignored in every possible way. You singlehandedly inspired me to paint again when my agent and even my own desire couldn't do it. Not even the certainty that Macom was mocking me for failing could do it. But you did. You supported my art when no one else has. Cared about why I felt things and what I was doing. Made me feel I could share my secrets with you."

I narrow my eyes on her, reading where this is going. "But?" I prod. "Because there is obviously a but."

"But you also shared some of my secrets with Abel without talking to me first. Told me how to spend the money I got from my art. Hired yourself as my attorney without really asking. You just told me. Paid my bills. Told me how to handle Kasey. All with good intent, I know that. But you have completely consumed me. You are like a drug that I am high on, but what happens when that drug is gone? I don't know if I have it in me to get any higher, and then crash without you, Nick. I don't know how I can get any more reliant on you, and survive that."

"Obviously we are not on the same page, Faith. Because every decision I make is with the assumption that we're going higher, getting closer, and that I'm protecting my woman. And that's what you are to me."

"I know that you're protecting me."

"And every reaction you have to me, and to us, is with the assumption that we're crashing and burning. That we're ending. That's not good enough for me or for you. And that's not *me* controlling *you*. That's something, or someone else, controlling you because you let it. You want control? Take it, Faith. For now, and despite every fiber of my being wanting to undress you, strip you naked, and never let you leave again, I won't. Because like I said, I still want you naked and willingly exposed. *Willingly exposed*, Faith. Like I am to you. I'll call the pilot." I turn and start for the door, the sum of my lies and her push to distance us, zipping through me like a razor.

"Nick, wait."

I don't wait.

Because besides the fact that "wait" isn't the response I'm looking for from her, there is a storm brewing inside me that I need to contain or she'll end up naked. And then I'll fuck her until this feeling goes away, which might be never since I want to force her wall down, but my lies say that I don't deserve to see it fall.

"*Nick.*"

She's no sooner said my name again then she is in front of me, her hands on my chest, heat radiating through me, but I don't touch her. I don't want to drown truth in the fiction by way of fucking. "I need to say something to you," she says, a seemingly nervous breath trembling from her lips. And I tell myself to think about those lips on my cock, that mouth sucking me deep and hard. I tell myself to strip her naked, fuck her, and send her on her way. I tell myself she's every other damn woman in my life that meant nothing to me because that would be easier, but she's not.

And it pisses me off.

"I'm done talking," I say, my hands coming down on her shoulders, and I fully intended to set her aside.

But she fists my shirt and steps into me. "What part of 'you are a drug' do you not understand? A crazy, wicked drug that consumes me. I'm afraid of taking another hit, and another, and depending on that drug, and then it's gone. I've never felt that about anything or anyone but my art. You and my art. I don't know what to do with that. But I can't—I won't—let your money and power take control of me or us."

Still I don't touch her. "In or out, Faith?"

"What does that even mean?"

"You either decide that we are reaching for those possibilities, and working through the ups and downs, not caving to them. Or you get out. But there is no in between for me. That's not how I'm wired. So. You have the control right now. Decide how this plays out."

Her lips tighten. "I *will* push back when you push too hard. And I won't back off."

"In *or* out, Faith."

"In," she says fiercely. "You know I'm in."

I'm not sold yet. I don't want a reply delivered by a cornered woman. "Maybe you need to think about it, because you weren't talking like you were in a few minutes ago."

"Because like most addicts, we try to deny we're addicted."

"That's not a good answer." My hand is instantly under her hair and at the back of her neck, pulling her to me. "Is that what you want? To deny the addiction? Because I don't deny mine,

101

Faith. I am very much addicted to you. I'm obsessed. And nothing but all of you will be enough."

"And if I want all of you, Nick?"

"You already have me, sweetheart. And you're clearly trying to figure out what to do with me, but that's okay. I'm here to offer suggestions." My lips slant over hers, my tongue licking into her mouth, a deep stroke followed by another, and when she moans, only when she moans, do I pull back, and add, "Suggestion number one. You have on too many clothes." I catch the hem of her shirt and pull it upward, over her head.

Before it's even hit the ground, my hand is back under her hair, cupping the back of her neck and pulling her lips back to mine. "Suggestion number two: It's okay to do drugs when I'm your drug." I kiss her again and she does that thing she does, which I swear I want to experience again and again for the rest of my fucking life. She sighs into the kiss, as if she can finally breathe, as if I'm the reason she breathes. She's damn sure the reason I breathe and most definitely the reason my cock is so damn hard it could break glass.

At the feel of her hands under my shirt, on my skin, a heady rush of lust and adrenaline pulses through me, while my mind conjures all the places her hands could be next. Namely, the same place I want her mouth—my cock, though just about any place on my body would do just fine. But as much as I want her to touch me, as much as I want to be naked with her right now, I can't focus on fucking. And holy hell, I want to fuck. But right now we have to have a conversation about control. And control isn't about having no limits. It's about controlling the ones you have, about owning them. And that means I'm keeping my clothes on, at least for now, while she is not.

I reach for her hands and pull them from my shirt, holding them between us, walking her backwards as I do. "Let's talk about the subject of the day. Control."

"You want it. *Sometimes* I'll let you have it."

My lips curve and I press her hands behind her back, shackling them with one of my hands. "Is that right?" I ask unclasping the front of her black, lacy bra, my hand settling between her breasts.

"Yes," she says. "*That* is right."

My gaze lowers, raking over her high, full breasts, her pebbled nipples, my finger lightly teasing one stiff peak, her back arching into my touch. "Can I have it now, Faith?" I ask, my eyes rocketing to her face. "Or am I being too controlling?"

"Not even close," she whispers, her voice low, raspy. Affected.

I respond to that bold sexual challenge in her that has been in the air between us from the moment we met and turned me on right out of the gate. I'm hot. I'm hard. My blood is pumping, but I am not blind to the fact that she ran from me minutes ago, vulnerability in that action, but now...There is none. Because being sexually daring is her emotional shield, something I suspect she learned at the club she and Macom frequented. Maybe that is even why the club worked for her. She didn't have to be present with him there. She didn't have to be present in life there. And that might have worked for her and him, but it no longer does for me or us.

I brush my lips over hers and release her hands, turning her to face the opposite direction, while I skim her bra away, my hand flattening on her belly, my teeth on her shoulder. "I'm going to keep asking for more, you know that, right?"

"Yes."

"Can I have it?"

"Yes."

"Are you sure about that?"

"Yes."

I settle on one knee, my hands on her hips, my lips on her naked back, my tongue licking the delicate spot. And when she draws in a shaky breath, I stand up, my hands falling away from her. "Undress, but don't turn around."

I want her to turn and look for where my head is right now. To look into my eyes, and see the test I'm giving her. To be present with me, right now, in this moment, in all possible ways. But she does it. She walks forward and starts undressing, so emotionally removed that she takes my commands that I'm giving her almost coldly.

And it both challenges me and pisses me off, and not at her. At me. I want her to be present, but I haven't given her a reason. I haven't let her know that I see her, *really* see her. Hell. Maybe I didn't until now. Until she almost walked out the door over a control issue we haven't even come close to solving.

Now I see that she is guarded in all the ways that matter, the ways that make her think we will end and I will leave. And now I refuse to let her hide. I walk around her and sit on the stool beside her workstation, directly in front of her. Our eyes meet and still I see no trepidation. No vulnerability. She verbally said she was in, not out, but she has shut down on me.

She watches me watch her, stripping away her socks and jeans, gauging her control over me. Making sure her façade of submission still gives her control and on that Faith understands sexual play, while I suspect Macom did not. The reality here is that submission, when done right, is all about the sub's control. But Faith is no submissive and I want more than her body.

Her gaze finds mine as she twists her fingers into the thin black lace of her panties at her hips, and drags them down the silky expanse of her legs. The way I plan to drag my tongue down them, in the very near future. The tiny triangle of blonde hair in the V of her body, sexy as hell, but then, everything about this woman is sexy as hell to me.

I stand up and move behind the stool. "Come to me, Faith."

Her lips curve ever so slightly, oh so sexily, and she walks toward me, her hips and breasts swaying seductively, stopping in front of the stool. I could tell her to bend over the stool, and stick that pretty ass in the air for me, and I suspect that is what she wants. For me to spank her. I give myself just a moment to think of her creamy, curvy perfect ass waiting on my palm. The way her back would arch in anticipation when I warmed her cheeks. How wet her sex would be when I slide my fingers between her legs. How hot she would be when my cock followed my palm. But now is not a spanking that would give her that ultimate rush, and force her to forget everything. I don't want her to forget. I want her to be right here, with me, willingly, emotionally exposed.

"Turn around and sit."

Her teeth scrape her bottom lip, and she does as I say, sitting down. I move to stand in front of her, squatting down, my hands on my knees, when they want to be on hers. "Open your legs for me," I say, the stool low enough to place her sex directly in front of me. My mouth exactly where we both want it.

Interestingly though, it's in this moment that I see a flicker of vulnerability in her eyes, but it is there and gone in an instant, the way we will be if I don't build our bond and build it now. To my surprise, she doesn't open her legs. "Are you going to get undressed?"

"No," I say. "I am not, but I am going to lick that sweet spot right between your legs, and slide my fingers in, and make you come. Open for me, Faith."

Her lashes lower, but not before I see the flicker of vulnerability, the emotional kind I am after, in her eyes. My hands go to her ankles and I slowly caress upward. "Look at me, Faith."

"No," she whispers, emotion radiating off of her.

I kiss her knees, tiny little clusters of kisses and her fingers slide into my hair. I flick my tongue between her knees, and then inch her thighs apart. She tilts her head back, looking skyward. Looking anywhere but at me. I don't force her to look at me. She's exposed when she didn't mean to be exposed. I stole the control she pretends to give to me. But this isn't about taking her control. This is about making her present and that I did it as easily as I have pleases me. Makes me want to please her and give her that escape, that sanctuary that is sex for her.

My mouth travels up her thigh and I lick her clit. Just once. A quick flicker before my mouth is at her other knee, my tongue teasing the inner curve. Faith trembles and I look up at her at the same moment her gaze lowers, colliding with mine, the vulnerability I'd seen moments before still present, and she doesn't seem to be able to hide it.

And for a moment I feel a stab of guilt. I'd come for her. I'd wanted to make her vulnerable to hurt her and for what? A bastard of a father I hated. But that bastard brought me to Faith. I caress a path up her legs, mouth on one and hand on the other, and I don't tease her any longer. I give her clit a gentle lick and then another, before suckling, my fingers stroking the slick wet heat of her body. And apparently vulnerability is arousing to Faith, because I don't even manage to slide my fingers inside her before she's pulling at my hair and trembling into release.

I ease her into her release, licking and stroking until she calms, falling forward and catching herself on my shoulders. I stand up and cup her face, forcing her to look at me, that vulnerability back in her eyes, etched in her beautiful face. "This is what I want from you."

"What does that mean?"

"You were willing to be naked physically while I was fully dressed, but not emotionally, not at first. You are always willing to give me control of your body, Faith, even from the first night we met, but you aren't willing to give me the ultimate control I've given you."

"I'm naked. You're not. One of us gave the other control. And it wasn't you."

"I can be naked and fuck a million women and they wouldn't have anything but my cock, Faith. But you Faith, are the one who is one hell of a drug." And I don't plan to say it, but suddenly the words are on my tongue, and I know I have to say them. I know she needs to hear them, "I'm falling in love with you, Faith."

She gasps. "What?"

"I'm falling in love with you," I say, my thumb stroking her cheek. "I've never said that to anyone. I've never felt it with anyone."

"I'm pretty sure lust and hate have evolved into something that I'm not sure I want to feel."

"Why, Faith?"

"You could hurt me, Nick."

"Sweetheart, you have pieces of me no one was supposed to ever have, and the many ways you could shatter them should have me running for the hills. But all I want to do is kiss you again. Hold you. Watch you paint." I brush my lips over hers. "Which you should do now. You have a show."

"Watch me naked," she says. "I need you inside me right now."

"As much as I like that invitation," I say, stepping back and pressing her knees together. "This was about you, Faith. Not me. I don't want it to be about me."

Faith is on her feet in an instant, her naked body pressed

to mine, her fingers curling in my shirt all over again. "Let's be clear, Nick Rogers. That wasn't just for me. That was for you. That was about control."

"Not this time."

"Maybe you believe that, but I don't. And I could drop to my knees and take it from you the way you just took it from me. We both know I can. But I won't because I now realize what I didn't before. You don't just want it. You need it. It's *your way, your wall*. It's how you keep people at a distance, me at a distance."

"I just told you I'm falling in love with you, woman."

"And you made sure I was vulnerable when you did because you were vulnerable. And I let you. I'll let you, but not forever, because I can't be as vulnerable as you just made me, alone." She releases my shirt and tries to move away, but there is no way in hell I'm letting her get away. Not now. And not ever.

Chapter Twelve

Nick

I CUP THE BACK OF FAITH'S HEAD, DRAGGING HER MOUTH TO mine. "Sweetheart, you aren't alone and if I have my way, you won't ever be alone again."

"That's a long time, Nick," she whispers, but I'm already kissing her by the time she finishes speaking my name, and as for that control she claims I am playing with, I let it go. I let her feel my unbridled need for her, and between the two of us, we are kissing, touching, all but crawling under each other's skin. That word I never meant to say—love—is now between us, and it's like freedom, a new kind of drug that stirs hunger in me for this woman, so fucking intense it damn near hurts.

My shirt comes off, my pants down, and it's only a matter of time before she's against the wall, and I'm pressing inside her, lifting her, pulling her back off the wall. Holding both our weights the way I'm willing to hold us both up every moment of every day, if she'll give me that chance. If she'll forgive me for the way we first met. It kills me right now not to tell her. Guts me and I have never wanted her trust so much. I urge her backward, and not just because I can now watch her breasts bounce as I pull her down on my cock and thrust it inside her, they are beautiful and fucking hot as hell, but she now has to trust me to hold her up. *She has to trust me.*

On some level, I know this is a fruitless endeavor. I can't force her to trust me, not and have that trust be real. And real is what she wants. Real is what I want. My hand flattens at her back, between her shoulder blades, and I drag her back to me, her head buried in my shoulder, our bodies melded together. I drive harder into her, wanting out of my own head. Wanting more of her. So fucking much of her.

"Nick," she pants out. "Nick."

Her voice, the grip of her sex, the rush of blood in my ears and in my cock, and a deep pull in my balls, says that I am here, in that place of no fucking return, only moments after she is. I quake, my thighs burning with the force of my release and our weight. I lose reality with the force of my eruption, and come back to the present to discover I'm leaning against the wall, holding Faith against me in a bear hug. And I don't want to let her go.

My legs have another idea and I shove off the wall, carrying her to the table next to her work station and ease her sideways to allow her to grab a tissue. "Ready?" I ask, before I set her down.

"Yes. I'm ready."

I ease her down my body, and set her on her feet, righting my pants as she tries to put her tissue to use, only to stumble. She laughs even as she's about to go down, which makes me laugh, but I catch her arms, preventing her fall. "I've got you," I promise.

Our eyes lock, the mood darkening, the pull between us fiercely present. "I know, Nick. Just don't let go, okay?"

"Sweetheart. I'm not going to let go. That's a promise, but don't forget you said that and how I replied."

Her brow furrows, and I turn away, hunting down our clothes, and kicking myself over the coded doom and gloom message I've just given her. I gather her clothes and set them on the stool, when my phone rings in my pocket. Assuming it's Beck, who's already called me with dead end leads today, I almost ignore it, but think better. I snake it out of my pocket, and glance at caller ID. "It's Chris Merit," I say, glancing at Faith, who is tugging her pants over her hips.

"Answer it," she urges quickly.

"Too late," I say. "He hung up."

"Call him back," she says, pulling her shirt over her head, sans the bra she seems to have forgotten.

I snag the bra she's not wearing and hold it up. "I sure as hell hope you get this eager when I call," I tease.

"Sorry," she says. "I only get this excited for Chris Merit." She snatches her bra up. "But you're the only one I take my underwear off for."

"I can live with that answer," I say, as my phone rings again and I glance at the screen again. "It's him again," I say, hitting the "answer" button. "Chris."

"Sara, actually," I hear instead. "I was wondering," she says. "Is Faith with you? I seem to have written her number down wrong." I glance at Faith. "She is. Hold on." I cover the phone. "Sara for you." I offer her the phone. She doesn't take it.

"Oh no. What's wrong. I wonder if my work got returned? What if—"

"Nothing's wrong," I promise, stroking her hair. "I'd sense it and I don't."

"God," she breathes out. "I hope you're right."

"I am," I say, handing her the phone.

She places it to her ear. "Sara. Hi." She listens a moment. "Yes, actually I'm still here in the city." She looks at me. "I'm staying with Nick all week." She listens again and those beautiful green eyes of hers light up. "I'd love to. Yes. Terrific. What time? Yes. I'll see you in the morning." She ends the call and now her entire face is glowing. "She wants me to help her set up the show. Her right-hand person had a family emergency. This is such an opportunity to learn another side of the business. Oh, Nick." She closes the space between us, her hands settling on my still bare chest. "Me being here opened that door. Once again, my love of art takes on a new life because of you."

My hand settles at her waist. "This had nothing to do with me. This is all you. All you. I'm just along for the ride and enjoying every fucking minute."

She pushes to her toes, kisses me. "I am too. The ride and you being on it with me." She smiles, this sweet, happy smile, and then moves away to finish dressing. I grab my shirt and present Faith with my back, pulling it over my head as I endure my own conflicting reactions to what just happened. On one note, I'm happy as hell that Faith not only has another reason to embrace her art, but to be here, with me, where I not only want her, but I can ensure she is safe. On the other note, she's embracing that art with Sara Merit, who knows I own the club, and whose husband used to be a member. The ticking clock gets faster and the balls I'm juggling multiply.

Inhaling, I turn around to find Faith perched back on the stool, staring at me with expectancy on her face, her mood back to sober. "We never finished talking about money. I don't want it to divide us again. I really would like to finish that conversation."

And the bullets just keep coming.

Chapter Thirteen

Faith

NICK'S RESPONSE TO MY REQUEST TO TALK ABOUT money again is slow to follow, his expression unreadable, his energy dark. The wisps of his dark brown hair around his face, torn from the clasp at his nape, the aftermath of our turbulent encounter. Certain we're about to have a repeat, I stand from where I've perched on the edge of the stool. But as surely as I'm prepared for another battle over the topic, yet again, his mood seems to lighten, and he steps in front of me, his hands settling on my neck, under my hair. "We do need to finish talking. Let's go back down to the kitchen to talk, but bring your paperwork from Abel. I want to go over it with you."

"I'd actually really like your thoughts before I form my own."

He kisses me and I hurry to the bedroom, and then to the bathroom, where I've left my purse, which now holds the documents I planned to read on the plane. Finding it on the counter, I reach for the paperwork, when my hand hits the money clip I'd found in my yard Friday night. Still puzzled by finding it, Nick's footsteps sound. I set the paperwork on the counter, and rotate to find him leaning on the doorway between the bathroom and the bedroom. "Is this yours?" I ask, holding up the gold clip with the imprint of an American flag on its side. "I mean, it looks like it's souvenir shop quality, and under your pay scale, but I thought it might be a sentimental thing." He pushes off the door frame and I close the space between us, stopping in front of him. "Then again," I add, offering him the clip, "you're actually not exactly sentimental. It's not yours, is it?"

"No," he confirms, taking it from me to give it a quick inspection. "Where did you find it?"

"My front yard as I was leaving for the airport. It must have been the delivery person who brought the package you sent me."

"Right," Nick says, the look on his face oddly serious, but he says little more. "A delivery person makes sense." He pockets the money clip. "I'll have my assistant call the delivery service. Do you have your paperwork?"

I grab the documents on the counter and hold them up. "All set."

"Well then," he says, "let's go have that talk." He backs out of the doorway, giving me space to exit. The idea that we're going to sit down and have a formal chat is a positive signal to me that he plans to take my concerns seriously.

Once I exit to the hallway, Nick steps to my side, and side by side, we start down the stairs, my curiosity piqued. "I just realized that I don't know much about your work life. I haven't even thought about you having an assistant, which of course, you do. And where is your office? How many staff members do you have?"

"Downtown. Twenty staff members. And my assistant is Rita, who is a mother, and has been happily married for decades. She also tolerates my arrogance about as well as you do."

I cast him a sideways look and a smile. "So I'll like her."

"Without question," he says, as we reach the living room, "and I'm fucked ten ways to hell if you two team up on me. That said, I'm brave. Once you know your schedule at the gallery, you should come to my office, meet her, and see the place."

"I'd like that," I say, stopping on this side of the island bar, as Nick rounds it and steps directly across from me.

"How long do you plan to work with Sara?" he asks.

"She said this is just for this week, but I'd love to help her get to opening day."

"That's weeks away," he points out. "And you have a show to prepare for. How much work do you have left to complete?"

"Two paintings," I say, pleased that he's aware of my deadline. "But one is half done and the gallery will inspire me. I should paint today, though. I'd actually really like to get a brush in my hand."

"I'm glad to see you embracing your work again. After we talk, just go hide upstairs and do what you need to do. We'll hang out here and order in dinner later this evening." He lifts the lid to a pizza box. "For now, we have this. Abel actually left us a few slices." He walks to the oven behind him and turns it on.

"You're hungry?" I ask incredulously. "How can you be hungry? We just ate not that long ago."

"Almost two hours ago," he says, glancing at his industrial-looking watch, with a thick black leather band and silver face that fits well with his black jeans and biker style boots. "That's a long time with all that fighting and fucking we just did."

I laugh, shaking my head, the laughter part, something I'm not sure I did all that often before I met Nick. "The things that come out of your mouth, Nick Rogers."

"You get special treatment," he says, grabbing a pan from the drawer under the stove and setting it on top. "You should hear what I say to those I don't like. Because I'm not a nice guy, remember?"

"All too well," I assure him, joining him on that side of the bar and helping him load the tray with pizza. "I can just imagine what your courtroom must be like," I say, lowering my voice to imitate him. "Tell me, Mr. Murphy. Right before her death were you fighting with her or fucking her?"

"First," he says, grabbing the other two pizza boxes. "My voice is much deeper than that. Second, I usually make those kinds of statements long before we ever get to court, and then we don't go to court."

"How often are you in court?" I ask, setting an empty pizza box on the counter beside me.

"A lot of my work is done for contracted, long-term clients, which means I negotiate and litigate on their behalf as needed. But overall, only about ten percent of my time is spent in court, while another thirty percent is spent in mediations." He sticks the pizza in the oven and sets the timer, his mood turning serious. "Let's sit and have that talk so you can get to painting. And to bed. You now have work tomorrow."

It's then that realization hits me. He starts to move and I grab his arm. He turns back to me, arching a brow, so very tall, broad, and bigger than life in too many ways to count. Bigger in *my life* than anyone else has ever been. "What's up, sweetheart?"

"I just needed to say something."

"You have my full attention." His hand settles at my waist,

and I swear I don't know how it's possible, but I feel this man everywhere when he touches me in one spot. "You *always* have my full attention, Faith," he adds, his voice low, intimate.

And what's really amazing to me is that I believe him. I feel his interest, his engagement, and not just now. Always. He is more present in my life than people I have known for years. "It just hit me that I didn't even consider saying no to Sara and rushing back to Sonoma."

"Is that a bad thing?" he asks.

"I don't know," I say. "That's what I'm trying to decide."

He tilts his head toward the table. "Let's sit and figure it out," he urges.

I nod and we both claim our barstools from earlier, and face each other. "Why don't you know?" he asks, returning to the point rather than moving past it, his hands bracketing my legs, our knees touching. "Just say whatever comes to mind, and you'll have your answer."

"I'm excited about working with Sara and painting and my show in L.A. and so many things, but the moment that I forgot to worry about the winery because of those things, tells a story."

And instead of telling me what I mean, he asks, "And that story is what?"

"That I'm counting on the winery running without me, and that means that I'm counting on your help."

"Good. I want you to. Because you can. I'm not going anywhere, Faith, and clearly, I'm doing my best to make sure that you don't either. I owe Sara for the assistance on that one."

"I'd already decided to stay," I remind him, wanting him to know that I'm here for him.

"I know you did," he says. "But let's face it. The winery comes with a long history of pulling you there. I have a short one of pulling you to me. I'd like to help you find a way to cut off the drain it has on you."

"You mean by paying off the debt and rewarding Kasey for taking charge."

"Among other things," he says, "but before we talk about money. I want to go over the documents with you, and with full disclosure, I drafted them for Abel."

I laugh. "That doesn't surprise me at all. You have to be the driver."

He doesn't laugh with me as he usually does, not this time. "I do," he agrees, his tone serious. "It's who I am. You need to know that. My instinct will always be to take control."

"Type A personality on caffeine," I say, "and the truth is that I can pretend to be a type A, but I'm not. But that doesn't mean that you get to be in charge."

He gives me a shrewd look. "Unless you're naked."

A knot forms in my chest with what is clearly an observation and a question I'm not ready to answer yet. "That's a different topic for another time," I say, cutting my gaze from his, and because I need to do anything but look at him in the next thirty seconds, I reach for my bottle of water and unscrew the lid.

Nick's watching me, I feel his scrutiny—heavy, intense, and it makes my throat dry. I tilt the bottle back, drinking deeply, and when I lower the bottle, Nick takes it from me, holds my stare and the bottle goes to his lips. I watch him chug the liquid, my fingers curling on my leg, acutely aware of the intimacy of sharing my water with him.

He sets the bottle down, and I don't even mean to, but I'm staring at him, and the look in his eyes tells me that his thoughts are with mine and I suddenly realize his message even before he says, "You can be naked with your clothes on or off, Faith." He reaches up and caresses my cheek. "And I do like you naked, but as you said to me, tell me whatever you want to tell me, whenever you're ready to tell me. I'll still be here."

"I just—"

"No pressure." He eases back in his seat. "For now. You were telling me my control has to have limits."

"Are you capable of limits?"

"Control is all about limits. Is that what you want, Faith? Limits?"

I'm instantly aware of where he's leading me and I go there. "Control is about limits. Possibilities are not. But me owing you money feels like a limit. It might not change you, but it *will* change me. I need to pay you back. And I need to give you that money I got from my art as a down payment."

He studies me for several beats, his expression unreadable. "You need this."

"Yes," I say. "I do."

"I won't agree to ever taking any portion of the winery. Period. No conversation. And no interest, Faith. I don't need the money. I won't take extra." I open my mouth to argue and he says, "Compromise. I'm agreeing to a payback for you, not me. Agree to my terms for me."

"Compromise," I repeat. "Okay. Yes. And for the record, I actually like that word. I like it a lot and perhaps I was unfair earlier. I know you just want to help and protect me. Just please communicate, Nick, and I think that makes all the difference."

"This seems like a good time to tell you, that if I have to spend money to take care of the winery situation, I'm going to spend money."

"And if I say I don't want you to?"

"I'm going to take care of this for you and for us. You can't be who you really are while being forced to be what you aren't."

That statement punches me in the chest with my mistakes, and pretty much defines a huge portion of my life. "I don't know how to take your help and not lose myself too."

"You're putting too much emphasis on the money. Eventually you're going to have to accept that is part of who I am. I'm not going to pretend that I don't have a large bank account. I work too damn hard to get it. And I'm going to spend that money on you and with you." He leans closer, softening his voice. "Make me understand why this is an issue. Who used money against you? Your father? Macom? Both?"

"Am I that transparent?"

"Not transparent enough, or I'd already know the answers to those questions. I need to know. Communication, remember?"

"Yes. Communication. Okay. My father was more about emotional baggage. As for Macom, I don't know if it was money or fame, or both, but it went to Macom's head."

"Meaning what?"

"He would throw the money and fame in my face."

"How?"

"Does it matter?"

"It affects you, Faith. So yes. It matters."

"He'd criticize me and then build me up and then do it all over again. I knew that he was inherently insecure, which made his actions about him, not me. I tried to build him up and support him. Eventually though, with him and my father talking in my ear, it wore on me. Their negativity became poison and I started to doubt myself."

"And the doubt led where?"

"I'm not sure it was the doubt that led me down a rabbit hole I couldn't quite escape." I think of the fight I just had with Nick. "Macom and I didn't fight like you and I fight."

"How do we fight, Faith?"

"We do what we just said. We communicate."

"And with Macom?"

"He never hurt me, but he threw volatile temper tantrums and destroyed things. The next day, he would buy me extravagant gifts to apologize."

"Well, to start. I'm not insecure, in case you didn't notice. I'm good at what I do but you have a gift that I admire. You are brilliant, Faith."

My cheeks flush not as much with the compliment, but the vehement way he delivers the words. Like he means them so very deeply.

He doesn't give me time to reply, "And as for money. I'm going to spend money on you. Because *I want to*. If I want to do it just because, I will. Because *I want to*. And if I want to do it because I piss you off, I will. Because *I want to*. He doesn't get to change that. He doesn't get that kind of say in our relationship."

"I don't need you to spend money on me but I don't want him to define me or us. I hate that we're even having this conversation."

"We needed to have this conversation. You lived with him. You must have thought you loved him."

"I did. The man I knew before the fame and the money."

"Money and fame don't change people, Faith. Those things simply expose their true colors."

"I don't dispute that, but I don't know how he hid those true colors so well. I've thought about that a lot. How did I miss so much?"

"Were you his submissive?"

"No. I told you. I'm not a submissive. You know that I'm not a submissive."

"But he tried to make you one."

"Yes. He did. I refused."

He narrows his eyes on me. "He found that world while he was with you, not before."

"Right after his first big sale, he was invited to an expensive, invitation only dinner club."

"That wasn't a dinner club at all."

"Exactly. And I agreed to go because he was still the Macom I thought I knew."

"And what happened?"

"For us, it was voyeurism and sex that felt daring and sexy at the time. Looking back, I think something was always missing for us, and that night, in that club, it felt as if we filled some void."

"And so you went back."

"Yes. And for a while I liked it. In some ways I always did, but why and how changed."

"Meaning what?" he presses.

"Starting out, we kept to ourselves. Just going there made things exciting. But then he got darker at home. More demanding at the club." I rotate and face forward. "The first time he crossed a line, he tied me up and then invited people to watch us without telling me, without *asking*. It spiraled from there."

Nick rotates forward as well, both of us side by side, arms resting on the table. "But you kept going?"

I glance over at him, daring to look into his eyes. "It's like you said earlier. I use sex to protect myself. That goes back to what I said a moment ago. I don't know when or how it happened, but that club became the place that I trained myself to be something that I wasn't before. It's was where I learned to be in control, even when I was seemingly not in control at all. Sex became a different kind of escape. I actually found those moments, when I could be in a room of naked bodies and still feel alone, sanctuary."

"From what?"

"Everything I didn't want to face. In reality, my control in that club was a replacement for claiming real control of my life."

"And then your father died," he says, and I cut my gaze. I look at his arm resting on the table, his tattoo partially exposed. The words etched there are taking me back to a place I don't want to be, but my father's death always leads me there. I reach over and cover those words with my hand. "An eye for an eye," I whisper.

"You keep going to it. You clearly want to tell me what it means."

Now I look up at him. "No. No, I really don't."

He studies me a beat and then says, "Then don't."

Just that easily he has accepted my answer and offers me an escape. I take it. "I need air." I slip off the stool and start walking but as I round the table, I realize that the past is in this room, when Nick is my present, maybe my future. I don't want to shut him out. I want to take him on the ride with me. I rotate to find him still at the table. "Come with me?"

His expression doesn't change—it's unreadable—but his actions are what matter. He stands, and it's only a minute later that we stand side by side on the balcony at the railing, and for several minutes we don't speak. We just stand there, the blue sky and ocean stretching far and wide before us, like paint perfectly inked on a canvas. The wind lifts over the balcony edge, and I can almost taste the salt water on my tongue and with it, the words to be spoken and not just for him. I need to face the past fully and be done with it. I inhale and let it out. "There was another artist who went to the club. Jim was his name." I rotate to face Nick again, and he does the same with me. "He was the one who got Macom the invite."

"They were friends then," he assumes.

"I believe that was Jim's intent, but he and Macom sat on a high-profile board for a charity together. They bumped heads and Macom got kicked off. The day it happened, Macom called me at work and told me about it. I got home that night to comfort him and found him with Jim's wife, in our bed. He invited me to join them. An eye for an eye, he'd said. I could help pay Jim back."

"Had you been with Jim and his wife before?"

"No. His wife was a submissive and Jim was very possessive and protective of her. I'd actually found it enviable until she hopped in bed with Macom. Anyway. They were still fucking when I got the call about my father. I left. Macom called the next day looking for me."

"And you never went back."

"No, and honestly I hated the L.A. scene. I went to college there and learned the world there, and it just made sense to stay. And it kept me from my parents' drama."

Nick moves then, turning me to lean against the railing, his big body trapping mine, his hands at my waist. "Faith, I need you to know some things about me. This isn't everything I need to share, but it's a start and an important one."

"I know you were in that world in some way, Nick. We've hinted at that in conversations."

"I was. Not now. But I've played in that world that you were playing in and I did so for many years."

"What drew you to it and why did you leave?"

"I was drawn there for the zero-commitment guarantee. There was just sex. No one believed I wanted more. No one asked for more. I left, because I met you."

She inhales and lets it out. "That was recent."

"Because I didn't want a woman in my life. Now. If I never see that place again, it will be too soon. I would never take you there."

"So it was one club?"

"Yes."

"And why wouldn't you take me there?"

"Because we are more than the sum of what I was there. Because we are better than that place. Because I damn sure have no intention of sharing you in any capacity and just walking into that place would make many a man and woman, want you."

"Did you have a submissive?"

"No. Never. I cannot stress this enough. Until you, I didn't do commitment and that is a commitment. But I liked the games and it was fucking without complication. Bondage. *Check.* Ménages. *Check.* Voyeurism. *Check.* No couple play though. I was never a couple and I don't need another man comparing dicks with me."

"And you're telling me this why?"

"I didn't want you to find out from someone else. And I didn't want you to think that I want to be there, not here. The past doesn't define me or you or who we are apart or together. It simply represents the paths that we each took to get here. To *each other.*"

I digest every word he has spoken with the realization that I am not shaken by Nick's confession, that is not so unlike my own. How can I be? He has been boldly forthright, brutally honest about his interests. And he's just told me that while Macom needed the club despite having me, Nick only needs me. And I choose to believe him. I choose to believe that he is right. All paths have lead us here, to a place where I have a paintbrush in my hand and this man in my life.

Chapter Fourteen

Nick

I ONCE TOLD FAITH THAT I DON'T DO GUILT. I MAKE decisions. I own them. I move on. But as I leave her in her studio to paint, just beyond our talk about sex clubs and that bastard Macom, guilt is gutting me. It's like I'm in a horror movie with some slasher sicko slicing and dicing me, and coming back for more. I fast-step down the stairs toward the living room, reminding myself that I told Faith all that I dared. I cannot risk sending her running for the hills and pushing me into the dog house. Not when it appears that someone wants the winery, or something connected to the winery, and that they most likely killed her mother and my father to get it. And Faith is the only person standing in their way.

Clearing the last step, I cross the living room, grab my briefcase in the kitchen, and then make my way to my office.

Once inside, I shut the door under the pretense of the client conference call I told Faith I'd scheduled. A lie to hide lies. Jaw clenching at that idea, I drop my briefcase on my heavy mahogany desk, and then walk toward the bookshelf-enclosed sitting area at the far end of the room. Claiming a spot in the center of the brown leather couch facing the door, I mentally prioritize the gaggle of fucked up shit in my head right now. My focus is on Faith's safety, which means keeping her close. Which means containing any threat that could push or pull her away from me. That means dealing with Sara Merit.

I pull my phone from the pocket of my jeans, and since I don't have Sara's number, I dial Chris. He answers on the first ring. "You're afraid Sara is going to tell Faith about the club. And I can tell you right now. She would not do that."

"You certainly know how to get right to the point."

"Then let me do it again. You have to tell her."

"I told her I was a member, with graphic detail," I say, and aware Chris has a bit of a history himself, I add, "She knows the world. It's not been kind to her."

"And living the lifestyle versus owning a club that says you can't live without the lifestyle are two different things."

"Exactly. And I never really wanted the damn thing. Mark owned it. Mark was a client and a friend, and I picked it up."

"You're known. Someone could tell her you owned it and even if that never happens, you really don't want that unspoken truth between you."

"I'll tell her at the same time that I tell her I dumped the damn thing."

"Smart move in my book," he says. "Do you have a buyer?"

"You interested?"

"Not a chance in hell, my man. But we both know money isn't an issue to you. Kurt Seaver runs that place from sun-up to sun-down. Give it to him."

"You read my mind. That's exactly what I plan to do."

"Good move. Good move." There's a voice in the background. "I'm actually walking into a meeting with a donor for my charity. Sara's with me. I'll fill in the holes she missed." He ends the call.

I pull up my text screen and Kurt Seaver's contact information, shooting him a message: *Ten o'clock in my office tomorrow.*

I move on to the next situation. I remove the money clip from my pocket, set it on the dark wood of the rectangular coffee table, and shoot a photo I then text to Beck. My superhero PI who had better start acting like a superhero. I punch his auto-dial and he answers on the first ring. "How's the black widow?"

"Since you're supposed to be an ex-CIA agent/ hacker, who I now pay one hell of a lot of money to do PI work, I'd think you'd know how to google "black widow" and find the meaning. She's never been married. She hasn't killed her non-existent husband or any lovers."

"Unless she was fucking your father right along with her mother."

My teeth clench. "Don't push me, Beck. You might be in high demand, but I'm paying you a hell of a lot of money to do your job. And that job now includes protecting Faith, not attacking her."

"Relax, man. I was just pushing your buttons. Faith isn't a killer, but considering that note you found, she was clearly fucking with your father's head. And I sent a gift to your inbox."

"Which is what?"

"That attorney she hired to go after her mother had a file on her that included correspondence with your father."

"How did you get that?"

"Don't ask what you don't want to deny later."

My jaw clenches. "Save me time. Summarize the findings."

"Validation of her story. She went after her mother. Your father nickel-and-dimed her into giving up. The interesting part of this to me is that your father was paying Meredith Winter while acting as her attorney. If he wasn't fucking her, I'd swear she was blackmailing him."

"I told you. My father wouldn't tolerate blackmail. He'd act on his own behalf and viciously. He was after the winery."

"Here's the thing. There are no dots connecting. I can't find Meredith's money. I can't find your father's money. This tells me that someone as good as me made it go away. I need to put feelers out in my underground circles and find out who, but that means two things: We need to offer cash in exchange for information. And we risk spooking someone into doing something we might regret."

"Do we have other options?"

"They're running out."

"Exhaust them," I say. "I don't want to spook the bank before I have time to steal the winery out from underneath them."

"If you do that," he says. "The net outcome could be the same as me going underground. You end up stealing someone's thunder and they come after you. Or Faith."

"What the hell is it about the winery that would make someone want it badly enough to kill for it?"

"There is no record, or anything, that remotely sets off bells. I checked for oil. I checked for real estate developments. There is nothing. And I went back a hundred years."

"It could be a business deal," I say, thinking out loud. "Some kind of merger that has never been put on paper."

"Or the same person who made Meredith Winter's money trail disappear made a whole lot more disappear."

"We just need to make sure they don't make Faith disappear."

"If the winery is at the core of all of this, and it seems that it is, make her put the winery up for sale. If it's gone, she's no longer a target."

"You do have someone watching her, correct?"

"I have a man watching your place and two in Sonoma, watching her place and the winery."

"Which brings me back to the purpose of this call," I say. "I sent you a photo of a money clip. Faith found it in her yard Friday. Does that belong to one of your men?"

"I see it. And my guys working the Sonoma area don't make stupid mistakes. And since Faith has no cameras on her property, I can't see who is. We need to upgrade her and I can do it without her knowing, but with her stamp of approval, we can get far better equipment installed."

"We're here until Thursday and there for the weekend. Schedule it for Friday."

"We're talking murder here. We need cameras at her house and at the winery, where we can watch her staff, now, not later."

I'm immediately hit by the fact that he's just stated: We're dealing with murder. He's no longer on the fence about how my father and Faith's mother died. He now believes what I do. They were murdered. "I'll get you in by tomorrow night," I say. "And Faith is working here at the Allure Gallery all week. I need you to be sure that you have someone watching her at all times."

"Done. And FYI, I hacked your father's autopsy reports. Nothing yet." He hangs up.

Fucker.

I set the phone down on the table and stare at that money clip with a bad feeling in my gut, my fingers thrumming on my knee. "What the hell were you up to Father?"

I pick my phone back up and dial my assistant. "And here I thought that new woman of yours would make you get a life,"

Rita says, bypassing a hello. In fact, I think she started bypassing hello with me seven years back. "Sundays are for church and reruns of Friends," she adds.

"And me," I say. "I need someone respected in Sonoma tomorrow, assessing the Reid Winter winery. They'll need to bring a full team. I need it done quickly."

"Tomorrow?" she asks incredulously. "No one is going to talk to me today, let alone be there tomorrow."

"Pay them whatever you have to pay them."

"That could be hefty."

"I trust you not to let me get raped."

"Oh good grief. I could do without your visuals sometimes, Nick Rogers. Tuesday is more reasonable, even with a bribe."

"I prefer tomorrow. If anyone can get it done, you can. Text me when you know the details. And yes, I'll bring the donuts you like in the morning." I end the call and stand up, walking to my desk, where I stick the money clip in the top drawer. I consider digging through the boxes of materials I have on my father, but that's risky with Faith in the house. And I'd rather be upstairs with Faith anyway.

With that in mind, I open my briefcase and pull out the sensitive material related to Faith and my father, filing it away in my desk. Selecting several client files I need to study, I seal it up, head to the kitchen where my computer still sits, and with it in hand, make my way upstairs. The minute I appear in the doorway, Faith turns to face me, a black cover-up over her clothes. Her hair piled on top of her head, little ringlets around her face.

She motions to her white Keds, now splattered with black and gray paint. "Maybe I could sell them to some clothing designer?" she says. "They're stylish, right?"

"Very," I tell her, walking to the wall behind her, where I can watch her canvas take shape. "It could be an empire." I sit down and open my briefcase.

Faith removes her cover-up and sits down next to me, her black pants now splattered with paint as well. "Isn't it going to be hard to work like this?" she asks.

"I'll manage," I say, leaning over and kissing her, when it hits me that she stopped painting the minute I showed up. "Unless," I say, pulling back to study her, "I'm making you feel uncomfortable."

She covers my hand with hers, a sweet gesture, when sweet has never been my thing. "I like you being here with me," she says, and when she lets go of my hand, I want hers back. Apparently, I like sweet now. A whole fucking lot. "I just wish you had a better place to work," she adds. "You should put a desk in here."

Or I could just buy a new house. A thought that stuns me, but I don't fight it. I'd buy ten houses for Faith, who is now flushing at her own words. "Not that I'm not suggesting I'll be here often, but—"

"Faith," I say. "I made this room for you. I want you here all the fucking time." I don't give her time to object. I move on. "And I'm fine right here. I have a ton of paperwork to review and emails to answer."

She rotates to face me, on her knees, her hand on my leg. "Hard limit: One night."

My lips curve. "That didn't go as you planned, now did it?"

"No," she laughs. "It didn't." She stands up and heads back to her painting station, and I decide I'll talk to her about extra security tomorrow morning. She's had enough hell today and she needs to paint. She has a show coming up. I watch her cover up before she turns back to me. "We need music."

I pull my phone from my pocket. "What are you in the mood for?"

"Surprise me and I'll see where it takes me on my canvas."

I tab through my music and choose Beethoven's Moonlight Sonata, and the moment it starts to play, she sighs. "Perfection," she says, a smile not just on her lips, but in her eyes.

I relax into the wall, intending to reach for my files, but when the music lifts with a dramatic chord, I find myself watching Faith. Every stroke of her brush mesmerizes me as I wait for that red streak that she has proclaimed the beginning of a story. To me this symbolizes a feeling of hope, a look forward, not behind.

My mind goes back to the night we'd met, sitting in front of her fireplace, talking over pints of ice cream:

"Why black, white, and red?" I'd asked of her trademark colors.

"Black and white are the purest form of any image to me. It lets the viewer create the story."

"And the red?"

"The beginning of the story as I see it. A guide for the viewer's imagination to flow. I know it sounds silly, but it's how I think when I'm creating."

I cringe with the words: The beginning of the story as I see it.

The beginning of our story is nothing like she sees it.

Chapter Fifteen

Faith

THERE ARE THINGS IN LIFE THAT ARE INARGUABLY perfect: Milk chocolate. Good ice cream. A perfect sunset. A cold night with a fireplace. And me with a paintbrush in my hand for the past few hours, while Nick sits a few feet away, working, with Beethoven lifting in the air. There is just something about that combination, that inspires me. Nick manages to calm and center me, which is really incredible considering he's intense, demanding, controlling and arrogant, while I am someone who is far more zen. But as I reach for the red paint to put the finishing touches on the mountain top of my painting, I debate the reasons that might be, and an amazing list of answers come to mind that I decide I might just talk over with Nick.

Satisfaction fills me as I stroke a brush through the red

paint to complete my work-in-progress. In another fifteen minutes, I set my brush down. I'm done and Nick is behind me almost immediately.

"Stunning, Faith," he says, his hands on my hips, and I find myself leaning into him, his big, hard body like a shelter in a storm that he's now helped me quiet. He really is a shelter, and there lies the core of why he calms me, why he works for me. He makes me feel like the rest of the world can't touch me.

"I like it," I say, inspecting my work. "But I'm not sure I'm going to use it for the show."

He turns me to face him. "Why?"

"It doesn't feel special. It's safe. I have to be cautious everywhere else. I don't want to do it on the canvas."

"You don't have to be cautious with me, Faith."

I reach up and pull his hair from the tie. "I know." I reach up and run my hands through his hair. "Because you're…"

He arches a brow. "I'm what?"

"Tiger."

"Tiger is for my enemies, remember. Not the woman I'm falling in love with."

There is that word again: Love. It's terrifying and thrilling. "It's okay to be Tiger, Nick," I say. "That name is a part of you. I've met him." My lips curve as I think of the many sexy times we've shared. "I'm okay with him coming out to play."

He doesn't smile. "Tiger's not a nice guy, Faith. You remember that, right?"

I flatten my hand on his chest. "He's tough. He's hard. He's cold. And I really like him best when he's naked."

He remains expressionless for two beats, and then laughs. "Ah, Faith. Woman, what you do to me. Maybe you need to put a little Tiger on your canvas."

My brow furrows. "What do you mean?"

"*You* are nice, Faith, but you have a darker side. That part of you that can take on the Tiger side of me, and hold your own. That's the part of you that wanted out when you were in the club, it just wasn't the right place or way for you to do so. *The canvas* is your place. Put whatever you found in that club on the canvas. We both know nothing about that will be safe."

It's as if a switch flips in my mind. I've been boxed by everyone's expectations of me on and off the canvas. I twist around in Nick's arms and walk to my canvas, and I start to pick it up and move it off the easel. Nick is quickly there to help. "Where do you want it?"

"Against the wall seems to be the best spot," I say, already grabbing a blank canvas and setting it on the easel.

"I'll order you extra stands for your completed works," he says as I turn to my blank canvas, inspiration starting to form. "We don't want your work to get damaged," he adds, as I reach for my brush. Nick intercepts, catching my fingers and walking me to him. "The food will be here any minute, sweetheart." He glances at his watch. "And it's almost ten. We both have early mornings."

I blink. "We ordered food?" I ask, and then shake away the cobwebs, giving a low laugh. "Oh right. We did."

Nick laughs, that deep, rough sexy sound I could really turn on and play like music, if it were possible. "We did." He motions toward the doorway. "Let's head to the bedroom and settle in so we can go to sleep after we eat."

"Well, as much as I want to argue, my hands are cramped and my stomach is growling."

He unbuttons the cover-up I have over my clothes. "You can spend some time with Sara at Allure tomorrow and then come back here and paint."

"Yes," I agree, "but you know what? Let me just put a few

strokes on the canvas. Just to get the inspiration started."

"You've painted for *eight hours*, Faith." He is suddenly lifting me, and I yelp as he scoops me up and over his shoulder. "Nick, damn it, the blood is rushing to my head." He smacks my ass and I arch my back.

"Nick!"

"Now where is that blood flowing, sweetheart?" he asks.

"You're evil," I say, thinking about the spanking he teased me with earlier today. "Really evil."

He keeps walking and doesn't stop until he's set me on my feet beside the bed. "Evil is your beautiful ass teasing my hand, sweetheart. You do need a good spanking."

Oh God. Why is just the promise of this man's hand on my backside so incredibly sexy? My nipples ache. My sex clenches and my hand settles at his hip, my thumb intentionally placed near his cock. "I asked," I remind him. "You didn't answer."

He cups my face. "Sweetheart, when I spank you again, you won't be hiding from anything, especially me. I'll do it because you trust me and you want to feel that trust, and no other reason."

The doorbell rings. "And that would be the food. I'll bring it up here." He kisses me and heads for the door. I inhale on his words, that were sexy, and intimate, and about us, but I turn and stare at the card from my father lying on the nightstand, where I'd set it Friday night, my mind replaying my exchange with Nick. It was the first time I'd seen his house:

"Where is your bedroom, Nick?"

"Up the stairs directly behind you."

I turn then and start up the stairs, my pace slow, calculated. I feel overwhelmed by him. I need to seduce him, to get back to a place I have control. I know every swing of my hips makes him burn. He doesn't immediately pursue, though. He's Nick after all.

Always dominant and in control, except when I make him want me. It arouses me and it's powerful when he responds, when he needs me the way I always need him.

I walk into his bedroom, taking in the king-sized bed, and the masculine décor, that fits him so well, and it affects me for no real reason other than the fact that everything about the man affects me. I need something now that I can't even name. An escape. That's what it was. I think this is the first moment I really realize how much this man could hurt me. I reach into my purse and grab the card from my father before setting my purse aside.

And then I sit on the bed with every intention of reading it, I think my subconscious just needs me to focus on something other than the man I am falling so very hard for. That I have fallen too hard for. He enters the room, and I swear he steals my breath with his size and just how damn beautiful he is, masculine and intense in his dark suit and white shirt in a way that only some men, very few, in fact, harness. But Nick does. So very well.

He looks at the card on my lap aware, I know, of what it is. "I need to read this," I say. "And you know that means I need you."

His chest rises and falls, expanding with delicious perfection. He closes the space between us, his stride long, graceful. He stands above me. I want to touch him but I don't. I need some control. I need him to touch me first, but he always wants to be first anyway. I know this. He shrugs out of his jacket and removes his tie, tossing both to the center of the bed. And then he surprises me by setting the card aside and taking me down on the mattress with him, rolling to face me. "I'm not going to spank you, Faith," he says, sliding his leg between mine. "Not now. Maybe not even this weekend. I want you to see and feel me. I want you to remember me this weekend, not my hand."

Inhaling, I return to the present with the certainty that he's achieved that goal. I see him and feel him in every possible way. And maybe he knew I didn't really want to read the card. Because I don't. I turn away from it now, rejecting its content, and walking toward the bathroom. I don't need my father's input on my career right before my show. Once I'm inside, I move my suitcase back into the closet, where I strip down. I'm about to pull on a sleep shirt I've brought with me when I spy Nick's row of t-shirts, the idea of wearing one of them winning me over and quickly. I search through the various graphic designs, and smile as I find a Batman shirt of all things. Oh how Nick it is.

I pull it on, letting it fall to my knees and then grab my pink fluffy slippers from my suitcase. Shoving my feet in them, I return to the bedroom at the same moment Nick returns as well, bags in his hand. "The Dark Knight?" I say, pointing at the shirt. "Really?"

"I told you, sweetheart," he says, walking around the opposite side of the bed. "I'm not a nice guy and neither are my idols."

"Batman is your idol?" I ask, settling onto the bed, and accepting one of the bags.

"That one should have your egg salad sandwich, and a bottle of water," he says, before answering me. "And I don't have an idol, but I like Batman a hell of a lot more than Superman. Better outfit, more money, no rules." He sits down and checks his bag, then takes off his boots.

We do some shuffling of bags and drinks and soon we are sitting facing each other with our bags as plates. "What about you, Faith?" Nick asks, unwrapping his sandwich. "Apparently, my club sandwich is a Philly cheesesteak."

"Do you like Philly cheesesteak?"

"It's greasy and unhealthy," he says. "Who doesn't like a Philly cheesesteak?" he asks, not waiting for a reply. "Back to more important things. Who's your idol?"

"At one point it was my father, but that ended. You know that. Aside from him, I have many artists that I admire. I think I told you that I really look up to Chris Merit. Aside from his talent, his family owed a winery here in Sonoma and became so famous that it felt within my reach."

"In reality, I happen to know that he lived in Paris when he started painting and was always filthy rich, so you two aren't much of a comparison."

"True," I say. "And it feels weird that I kind of idolized him now since I know him personally. But I did and I still admire him."

"He's a good guy," Nick says. "And talented. I have one of his paintings in my office."

"I need to see that," I say, about to take a bite of my sandwich when a thought hits me. "I haven't even told Kasey I'm not going to be there tomorrow. I should text him."

"I'd like us to take him to dinner Thursday night," Nick replies. "We need to make him believe that I'm a co-owner, just like we do the bank."

"Kasey too?"

"Everyone. It's the only way we make the bank buy into this. Is that a problem?"

"No. Whatever we have to do."

"On a positive note and another topic to discuss with Kasey," he says. "While you were painting I heard from my assistant. She's lined up a team to do the assessment at the winery, starting tomorrow."

"Oh. Great. That was fast, but I need to warn Kasey about that too. I need to grab my phone." I scoot off the bed and walk into the bathroom, where I find it in my purse. Once I rejoin Nick, I text Kasey. "How soon will we get the assessment results?"

"It's a big place. I expect it will take a few days."

My phone buzzes and I glance at Kasey's reply. "All set. Dinner Thursday night and he knows about the assessment."

"While we're on the topic of business," Nick says. "One more thing. Beck, the private investigator I told you I hired, wants to install cameras at your house and the winery. And he'd rather the staff not know."

My brow furrows. "Is there a problem I need to know about with the staff?"

"He didn't express a specific concern, but did stress that he absolutely doesn't want the staff to know. It's his job to trust no one."

"Right. That makes sense. When does he want to do it and how should I coordinate getting him into the locations?"

"He can get into both locations on his own."

"Okay well, the fact that he can get into both locations on his own says I need a new security system. But yes. Whatever he needs to do. Tell him to do it." I take a bite of my sandwich.

He pulls his phone from his pocket and sends a text message before snatching up a few chips. He is about to set his phone down when it buzzes with a reply already. He reads the message and glances at me. "He's going to get it done tonight." He takes a drink of water and sets it on the nightstand, while I manage another bite of my sandwich.

"And he's had no other luck on anything?" I ask, before taking another bite of my sandwich.

"No, which is significant considering his skill set. He's concerned there is more going on than we know and someone has covered it up."

My brow furrows. "Like what?"

"Is there any reason the winery might be worth more money than you think? Something no property assessment can find?"

"I don't even have to think about that answer. Absolutely nothing comes to mind and I can't believe my father knew of any such thing. He'd have told me, or at least, left the details in his will." My eyes go wide and I rotate to the nightstand, picking up the card. "Could this be where the answers lie?"

"No," Nick says. "He left this for a specific birthday, knowing that you could inherit before that date. And your attorney gave you no indication it needed to be opened sooner, upon his death."

He takes the card from me. "He didn't support your art. If you want to open this, do it after you prepare for your show, and preferably after the show itself."

"That was my preference actually, but if there could be answers we need inside—"

"I'll make you a deal. If I can't shut down these issues with the bank this week, we'll open it. Together, and if you want that spanking for just that reason," his lips curve, "this time, I'll be happy to oblige."

My cheeks flush. "Thank you."

He laughs. "Thank you, sweetheart, for having such a sweet little ass." He sets the card on the nightstand, when my cellphone rings my brows furrow. "What time is it?" I ask, as I'm digging in the blankets for my phone I've now lost again.

"Eleven," Nick says, glancing at his watch.

I locate my phone right as the call ends, drawing in a breath at the number on the caller ID, and sucking in hair.

"What's wrong?" Nick asks.

"It was Macom," I say, tucking the phone under the pillow. "Josh called earlier and warned me that he's become obsessed with talking to me. He didn't want me to talk to him. He said he messes with my creative process." My phone starts to ring again.

"Let me talk to that bastard," Nick says, reaching for it.

143

"No," I say, grabbing it first and standing up. "That would just turn into him calling Josh and Josh calling me."

"Block him."

"I almost did that earlier today, but that gives him power and satisfaction, too."

He stands up, hands on his hips. "You know, Faith. I'm starting to get the feeling that he has a hell of a lot of power and presence in our relationship." He doesn't say anything more. He rounds the bed, but he doesn't come to me. He passes me by and I rotate to watch him disappear inside the bathroom. And while he doesn't shut the door, he's just shut me out.

Chapter Sixteen

Faith

I AM STUNNED BY NICK'S REACTION, BUT I AM QUICKLY reminded of the many ways this man has put himself on the line for me. He's pursued me. He's set up an art studio for me. Fought for me with the bank and today, professed budding love. And now, I've given him a proverbial punch, maybe I've even hurt him. I don't want to hurt him.

Dashing forward, I enter the bathroom as he enters the closet. Crossing the room, I step into the doorframe dividing the bathroom and the closet, to find Nick standing with his back to me at the same moment that he peels his shirt over his head, muscles rippling, the small space suddenly even smaller.

"Nick," I breathe out.

He hesitates, not just in action—I feel the emotional hesitation and I know that my instinct was right. I've hurt him and that means that *I* can't have that same hesitation. "I don't love him. I don't even like him but he, and my mother, taught me not to trust. I can't just make that go away and I wish that I could. It's going to take time, but what I can tell you is that you, and you alone, are the reason that I'm learning to trust again."

Still he doesn't turn, shutting me out, keeping me at the distance he rarely tolerates. He inhales, his face lifting to the ceiling for several beats that are just too long for me. I close the space between us, and I pretty much collide with him as he turns to face me, my hand flattening on his chest, his catching my shoulders. "I will make him go away," I vow.

"I don't expect him to be out of our lives any more than I do my fucked up father or your mother. They fucked with our heads. They made us and they still play us."

This is a revelation about Nick he's never shared. "Your dad fucked with your head?"

"Of course he did. You know that I was raised by a rotation of nannies he fucked. He's why I am who I am today. Everything I do is to be better than him and different than him. But I know it. I admit it. I deal with it. You have done a lot of avoiding things in your life, Faith."

"You're right. I have."

"I'm in your life or I'm not. It's me. Just me. I can deal with the aftermath that he's created because I understand it. But only the aftermath, when he's past tense."

"He is."

"He just called you and you didn't shut him down. That makes me feel like you aren't ready to let him go. And if you aren't—"

"He is *nothing* to me. *You are.* I just didn't plan to talk to him ever again."

"You're an artist and so is he. You're going to see him. *We're* going to see him. Are you prepared for that?"

"Honestly? Not yet, but I will be. I didn't think or even dare to dream about being in a high-profile show while I was trapped by the winery. I didn't mentally prepare. I'm not like you, Nick."

"If you want me to make him go away, I will."

"And then you'll wonder if I would have done it without you. I need to handle him and I will. Actually, I just want this done and over with." I twist out of his arms and charge through the bathroom into the bedroom, only to discover my phone ringing again.

Anger burns inside me for about ten different reasons: I've let Macom get into my head and inside my relationship with Nick. The man actually expects me to answer his calls when I haven't spoken to him in over a year. And I could keep going with the list of reasons but I'm at the bed holding the phone and I hit answer. "What do you want, Macom?" I demand, turning to find Nick standing in the doorway between the bathroom and the bedroom.

"Faith," Macom replies, his voice low, intimate, familiar, and I feel it like a punch in my belly and not a good one.

I sit down on the mattress, my eyes on Nick. "Why are you calling, Macom?"

"I heard the good news about the show. Congratulations."

"*Why are you calling me, Macom?*" I repeat.

"I want to see you. Come here. Our bed misses you."

I laugh bitterly and cut my gaze from Nick's. "Are you kidding me right now?"

"I messed up."

"Let me be clear. We are *not* friends. We will never be friends. I don't think we were ever friends. We will *never* be anything but a bad mistake. Don't call me. Don't even talk about me. Stay away from me at the show. And be professional. Leave

Josh out of this."

"I'll come there and help you make your show selections," he says, as if I've said nothing. "I want you to do well."

"I've moved on, Macom. I'm in a relationship."

"Of course you are, but I'm up for the challenge."

"There is no challenge. *Do not* come here."

Suddenly Nick is on a knee in front of me, taking the phone. "This is Nick Rogers, Macom. I'm the challenge. Faith was done with you long before she left you, and you were too self-absorbed to see it. But if we need to talk this out, I have a private jet fueled and ready. I can fly you here and we can sit and chat. You can tell me all about your art."

Nick abruptly lowers the phone and tosses it on the bed. "He hung up."

"You were supposed to let me handle this."

"Yes well, sweetheart, I'm a little more possessive than I realized." His hands slide under his shirt on my bare thighs. "And if you're angry—"

"I'm not angry," I say, leaning forward and tangling fingers in his loose hair, his protectiveness, possessiveness even, hitting a nerve and not a bad one. "I'm not," I say, shoving away the memory now stirred, and focusing on this man, the man that matters. "I need you too much, Nick. I need you to know that's scaring me because I'm afraid you'll see it as something it's not."

"Then we'll be scared together, because I need you, Faith. So fucking much it hurts. Don't make me feel that alone because you're afraid of getting hurt. Because I'm just as afraid."

I pull back to look at him. "You're afraid."

"Yes. And I don't do fear. I don't wear it well, remember?"

"God, Nick. You are—"

He kisses me, a deep, drugging kiss before he pulls back, those deep dark blue eyes meeting mine. "I am what?"

"Everything."

"I like that answer," he says softly. "And in the midst of everything, I am the man who very much wants to fall asleep with you in his arms and wake up the same way, ready to go kick the bank's ass. Let's make that happen."

I nod. "Yes. I'd like that."

"What's your bedtime ritual?"

"Before I stopped painting, I would lay in bed and listen to music and think about what I might put on the canvas. What about you?"

"I go to bed."

I laugh. "That's pretty basic."

"I keep what I can simple." He kisses my forehead and stands up. "I'll be right back." He walks into the bathroom, and it hits me that I haven't taken off my make-up, but right now, I just don't care. I slip under the blankets and flip out my bedside light, inhaling the spicy, wonderful scent of Nick clinging to the blankets.

Nick reappears in the bathroom doorway, still shirtless, his hair tied back again, his jeans replaced with pajama bottoms. He flips out the bathroom light and it's not long before he's in bed with me, propped against the headboard, his phone in his hand. "Music," he says, and with a punch of his finger, the soft, soothing sound of Beethoven's Moonlight Sonata fills the air.

My lashes lower a moment, and I take in the delicate notes. "I love it."

"I thought you would," Nick says, flipping off the light. A moment later, he's lying on his back, and pulling me to his chest. "Name one movie this music was featured in," I challenge, snuggling close to him, my hand on his chest.

"Interview with a Vampire," he says correctly. "Your turn."

"1970. Love Story. And it was a tragic love story that my

149

mother loved."

"What's your favorite movie, Faith?"

"I don't have one. You?"

"Me neither."

"What's wrong with us?"

He laughs, that low, sexy laugh that is both soothing and arousing. "Let's find one together," he suggests. "It can be the first of many firsts for us."

"The first of many firsts," I murmur. "I like that."

He strokes my hair. "Good. Now close your eyes and paint."

I shut my eyes. "Paint," I whisper, listening to the music, the delicate touches of piano keys, thinking of my canvas. I can see myself painting, feel myself slipping into slumber. I have red paint, not black, and my brush is moving with purpose, speed. Emotion. The scene fades away and suddenly I am cold and hot and cold again. I fight to open my eyes and for a moment I do, feeling myself slipping in and out of a dream or a nightmare, but I can't seem to escape it. And then I'm back in time, inside the memory Macom and Nick had stirred tonight with that phone conversation. I'm at the dinner club with Macom, and I don't want to be there again. Not tonight. Not ever again. I don't want to relive this. But as hard as I try, I can't stop it from happening now any more than I could then.

In my mind's eye, I see myself in a short, silk, red Versace dress with deep cleavage that Macom had bought for me that night. Too much cleavage to suit me, but Macom likes to show me off. Maybe this should please me. Maybe it's pride. It doesn't please me, though, nor does it feel like pride. Macom himself is dressed in a black sweater and dress pants, his dark, curly hair neatly trimmed on the sides, longish on the top.

We enter the fancy, five-star dining room, his hand at my waist, and men turn to look at me, when they would not look at

*other women in this part of the club—only those whose men allow
their woman to be shared. I would not allow such a thing. I expect
us to sit down, but instead we pass through a curtain, entering a
sitting room that I've never visited, complete with a couch and two
chairs framing a fireplace. Tom, a young and good-looking investment banker who often flirts with me, is standing at the fireplace.
He looks up at our entry, eyes lighting in a way that tells me he's
waiting on us.*

*"What is this?" I ask, but Macom doesn't answer. His grip at
my waist tightens and he urges me forward. "Macom, damn it," I
say, digging in my heels.*

*He rotates me to face him, tangling fingers in my hair. "A new
game."*

"No, I—"

*His mouth closes down on mine in a deep kiss I cannot seem
to escape, but I press on his chest and he finally pulls back. "Relax,
Faith. Every game we play makes us hotter and better."*

"You want to share me? Is that what this is?"

*"You're mine. He's just to borrow." I shove back from him and
I'm pissed. I start to walk out of the room, but anger gets the best
of me. I turn and storm a path to Tom, stepping to him and kissing
him. He molds me close, his hand quickly on my breast but I am
done.*

*I push away from him and find Macom standing almost di-
rectly behind me. "He tastes better than you." I step around him
and keep walking, straight out of the club door. And I keep walking, tears streaming down my face. I wanted my man to be protective, possessive, even. I'd wanted him to want me that much. But
he doesn't and I either have to leave or find a way to deal with the
reality: There is no such thing as a fairy tale. And maybe that's the
problem. I wanted that fairy tale romance that doesn't exist and I
have missed that point. Everyone in that club, including Macom,*

knows that but me.

The images go dark again, and I feel my heart racing, but the music returns to me. Moonlight Sonata. Soft piano playing. My hand on Nick's chest, his breathing steady. Calm returns, and I slowly sink back into the music, reveling in the feel of Nick next to me. I fade into sleep, and my mind goes blank, a sense of relaxation overcoming me, but somehow I'm now standing in my mother's garden. Or above it, looking down. My mother and father are there, kissing and laughing like young lovers, the way I remember them from my youth, but then my uncle walks up, taps my father on the shoulder and my father backs up. My uncle takes my father's place with my mother and starts to kiss her. My father just watches. I start screaming at him, not them, but it's like I'm not really there. Like he can't hear me, or won't hear me.

I gasp and sit up, blinking into sunlight, a new day already upon us, and Nick is no longer in bed with me. "Faith," Nick calls out, rushing from the bathroom, now dressed in sweatpants and a t-shirt. "Sweetheart. Are you okay?"

"Nightmare," I say, throwing away the covers and scooting to the side of the bed. "Why are you dressed like that? Don't you have work?"

"I have a gym in the basement of the house. I was going to ask you to join me, but you were dead to the world. You want to talk about the nightmare?"

I inhale and let it out. "Yes and no."

He settles on his knee in front of me, his hands under his shirt, and on my knees this time. "You have a few hours before you leave for the gallery, in which you could paint. Maybe you need to paint to clear your mind?"

"How can you know me this well?"

"Because I care enough to pay attention, Faith."

"Would you ever take me to your club?" I blurt, before I can stop myself.

Something flickers in his eyes, there and gone, in an instant. "Do you want me to?"

"Would you?"

"Never. Not even if you asked."

"Why?"

"Because you're mine, Faith, and I don't share. And for the record, in case you forgot already: I'm yours, too, in all my arrogant glory."

I'm his and he's mine. "It was about Macom," I say. "The nightmare was about Macom. And oddly, my mother."

"I'm listening," he says, his expression unreadable.

"I relived the first night Macom tried to share me at the club."

"Tried?"

"Yes. There was a man who'd always flirted with me, and Macom wanted to watch me with him. I was furious. I left him there to do what he would. I walked home and at first I said that I'd never go back. But then I decided that everyone at that club was smarter than me. They knew that pleasure was pleasure and expecting fairy tale endings was pain. That's how I went back. That's how I became truly involved. And that's how I survived Macom. That's how I convinced myself we were the best I would ever have."

"Where does your mother come into play?"

"The images shifted and I was in my mother's garden. I watched my father kiss my mother and then my uncle showed up, and he backed away. He gave her to him. I was screaming at my father, but he couldn't hear me. It's like I wasn't there. He settled for my mother. He convinced himself they were the best he would ever have. I decided before I ever met you that I was done settling. I just didn't know where that would lead me or how to get there. Just that I needed to go."

"And you needed to tell me this why?"

"It led me to you, and while I do not want you to be controlling, I needed you to be the man you were tonight with Macom."

"Explain, Faith. I need to understand."

"We have the clubs in our backgrounds. I think I needed… When you took that phone, you made it clear we are just us. I needed to know that we are just us. That you will protect us, not give us away."

He cups my face, his voice low, raspy. "I will always protect not just us, but you, Faith. And everything I do, I do for you. I need you to remember that. Promise me, you will remember that. Tell me you know that."

"I do now. I know."

He pulls away and looks at me. "Don't forget," he orders, and on the surface his warning is all alpha male, but beneath it, in his deep blue eyes, there is something more. He lets me see that he is not unbreakable—that perhaps I alone could break him. The way he could break me. Something shifts and expands between us in those moments that I have never felt before. A bond forming that creates a need between us. We need each other. It is wonderful. It is divine. But long minutes after he's departed for the gym and I stand at the easel with a brush in my hand, I cannot help but wonder—when two people become this vulnerable to each other, when we need each other to keep from shattering, does this mean together we are weaker, or stronger?

Chapter Seventeen

Nick

"**W**OULD YOU EVER TAKE ME TO *YOUR* CLUB?"

That is the question beating me to death while *I* beat a treadmill to death with a fast, hard run, the torment of her question lessened only by my fantasy of beating the shit out of Macom. Though another part of me wants to shake the man's hand for being stupid enough to lose Faith. I'm the winner in this one, but he also hurt Faith and that part of me that isn't a nice guy really wants him to pay.

I finish running, and the idea of Faith upstairs waiting on me, has me flipping out the light and skipping the weights. And when I would normally stop by the kitchen for a bottle of water, I continue onward, up the next level of stairs and into the bedroom, where Faith is not. Certain she's forgot the time and is still painting, I walk down the hallway to her studio, and step through the doorway. Sure enough, Faith is painting, but from the silky sheen of her loose blonde hair, and the faded jeans peeking from her cover-up, she's already showered and is completely unaware of my presence.

Being absorbed with her work, she doesn't look up, and God, she's beautiful when she's this focused on her art: The graceful way she moves. The way her brow furrows randomly with the strokes of her brush. The way her teeth worry her bottom lip as she tilts her head to study another angle of her work. Curious myself about what is newly developing on her canvas, I ease several feet deeper into the room, and behind her, keeping a distance so as to not break her concentration, but still she doesn't seem to know I'm present. Bringing her canvas into view, I'm surprised to find red as her master color, rather than her favorite black or gray, the image created appearing to be some sort of skyward half-moon with a circle beneath it. I don't know what she's creating, but the red tells me that she's doing what we discussed and unleashing a different part of herself.

Several beats pass and she remains immersed in her work, which is my signal to get lost and let her work. I'm about to exit the studio when Faith laughs. I glance back at her and she grins. "You're pretty easy to fool, Tiger. Did you really think you were that stealthy?"

I laugh and take a step toward her. She points her brush at me. "Stop right there. You go shower and get focused on your game, counselor. That's the point in this little exercise. You motivate me to paint. I expect you to keep being a bad-ass attorney who doesn't lose."

"I don't know *how* to lose, sweetheart," I say, giving her a wink and heading down the hallway, and I hit the shower, following Faith's order. I'm one hundred percent focused, but that focus is on her. She's worried about my career. She's worried about paying me back. She's a good person who deserves the world. I'm an asshole who plans to give it to her, when I would give it to no one else. Maybe that's the definition of love. Heartless bastards like me grow hearts. Whatever the case, I'm her asshole and she's stuck with me. I'm going to make sure of it.

Twenty minutes later, not only shaved to the fully outlined goatee I prefer when headed to court, as I will this week, I've dressed, in a grey, pinstriped suit with a vest and a pressed white shirt. I'm standing at the mirror, fitting the black tie I've chosen to match the pinstripe around my neck when Faith not only appears, but scoots between me and the counter.

"I'll do it," she says. "If that's okay with you?"

"Sweetheart, if it's on my body, you can touch it."

She laughs. "That is such a you thing to say." She works the tie with expert technique, and I dislike the idea of her doing it for Macom and I don't even care how possessive that makes me. "How did you learn to do this?" I ask.

"My father," she says. "He always wore a tie at the winery and I had this obsession with artsy ties even before I started painting. I'd pick his tie and then tie his tie." She pats *my tie*. "Done and you look good in this suit. Powerful. But then, you always have that alpha power thing going on."

"Do I now?"

"You do. It's very sexy, but I'm pretty sure you know that."

I stroke the hair behind her ear. "And I know you didn't know I was there until the end. I watched you with your paintbrush and, sweetheart, that is what I call sexy."

"I knew," she says. "I always know when you're close, Nick, but I was finishing one little spot that I didn't want to screw up, and then you were leaving." She reaches for my arm and glances at my brown Cartier watch. "It's seven. You have to be at work at eight."

"I'm the boss. I won't get fired if I'm late."

She pushes to her toes and kisses me. "The boss of everyone but me. I'm going to change shoes and touch up my make-up and I'm ready to go."

She tries to move away and I bring her to me, my hand tangling in her hair, as I drag her mouth to mine. Taking a long, good morning drink of this woman before I say. "Sometimes you like it when I'm the boss. At least when we're naked and that's not a bad thing. You like it. I like it."

"I know that."

"Just in case you *don't know*. I'm never going to hurt you and I damn sure will *never* share you. You know that, right?"

"I already told you. I like when Tiger comes out to play. And don't start thinking I'm some shrinking violet, Nick Rogers. I told you some stuff. You know. Move on. And if you underestimate me, I'll end up on top every time that way. And sometimes l prefer *you* on top."

"As long as I'm inside you, sweetheart," I say. "I'll be on top, bottom, sideways, or any which way."

She shoves against my chest. "Go make coffee or whatever you do before work."

I laugh and step away from her and leave her in the bathroom, taking a path toward the stairs, but once I'm there, I pause, my curiosity over how Faith's new work is developing winning me over. Walking in that direction, I enter the studio, cross to the painting and stare at what has become a dramatically changed image that downright punches me in the gut. I'm looking at two eyes that I know represent 'An eye for an eye'. Words she connects to Macom's betrayal. Macom, who she dreamed about last night. Suddenly, I feel like the fool, on my knees for a woman who's on her knees for another man. I don't want to believe that's true, but I don't know how else to read this, either.

I cross the studio and don't even consider the bedroom. I have a job to do, and as Faith herself said, a focus I need to maintain. I gather my work from my office and end up in the kitchen, where I set my briefcase on the island bar. Faith hurries down the stairs, her blonde hair bouncing right along with her beautiful fucking breasts in a light blue V-neck t-shirt, her purse on her shoulder. In this moment, I do not want to want her, and yet, as she nears, and I watch the sway of her hips, my damn cock decides to stand at attention.

Where the fuck is my discipline?

"I thought you'd be on cup number two by now," she says, stepping to the counter directly across from me.

"I took another look at your painting," I say, deciding my focus is important. And she's distracting the fuck out of me.

"And?" she asks, sounding almost hopeful.

"And what, Faith?"

"What do you think? If you hate it—"

"You dreamt about Macom and now you're painting about Macom."

She blanches. "What? No. That is *not at all* the case."

"It seems pretty damn clear."

"Then it's you who doesn't trust me, Nick. You who don't trust us. Because I told you about the dream and I told you that dream was about us. And I did what I told you I was going to do. I'm getting Macom the hell out of our relationship. I'm facing the past. I'm owning it. And I own things by painting them."

"Is that painting going in the show? Is it to get his attention?"

"Oh my God. Did you hear anything I just said to you?"

"Answer the questions," I bite out.

"You're being a complete asshole right now, Nick Rogers. That painting is for me. For us. It's not meant for any other eyes."

I stare at her several beats, and she stares right back at me, not a blink. And I believe her. "I'm an asshole," I say.

"Yes, Nick Rogers, you are. You *really* are."

"Because you make me crazy."

"So, it's my fault that you're an asshole? Considering you were an asshole the night I met you, I'm pretty sure you mastered that skill long before I met you."

"I'm apparently practicing that skill right now. How am I doing?"

"Exceptionally well."

"I might end up in jail when I meet this guy."

"At least you'll have Abel to represent you."

I laugh, never a step ahead of this woman. "Indeed. At least I do. Will you visit me in jail?"

"I'd prefer to just keep you out of jail." Her mood shifts, darkens. "He's not worth it."

"But you are."

"Is that your way of apologizing for being an asshole?"

"If I want to apologize, I'll apologize," I counter.

"So, you don't want to apologize?"

My cellphone starts ringing and I grimace. "And so Monday begins." I grab my phone from my pocket and glance at the caller ID, then at Faith. "A client that never uses my cell," I say, answering the line. "Devon."

"Holy hell, Nick. The Feds want to talk to me. I have a deal that went sour. I'm scared man. I need help." When a hedge fund billionaire sounds like he might just start crying like a baby, you know he's in trouble.

"What the fuck did you do, Devon?" I demand, and then

quickly say, "Don't answer that on the phone. Meet me in my office in twenty minutes." I end the call and dial Abel. "Heads up. Devon Stein. He's getting a visit from the Feds. I need you to consult."

"When?" Able asks.

"Now. My office. Can you do it?"

"I have court. I'll call you when I get out, but make sure he keeps his mouth shut." He hangs up and I end the call. "I need to run, sweetheart."

"I can take an Uber, no problem. Go. Do you job."

"You're not taking an Uber," I say, reaching in my pocket and setting a key on the counter. "Take the BMW."

"No, I—"

"*Sweetheart*. Take the BMW. I'll drive the Audi. The code to get into the house is 1588 in case you need to come back here. I could have a late night. I hope that I won't." I round the counter and pull her to me. "I'm sorry and I said that because I want to say it. And I meant it when I said that I'm crazy for you, woman."

"You said that I'm making you crazy."

"That too," I say, kissing her. "Enjoy today. You belong in the art world and you belong with me." I release her and head for the door, and as I step into the garage, eyeing my custom BMW, my pride and joy, Faith will be driving today. And I no longer care if Faith drives it as well as she rides me. I'll let her keep the damn keys and the car, for all I care. If Abel heard me say that, he'd already be planning a wedding. And it might just take something that dramatic to make sure she doesn't leave me.

Chapter Eighteen

Nick

I ARRIVE IN THE FINANCIAL DISTRICT AND TO MY OFFICE IN fifteen minutes. I'm on my floor in another five to find Devon pacing in front of Rita's desk and looking like he's slept in the wrinkled mess that is what I know to be his standard ten-thousand-dollar suit. A symptom of his excess, and while I enjoy luxury, there is a point where money starts to control you, not you it, and that can lead to trouble, which I saw coming a year ago with Devon.

Rita spots me moments before him, her relief palpable, her red hair worn long today, while her patience is eternally short. Devon follows her gaze and rotates to face me. "Nick," he breathes out, and he really looks like he might implode if he doesn't spill out his confession here and now.

Exactly why I need him out of this lobby. "Have a drink in

my office, my man," I say. "I'll be right there."

The minute he's gone and my door has opened and shut, I step to Rita's desk and she lets out a breath. "He's guilty of whatever he's here to talk about. He's a guilty, walking-dead mess."

"Which is why I need North on standby to file an action, if it becomes necessary," I say, speaking of my associate "And get him on the response to the bank on the Reid Winter Winery that needs to be done today."

"He already has the documents and is working on them now."

"Any further information on the inspection?" I ask.

"A team of five will be there any minute and they plan to finish by tomorrow night."

I grab a sheet of paper and write down Faith's number. "Faith isn't at the winery. She's here. Kasey is in charge, but text myself and Faith when the team arrives. If you have any trouble at the winery, call Faith. She knows who you are, but I left quickly this morning and didn't tell her you might be contacting her."

"Left quickly? As in she's at your house?"

"Drill me about my personal life later when you can really dig your nails in and do it with full, irritating force. I need to see Charles tomorrow after that inspection is complete," I say of my banker. "Get him on the schedule and if anyone from SF Bank calls, put them through." I consider a moment and write down instructions for North before handing it to Rita. "Have North ready to file these documents with the court the minute we receive the new evaluation of the winery."

She glances at the information. "This will put you in court Wednesday. I'll move your morning appointments. What else?"

"If Faith calls, put her through. And I need Frank Segal, an attorney practicing out of Sonoma, on the line."

"Now?" she asks incredulously.

"The minute you can reach him," I say, pausing at my door, "so yes. Now."

"You are clear on the fact that one of your largest clients who's about to wet his pants is in your office, correct?"

She's right. He'll melt down if I take a call when I'm with him. "Get Segal on the line the minute Devon leaves." I turn and head for my office.

"I really deserve those donuts, Nick."

I pause at my closed door. "Which is why you will have them as soon as you send someone to get them that is not you or me," I say, before entering my office.

And holy hell, the minute I shut the door, Devon spews a mess of shit out at me, that all but guarantees he'll be needing Abel a hell of a lot more than me. I listen to him, and despite all I have seen in my years of practice, this man manages to blow my mind. He's brilliant, with a wife and kids, and a hell of a lot to lose, and yet he made stupid choices. When he's finally done, and we have a plan to connect him to Abel, I watch him exit, with my father in my mind. Greed catches up to people and I tracked my father's business dealings. When he wasn't banging a new woman, he was banging a new payday, and usually at the price of others. And that shit catches up with you. For some, it lands them in jail. Others in a grave.

That's not a hard place to go with my father, but how the hell did Meredith Winter end up dead, too?

Kurt arrives right at ten as scheduled, and I meet him in the conference room where Rita has him waiting at the rectangular glass table. I like glass tables. There's nowhere to hide, no hidden hand gestures or body language. As for Kurt, an ex-SEAL, he's a casual guy who prefers jeans and t-shirts, but wears discipline like a second skin, and today is no exception. He stands when I enter, his expression stoic, all six foot four inches of him pure steel. An intimidating guy to most, and in physical combat, I'd keep my gun pointed at him and never let go of the trigger. In a boardroom, I'm the one everyone fears, but guys like Kurt usually take a bit longer than most to figure that out.

"I'll cut to the chase," I say, motioning for him to sit and claiming the spot directly in front of him. "The club is your life, not mine, therefore I'm gifting it to you. I'll have the paperwork ready for you tonight, and your only expense will be the taxes on the value of the gift. I'll front you that money in the form of a loan, if you need it. Or you can sell. I paid three hundred and fifty thousand for it. You can easily turn it for that, or more, and I'll broker the deal for you."

He narrows his eyes on me. "Why wouldn't you broker it for yourself?"

"I don't need the money, and after years of service to that club, you deserve the reward."

"Why wouldn't you broker it yourself?" he repeats.

"A woman," I say simply. "I need it gone."

"That's becoming a familiar theme, considering you bought it when Mark Compton met a woman."

"Technically I bought it because of his legal issues but she wasn't just a woman. She's his wife."

"A woman is why he stayed away," he says. "And I will never let a woman dictate my life." Words that echo my own sentiments before I met Faith. "If the club is now mine," he continues. "I'm not selling and I don't need a loan. You pay me well and I've recently made a smart investment that paid off."

"Well then, I'll have the paperwork to you tomorrow," I

say, standing and offering him my hand as he pushes to his feet. "But I need it signed tomorrow as well."

"Get it to me tomorrow, and I'll have it back to you by Monday. I need time for my attorney to look it over."

"It's a gift," I bite out.

"That comes with potential liability. I'll look for the paperwork." He heads for the door and exits.

I smile, that hard-nosed SEAL in him predictable in his skeptical pushback. I knew he'd want to have an attorney review what seemed too good to be true, even if he didn't act like it was too good to be true. And I knew he'd push for Monday, which is after Faith and I get back from Sonoma, and a full two weeks before Macom fucks with her head again in L.A.

The phone on the conference table buzzes. "Segal is on the line," Rita announces.

I sit down and grab the receiver. "What do you know that I don't know?" I say, skipping the formality of a greeting. "What is it about the winery that makes the bank want it?"

"I have no idea," he says.

"What makes that property valuable beyond the obvious?"

"Asking your question ten different ways doesn't change my answer."

"The note Faith's father left for her," I say, hitting him from another direction. "Do you know what's inside?"

"That note is between Faith and her father."

"She hasn't opened it. Do you know what's inside?"

"Yes."

"Is there anything in that letter that tells us why the bank is after the winery?"

"Absolutely nothing. It's personal. It's not business and she'd know that if she just opened it."

"Right. I'll be in touch." I end the call, my fingers

thrumming the table, when Rita buzzes again.

"Beck is here."

She sounds uncomfortable. Beck has that effect on people. "Send him back."

"He sent himself back," she says, and sure enough, Beck opens the conference room door.

He's thirty-five. Tall. Quiet. Lethal. The difference between him and Kurt: CIA vs SEALs. No conscience vs conscience. I don't get up. I let him come to me. He saunters toward me, dressed in black jeans and a Metallica shirt, his longish, black hair spiky. He claims the seat occupied by Kurt, his stare meeting mine, his blue eyes so damn pale, it's like looking into the eyes of a husky on the prowl, ready to attack. You want this man on your side, but you protect your throat.

"I hope this visit means you finally did your job," I say dryly.

His lips quirk sardonically. "Meredith Winter had a gambling habit most of her adult life. Ten years ago, her husband reined her in and put her on a budget."

"And made no provisions to control her when he died."

"Exactly. And when he hit the ground, she did, too. The underground poker rooms, and those dudes are bad news. She lost her touch. She took out markers against the winery, which explains why there was no money trail for her spending and why your father was paying her cash."

"If you want me to believe they both ended up dead over a gambling debt, you're barking up a fool's tree. My father would not just pay off her gambling debt no matter how good a fuck she was. Not without leveraging her for the winery and he'd put that in writing. You need to find it."

"I told you. Someone wiped the phone and computer records. There are entire periods of time missing from your father's and Meredith Winter's records. But there is an obvious suspect here. The next person in line to inherit, even if he had to force it through the court system."

"Faith's uncle," I supply.

"That's right. Keep her away from him."

"He fucked her mother. She hates him."

"Interesting," he says, though he never sounds overly interested in anything. "When?"

"The year Faith graduated college."

"He was married then," Kurt says, proving he's been studying up. "And his wife is the female Mark Zuckerberg, her company is Facebook's biggest competitor. He wouldn't want his wife finding out he bent over his brother's wife, as she, from what I understand, gives him an allowance and keeps him on a leash."

"He's filthy rich. No prize at that winery would be worth killing over."

"But protecting his secret would be."

"None of this connects dots that make sense." I circle back to where we were. "This gambling debt was a tool my father used as a weapon. You need to find out why he needed that weapon because that's why they both ended up dead."

"If you're right, and I believe you are, Faith is now the target."

"Which is why I'm taking attention and pressure off of her. I'm going to get my bank to buy out the bank note, and we've done up dummy documents to make me a key stockholder. That brings the attention to me."

"Or you trigger a reaction you don't want by making whoever wants that winery think they can't have it."

"Pissed off people make mistakes, and we'll be watching."

"Or your actions ensure that history repeats itself. Your

father and Meredith Winter got in someone's way. Now you and Faith are in the way. They died. You two die."

"And would you suggest I do something differently?"

"No," he says, standing up, and without another word, heads for the door.

Chapter Nineteen

Faith

I ARRIVE AT THE ALLURE GALLERY RIGHT AT NINE, PARKING the BMW in the rear of the gallery, running my hands over the logo on the dash with a smile. And not because it's a BMW but because it's *this* BMW. Because this one is custom, sleek and sexy, just like the man who owns it. I'm just about to exit the car when my phone buzzes with a text from an unfamiliar number and a message. *Faith, this is Nick's assistant, Rita. He's in a meeting but wanted you to know the minute the inspectors arrived at the winery. They are there now, and have already checked in with Kasey.*

I am pleased by this text. It tells me that Nick listened when we talked. He's trying to keep me involved and informed. I text Rita back: *Thank you. I am looking forward to meeting you.*

Rita replies with: *When will that happen?*

This week I hope, I reply.

Looking forward to it as well. Let me know if you need anything, is her message.

I smile at her offer, but as my mind turns to Kasey, I suddenly feel selfish for being here, not there. He's dealing with everything I don't want to deal with and I've never put that on him, or taken that off of me. I hit his auto-dial and he answers almost immediately. "Everything is fine," he says, greeting me. "I'm quite capable, in case you've forgotten."

"You are incredible," I say. "Which is why I never want to take advantage of you."

"Please, Faith. Use me. Your mother did."

"My mother abused you."

"Okay. Your father used me. Use me like he did, but with less involvement."

"How is the inspection going?"

"They're on the other side of the property," he says, "and we don't even feel like they're here. Does this inspection get you out of probate?"

"It's a step to getting us out of all this mess soon," I promise, reading the concern beneath his question. The winery has been his life, all his adult life. "And we're close. The bank note is caught up. The bills will be by Monday. And Thursday, I'm going to talk to you about finally getting you the appreciation you deserve."

"I don't need anything from you but some trust. Your father trusted me. Now it's your turn. Let me run this place."

"My father would roll over in his grave if he knew I didn't plan to run the winery."

"I loved your father, kiddo, but on this he was wrong. His obsession with you running this place was illogical. You have a dream. Most of us never make ours come true. Be the exception."

"Thank you, Kasey. I'm looking forward to talking Thursday."

"Me too. Now. Am I safe to promise vendors money by Monday? Because I have someone waiting for me right now."

"Yes," I say. "Monday at the latest."

He lets out a breath. "I have to tell you. I'm relieved."

"Me too," I say. "All is well."

"That is good news for us all."

We exchange a few more words, and when we disconnect, I am feeling really good about Nick's idea to offer incentives, maybe even some ownership, to Kasey. He deserves it, and with the financial troubles moving behind us, he'll be the reason that I can keep the winery and focus on painting.

Exiting the car, I lock up, slip my purse over my head, a flutter of anticipation in my belly as I race toward the door. Sara must see me on a camera somewhere, because she opens the door before I can knock, greeting me in a pink Allure t-shirt. I step inside the gallery and she pulls me into a hug, greeting me with such warmth that I feel like we are old friends. Only I don't have any old friends and certainly none I'd want to call friend again. It's not long before I have my own pink Allure t-shirt on and we begin touring the gallery while she shares her vision for the structure of the displays, and actually asks for my thoughts. We get excited together talking about random ideas.

By ten, we enter the private business area, pass the reception area, and several offices before Sara presents me with an office. "This is yours for as long as you can help." She shoves her long dark hair back from her face. "There is a break room on the other side of the office area with lots of coffee options. And," she sits down in front of me, "these are all the new artists who have submitted for the gallery's consideration. I picked my top ten. What I'm hoping is to see what your top ten will be and then we can debate, narrow it down, and take ten options to Chris. He's basically endorsing them, so he gets the final say, even though he says he trusts me. I want him to pick."

And they already picked me. Chris Merit endorsed *me*. "I'm excited to do this."

"I'm excited to have you here. Take your time. Chris is deeply absorbed in finishing a painting right now, and he won't look at our picks until he's done. I just need to pick this weekend. I'm in the back far corner office if you need me, or," she grabs a sticky note and pen, and scribbles down her number, "just text me." She laughs. "Because why wouldn't you text me a few doors down?"

We share a laugh and she leaves me to work. I stare at the painting in front of me, which is, of course, an incredible Chris Merit black and white cityscape. I study the technique and I really don't notice anything else about the office for a good ten minutes. Only then do I notice bookshelves lining the wall to my left, filled with art books I'd love to study at some point. Right now, though, I have work to do and I remove my purse and I'm about to stick it in a drawer. It's then that my phone rings and I pull it from my purse and note Nick's number.

"Hey," I say, answering. "How is that client situation?"

"Bad. He needs Abel. We're meeting with him at two. How are things there?"

"Fabulous. I love this place and Sara. Thanks for having Rita text me, Nick."

"I'm not trying to run your life, Faith," he says.

"Not on purpose," I say. "It's your nature to take control and in case I've sent you confusing messages, I do want to be informed, but I feel immense relief to have you handling this situation for me, Nick."

"I actually need to talk to you about your mother. Were you

aware that she had a gambling problem?"

"No," I say, shaking my head. "But isn't that just perfectly priceless. That's where the money went, isn't it?"

"That's where this seems to be headed," he says.

"And here I thought her only destructive vice was sex."

"Sex is not a vice."

"It is when you're married and fucking half the state," I say. "Unless of course, my father liked to watch her with other men as she claimed. In which case, he was more screwed up than her. I don't know why I was hoping for her bank account to save me. I need to save myself."

"You have me now, Faith."

"I know."

"Do you?"

"I'm trying to get us to that."

"Try harder. And just so you know, we should have the new evaluation by tomorrow. I'm meeting with my banker tomorrow to be ready to move the note, but I'm going to decide when to act based on how all the players are responding to the situation at the time." His intercom buzzes and a female voice I assume to be Rita's, says, "Devon is melting down again. He's on the line."

"I'm not babysitting that stupid crybaby prick," Nick bites out. "Feel free to tell him that."

"Now that you got that off your chest," the woman says. "What would you like to me to say to him?"

"Whatever the hell you want to tell him, Rita."

"You're in a deposition," she says. "Remember that."

I laugh. "I like Rita."

"She's a pain in my ass today."

"Isn't everyone?"

"Yes, which is why I really need you here, to fuck me into amnesia. I'd come over there and do a little artistic fucking with you, but I have a lunch thing I need to prep for. Think of me, sweetheart. I'm damn sure thinking of you." He ends the call and I laugh, but it fades quickly.

I really want to end this nightmare with the bank. I need to do something other than wait on Nick to be my hero. I inhale and tell myself to make the call I know I need to make. Only I don't even know the number to call. I turn to the MacBook sitting on the desk and key it to life, looking up Pier 111, the business my uncle's wife founded, and that he helps run. Finding the main number, I punch it into my cellphone.

"Pier 111, can I help you?"

"I need Bill Winter, please," I say.

"May I ask who is calling?"

"Faith Winter."

"Hold please." A few beats later she returns. "He'll call you back. What number can he call you back on?"

I give her my cellphone number and end the call. Why did I even bother to make that call? He's a bastard. My cellphone starts to ring with an unknown number.

Expecting it's him, I answer. "Hello."

"Faith. What a surprise that you called. We've needed to talk."

I open my mouth to ask him about the bank and the value of the winery when it hits me. He's a bastard. He could try to take it as well. My mind races for a reason for this call. "Faith?" he presses. "Is something wrong?"

"I had a dream last night," I blurt.

"About?"

"You. My mother claimed that my father liked to watch her with other men. Last night I dreamed that you were one of those men. Were you?"

Chapter Twenty

Faith

HE DIDN'T SAY NO.

That's what haunts me for the rest of the afternoon while I sit at my desk evaluating the files Sara gave me. Even after Sara and I dine on Chinese food and enjoy great conversation, I replay it again. And now, at nearly five o'clock, I do it all over again.

"My mother claims that my father liked to watch her with other men. Last night I dreamed that you were one of those men. Were you?"

"Sex is what put us at opposite ends of the world," he says. "We're the only Winters left. We need to put the past behind us."

"That's a yes," I say.

"That's a refusal to discuss my sex life with my niece. How are things at the winery?"

"We are not friends or family," I say. "I have zero desire to discuss my life with you. I simply wanted to know if you and my father were both sick enough to share my mother. That simple. I got my answer. What I don't understand is why my father was upset when he found out you fucked her on your own? I mean, what difference does it make? You know what. This was a mistake."

My phone buzzes with a message, pulling me back to the present, and I glance down to find a message from Nick: *Client losing his fucking mind. I'll be another two hours. I'll bring home dinner.*

My stomach does this funny loopy thing it's never done in my life with the words: Bring home dinner. Like home is something we share. It's just a phrase, of course. It means nothing, but then, Nick does nothing by accident. And I'm officially falling so damn hard for Nick that there is no turning back. I'm in this, no matter how broken I end up.

I text back: *I can make my famous pancakes.*

He replies with: *Only if you make them naked.*

I laugh and type: *Batter splatters.*

Good point, he replies. *I want every inch of that gorgeous body feeling good next to mine. Call you soon, sweetheart.*

Sara appears in my doorway. "It's getting late. Are you staying a while?"

"Are you?"

"Chris isn't answering his phone, which means he's lost in his work. I figure I'll work another hour or so and then take him dinner."

"Nick is working late. I figured I'd stay another hour and then head home." Home. Now I said home.

Sara catches it too, her lips curving. "It's nice to have you here in the city. I want coffee. You want coffee? They make a killer white mocha next door."

"White mocha?" I ask, perking up. "I'm in." I grab my purse and slip it over my shoulder before sticking my phone inside.

"Great. We can dash over there and be back in a few minutes."

We make our way to the door, and step outside, both of us hugging ourselves against a chilly wind, the smell of the ocean air touched by the scent of fresh, hot nuts from a nearby vendor. In that moment, I decide I love this city. The smells. The art. The energy. *Nick.*

"We have arrived," Sara announces, indicating a door only a block from the gallery.

"Rebecca's," I murmur, reading the writing on the door. "Didn't Chris paint something dedicated to Rebecca?"

"He did," she says, and rather than offering more detail, she opens the door, motioning me forward.

I enter the adorable little shop, with paintings of people drinking coffee on the walls, and clusters of wooden tables, while booths line the left wall. Sara joins me and we approach the register, where a glass display case allows me to drool over a tempting selection of cookies and sweets.

"Usual, Sara?" a tall man, with dark brown hair and glasses asks.

"You know it, Mick," Sara replies, "and anything Faith wants is on the house now and forever." She glances at me. "We own this place, too. Mick is our manager, and co-owner."

"Oh well then, thank you to you both," I say, placing my order and it's not long before Sara and I claim one of the cute wooden booths in the back of the shop, with Mick's promise to bring us our drinks.

"So, you own the gallery and the coffee shop," I say. "That's a great combination so close together."

"Well, there is a connection, which is Rebecca. It's a long

story, but she worked for the gallery. She spent a lot of time here. We were going to re-name the gallery Rebecca's, but had some name recognition issues and decided to make the coffee shop Rebecca's. We remodeled it to add these cute booths, and over-hauled the menu. We wanted it to be her place."

Our order arrives and by the time we're alone again, despite my curiosity about Rebecca, I never get the chance to ask questions. "Oh yikes," Sara says. "I just realized I left my purse and phone next door. I need to run back."

"Of course," I say, and we hurry to the door, and back to the gallery.

"Before you go back to work," Sara says, "I want to show you something in my office."

I follow her to the corner office and step inside, my lips parting instantly. "Oh my God," I whisper at the sight of a mural on the wall behind the massive mahogany desk. A painting of the Eiffel Tower in Chris's signature black and white. "It's incredible," I murmur, crossing to stand behind the desk, studying the tiny details that few artists ever master.

"Look up," Sara says and obediently, my gaze lifts to find another European scene.

"The Spanish Steps," I say, and I can't help myself. I set my cup down and lay down on the floor, staring up at it. More details. More perfection. "Wow."

Sara laughs and appears above me. "How's the view from down there?"

"Spectacular. He's incredible, Sara. Each step is different. The shadows. The shading. The texture."

"Sara."

At the sound of Chris's voice, my eyes go wide, a cringe following. How did I let myself end up on the floor?!

"Chris," Sara says, whirling around to greet him.

"Fuck, Sara," he says, his voice growing closer. "Why aren't you answering your phone?"

Sara is around the desk in a heartbeat, and I don't know what to do. Stay down or get up?

"I forgot it when we went to the coffee shop."

"Baby," he breathes out. "It's only been a few months."

My brow furrows at the curious comment that seems to explain his over-the-top reaction.

"Seven months," she says. "I know that's still not a long time, but we both need to let it go. We need some semblance of normalcy."

"Normal?" he asks. "Have we ever been normal?"

"No," she says, her voice softening. "And I love that about us."

"Keep your phone with you, baby," he says. "Please."

"I will," she promises. "Stop worrying."

"I won't," he promises. "Did Faith already leave?"

"Actually," Sara says. "She's on the floor behind the desk."

I cringe all over again and suddenly Chris is standing over me, big, blond, and wearing a t-shirt that displays the artistically perfect, multi-colored dragon tattoo sleeve covering his right arm. "Why are you on the floor?" he asks.

"I was admiring your work. It's stunning. The detail is perfection and yet you had to do it on a ladder." I sit up, hands behind me, holding me up. "Is it bad for me to admit I have a crush on you right now? Completely professional, of course, but it's powerful."

Sara laughs and hitches a hip on the desk. "A lot of people feel that way about Chris."

Chris squats down in front of me, his intense green eyes boring into mine. "But not you," he says.

I blink. "What?"

"Don't idolize another artist," he scolds. "Appreciate their skills. Study their technique, but when you idolize them, you can't see your own work clearly. Focus on your own work and based on what you're doing thus far, I can promise you, success will follow."

"In fact," Sara says. "Why don't you come to work here full time? Chris can mentor you and I get two gifted artists helping me make this place a success."

I blanch. "I...I wish that I could, but I can't. I have the winery to think about."

"Don't you have a management team to run it?" Sara asks.

"Yes, but it's complicated. And I can't afford a misstep. I'm alone—"

"What about Nick?" she asks.

"Nick and I are new and I don't expect him, or want him, to take care of me."

"That's a conversation for you and Sara," Chris says, "But all I can say is that painters paint."

"I know," I say, "but my family has owned this winery for generations. It was everything to my father. He expected me to run it."

"Your father," Chris says flatly. "That's another topic for Sara. And on that note, I'm leaving." He stands up and turns to Sara, and I swear he doesn't even touch her, and they sizzle.

"I'll meet you at home."

"I'll be there soon."

"Your phone," he says.

"I know," she says.

They stare at each other for another few sizzling moments and then he's gone. To my surprise, Sara then sits down on the floor next to me, cups in hand, and hands me my coffee. "Sorry about that."

"I'm sorry. I feel like I eavesdropped."

"You didn't. And Chris is protective, but he's not that over the top. There was…an incident in Paris." She cuts her gaze and visibly shakes herself and then rotates to lean on one shoulder and face me. "I can't talk about it. Maybe one day, I'll tell you. Not now. Even if we knew each other that well, I'm just not ready, but let me say this, Faith. The past year has reminded me that life is short. We only get one chance to live it. Painters paint."

"I know, but it's complicated."

"My father is very rich."

"Like Chris."

"My father is nothing like Chris," she says. "Chris is strong, tough, dark in ways I understand, but he is kind, generous, gifted, generous. Did I say generous?"

"And your father?"

"Brutal. Self-centered. He treated me and my mother horribly. And he wanted me to live the life he designed and when I refused, he disinherited me. But even then, when I had the courage to walk away from him, I took a teaching job, when art was what I'd studied and loved."

"Why?"

"Fear. Money. Stability. You know galleries don't pay much."

"What changed?"

"I found a journal. Rebecca's journal. Inside it was all her deepest thoughts, fears, and confessions. Impossibly, it seemed, she wanted to be in this world, too, but resisted for the same reasons I did. But then one day she walked into a gallery, this gallery, and her life changed. She dared to chase her dream. And she was younger than me. Braver. She inspired me. I came to look for her, and she was gone. I never met her. I took her job. She led me to my dreams. To Chris. And now…"

"I'm here," I say, rotating to lean against the desk. "And with Nick."

"Yes," she says.

"I don't want to get ahead of myself."

"Is that comment about your art or Nick?"

I glance over at her. "Both, I think. Nick and I are new."

"I moved in with Chris a few weeks after meeting him and I was terrified. He was bigger than life."

I face her. "Yes. Nick is so—everything."

"Good. He should be."

"I'm not ready for him to be everything."

"Because you're scared?" she asks.

"Yes. He hasn't revealed all of himself. I know this. I sense it."

"Chris once told me that we are all the sum of all of our broken pieces. You can't grow if you don't risk more damage, Faith. You can't find the person who makes you whole again if you're afraid. Nick. Your art. Whatever it is, ask yourself: What if there is no tomorrow? Because there was no tomorrow for Rebecca. It can happen to any of us." She cuts her gaze and swallows hard, seemingly shaken, before she stands up. "I want you to work here," she says, pushing past the obviously upsetting topic. "I want you to paint one of the offices the way Chris did this one," she adds. "Pick one. Any one, but if you say you'll do it, you can't stop coming here until it's done."

"You want me to—"

"Yes. Say yes, Faith."

"Yes."

She opens a drawer and pulls out a key, offering it to me. "Your key. I'll pay you two hundred thousand dollars a year. I'm going home to my husband. The security system arms if you hit the button by the door." She starts walking toward the door.

"Sara," I say.

She turns to face me. "Yes?"

"Thank you."

"No thanks needed. I'm really glad to have you here." She disappears into the hallway and I believe her. Sara and I are alike in ways few people could understand. And suddenly I have two people in my life who fit.

I've never had anyone in my life that fit.

But she fits. *Nick* fits.

I inhale on a ball of emotions. Fear? Is that what is controlling my decisions? And if it is, how did fear become that powerful in my life? How did I convince myself that fear was strength? Because I did. And it makes me angry. I hate that this is what I've become. My purse vibrates with a text and I open my purse to find a message from Nick: *I'm outside.*

He's here. He is always here when I need him and if I let it happen, that will be always. And needing him doesn't make me weak. It makes me brave. Suddenly, I want to see him, I want to feel what he makes me feel, and see if it feels different after that conversation with Sara. I exit Sara's office, and hurry to my new office, pausing with my hand on the light switch, envisioning Sonoma on the walls. Or maybe something new and daring. My lips curve and I shut out the light, my pace hurried as I exit into the gallery, a little thrill in my belly as I think of my art on display. I reach the exit, and open the door, punching the security button before I step outside. And there is Nick, looking like sin and sex in his tan suit, leaning against his Audi, the beam of a streetlight illuminating him.

My heart starts to race and I start walking, his eyes, those intense, blue eyes, following my every step, a curve to his mouth. And the minute I step in front of him, he pulls me to him, that raw, sexy scent of his consuming me. "How the fuck did I miss you this much?" he asks, his mouth closing down on mine. And oh, what a kiss it is. Deep. Passionate. Hungry. Like he has been starving all day and I didn't know until this minute that I have been, too. "I have something for you."

"That wasn't it?" I ask, sounding breathless. Feeling breathless.

"That was just hello sweetheart." He strokes a lock of hair from over my eyes. "I was going to save it for your show, but I think it's a good way to celebrate you being here today instead of in Sonoma." He pulls a box from his pocket and opens it to display a jeweled necklace, shaped like a paintbrush and color palette.

"Nick," I whisper, completely blown away and not because the stones glisten with reds, blues and greens. It's the sentiment, the thought he's put into this. I push to my toes and kiss him. "Thank you. It's perfect."

"You're perfect, Faith."

"No Nick. I'm broken. But I'm pretty ready to be broken with you, if you think you want to be broken with me."

"Not broken. Together. Whole. Us. We. You and me."

"Yes." My heart swells all over again. "I like how that sounds."

"Me too, sweetheart. And how's this for a plan for the night? We walk two blocks to the best Mexican food place in town. After we eat at Diego Maria's, we go home where the process is: Fuck. Paint. Fuck. Paint. Sleep. No nightmares tonight."

I smile. "I like that plan."

"But do you love it, Faith?" he asks, his voice low, raspy, and I'm not sure we're talking about the plan or us. Either way, I don't let fear win this time.

"Yes," I say. "I do."

Chapter Twenty-One

Nick

FAITH AND I ARE UP EARLY THE NEXT MORNING, HER IN her studio painting again, and me back in the basement on the treadmill. I run with the same fierceness I did yesterday, but this time, my mind isn't on the club, but rather a replay of Beck's ominous warning about history-fucking-repeating itself, with a repeat of a double murder the outcome. I am stuck in one of those rock-and-a-hard-spot places that I've always called myth, and it pisses me off. I can't delay my actions and risk Faith losing the winery, but before I act, I need a better plan than "I hope like fuck not" when it comes to Faith and I living or dying.

I punch the stop button on the treadmill, and by the time I step off the belt, I'm already dialing Beck. "Once the inspectors give me an evaluation on the winery," I say, the minute he answers, "I have to move. I have to file a petition and claim Faith's rightful inheritance. I can't give the bank time to undervalue it with their own inspectors, which could well lead to Faith losing the winery."

"What's the timeline?"

"We get the evaluation back today. I meet with my banker later this afternoon. If the evaluation comes back where I need it, we'll file an emergency request to be in court Wednesday or Thursday, at which time my bank will buy out the note. If the evaluation doesn't come back where I need it to be, I'll package it to get it there, and we'll be in court Thursday or Friday." I look up to discover Faith standing in the doorway, hugging herself, the look on her face telling me that she heard every word.

"I have dirt on three people in the bank, and I've used it. They aren't breaking. That means they are either scared or we're wrong. And I don't think we're wrong."

"And your solution is what? And don't tell me you need to think this time."

"Whatever action you take, at least getting rid of both of you is harder than getting rid of just Faith, especially with my team watching."

"Holy fuck. Is this really what I'm paying you for? Get me *answers*." I hang up and focus on Faith. "Hey, sweetheart," I say, crossing to stand in front of her, my hands on her shoulders. "How is painting going?"

"Why would you want to delay claiming the winery?"

"When you take someone out at the knees, you want to know what their reaction will be."

"If we're already with another bank, what can my present bank possibly even do?"

"The question is, what are they motivated to do and why," I say, sticking to the truth, but leaving out murder as an option.

"Let's grab some coffee while we finish this conversation."

"Nick—"

I kiss her. "Coffee. Conversation. Me. You. Upstairs." I turn her toward the stairs, and place her in motion.

Once we're in the kitchen, coffee in hand, we lean on the same side of the island facing each other. "I'm very confused by the conversation I just heard. And even your response. Is the bank going to lash out at you? Because I don't want you to end up with trouble over me."

"Sweetheart, you and I are in this together. And when someone goes to this much trouble to get something and you keep them from getting it, you have to be prepared for anything. Especially when you don't know all of the facts, and we don't."

"I need to just open that card from my father. Now. This morning."

She starts to move away and I catch her arm. "I called Frank. He knows what it says and it's not what we need."

"Did he tell you what it says?"

"Only that it's personal and it has nothing to do with business."

She inhales and sinks onto the edge of the stool. "Okay. Well, I always thought it was. You know. A good ole personal punch in the chest. The whole: Your destiny is the winery. It's in your blood. I'm counting on you. Art is a hobby. Set it aside. Focus."

I step to her and run my hand down her hair. "Don't do that. Don't let this get into your head. You're an artist. That is what you want. That is what *you are*."

"I called my uncle," she surprises me by saying.

Alarms go off in my head and I pull back and rest my elbow on the table. "When and why?"

"Yesterday. I meant to tell you sooner, but last night was

good, and I didn't want to ruin it with him."

"Why did you call him and what happened?"

"I got this idea in my head that he might know what the value of the winery is outside the obvious, but the minute I heard his voice, I had second thoughts. I don't trust him. I was afraid that if I alerted him to a potential payoff, that despite being a wealthy man, he might try to take it."

Smart girl, I think. "Then what did you say to him?"

"I blurted out that my mother said that my father liked to watch my mother with other men and asked if he was one of them."

"Holy shit, woman," I say, scrubbing the new day stubble on my jaw. "What did he say?"

"He didn't say no. He talked around it."

"Holy *fuck*."

"I know. But what doesn't make sense is why my father would be furious about him sleeping with my mother if they'd already been together. As in all of them. Unless their fallout wasn't about sex at all." She shakes her head. "But then he swears he and my father made up before my father's death."

"Something with him doesn't add up, but Beck can't connect the dots between him and the bank. Whatever the case, I'm moving forward. I'm going to get in front of a judge and get you out of probate. But from a timeline standpoint, I may have been overly ambitious with that Thursday night dinner with Kasey. Let's make it Friday night."

"He'll be fine with that. I talked to him today and I'm feeling really good about him running things without me."

"Good. You've come a long way in a short while, sweetheart. And on that note. Show me what you painted this morning."

She stands up. "Not what I was supposed to be painting," she confesses as we start walking.

"What were you supposed to be painting?"

"Something appropriate for the show," she says. We start up the stairs and she adds, "I'm obsessed with those eyes. And I don't even think it has anything to do with the whole 'face the past' motto I'd used when I picked up the brush. It's just different and challenging. I'm enjoying it."

"You know the saying. Do what you love and success will follow."

"I need to move on and work on my final show piece. Oh, and that reminds me. Sara wants me to do a mural in one of the offices."

"What kind of mural?"

"It will cover one of the walls and it can be anything I want it to be, but it's kind of intimidating. Chris painted her office."

"You need to stop comparing yourself to Chris."

"Funny you say that. *He* said that."

"Maybe he'll be the mentor you need then," I say, as we enter the studio and cross to stand in front of her canvas, which is now well developed. One of the eyes is now filled with a rainbow of colors. The other is red and black. Almost as if it's her past and her present. And I can't explain what it is about two eyes on a canvas, but it's brilliant. "You have to put this in the show."

"No," she says. "Macom will read into it and I don't want that drama. The entire point in this painting was to face the past and get rid of it."

"You just said it had become about the challenge. And it shows. And if you want to stick to the original theme of facing your past, face Macom with this painting. Get rid of him in person. And if he doesn't get the idea, I'll handle him."

She narrows her eyes on me. "You want trouble."

"I love trouble."

"You want trouble with him."

"I want to beat the shit out him."

"Nick. You can't—"

"I can," I say, pulling her to me, "but I won't."

"Promise."

"I promise, unless he makes it impossible to resist."

"*Nick.*"

"Sweetheart, I'm not violent, but I am brutal. Come get naked with me and I'll show you."

"How did you just make that sound sexy?"

"Must be love, sweetheart," I say, "and now, I'm going to do things to you that you won't forget for the rest of the day. And *that* is a promise." I scoop her up and start walking toward my bedroom, and my bed, where she belongs. And I'm going to make sure she knows it.

I arrive at work with a box of donuts, which I set on Rita's desk, earning me a smile. "You remembered."

"I did," I say. "Because you, Rita, are like Glinda the Good Witch, who's a really good bitch to everyone but me, when *you are well fed.* I like you well fed." I head to my office. "Whatever I'm doing today, when that property assessment arrives, get it to me." My mind turns to my personal banker. "What time will Charles be here?"

"Four o'clock," she says. "And North is on standby for the emergency filing the minute you say go. It's prepped and on your desk. He, on the other hand, is sleeping in his office. He's sick. The kind of sick that makes being sick look good."

"Fuck. Send him home."

"I tried. He refused."

I walk back to her desk, pick up her phone, and dial his office. "North?"

"Yes?" He starts coughing.

"Get the fuck out of my office before you make me sick." I hang up and Rita opens the donut box, pointing to a certain donut. "Your favorite."

I turn away and walk into my office. About the time I reach my desk, my cellphone buzzes with a text and I have to sit down when I see it. "Holy Mother of Jesus," I murmur at the sight of Faith's uncle, naked, tied up, and with a woman—I think she's a woman—but whatever the case, he or she is spanking him. Rita's voice lifts from the lobby and suddenly Beck is walking into my office without knocking. My intercom buzzes. "I told him to wait," Rita says. "He's impossible."

"Yes," he is, I say. "But it's fine. I'll deal with him."

Beck's lips twist sardonically with my comment, and he shuts the door, his dark hair extra spiky today. His t-shirt—an image of a middle finger with a "fuck you" printed above it—somehow appropriate considering that photo he just sent me. He crosses my office and sits down on the arm of a visitor's chair, always a rebel, even in the smallest of ways. "You got my good morning calling card, I assume?"

"I did." I lean back in my chair. "Did he?"

"Not yet," he says, "and here are my thoughts. We both know that you already decided you're making your deal with your bank and hers. If her bank simply thought they could cash in on the winery, it's over. If there's more to it, it's not and we have two sources of potential trouble: Someone at the bank and the naked, perversely kinky uncle." He holds up his hands. "Married uncle. We both know you'll use your extremely large bank account to influence her bank. *I* will handle the naked married uncle."

"I didn't hire you to fly blind and tape on Band-Aids, Beck."

"We both like trouble," he says. "Maybe there isn't trouble to be found. Until we get the autopsy report, we don't know, and unless you want to wait on that report, this is where we're at."

"Are the cameras in place at her house and the wintery?" I ask, concerned about Faith's safety.

"Yes, and we're watching her so closely that I can practically tell you what color Faith's panties are." He holds up his hands. "Don't worry. I'll ask if I'm curious. I'm curious. What color—"

"Get the fuck out."

He laughs and heads for the door. The minute he's out of my office, Rita is inside. "Seems a good bribe works wonders. We have the winery's new evaluation."

"How much?" I ask.

"Forty million," she says. "Five million more than Faith's note with the bank."

"Fuck me in a good way. Get Charles—"

"He's on his way over now. Look over the filing and I'll get it done myself. North and the trashcan are now one."

I reach for the documents she needs, do a quick review of the key points, then hand them to her. "File it at four o'clock. I don't want the bank to have time to get someone to the winery before we end up in court."

"Can you get an emergency hearing tomorrow? Because the Nichols family is coming in at ten and you know—"

"How they are. Yes. I do. Plan on Thursday."

"Got it," she says. "Is Faith prepared for court? She'll need something to wear."

"Fuck. Yes, she will, and no she isn't."

"I can order her some clothes, but I have no idea on shoe size."

"Negative. If I just order her a wardrobe, she's going to be pissed."

She arches a brow, her hands settling at the waist of her navy dress. "Really? Most women would love for a man to buy them clothes. Interesting. I *like* her already. Did you say, or did I overhear, that she's working at a gallery here locally?"

"Allure Gallery."

"I'll put your black card on file at several boutiques nearby." She pulls her phone from her pocket and tabs to the Gallery. "Chanel and Dolce & Gabbana are two blocks away. I'll get it done right away." She glances at me. "When do I meet her?"

"Go file the paperwork and eat a damn donut," I say.

She smiles and walks toward the door.

She's barely had time to get there, before I've sent a text to Beck with the details. Next up, I dial Faith. "Forty million, Faith."

She breathes out. "Oh, thank God. It's lower than I expected but still good and I can't believe the bank really thought that I'd come in under that."

"I suspect they would have come in with a much different number than our person came in with. Whatever the case, it's done. We beat them to the punch."

"So now what?"

"I work my magic and you're not only out of probate, my bank owns your note by the time we return to Sonoma. But I need a complete ledger of all your vendors and outstanding accounts payable."

"You're going to pay off the bills, aren't you?"

"We talked about this, sweetheart."

"Yes. I know."

"And?"

"And I'll have Kasey and Rita connect. Does that work?"

"Yes. It does. This is good, Faith. If all goes as planned, we'll be going to court Thursday." I decide a conversation about money and shopping is better saved for in person, but she goes there on her own.

"I need to be in court?"

"Yes." I say. "You do."

"I have nothing to wear here. I have to go buy something."

"About that—"

"No. You're paying off my debt. I will not use your money to go shopping. End of subject."

"Faith—"

"No."

"Rita is putting my card on file for you at Chanel and—"

"No. *Move on*, Nick."

I move on. For now. "I'll have a plane on standby for either Thursday night or Friday morning, whichever we decide we prefer. Any thoughts?"

"Friday," she says. "I don't want to put that pressure on us Thursday."

"Friday it is," I say, pleased that she so easily chose to stay here, instead of go there.

She's silent several beats and then, "Nick."

"Yes, sweetheart?"

"Thank you. For *everything*. Even trying to spoil me with clothes."

"The only thank you I need is you naked in my bed tonight. I'm going to be late but I'll update you soon." I end the call and push away from my desk and stand up, walking to the window. Maybe there were no murders. Maybe this is over the minute I get that autopsy report but every day that passes, I feel the betrayal of my lies, as much as I dread telling Faith the truth. How the hell do I tell a woman who has become every-thing to me, who I've asked over and over to trust me that I thought she was a killer? I press my hands to my desk. I have to make her love me more than she can possibly hate me.

Chapter Twenty-Two

Nick

THE "STUPID" DISEASE ERUPTS NOT LONG AFTER THE evaluation comes in on Reid Winery. Every client I personally handle needs me personally, and why? Because they've done something stupid and the only pill that will fix them is me. It's nearly six pm by the time the eruption calms down, but I've still managed to secure my Thursday court date, coordinate action with Beck, and pound on Abel until he confirms that the autopsy on my father has become one big fuck up. We are weeks from answering the murder question, and therefore weeks before I can risk telling Faith the truth.

Rita appears in my doorway. "Your broker has called four times," she says, walking to my desk, an envelope in her hands. "I suspect that means he's called your cellphone at least that many times."

"I'll call him back."

"I know," she says. "You've told me that four times. And I know, Nick Rogers, that you're this mega-superstar attorney, but apparently, I'm older and wiser. So here is some sound advice. When someone controls as much of your money as that man does, and he calls that many times, call him back."

I scrub the back of my neck. "Right. I will."

"When?"

"Before I leave."

She gives me a keen inspection. "You haven't even started prepping for the Nichols meeting tomorrow, have you?"

"No. I have not."

"What do I need to do?"

"Go home. I've got this."

"You're sure?"

"Positive."

"A few updates first. Number one: Kasey sent me the accounts payable for Reid Winery. All the bills are now paid in full and I have it set up for him to send me the bills once a week."

"Excellent."

"Number two." She sets an envelope on my desk. "This came for you. It's from Faith. And if it includes further accounts payable, I haven't paid them. I didn't know if that's what it was and I didn't want to risk invading your privacy."

I arch a brow. "And you've cared about my privacy since when?"

"Since your privacy became Faith's as well. Do you want me to arrange dinner delivery?"

"No. I'll wait."

She gives me a knowing look. "To eat with Faith."

"*Yes,* my nosy-ass assistant. To eat with Faith."

"Good," she approves. "You've been alone too long. And on

that note. I'm going home and leaving you alone."

She heads for the door and I reach for the envelope, opening it up to find a check for sixty thousand dollars and a note:

Nick,

You promised to take this and I believe that you're a man of your word. And I owe you this and so much more and I'm not talking about money. I'll be waiting on you when you get home.

Naked.

Faith

My lips tighten and I re-read the note a total of three times before I set it on the desk. I don't want her damn money, but I do want her. And naked or not, I like the idea of going home to her. I exhale and tap the desk, and while it matters to me that she isn't in this for the money, I want her to take the damn money back.

My cellphone buzzes where it rests on my desk and I grimace at my broker's number on caller ID yet again. *But* Rita *is* right. The man has a shit ton of my money.

I take the call. "Ned," I greet.

"What the fuck is this fucking shit you're fucking doing to me?"

"Once a New York fuck-mouth, always a New York fuck-mouth," I say.

"I'll fuck-mouth you, Nick Rogers." He pauses. "No. No I won't. Fuck you for even tricking me into saying that. I got you out of Blue Textiles. They were tanking."

"I had 200 in them. How badly did they tank?"

"I got you out before you lost your original investment and fifty more."

"I was up a hundred and fifty."

"Fucking call me back when I call. In case you've forgotten, I shouldn't have pulled you without your approval. Bottom line.

I got you out fifty up, man. And I have a deal now that will make up your loss and then some. This is a 200k buy-in and it's hot. I need you in now and the money will be big and fast." He gives me the pitch and it sounds worth the risk.

"Do it," I say, and when I would hang up, I hesitate, "And," I say, an idea hitting me. "Do a separate buy-in of sixty thousand dollars, under the name of Faith Winter. Whatever you need on Faith, Rita can get you tomorrow."

"That's one hell of a gift."

"Do it without comment," I say, ending the call.

And now, I feel good about taking Faith's money.

It's two hours later by the time I've finished my prep for tomorrow's meeting, and I'm just about to call Faith and see if she wants me to pick up dinner, when I hear footsteps in what I'd thought was the empty offices. A few seconds later, Faith appears in my doorway, the sight of her setting my blood to pumping, and not because her black jeans and light blue t-shirt accent every one of her many curves. It's simply because she's here. She's Faith. And she rocks my world.

"Hey, sweetheart," I say.

"Hey," she replies, leaning against the door frame and looking a bit tentative. "Rita helped me get past security."

"Remind me to give her a raise tomorrow."

She pushes off the door, shuts it and the leans against it. "So, I'm not interrupting?"

"Come here," I order, softly.

She gives me one of her seductive looks that tells me she's feeling out of control, which means sex is her weapon, her way of getting it back. That's going to be a problem because in this,

I'm not giving it away. She walks toward me, the sway of her hips a seductive, sweet dance, and I don't remember a woman ever making me this hard and hot this easily, but Faith does. She rounds my desk, and I roll my chair just enough to allow her between me and the desk, my hands settling at her hips.

Her hands going to my hands, her perfect backside resting on my desk. A fact that I'm certain I will think about many times in the future. "I like you in this office, behind this desk."

"Do you?"

"You're Tiger here. Powerful. Confident. Sexy."

I don't let her take me to the fuck zone. Not yet. "I'm always Nick to you, Faith. You know that."

She inhales, her mood shifting, softening, a tentative quality to her voice as she asks, "Did you get my note?"

"I got your note and the check. And I *still* don't want your money."

"You promised to take it."

"As you pointed out in the note. And I did promise, therefore, I will take the money. But we are at that place in our relationship where there is more ahead of us, not less. I won't try to define what that is right now, in this moment, but it's a hell of a lot more than how badly I want to be inside you right now."

"You want to be inside me right now?"

"I always want to be inside you, Faith. You know that, too. And you know that gives you control. You have a lot of control but I need you to let me be who I am. And who I am is the man who wants to take care of you. I want to handle the bank. And I damn sure want to buy you the outfit you need for court."

"I bought something today."

"Faith—"

"You paid my bills at the winery today, Nick. I just couldn't let you do more today."

"I'm not Macom, Faith."

"Stop saying his name." Her hands come down on my shoulders. "I am not thinking about him. Nothing about you feels like him. Nothing about us feels like what I was with him."

"Then let me be me."

"Then you have to let me be me, too. It will take me time to lean on you, Nick. Because it's not natural to me."

"Because when you leaned on Macom, he abused that trust."

"Now who is making him a part of our relationship? But if you're going to go there, I *always* on some level felt alone with Macom. So. I've *always* been alone."

I stand up and cup her face. "So have I. But we aren't alone anymore."

"I'm going to protect you just like you do me, Nick. You need that, too."

"Sweetheart, you can't protect me by protecting my money. Money's been saving me my entire life. *You* are what I need." I kiss her, my mouth closing down on hers, tongue licking into her mouth, the taste of coffee, and sweetness, *her* sweetness, exploding on my taste buds. It only makes me hungrier for her, for that certain little sexy thing she does and doesn't even know she does. And she gives me exactly what I crave. She breathes into the kiss in that way that says, "Now I can breathe." Now I have what I need and it sets me on fire, burns me inside and out, and I don't play the control game I'd been ready for when she entered the office. I let myself go, deepening the kiss, letting her taste the hunger in me, the unleashed passion and she seems to feed off of what I feel, molding herself to me.

I drag her shirt over her head and I don't stop there. Her bra follows. Her zipper is next and then I set her on the desk, my gaze raking over her breasts, before I reach for her leg, and settle the high heel of her boot on my leg. I unzip it and pull it away.

Repeating the process with the other leg before I set her back on the ground, our bodies melding together, lips following, but I want her naked. *Need* her naked. I drag her jeans down her hips, and since impatience is my virtue right now, her panties with them. I lift her and maneuver her jeans away from her feet. And now, once again, she is naked and I am not.

Trust.

The word comes to me, clawing at me, my lies cutting me, the way I fear they will cut her, and I am not a man that feels fear.

She pushes off the desk and reaches for my pants, my zipper. I shrug out of my jacket, and by the time it's off, her hand is slipping inside my pants, pulling my cock free. I wrap my arm around her and lift her, her legs wrapping my waist just long enough for me to walk us to the sitting area to my right. Ignoring the couch, I stop at an oversized chair, which I sit in, and I pull her on top of me, straddling me.

"You have on too many clothes," she whispers, reaching for my tie that I really don't give a damn about right now.

I cup her neck under her hair, bringing her closer, breathing with her as I say, "I don't know if I've ever needed inside you as much as I do right now," before I pull her lips to mine, letting her taste how real those words are, and she sinks into the kiss, into the heat of the moment.

In the midst of that kiss and the next, I manage to get just what I hunger for. Her sliding down my cock. Her taking all of me, naked, exposed, *mine*. "The next time I sit in this chair with a client across from me, I'm going to be thinking of this." I press her backwards, wanting to see her, all of her.

She catches herself on my knees, arching into me as I thrust—her hips, her back, her breasts high in the air, nipples puckered. We grind together, a slow, hard, melding of bodies, and I wrap my arm around her waist, my free hand cupping her breast. My mouth lowers, tongue lapping at her pink puckered nipple. She pants out my name and I drag her to me again, her lips to my lips, and a frenzy of kissing and swaying follows— slow, fast, hard, fast again. Hard again. Harder now. Faster now. Her arms wrap around my neck, breasts molded to my chest, her body stiffening a moment before she trembles in my arms, and quakes around my cock. I shudder into release with her, and I lose time. There is just how she feels. The way she smells of amber and vanilla. The way her taste lingers on my lips.

When I finally come back to the present, I am instantly living that clawing guilt from my lies, remembering my own thoughts from earlier. I need her to know how much she means to me. I need to know when the truth is revealed, she can't just walk away. Because I can't lose her. "Faith."

She leans, back and I rest my hand on her face. "I can't lose you."

"Then you won't," she says. "Because if there is one thing I know about you, Nick Rogers, it's that you don't lose anything you really want."

She's right. I don't and I want her. "Move in with me."

She blanches. "What?"

"Move in with me, Faith. We'll split our time between Sonoma and San Francisco, but wherever we are, we're together. We're home."

"We've only known each other a few weeks, Nick."

"And I want to know more. I want you to know more. Find out who I am, Faith. Find out that my money won't change us or me. The dynamic we've shared this week here won't change. You don't have to answer now. Think about it. Decide when you're ready, but expect me to ask again. Expect me to—"

"I should say no."

"Why?"

"Because it seems smart."

"But what feels right, Faith?"

"You. Us."

"Then move in with me."

"Yes."

"Yes?"

"Yes."

Chapter Twenty-Three

Faith

I SAID YES.

This is my thought as I fall asleep in Nick's arms only hours after actually doing so. And I said yes without hesitation, with Sara's words in my head: *What if tomorrow never comes?*

I wake Wednesday morning with a smile and those same words in my head: *I said yes.* I feel lighter in some way with this choice I realize, as Nick kisses me before he heads down the stairs to run while I head to my studio. It's as if a weight has been lifted from my shoulders. I'm no longer fighting my connection to Nick. No longer letting that fear, I'd inadvertently let rule me, rule me. And as I step to a fresh canvas, preparing to work on my final show piece, I step back to what I call 'An Eye for an Eye'. I want to finish it. And I do. I finish what I know to be the most daring piece I've ever painted. It's not my trademark black and white and red. It's not my trademark landscape.

I love it.

I love Nick.

And when I walk back into the bedroom to shower, I spy the card from my father lying on the nightstand, and I realize now that the reasons I don't want to open it run deeper than I've allowed myself to admit. On some level, even after I left Sonoma to chase my dreams, I still needed his approval. I feared never having it. I really don't need to open a card that tells me I never had it. But one day, when the winery is running magically again and my art is just as magical, maybe I'll read it to prove to myself that I never needed his approval.

It's in that moment, that Nick walks into the bedroom, loose hair dangling around his face, obviously having escaped during his run, his snug t-shirt damp, his body hard. He glances at the card in my hand. "It's calling to you?"

"No," I say. "Actually, it's not calling to me at all. Nothing that drags me back to the past is calling to me." I shove it under the mattress, and like the past, I leave it behind me.

Nick steps to me, his hands settling on my shoulders. "One day it will feel right."

In that moment, I think of the shadows I sometimes see in his eyes, the secrets he hasn't shared, hoping that this new chapter in our relationship will free him to share them with me. I push to my toes and kiss him. "One day," I say, but I'm not talking about the card.

He knows. He always seems to know. He inches back, his navy blue eyes meeting mine, and for just a moment, I see what he never allows me to see: Vulnerability. And that is progress. That is one step closer to him being as exposed as he's made me.

By the time I reach the gallery, I'm leaning toward including 'An Eye for an Eye' in the L.A. show. Excited about my choice, I chitchat with Sara, and then settle into my new office with a cup of coffee beside me. And then I do it. I pull up the forms for my submissions and type in my selections, but I can't seem to get myself to push send. Sara appears in my office and claims the seat in front of me, setting a photo on the desk. "What do you think of this painting?"

I study the waterfront beach scene and smirk. "Average."

She sighs. "My thoughts, too. The artist is quite lovely, but she just isn't ready for the big league. I dread telling her we won't be selecting her work. Anyway. On to brighter topics. Have you thought about painting the office?"

"Yes. I'm excited to start, but it's going to have to be next week. I need to take care of the management side of the winery. I'll be gone Friday to Sunday and back Monday. But can I ask your opinion on something?"

"Of course."

"I made it into the L.A. Art Forum."

"Oh wow. That's a big deal. Congratulations, Faith."

"Thank you. I need to pick all my pieces and submit them this week."

"And you're having trouble picking?"

"Yes and no. See, they picked me after they saw my work at the show you guys set me up with. That show had my classic work. The definition of who I've been publicly as an artist. But I want to include something different and daring for me. But should I? Or should I stick to safe over daring?"

"Safe is average," Chris says, stepping into the doorway. "Decide if you want to be average, and you have your answer." He disappears into the hallway.

Sara lifts a hand. "There you go. Your answer."

"Well the thrust is that I'm not feeling like playing it safe or being average. As proof, I'm not only here instead of at the winery, I agreed to move in with Nick."

"You did? Wow. Yay! That's huge."

"It is and it was also an easy decision thanks to you."

"Me?"

"Yes. You. You said: *What if tomorrow never comes?* Those are my new words to live or die by."

She smiles and stands up, exiting the office. I pull up the Forum paperwork in my email and fill it all out. I enter 'An Eye for an Eye' as my final piece. I then text Nick: *I did it. My entry for the Forum is complete.*

He surprises me by texting back a picture of 'An Eye for an Eye', I didn't know he'd taken: *Did this masterpiece make the cut?*

I smile and type: *Yes. It did and why do you have that picture?*

His reply is instant: *Reminding myself to be the same kind of badass you are today.*

I smile, warmed inside and out by this man in ways I didn't know I could feel warm. As for being a badass, Nick is the ultimate badass, while Macom is the ultimate asshole. I try not to think about how that might look when the two meet. Because they will meet, no matter what painting I place in that show. And they will clash, no matter how I try to stop them. And I'm not sure Nick is capable of war and peace. I'm pretty sure it's all war to him.

And Macom aside, God, it's sexy.

Our Thursday morning court date has arrived, and I'm a nervous wreck. I can't paint and I'm done with my show pieces, so I work out with Nick, and even a hard run doesn't calm me down. Nick's attempts at distracting me in the shower, are completely effective, but the minute we're dressed, my nerves are back. He dresses in a navy blue suit and I pick a blue and silver tie to match and then help him knot it. My dress is black, with a tapered waist and flared skirt. My shoes, classic pumps. I have no idea why I picked black when funeral black is the last thing I need to be wearing today, but it's too late. It's what I have.

"Let's go on to Sonoma when we're done today," Nick says, leaning on the door frame.

"I thought we were going to wait until tomorrow? What if something goes wrong today?"

"It won't. It's going to go well. And rather than flying, we'll drive. It's not far and we'll have the BMW when we're there."

"You don't want to drive my broken down Mercedes?"

"Nothing against your broken down Mercedes. But I prefer the BMW."

I laugh. "Okay then. Let's pack."

"You don't have to pack. You live here now. But I do, because I live there now, too."

"Yes. You do. You need things there. Your things."

His lips curve and he says, "You're my thing. But I'll take some stuff anyway."

"I'll help you," I say, and for the next few minutes, I busy myself gathering items for his suitcase, and packing up the few items I want to carry back and forth with me. Once we're done, we load up the car.

And then for the first time all week, Nick and I leave in one car, him behind the wheel of the BMW. By the time we get to the courtroom, my palms are sweaty. "Relax, Faith," Nick says, after opening my car door and helping me to my feet. "I'm an arrogant bastard for a reason. I'm good. Really damn good and we're going to win today."

"But we've talked about this. But what if someone is angry you got me out of this nightmare and they lash out at you? What if I'm the reason—"

"Stop," he says, his hands on my shoulders. "Don't start fretting over me. I pack a big punch. Anyone who comes at me is going to feel a hell of a lot of pain and they know it. I got this, sweetheart, and I got you. Okay?"

"Yes. Yes, okay." I flatten my hand on his lapel. "You *are* a bad ass."

He rewards me with a curve of his delicious mouth. "You inspire me."

I manage a laugh. "I'm not sure that is the way a woman wants to inspire a man."

"If a woman doesn't inspire her man, he's not her man. Now. Come see me in action."

Literally thirty minutes later, Nick and I step out of the courtroom, and the bank has approved the buyout, I've inherited the winery, and Nick has shut down every attempt my bank made to stop it from happening. "I don't believe it," I say, as soon as we're in the car. "It's done."

"You doubted me?"

"No. I did not doubt you."

"Sounds like you doubted me." He leans over and kisses me. "And that, I do believe, earns that sweet little ass of yours a spanking."

"Hmmm. Promise?"

"Oh yeah, sweetheart. I promise." He settles back in his seat. "Let's go to Sonoma."

A few minutes later, we're on the road, and life is good. Almost too good to be true.

Chapter Twenty-Four

Faith

"**W**E'RE HERE, SWEETHEART."

I blink and open my eyes. "Nick?"

"Yes, sweetheart. *Nick*. You fell asleep. We're home."

I blink again. "Home?"

"Sonoma."

"We are?"

He strokes my hair. "Yes." He smiles. "*We* are."

I sit up and look around to find we're parked in the drive-way of my house. And instead of the warmth and happiness "home" should create, there is an instant ball of nerves in my belly made better by only one thing: Nick. "We," I say, glancing over at him, "because we're really doing this thing, right?"

"We've been really doing this since the moment we met."

He leans over and cups my head in that way he does and kisses my forehead. "Come on. Let's go inside and get settled. And I vote for taking you out to lunch and a trip to the grocery store or I'll starve this weekend." He grabs his jacket from the back seat, where he'd apparently put it during the drive, and then exits the car. I grab my purse from the floorboard, where I'd left it when we'd gone into the courthouse. Slipping it over my shoulder, I exit the car and join Nick at the trunk and the minute I'm beside him, the intimacy between us seems to take on a living, breathing, life of its own. It thickens the air, wraps around us like a warm, soft blanket that I want to snuggle inside of and never leave.

He opens the trunk and pulls the two suitcases out before shutting it again. And then, together we roll the suitcases toward the house. "I'll get them the rest of the way," Nick says when we reach the stairs leading to the porch.

I hurry up the steps, key in the code to the door, and push it open. Nick joins me, and that charge between us intensifies the instant we are both over the threshold. He sets the suitcases inside the foyer, and drops his jacket on top of one of them. I shut the door. And suddenly we are facing each other, our eyes colliding, that word "home" radiating between us.

The air thickens, crackles, and I move. Or maybe he moves. Maybe it's both of us but suddenly my purse is on the ground, and we are kissing, a deep, drugging, intimate kiss. His hand is on the back of my head, and God, how I've come to love the way he does that. I breathe into the kiss, sink into it and him, and it only seems to ignite us further. And of course, my phone rings. I ignore it. Nick ignores it. I reach for his tie. This time I'm getting it off and every inch of clothing he's wearing. My phone stops ringing. I pull the silk from his neck, letting it fall to the ground. My phone starts ringing again.

Nick and I both groan. "You better get that, sweetheart," he says.

"It's not important." It stops ringing again and starts again. "Okay. It might be." I squat down to open my purse and remove my cellphone, frowning when I see the number. "Kasey," I say, standing up and answering the line. "Is everything okay?"

"Of course. Why wouldn't it be? The bills are paid. All is well."

"You called three times."

"No. I just called once."

"Oh. The other calls must have been someone else. Hold on one second." I glance at the caller ID. "Josh," I mouth to Nick, and I don't miss the tiny smirk on his face at the reference to my agent, who he clearly does not like.

"Rita was fantastic," Kasey adds, pulling me back into our conversation, while Nick's own phone buzzes and he pulls it from his pocket, looking at the Caller ID. "I gave her the accounts payable list," Kasey continues, "and within two hours everything was paid to date."

Nick points to his phone and motions down the hallway off the foyer. "No more bill collectors," I reply to Kasey, following Nick, but as he continues to the living room, I cut right into the kitchen, rounding the island to sit on a barstool.

"Are we sure?" he asks. "This isn't a one and done kind of thing?"

"Not at all," I assure him settling onto a barstool, "We're past the challenges that started when we lost my father."

"Then you finally got into the bank accounts."

"Everything is now in my name," I say, avoiding the topic of my mother and the bank accounts I won't have access to until Monday, but I already know are empty. "That means I'm free to discuss the future with you, because I know we have a future and one worth your time."

"Hiring Nick Rogers really made a difference it seems."

"Nick has made an incredible difference," I say as he appears in the doorway, his eyes meeting mine, as I add, "In every possible way."

Nick's lips curve slightly and he walks to the island, sitting down on the barstool across from me. Meanwhile, Kasey delivers a stilted, "That's great news," followed by an awkward pause.

Dread fills me. "Oh God. You're quitting."

"No. Of course not. This place is my life."

Relief washes over me. "Then what is it that I'm sensing?"

"Full disclosure. I just had coffee with your uncle. And since I know how you feel about him—"

My gaze rockets to Nick's. "Why did you have coffee with my uncle, Kasey?"

Nick doesn't react and I have a sense that he knew before I did, perhaps from his phone call. "He bought a thousand bottles of wine for a weekend event," Kasey says. "And not the cheap stuff. Once the transaction was complete he cornered me about you. He wanted me to try to convince you to talk to him. Apparently, he's left you several messages you haven't answered."

"He hasn't left me any messages," I say. "Okay. Not recently. And I talked to him two days ago and have no desire to talk to him."

"I know that your father had issues with him as well, but they did make peace in the end. And now Bill wants to make peace with you."

I stand up with the impact of that statement. "My father and Bill reconciled?"

"They did. And just in time. It was only about a month before your father's death."

"Do you know what the falling out was about, Kasey?"

"No. Do you?"

"I thought I did, but I have a hard time believing they reconciled under the circumstances as I thought I knew them."

"I can't help you there. Your father never shared that with me and Bill didn't either. All I know, is the man seems sincere in wanting to call you family." He hesitates. "Look. I'm just the messenger and I wanted to talk to you about this now, not tomorrow night, simply because I didn't want you to hear I'd met with him through another source. We do have some wagging tongues in this town."

"I appreciate that and I'm sorry to put you in the middle of this. I'll call him. I'll make sure he leaves you out of this."

"I'm not concerned about me, but I am concerned about you. You're alone, Faith. He's family."

"He's not my family," I say, and suddenly I want to get the meeting with him over and done with. "Hold on a second." I cover the phone and speak to Nick, "Dinner tonight?" He nods and I uncover the phone. "Nick and I actually just got into town. Can we move dinner back to tonight?"

"Of course. Where and when?"

"How about the Harvest Moon Café at eight? That gives you time to close up shop there."

"That works. I'll see you then."

I end the call, setting my phone on the island. "Your uncle's timing is suspect," Nick says. "What did he want?"

"He bought a thousand bottles of wine and then convinced Kasey to soften me up and look at him as family."

"On the day you now own the winery," Nick says. "I've thought for a while now that he was behind the bank withholding your inheritance."

"He's filthy rich," I say. "He doesn't need the winery, nor has he ever approached me to buy it."

"But he might have approached your mother."

"Yes. He might have."

"And she would have told him that you wouldn't sell."

"That's true, too."

"His wife is filthy rich," he says. "And the word is that she treats him like a kept animal on an allowance."

"So, he wants his own assets?"

"It could be that simple," Nick says, "but I'm still of the belief that there is a hidden financial resource within the winery. And that call I got. That was Beck, letting me know about Kasey and your uncle. He didn't like how familiar they seemed."

"They've known each other longer than I've been alive," I say. "And they were friends at one point. But I can tell you this. When my father shut Bill out, so did Kasey. He was my father's best friend. And this is over now, anyway, right?"

"It is, but if I'm right and your uncle was behind this, expect him to try to buy you out."

"You think he's still a problem."

"I think he upsets you and that's a problem I'm going to make go away. Send him to me. I will bust the fucker's balls. The end."

My phone rings again. I glance at the number. "It's just Josh." I decline the call.

"We're here for thirty minutes and you're ignoring your agent who is suddenly 'just' Josh. Call him back."

"You don't even like him."

"Irrelevant point, pulled out of a hat, and meant to deflect. He's a horny piece of shit asshole, but he's your agent and your career is connected to him."

"He can wait. Right now, I need to finish this conversation about my uncle, and talk about Kasey's incentives."

"Call your agent back." He rounds the counter, snags my

hips and pulls me to him. "The man wants in your pants. I don't like it, but professionally he's your agent and your career is taking off. Everything else can wait and will be far more tolerable if he's delivering good news. *Call him back."*

"You're being obnoxiously pushy."

"And this is unusual why?"

"Nick—"

"Faith."

"Nick—"

"Faith. How many times are we doing this? Because I have all weekend, but just in case you've missed the obvious. If you won't fight for your art, I will. That's what I do. I fight. And you could have already called him back in the time we've had this exchange."

"Fine." I grab my phone and Nick releases me while I hit re-dial.

Josh picks up on the first ring. "You have another sale from the Chris Merit show, darling."

I perk up, that ball of tension that had formed when we arrived, eases just a bit. "I do?"

"Yes. You do."

I turn to Nick and mouth "another sale." He gives me a wink that does funny things to my belly, while Josh adds, "And thanks to Chris Merit, and your amazing skills, your price is now twenty thousand a painting. After this show, we're going to make it thirty. You need those paintings shipped out in a week. How are they coming?"

"I'm done. I copied you on the submission form."

"Done? As of when?"

"Yesterday."

"And you didn't run the pieces by me?"

"I knew what I wanted in the show."

"I need photos. Send me photos. We can still change them out if—"

"No. I'm not sending you photos or changing things out. I told you. I'm painting for me now, not for you or anyone else."

"As you should be, but come on, Faith. I've been in this with you a long time. Send me photos."

"On the condition that you offer no opinions."

"Agreed. And get them shipped in advance. Don't take risks. The details on how to ship, and where to ship, are on your forms."

"I'll pull it, and it will be handled."

"You need to have all pieces there in a week."

"I know, Josh. Deep breath. I'm not going to let either one of us down on this. And you know what. I'm not sending you photos. I don't want you to freak yourself, or me, out over my choices. They are made. I stand by them. You need to just see them when I get there."

"Faith—"

"No, Josh. No. And FYI. I'm working at the Allure Gallery with Chris and Sara Merit now."

"What about the winery?"

"I have a staff."

"You've always had a staff. That didn't keep you painting."

"My situation here has changed."

"Here. So you're finally back in Sonoma?"

"Actually. I'm moving to San Francisco. Sonoma will be my weekend home."

"You're moving in with Nick Rogers."

"Yes."

"I told you—"

"That he'll fuck me and leave me? I think it's pretty clear that's not the case. I'll get you the new address."

"Okay. I get it. You want me to back off. And I will, after I say *be careful*, Faith."

"I've done a lot of that all my life. It's not worked out so well. I'll see you in two weeks." I end the call and face Nick, both of us settling elbows on the island.

"You sold another painting," he says, warmth in his eyes. "You're going to be famous before you know it."

"I don't want to be famous. It's about being good enough and as is the case in many careers, money is one of a number of validations. I've made eighty thousand in a week, Nick. From my painting. That's crazy good."

"Yes," he agrees. "It is. You told Josh you were moving to San Francisco."

"Because I am."

"What about here?"

"What about it?"

He snags my hip and walks me to him. "The minute we arrived here, you tensed up. I don't like what this place does to you, but we're both going to like what I'm about to do to you." He scoops me up and starts walking and doesn't stop until he's laying me down on the mattress, and his big body is over mine.

"Now we celebrate. You sold another painting. And we won the war."

"Are you sure we won?"

"Yes. I'm sure we won."

"Why do I feel like there is more?"

He rolls us to our sides, facing each other, his leg twined with mine. "There is more. More fucking. More loving. More us."

"Because you think you—"

He strokes hair from my face. "I know I love you, Faith."

"You do?"

"I do."

"I love you, too."

"Then there's more. There's always more. But whatever it is, good or bad, we do it together. Say it."

"We do it together."

Chapter Twenty-Five

Nick

MORE.

That word stays with me as I make love to Faith, and even afterward as we dress in casual wear—Faith in jeans and a V-neck blue t-shirt that shows off her necklace, which she keeps touching. I like that she keeps touching it, as if she's remembering me giving it to her. As if she connects me to her art, and since she loves her art so damn much, I'll say, paint me, baby, any damn day.

I dress in black jeans, boots, and a black t-shirt that reads: *Lawyer—Let's just save time and assume that I'm right*, which gains me the laugh from Faith I'd been looking for. Because her laugh is sexy as fuck and damn addictive. Like the woman herself.

"You are not always right, Nick Rogers," she proclaims

when she sees it, stroking my cheek. "But don't worry. I'll catch you when you fall."

"Don't I owe you a spanking?"

"It really is starting to seem like you're all talk and no action," she replies, twisting away from me and giving me a sexy glance over her shoulder. "Come, my hungry man. I have the world's most perfect burger for you."

My man.

She's learning.

I am her man.

I follow, but not for the burger. For the shake of her curvy and perfect ass in those jeans, and somehow my mind still works enough to ask, "Do you have the instructions for shipping your paintings? We need to arrange to have someone pick them up."

She pauses at the door, and faces me. "I looked it up when I submitted my final paperwork. They have special arrangements with FedEx and there's a location right up the road."

"Then we'll go after lunch," I say, stepping beside her, and because I just can't help myself, which is pretty damn unfamiliar to me, I give her a quick kiss and open the door.

"Food is literally three minutes away," she says once we're in the car and pulling onto the main road. "Just turn right, drive a mile, and we're there."

"Got it," I say. "Food. One mile." I glance over at her. "Dessert when we return home, and it's not ice cream."

"Oh. We need more ice cream. I have to have ice cream when I'm here. It's kind of like Sonoma survival. A survival kit that is cream, sugar, and calories."

"Why do you need a survival kit?"

"You're about to find out," she assures me, but doesn't give me time to press for details. "So," she continues, "we eat. Then we need to go by FedEx and the grocery store."

"And to get boxes so you can pack some of your things to ship to San Francisco. We can arrange to have Fed Ex pick them up tomorrow with your paintings. Then it can all be waiting on you when we return Sunday night." I pull us into the restaurant driveway and park.

"That's expensive, Nick." I open my mouth to object and she holds up a hand. "Don't tell me not to worry about money. You didn't get rich by throwing away money. Don't expect me to start throwing it away for you."

"And I appreciate that, sweetheart, but the sooner you're with me in San Francisco, the happier a man I'll be."

"I said yes for a reason. I'm already with you, Nick."

I lean over and kiss her. "Keep saying yes. I like that answer." She smiles, and I like that, too. I'm so fucking in love with this woman, it's insanity, and I am happily insane. I have no fears. No regrets. No second thoughts. I want her. I need her. She's mine. "I'll come around and help you out," I tell her.

"Because you have such good manners," she teases, a reminder of our little bathroom encounter on the first night we fucked, when I promised to make her come about a half-dozen ways, but only when I thought she was ready.

"You know it, sweetheart," I say, exiting the car, and the moment I'm outside, a sense of being watched hits me, right along with a blast of cool wind. And yes, logically, it's Beck's people. It had better be Beck's people, but I don't like how it feels. I round the car and help Faith out, wrapping my arm around her shoulder and holding her close. Making it clear she's mine. She's under my protection.

We enter the restaurant and that feeling doesn't fade, even as the rush of attention falls on us, as people who know Faith greet her. By the time we are at a table it becomes apparent that pretty much everyone in this city knows her, and *her mother.*

Her dead mother, who is connected to my dead father. And that sensation of being watched is magnified with that realization.

Faith hands me a menu. "Now you know why I need a Sonoma survival kit. Everyone knows your business here."

As if proving her point, another guest steps to Faith's side and after I am introduced, I text Beck: *Are your men following us?*

His reply: *Of course. Why?*

Mine: *Because I don't see them but I feel them.*

His: *Huh, is his answer.*

Mine: *WTF does huh mean?*

His: *I guess lawyers are never wrong. And if you believe that, I have a million dollars I want to sell you for fifty bucks.*

He's obviously referencing my shirt, telling me he has eyes on me and us. But something still doesn't feel right, and I discreetly scan, not just for his men, but for the source of my discomfort. An old lady to our right. A cluster of businessmen in deep conversation in the corner. A mid-fifties man by himself in the corner in jeans and a t-shirt. Another cluster of businesspeople. A college-age woman by herself, with headphones on. My gaze shifts to the hostess stand where a fit man in his mid-thirties is flirting with the woman showing people to their tables.

"The entire town is going to be talking about us now," Faith announces, drawing my attention back to her.

"Hopefully they mention my shirt."

She laughs. "I'm sure they will. You can't hiccup and not have it be part of the story."

"But you want to live here?"

"If I gave you that impression, it's wrong. I love my house, because it was an escape, and my home outside of the winery. But I went to school in L.A. and stayed in L.A. for a reason, beyond my aspirations in art. I never wanted to live here."

"And you do want to live in San Francisco?"

"I do," she says. "You're there."

"But do you like it? Because if you don't—"

"I do," she repeats. "I *really* love it there, and I always have. The art. The food. The way it's a small city but you can still get lost in a crowd. The views. The art."

"Always the art. San Fran is a great hub for your craft. Why L.A.?"

"L.A. had wider opportunities for school, work, and a connection to agents and industry professionals."

Our plates arrive and once we've tasted our food, and I've given the burger the thumbs up Faith is looking for and that it deserves, I focus on what she's just told me. "You don't want to be here. That means we need to make sure the winery is self-reliant."

"I feel like I should offer Kasey stock."

"I suggest you start with a large bonus plan. Make sure he really does handle things when you, or your father, aren't looking over his shoulder."

"I'm sure he will. Of course, he will. But what kind of bonus?"

"I have several plans I've helped clients set up over the years in my briefcase. You can look them over, but I'd suggest feeling him out tonight. We can send him whatever you decide on Monday. But, that said, I would like him to work with Rita on the accounts payable and have our CFO audit the books once a month."

"Is that really necessary?"

"I've seen people get screwed, Faith. And it's always by people they trust. Additionally, you need someone to play your role."

"That'll be expensive."

"The right person will grow revenues and more than pay for themselves. And since you don't want to sell and you don't want to work at the winery, the idea is to make it an investment. It pays you profit monthly. And when your art starts generating million-dollar payouts, you spend more money on the winery, and end up with tax write-offs."

"I'd love to have that problem," she says, despite the fact that her inability to see her own success and skill is a product of a past she hasn't quite escaped.

But she will.

"Eighty thousand in a week," I remind her. "Success isn't an option. And I get to call you my crazy talented woman."

"And I get to call you my arrogant bastard?"

I laugh. "I told you. Anything but Mr. Rogers. And you forgot that when you were drinking."

"I didn't forget. I saw opportunity."

I laugh and our waitress chooses that moment to re-appear and present us with the check, and damn, I want her to go away. Or maybe I just want to take Faith away from this place, and this intrusive little town. I reach for the ticket, and as I hand the waitress my card, I have that same sense of being watched all over again.

We stand up to leave and my gaze travels toward the sensation, and the man in the corner, sitting at a table, flirting with our waitress, when he'd started out flirting with the hostess. Faith and I start walking and my eyes catch on the tat on his hand: A flag, like the money clip. It's a long shot, but it could be a connection, and I don't let long shots go just because they're hard. I pause and turn back to the table, looking for something I haven't lost. Faith turns to help me, and my hand settles on Faith's shoulder, lips near her ear. "Be discreet," I murmur, and trying not to scare her, I say, "the guy talking to our waitress is familiar, but I can't place him. Glance over as we exit."

She nods, and we start walking, passing through the restaurant and stepping outside. "I've never seen him," she says. "He must be a tourist. Maybe from San Francisco?"

"Maybe," I say, opening her door for her, and pulling out my phone.

I round the trunk and text Beck: *If the guy at the corner table isn't your guy, find out who he is. He has a flag tattoo.*

Once we're on the road, stopping at FedEx and then the grocery store, the trend of a waxing and waning feeling of being watched continues, as do the references to Faith's dead mother. By the time we arrive back at the house there is no denying the relief I feel when we step inside and shut the door. And the word in my mind is no longer *more*—it's murder. It's not a good thought, but not one I can risk setting aside. Murder brought me here. Faith kept me here.

We're unpacking the groceries when Faith's phone rings on the counter where it rests. "Josh again," she says, answering the line, in a short conversation that finishes with, "No. No. No. I'm not. I'm hanging up now." And she does. "He wants to see my submissions so he can make me second guess my choices and I'm not going to do it."

"Good for you," I say. "So now I say we pack you up. Where do you want to start?"

"My closet. My clothes are the most important thing for me to take. And my shoes, of course. A girl has to have her shoes."

I'd tell her I'd just buy her all new things, but I'm smarter than that, and her phone rings again anyway. She grimaces and answers it without looking at the caller ID. I walk to the fridge and grab a bottle of water, as she says, "No, Josh. Stop calling." I've just opened my bottle and tilted it back when she snags my shirt and I turn to face her as she says, "Bill. Why are you calling me?" She places the phone on speaker and I join her at the island and set my water bottle down.

"I'm concerned that I gave you the wrong impression when we talked," he says. "I wasn't inferring anything about your mother or father. I simply don't feel the topic is appropriate between myself and their daughter."

"They're dead," Faith states flatly.

"I'm aware of this fact every day of my life. We're family, Faith. Your father and I found our way to a truce. I'd like to do that with you as well."

"No," Faith says. "I have no interest in reconciling with you and you've already proven that you won't answer my questions."

"Not if they're related to their sexual preferences."

"You did have a threesome with them, didn't you?" She doesn't give him time to answer. "Why, if you already had sex with both of them, did he get pissed when you had sex with just her?"

"Our falling out wasn't about sex."

"Then what was it about?"

"Brother stuff. We're family, Faith."

"Stop saying that," Faith bites out. "Don't call me. And don't call or visit Kasey."

He's silent for several beats. "I have some old photos I just stumbled onto of your father. I'll drop them by the winery. I think you'll enjoy them. Maybe we can have coffee." He softens his voice. "I really hope that you have a change of heart, Faith." He hangs up.

I reach for the phone and ensure the line is disconnected. "He had a threesome with my parents, Nick."

"Yes," I say. "I believe he did. He also wants to buy the winery."

"Even if I was willing to sell, which I'm not, I'd never sell to him. You'd think he'd be smart enough to just lie and say he didn't do the whole ménage thing with my mother and father."

"He doesn't know what you know. That's obvious. And he knows that right now, you won't sell to him."

"So, he tried to drive me into the ground so I'd be desperate."

"Most likely," I agree. "And it's a smart guess that he made a deal at the bank to pay someone off for helping him pick it up for a steal."

"I will never sell it to him. I'm not going to sell."

"But he knows, everyone knows, that you want to paint."

"Oh God. You don't think he bought my work to give me some façade of success so I'd dump the winery, do you?"

"Don't do that. Don't let him downgrade your success. It's yours. You own it."

"Can you do what you do and make sure he didn't buy those paintings?"

"Yes. I will. But those sales are your sales. You own them, but if I confirm that he owns the hell you just went through, I'm going to ruin that bastard."

"No," Faith says. "Don't ruin him. I don't need justice. I just need him to go away."

"Faith—"

"No, Nick. Promise me."

"I'm not going to make that promise, because it would be a lie."

"I just want to make this go away." She grabs my arm and covers my tattoo with her hand. "Revenge: An eye for an eye. That's you. Not me." She lets go of my arm. "I'm going to start packing." She heads out of the kitchen and I don't immediately follow.

I text Beck: *Bill Winter is trying to get into Faith's good graces.*

He's behind all of this.

Beck: *Agreed. I'm working on it.*

I inhale and press my hands to the counter, the word murder in my head again. Bill might be trying to get into Faith's good graces now, but as Abel has always said, once a killer, always a killer. Only I'm not my father. I won't just cause pain. I'll draw blood and I'll make sure it's first blood.

And I'll do it for Faith.

I push off the counter and seek her out, her frustrated groan drawing me toward the front of the house. I find her in the foyer trying to put together one of the boxes we picked up earlier, frustration in her face before she tosses it. "I can't get the stupid thing together. I've been living alone and doing just fine, but now, I cannot get that box together."

I walk to her and ignore the box, pulling her to me. "Inferring that I've made you weaker?"

"No. No, that's not it. I'm sorry." Her hand goes to my chest. "If anything, your badass-ness has brought out my own."

"The eye for an eye revenge thing is a trigger for you. I know that. But he broke laws if he did what we think he did. And if he will go after his own niece, think what he'll do to others. He deserves to pay."

"You're right. But that means justice, not revenge. To me, they're defined with different intent."

"You're right. They are. And I might be brutal, sweetheart, but the law is my bitch, and so are your enemies."

"I know that. I'm not really upset at you, Nick. I wasn't even reacting to you. I'm upset to realize my father was someone I didn't know him to be."

"His sex life doesn't change who he was as a man, Faith."

"A little kinky sex doesn't. I, of all people, know that."

"Then what's bothering you?"

"He played the victim and that feels like a lie. It's like I didn't really know who he was and that is such a deep betrayal. I don't want to talk about this anymore. Not before we meet with Kasey. Can you just please help me with the stupid box?"

"Of course." I kiss her temple, my lips lingering there, because damn it, it's like she was talking about me. And it feels like she has that kitchen knife in her hand again and she just plunged it in my chest.

Chapter Twenty-Six

Faith

I DON'T LIKE WHO YOU ARE HERE...

Nick's words play in my head the entire afternoon as we box up my belongings for the move to San Francisco. Namely because there isn't much to do or that I want to take with me, most certainly not how I act and feel here. All I want are my clothes and shoes, and basic items I use every day. Nick notices too.

"You know," he says, about an hour into packing my bedroom, "you can take anything you want. You can take *everything* if you want."

"I'm taking what matters," I assure him, holding up a pair of pink panties. "See?"

I successfully distract him and we move on to the living area and make the rounds from there. The entire time, he builds the boxes and tries to overstuff them, and I pull things back out. Time gets away from us and it's nearly sunset and time to get ready for dinner when it hits me that I haven't packed a box of random items like gloves and scarves I keep in the closet. Afraid I'll forget again, I rush to the bedroom and the closet. Grabbing a decorative wooden container where I have various accessories stored, I stick it in an empty box in the center of the small room.

I rotate to leave and find Nick leaning in the archway, his hair half around his face, and half tied at his nape. His blue eyes are stark. "Are you having second thoughts?"

"What? What are you talking about?"

"You aren't taking anything with you, Faith. It's as if you aren't committed to leaving or rather, staying with me." There is a hint of vulnerability in his voice, his eyes, that Nick Rogers doesn't allow anyone to see. But he does let me now. He lets me see that I could hurt him the way he could hurt me.

And I am instantly in front of him, my hand settling on his chest. "I am committed," I assure him. "I want to be with you."

"Then why do you read like someone packing for a vacation and planning to come back home?"

"Because you're looking for one thing, and not seeing what's really going on."

"Which is what?"

"I just don't feel connected to anything here. Only my studio."

"You bought this house. You designed it."

"Because I needed something of my own."

"And now you're accepting something that's mine."

"No. It's not like that. I don't want your place to look like mine."

"It's not my place anymore. It's ours and I've never wanted to share my home with anyone and I have zero hesitation in this.

I need to know you feel the same."

His cellphone rings and he draws in a breath, breathing out. "Why do our phones ring at the worst possible times?" And when I would expect him to ignore the call, he doesn't, which tells me he's the one shutting down now, withdrawing.

"Nick," I say, but he's already looking at his caller ID with a frown.

"Rita. This is an odd time for her to call." He answers the line. "Rita?" He listens a moment. "Kasey?" he asks, and after a pause, "Right. She's standing right here. She'll call him." He ends the connection and offers me his phone. "Call him. There's a problem."

"I guess I don't know where my phone is," I say, punching in Kasey's number and the minute it rings, he answers.

"Faith?" Kasey asks.

"Yes. Sorry. I was—"

"We have several busted water lines in the west vineyard. It's bad. I'm trying to get someone out here, but struggling at this hour."

"How bad is bad?"

"It's flowing from numerous locations and flowing isn't even an appropriate description. Gushing is more like it. If we don't get someone out here soon, it's a total loss."

My stomach knots. "We'll be right there."

"Faith, I don't know if we can save it even if we get someone out here," he adds, pretty much repeating what he's just said but obviously trying to prepare me for what he feels is the inevitable: We've already lost the west side.

"Do what you can," I say, ending the call. "We need to go there. There are several broken—"

"I heard," Nick says. "Grab your purse and phone. We'll go now."

I head into the bathroom, grab my purse, and hunt for my phone that I can't find. Frustrated I shout, "I can't find my phone!" and Nick appears in the bathroom, holding it. "Oh, thank God," I breathe out, racing toward him and grab it. "This is bad, Nick. He can't get anyone out there."

"You drive," he says, handing me the car keys. "Let me make some calls."

"Thank you," I say, nodding, and it's less than a minute later when we're in the car and he's already on the phone. "Rita. Be a superwoman right now. We have several broken water lines in the west vineyard. Pay whatever you have to get help out there now." There is a pause. "I should have known. Yes. Call me." He ends the call and glances over at me. "She already knew and is already looking. And the woman is magic. She'll get us help." He's already dialing again. "Beck," he says. "Do you know what's happening?" He listens for a few beats. "Right. I'll find out if it's intentional once we're there, but get fucking cameras on the vines. I want every inch of the property covered." He doesn't wait for a reply. He hangs up.

That knot in my stomach doubles in size. "You think this is payback for us winning in court."

"I'd bet my bank account on it, sweetheart. Beck has the cameras in place that we discussed, and men here locally watching the place, but he didn't have eyes on the vines."

"I'm sure that didn't feel important," I say, turning us down the main road leading to the vineyard. "Why would it be? Until it is, obviously."

"Aside from us winning in court," he says. "You shut your uncle down today."

"Why would he do this? This isn't squeezing me financially. This is destroying the vines that produce profit for the winery we're assuming he wants to own. It doesn't make sense."

"It does if the real treasure isn't the vines, but the property."

"You've said this before, but what treasure, Nick? What could it be?"

"The options are many: A highway or development coming through here that he's gotten an ear on. Some natural resource. Leverage on another deal. Even some sort of big-dick play for his wife. *See me. I have this family vineyard worth forty million dollars. I'm the man.* The reasons are many and they don't matter at this very moment. Bottom line, I don't believe this is an accident even if it ends up staged as an accident. And about those cameras that I just ordered Beck to put in place. Those are between you, me, and him. No one else."

"Not even Kasey?"

"No one. And it's not about me not trusting him. I don't know him to trust him or not trust him at this point. But even if I trusted him, we have to worry about who he might decide to trust himself. There's a saying I never forget: Betrayal doesn't come from your enemies."

"That's the bitter hardcore truth," I say, turning us down the drive to the mansion, the now familiar flutter of dread in my belly. It's present every single time I've come here since my father's death, no matter how many times I come here, and even when I was living here. I pull us up to the valet area, and Kasey waits for Nick and me at the top of the steps, his gray suit uncharacteristically rumpled, his thick, dark graying hair also in rare disarray, as if he'd been running his fingers through it.

Nick and I walk up the steps and the two men greet each other, shaking hands. "We aren't saving those vines, are we?" Nick says, giving him a keen look.

Kasey's hands settle under his jacket on his hips, his expression stark. "No," he says, proving Nick has read him right. "Now we just need to stop the bleeding of gallons of water, and start thinking about recovery. A witness saw two teenage boys in the fields but that makes no sense to me. The pipes were hammered and broken in numerous locations."

"Do we need to go out to the vineyard?" Nick asks.

"Every staffer I could get my hands on is out there, knee high in water with buckets," Kasey replies. "You don't want to be out there."

"Knee high," I murmur, acceptance sliding through me. "Yeah. The vines are lost."

Nick's phone buzzes with a text and he pulls it from his pocket, reads it and says, "Rita has a team on the way."

Several customers exit the door behind Kasey at the same moment the crew Rita sent turns down the driveway. From there, chaos erupts. I leave the vineyard to Nick and Kasey, while the customers are mine to manage. It's nearly two hours later that the guests are cleared out of the mansion, the staff that can be sent home are home, and I find my way to the closed restaurant, and sit down at a corner table, a number of things rushing through my mind. One of them is giving whoever did this exactly what they want. *I need to sell this place.* But I won't be bullied into doing it now or to sell to any one person.

Nick appears in the entrance and crosses to sit next to me, his hand on my leg. "The crew is good. They shut down the water flow in ten minutes, and they're extracting the water. We'll get the right kind of teams out here tomorrow to start the repair process."

"Thank you, Nick, for helping."

"No thanks needed. Ever. You okay, sweetheart?"

"Whoever did this won."

"No. They did not. We'll rebuild the west vineyard."

"That's not what I mean." I rotate to face him, the realization coming to me. "Keeping this place wasn't just about satisfying my family legacy for my father. It was safe, although that's almost a laughable statement right now."

"An excuse to fail at your art."

My throat tightens. "How did you know that? I didn't even know that until just a few moments ago."

"I pay attention," he says, and not for the first time. "I care. Everyone was telling you that you'd fail, and this place was both a sanctuary and a prison. But you need to think about this when we're out of the heat of this fire."

"I want to sell it, Nick, but I have to rebuild those vines first or it won't give me a nest egg."

"Agreed and anyone who thought I'd let you be crazy enough to sell it under those conditions, didn't think ahead. A year from now, we can not only have it rebuilt, we'll have time to figure out the hidden value. We'll get you that nest egg, sweetheart, and I have a pretty good nest egg for us both."

Trying really hard to get out of my past and my own head, I don't reject that idea. Instead, I press my hand to his face. "Is it okay if I contribute to it?"

He presses my hand to his lips. "I'm really turned on by the idea of having a famously wealthy artist in my bed."

My lips curve. "That was a pretty perfect thing to say for such an arrogant bastard."

"Even arrogant bastards have our moments."

Footsteps sound and a frazzled-looking Kasey appears and he doesn't hesitate to cross the room to sit with us. "I need to know a number of things," he says, his focus landing on Nick. "You're a stockholder now? Because Rita said that you are."

"I am," Nick says, "which means you have the resources to fix today's problems."

"You'll want a return," he says. "Do you plan to sell?"

Nick squeezes my leg. "Have you heard a rumor?"

"This place has always drawn offers," he says, "and you're filthy rich, man. Money loves money."

"Did my father consider selling?" I ask. "Is that why you assume I will?"

"You know your father would never let go of this place, though yes. People tried to buy it."

"What is it about this winery that makes people want it?" Nick asks.

"We are part of the core history of Sonoma," he says. "It appeals to buyers. I know one wanted to restore the house and get it designated as some sort of landmark." He refocuses on Nick. "Are you going to force a sale?"

"I don't need a return," Nick says. "I'm here for Faith. And what she wants, I will make happen."

His attention turns to me. "Are you going to sell?"

"I'd be a fool to sell now," I say. "I'd lose money."

"That's a maybe," Kasey says. "Just not now."

"Not for a long time," I correct.

"And now you're devoted to being here and fixing things," he assumes.

"No," I say. "I'd like to offer you a new compensation package with bonuses. And if I sell, I'll include an incentive for you. I want to take care of you."

"Are you saying you're going to let go of the day-to-day operations?" he presses.

"I'm moving to San Francisco with Nick, unless you tell me I need to be here to run this place?"

"You don't," Kasey says. "You're free."

Free. Am I ever really free of this place as long as I own it? I have to try to be. "Would you like to take over the living quarters in the mansion?" I offer.

His eyes narrow. "You're offering me the mansion?" His

tone is incredulous.

"Yes," I say. "Rent free."

"I'll draft a contract with your compensation," Nick interjects. "We'll include the mansion, but I will need you to work with my team to manage the finances. If this sounds acceptable to you?"

"It does," he says, looking at me. "This place was never your place."

"No," I say. "But it has always been your place."

"Yes," he says. "It has been. And yes. I want the mansion quarters."

"Great," I say. "I ah…I haven't cleared out my mother's things."

"I wondered about that," he says. "I can do it."

"Thank you," I say. "Donate what you don't want. And my mother's car. It's yours. Sell it. Keep it. Whatever you want. I'll sign the title over to you."

"We'll authorize additional staff as well," Nick says. "Someone to report to you, but do what Faith would have done to support you." Nick grabs a paper napkin. "Can I borrow your pen?"

Kasey removes it from his pocket and Nick sets it on his knee, writes down a number and a percentage, showing it to me for confirmation. I nod at the numbers that equal a substantial, and deserved, pay increase for Kasey. Nick slides it in front of him. Kasey looks at it and then between us. "Very generous. Thank you. And on that note, I'm going to go check on the work crew."

Nick quickly adds, "Coordinate with Rita to get a new team out here to start the repair process."

He gives an incline of his chin, stands up, and leaves. "Could a historical marker be a reason to want this place?" I ask when he disappears around the corner, while Nick sends a text message.

"I don't know enough about that topic to say, but we'll find out. I just told Rita and Beck to investigate in different ways, but I'm doubtful. Otherwise your father would have done it on his own and pushed up the value of the winery."

"Unless it costs a lot of money to do it, and my mother was gambling then, too," I say.

He glances over at me. "Good point."

A thought hits me. "And I'm officially brilliant," I murmur. "I just gave him the only working car I have."

Nick turns to face me. "Don't get angry, but—"

"You had it fixed."

"Weeks ago and that old car is beneath my woman. We'll buy you something you want that I know is safe."

"You can't just—"

He leans in and kisses me. "Give him both cars, Faith. And if you don't want something new, there's two cars to choose from."

"You'd let me drive your Audi instead of your BMW?"

"Fuck. I must be in love because, yes. I'll not only let you drive it. I'll let you call the damn thing your own if you—"

I lean in and kiss him. He cups my head and slants his mouth over mine, his tongue licking into my mouth before he glances at his watch and says, "It's half past, you should be naked and riding my cock right now."

"That's crass and horrible."

"And it turns you on, right?"

I sigh. "Yes."

He laughs. "Let's get out of here."

Leaving the winery behind in the many ways that currently

apply, comes with relief, but arriving to the house I'd bought as an escape from it doesn't feel like an escape anymore. It feels like a part of that excuse this entire town had, unknowingly, become to me. Once we're on the porch, we find packaging left by FedEx to package up my art. Nick and I pull them inside and start carrying the supplies upstairs. Once we set the first lot down, he heads for the stairs. "I'll get the rest, sweetheart."

Scanning the work I'll soon ship off to L.A., my attention lingers on the painting of Nick—his eyes, and the secrets in their depths, my focus. I don't have any secrets left. He knows who I am. He knows what I am and yet, still he holds back. I grapple with an array of varied thoughts, and where they lead me, but Nick's footsteps sound before I reach a conclusion.

I walk to the floor-to-ceiling window and stare out at the night sky, the canvas of a full moon and the twinkle of at least a dozen stars. Nick steps to my side, his hand at my waist, a possessive quality to his touch. "You need a studio like this in San Francisco. We'll hire someone to build it or we'll just buy another house."

I face him. "You want to buy a new house because of me?"

"I want a place that you feel is yours, not mine."

"Because I didn't pack this one up to take with me?"

"I want you to feel like you're home. Like you did here."

Like I did here, I think, those thoughts I'd started to have when he'd been downstairs charging at me again. "The day I moved into this house with all my renovations done, I stood right here and watched the sun set, and told myself: Now I could be happy in this town. But once the sun set, do you know what I did? Nothing. I didn't paint. I built this beautiful studio and told myself it would inspire me, but I didn't paint. And when I was packing today, your words kept coming to me."

"My words?"

"You said you don't like who I am here. And I don't like who I am here. So, no. I don't want to take a lot of my stuff with me. This place was a placeholder. It's time to move on. I don't want to be here. I want to go home, to San Francisco, with you, Nick. Tonight. Or tomorrow when FedEx picks up my art."

"Then we'll leave tomorrow."

"Good. But I do think that, if I'm honest with you, I'm not without hesitation. I keep thinking that you will break me or me you."

"We've already determined that we're both broken. But we're better together than we are apart."

"Anything too good to be true, is too good to be true."

"Sometimes it's just good, sweetheart."

"But you're not a good guy, Nick, remember?"

"I'm not good," he says, "but I'm a hell-of-a lot better with you than without you."

"Then you need to confess your sins, Nick."

He goes completely, utterly still. "What sins, Faith?"

"The ones you haven't told me. The ones you don't want to tell me. Trust me that much. Because it's not about what you haven't told me that feeds distrust. It's about your unwillingness to tell me."

He snags my hips and pulls me to him. "When I'm ready, remember?"

"Yes. Agreed. But I'm already exposed and on the line with you, more so than ever by moving to the city with you. So, when do you think you'll be ready?"

"When I've made it impossible for you to live without me."

"Because you think I'll want to leave when you expose yourself?"

"Yes," he says, solemnly. "I do. But you need to know that I'll fight for you."

Chapter Twenty-Seven

Nick

TONIGHT, I TELL FAITH ABOUT THE CLUB.

After a hell of a good weekend with Faith, I arrive to work early Monday with that vow in my mind, and a sense of relief. Not only will she know that I owned the club, she'll know that I sold it, and that she was far more important to me than it ever was.

By eight, I've already drafted Kasey's documents, contacted Faith, and sent them to her to review. Rita shows up about the time I've hit send, dressed in a red dress, with the red headed attitude. "Oh look," she says, waving her hands over her voluptuous figure. "We match. Your tie and my dress. Aren't we adorable?"

I give her a deadpan look. "Sometimes I think you forget it's me you work for."

"Sometimes, I think you forget it's me that works for you. And moving on. Landmark properties. It comes with regulations on property improvement, but the potential to create a tax-exempt organization."

"Yeah. No. That would be tricky and potentially illegal."

"Everyone doesn't care as you know." She sets a document on my desk. "That is the detailed breakdown, but from what I can tell, it might push up revenues, but not much. And I still cannot find any documentation that indicates a development, highway or otherwise, that would affect Reid Winter Winery. As for oil or minerals, there's certainly been gold and various other findings in the state, but nothing specifically in Sonoma or on that property. At least, not that is properly documented."

The same answers Beck gave me yesterday, but I'm still not satisfied. North walks into my office, still just as Clark Kent, super geeky, but extra damn skinny. "Did you almost die or what?"

"Yes," he says, shoving his thick glasses up his nose. "I did."

"You're fine now?"

"Yes."

I eye Rita. "Have him do everything you already did on Reid Winter Winery. See if he finds anything else."

"Typical Nick Rogers," she says, not even the slightest bit offended. She sets a stack of documents on my desk and spreads them out. "Sign. Sign. Review. Review. Sign. I'll be back in thirty minutes." She heads for the door and motions to North. "Follow."

They exit my office and my cellphone rings and a glance tells me it's Beck. "Tell me something I fucking want to hear for once," I say.

"Well, hello sunshine," he replies dryly. "Fuck you in the morning, too. You never asked about flag dude again."

"I wasn't aware I needed to micromanage you to do your job. What about him?"

"Jess Wild. Ex-CIA. Does contract-to-hire work and makes my kind of bank."

"Which tells us what?"

"He has a thing for wine. He spent time in wine country investigating a French operative who also liked wine."

"You're telling me he was vacationing?"

"I'm telling you he showed up there last week, at the same time that a married female executive of Davenport Data showed up. And since he's banging her, we suspect she's either his client or his target."

"Does she connect to Faith or anyone connected to Faith?"

"Not that we know of, but we aren't stupid, despite your general opinion that we are. Banging a powerful hot chick as a cover is what I'd call brilliant. We're watching him."

"And the problems at the winery?"

"I have nothing new. Obviously, someone is still squeezing Faith to sell. And all I can say, is history—"

"Do not repeat that history repeats shit again."

He changes the subject. "I hacked the autopsy report again."

"And?"

"The written form filled out to order the proper testing was scanned and marked correctly, but when it was input into the database for actual completion the data was incorrect. The important tests were left off. It could have been an input error but per the internal memos, the person who input it insists she didn't make an error."

"It was hacked."

"That's my conclusion," he says. "Someone knew you ordered the autopsy and made sure certain toxins were not checked for. And we both know that there are substances that won't show up if you aren't looking for them."

"Jess Wild," I say. "That flag wearing ex-CIA agent. It has

to be him."

"Except that he let you know he was there. That's a stupid move with someone like you. Then again, he could be such an arrogant prick that he wants to challenge you."

"I need to buy us some time," I say. "Play the game. Give them what they want."

"If you mean put the winery on the market, you risk some-one like Bill fearing the bids will get too high. Once a killer—"

"Always a killer," I supply, as he repeats my thoughts from the other night. "We need to reel in the uncle. Make him think he can get in with Faith and that's a big order."

"You can be her voice of reason," he says. "Of course, you'll have to convince Faith that this makes sense without sharing your suspicions." He laughs. "Good luck with that one."

My phone beeps and I glance at the caller ID to find Kurt's number. "I'll be in touch," I say to Beck, and disconnect, an-swering the line. "Kurt," I greet, eyeing my watch. "I'm expect-ing you in the next hour, correct?"

"My attorney can't look at this until this afternoon."

"Then get another attorney," I say. "You've had time and this is a gift. I can insert another name in this paperwork in six-ty seconds. Have the signed documents here by three or I will." I hang up and start counting. One. Two. My phone rings again.

I answer the line. "I'll just sign the damn thing. I'll be there at two." He hangs up.

And I have the outcome I'm after. That club is not mine. Faith is.

I spend the fifteen minutes that I manage to spare for lunch on the phone with Faith, sharing her excitement that her paintings have officially been received. By two, I have my document from Kurt. By four I have about ten crisis situations that ensure I'm going to have to work late. I text Faith: *I'm going to have a late night. I'll text you on the way home about dinner.*

Faith replies with: *Why don't I bring you dinner?*

I reach for the sandwich I've had sitting on my desk since noon and toss it in the trash and type: *Chinese?* Because she was craving it before bed last night.

Perfect, she replies. *I'll text you when I'm on my way.*

I think of her spending her money to pick up that meal and I dial Charlie, arranging to add Faith to my fast cash account, and ordering her a credit card. Once I'm done, I buzz Rita. "Come."

She appears in my doorway almost instantly. "Come? That doesn't work when my husband says it and it won't work when you say it."

"I said come and you're here," I say. "It worked."

"Only because I have work for you." She marches to my desk and again sets a stack of documents in front of me. "Sign. Read. Sign. Call about this and be the bastard that you are. Sign."

"I need the top three realtors you suggest and the top three remodeling services."

She gives me a keen look. "Are you buying a new house?"

"Faith and I are going to buy a new house."

"And she hasn't agreed, thus you want to make her feel in control by her choosing the contacts you work with."

"You know me a little too well sometimes."

"I'll get you the names." She starts to turn and seems to change her mind. "A jeweler takes quite some time to customize a ring, perhaps six to eight weeks. Shall I line up a few for you to interview?"

A ring. A wedding. I wait for the hesitation, the wall, the

push back, but there is none. "Yes. Line them up."

"Price range?"

"Whatever it takes to get perfection."

Her lips curve. "I'll let them know."

A ring, I think. A wife. Holy fuck. This is happening. I'm going to make it happen.

I send Rita home at six. Faith sends me a text at six-thirty on her way to pick up the food. At seven, I toss down my pen, pressing fingers to my eyes, finally done with a brief I need by morning. The elevator dings and Faith appears in the doorway, giving me a shy smile, her pink lipstick the same pale shade as her Allure Gallery t-shirt, which she's paired with faded torn jeans.

"Hungry?" she asks.

"Starving," I say, standing up and closing the space between us to take the bags. "For you, but I'll settle for what's in the bags until we get home."

"Home," she says, biting her lip. "I can't get used to that."

"You will," I promise, motioning with my head and leading her to the small round conference table to the left of my desk. Once we've settled into our seats, takeout containers in front of us, I reach into my jacket and set a small sheet of paper on the table. "That's the names and numbers of the top realtors and remodelers in town. I want you to pick the ones you want to work with."

"You really want to do this, don't you?"

"I do. Don't you?"

She hesitates, but a smile hints at her lips. "I guess it couldn't hurt to look."

Baby steps, I think, but I don't heed that warning. I reach

into my pocket again and set a bank card on the table. She stiffens instantly. "What is that?"

"You're with me now, sweetheart. All the way. No half way. I had your social from the legal filings I did. I had you added to my account and ordered you your own card. I keep two hundred in that account so you can get pretty much whatever you want when you want it."

I blanch. "Two hundred thousand dollars?"

"Yes."

"Nick—"

"I know you're going to fight me on this."

"I still owe you money."

"You don't owe me money, but we won't beat that up. Humor me. Put it in your purse. Have it with you in case you need it." I pause. "Please."

"Please? Nick fucking Rogers just said please?"

"I have very good manners, remember?"

She scowls. "No. You have horrible manners." Her voice and expression soften. "I'll keep it, but I'm—"

I lean in and kiss her. "Going to fight me on this. I know. Put it in your purse." She nods and unzips her purse where it rests at her hip, and sticks it inside a zipper pocket.

"Now," I say. "Tell me about the L.A. show. Did you hear anything more about your work?"

"What the fuck, Nick?"

At the sound of Abel's voice, alarm bells go off in my head, I'm on my feet in an instant. "Abel—"

He appears in the center of the office. "You sold the fucking club and didn't give me a chance to buy it? Nick? Where the hell—"

"Abel," I bite out, and holy fuck I'm going to murder him.

Faith stands up at the same moment that Abel rotates to

look at us, his eyes going wide. "*Oh* shit. Nick, man—"

"Get out," I all but growl at him, stalking toward him as he turns to leave, shutting the door behind him.

I face forward and Faith is in front of me, hugging herself. "What club, Nick? What was that and why do you, who is always cool and calm, look like you want to throw up right now? Is it the club you used to—"

"Yes."

"You own it?"

"Owned. I sold it. And I only owned it for a year. I bought it from a client to save him—"

"You didn't tell me. You know what that world did to me and you didn't tell me you *owned* a club."

"I planned to tell you tonight."

"Of course you did. Tonight. The night Abel spills the secret."

"Abel burst in here because he heard I sold it today. Today, Faith. Actually, I gave it away. I took a three hundred and fifty thousand dollar hit because I just wanted it gone."

"You didn't tell me," she repeats, rotating to face the opposite direction and starting to walk toward the window.

I move toward her, intending to pull her in my arms and she seems to know. She stops dead in her tracks. "Do not even think about touching me right now."

Chapter Twenty-Eight

Nick

I IGNORE FAITH'S ORDER NOT TO TOUCH HER, SNAGGING HER wrist. When she tries to pull away from me, I step into her, catching her hips and guiding her to me. "You are what matters to me. You, Faith. Not some damn sex club."

Her chin lifts in challenge, her eyes meeting mine. "Take me there."

My rejection is instant. "Not a chance in hell."

"Take me there or I will go there on my own."

"You're not a member. You won't even find it."

"I've been in that world, Nick. *Your* world. Because I'm not naturally a bull like you does not mean I can't be one if I need to be. And if you think I can't make a few phone calls and find out where that club is, you underestimate me."

"I have never underestimated you a day that I've known

you, but you won't get in the door."

"Then I'll stand there until they call you and you can let me in."

She will. I see it in her eyes. "Why do you need to do this?"

"I need to know who you really are."

"*You know* me, Faith."

"I don't want any more surprises."

Those words grind through me and make my decision. Because there are more surprises to come. I have to let her resolve this one from start to finish before we get there. I take her hand and lace our fingers together. "Come with me," I say, and I start walking, opening the office door and leading her into the lobby. I don't stop until we're at the elevator, and I don't give her a chance to withdraw any more than she has already.

I punch the call button and pull her in front of me, and when the doors open, I say, "There are cameras inside."

"Which won't matter if I'm alone. I need space."

"Too bad," I say as I walk us inside, holding onto her every step of the way. In a matter of seconds, I'm holding her in front of me again, nice and close, my hand on her belly, and we're riding toward the garage. "You don't have to do this," I say near her ear, as if me saying this will miraculously make her believe it.

"I do," she says, her hand coming down on mine, fingers closing tightly around it, barely contained anger in the death grip. "And on some level, I know you know I do."

I didn't know this would be her reaction, but in hindsight, I should have. I know Faith. When she spins out of control, she rebels against the free-spirited artist that she is at her core, and tries to force control. The car halts and the doors open and I take her hand again, leading her into the garage. She digs in her heels. "I'll follow you. I'm parked—"

"Negative," I say. "You ride with me. You stay with me. Or

you don't go. And before you even think about arguing, this is non-negotiable, Faith."

Her expression tightens but she clearly reads just how insistent I am on this. "Fine," she says. "I'll ride with you."

I'm already walking, leading her to the Audi and clicking the locks. I open the passenger door and hold it open for her, reluctantly letting go of her hand. She inhales, as if steeling herself to be trapped in a cage with me, before ducking into the vehicle and settling into her seat. I stand there for several beats, fighting the urge to pull her out of the car again, kiss her, and force her to listen to reason. But I can't force Faith to do anything, and if I could, I doubt I'd want her so fucking much. She's made up her mind and I have to ride the ride with her.

Still, as I shut her inside the Audi and round the rear of the vehicle, I mentally argue a case to go home instead of the club, knowing she'll rebel, but wanting to do it anyway. I'll take her there. I'll tie her to the bed and I'll make her come so many times she forgets the club ever existed.

But she won't forget.

Fuck.

I open the driver's side door and join Faith inside, that sweet amber and vanilla scent of hers colliding with the punch of anger filling the car, and proving to be a brutal cocktail. Wanting this over with, I crank the car in reverse, and pull us out of the space. I don't turn on the radio. I want Faith to talk to me, to ask questions, but she doesn't. Once we're on the road, silence consumes us. Thick, heavy, a weight that promises to bury me, and us, alive. I want to say something to fix this, but I go back to knowing Faith. If I push her right now, she will thicken the wall she's now thrown between us.

So, for fifteen minutes, we endure a wordless ride, until finally we pull up to the private gates of the club, a mansion that sits on the edge of an elite neighborhood. I roll down my window and key in the entrance code, making it painfully clear that I still have access to the facility. The gates open and I pull us through them and we travel the long path hugged by trees and manicured foliage. Once I turn us onto the horseshoe drive, I stop in front of the mansion, holding up my hands to both windows and valets.

I turn to her and before she knows my intent, I have cupped her neck and pulled her to me. "While we are here, I am your fucking king. You do what I say. You stay by my side. You hold my arm or hand. This, too, is non-negotiable, and I swear to fucking God, Faith, if you disobey me on this, I will throw you over my shoulder and carry you out of here. Do you understand?"

She breathes out. "Yes."

I want to kiss her, but I don't. I hate her being here too damn much and I will not risk her reading me in any other direction. "Stay," I order instead. "I'll come around and get you."

I don't wait for her agreement. She doesn't get a fucking opinion while we're in this place. I exit the car and speak to the valet, a thirty-something guy named Rick, who's been with the club for a decade. "Hold the car up front," I tell him. "We won't be long. Is Kurt here?"

"He is."

"Have him meet me in the foyer if he's not indisposed at the moment." I palm him a large bill, and round the car, where Faith thankfully has listened and stayed inside. I grind my teeth and force myself to open her door. She slides her legs to the ground and I offer her my hand. She hesitates, damn it, she hesitates, and it kills me. It also pisses me off. I squat down, lowering my voice for her ears only. "You aren't getting out or going anywhere without touching me," I assure her, "so slide back in and we'll leave or," I offer her my hand again, "take my fucking hand."

She presses her palm to mine and I stand, taking her with me and moving her to the curb. The car door shuts behind us and I lace my fingers with Faith's, bending our arms at the elbows, and fitting her snug to my hip. We start the walk up the stairs leading to the entrance, each of the dozen steps a walk of doom I reject. If this goes badly, I will lose her.

I'm not losing her.

We reach the top and a doorman in a suit—everyone in the place wears suits—well trained at the kind of discretion the club requires, does not make eye contact. He simply opens the door for us. Stepping inside the foyer, the mansion instantly drips of money, from the expensive paintings on the walls, the tiles and thick, oriental rugs on every floor, to the enormous, glass chandelier above our heads. "Where do they lead?" Faith asks of the set of wooden winding stairs directly in front of us, a red and multi-colored oriental carpet up their center, while a second stairwell leads downward.

"No place you want to go," I assure her, redirecting her attention. "To the left is a cigar and whiskey room that is just that. Nothing more. No sex. No play allowed."

"The stairs, Nick," she says tightly, still keenly focused on them.

"Upstairs is group play. Downstairs a dungeon and bondage area, among other things. I didn't go to those places without you, and we won't be going to them now."

She faces me. "I want to go to both areas. All areas."

"I told you, Faith. I didn't go to those places without you. I won't take you to them now or ever." I glance to the left to find Kurt, looking stoic in a black suit and gray tie.

Faith follows my gaze and Kurt closes the distance between us, standing in front of us in a few moments. "Faith is my guest," I announce. "She is not, nor will she ever be, applying for membership." He doesn't react, but he's smart enough to know that she's why he now owns the club. "Faith," I add, moving on. "This is Kurt. The new owner of the club. Kurt. How long did I own this place?"

"Roughly a year," he says.

"Who owned it before me?"

"I'm not at liberty to name names, but one of your clients."

It's a good answer, the right answer, which sets up the story I'm trying to tell right now. "And this person owned it how long?"

"He created it," Kurt explains. "It was his from day one ten years ago."

"And did I ever claim the ownership duties?"

"You did not."

"Did I ever spend time in any of the places those stairs lead?"

"No, you did not," he says.

"And why should Faith trust that you aren't simply protecting me?"

He looks Faith in the eyes for the first time since joining us. "I protect my members, but I don't lie. I'd decline to answer rather than lie as I did when asked about the prior ownership. This was never Nick's place. It was mine. It's simply official now." He looks at me. "Room eleven is yours."

I nod and he gives Faith another look, but says nothing more. He simply turns and walks away. I don't speak to Faith. I lead her down the hallway and I don't stop until we're at room eleven. I open the door, and allow Faith to enter what amounts to a giant bedroom with a wall of sex toys on the left. A massive canopy bed is on the right. A bondage stand is in a half-moon space at the back wall that is covered by a curtain. Beyond that curtain are seats, should you decide to invite viewers, which I never did.

I've barely shut and locked the door before Faith is already moving deeper into the room, walking up to the wall of toys. She pauses and grabs a black silk face mask, and then walks toward the bondage stand. She steps inside it, her back to me, as she starts undressing. I move to a spot a foot back, watching her, waiting, telling myself I'm about to show her that we are still us here, and anywhere. That I am still me. Once she's naked, standing there, her perfect, heart-shaped ass on display, she puts on the mask and then turns to face me. Her arms are at her sides, hands gripping the bars on either side of her. Her breasts are high, full, nipples tight pink nubs. And yeah. My cock is hard. Hard as sin city is to beat on a good day for a casino, which is every fucking day. This is Faith. She can smile and my cock sees it as an invitation.

"Tie me up," she demands, her voice quavering, and I don't miss the way her knees tremble, and that jolts me with realization. She's trying to be that person she was in the club with Macom. But she's not that person. And I'm damn sure not Macom.

I walk to her and I grab the bars above her hands, but I don't touch her. I lean in, my lips near her ear. "You will never learn how to fuck me and still be alone because you will never be alone again, Faith. And I won't touch you in this place." I remove her mask. "Get dressed. We're leaving."

"No. Nick." She grabs my lapels, her naked body pressing to mine. "I need—"

"To put your fucking clothes on," I say. "And let me be clear, Faith. If you don't get dressed, I will dress you and that's going to be awkward for us both. I'll be in the hallway." I turn and walk to the door, opening it and stepping outside, running a hand over my face, adrenaline I didn't know I'd triggered pumping through me.

I lean against the wall, inhaling and willing my body to calm the fuck down. I am always calm. Until now apparently. The door opens and Faith exits the room, thankfully fully dressed, and I don't look at her, nor do either of us speak. I take her hand and lead her down the hallway, getting us the hell out of here. We exit the mansion, and start down the stairs. By the time we're at the bottom, the car is pulled directly in our path, and I open the door to allow Faith to enter. A minute later, we're in the car and are back where we started. Her scent and her anger is a powerful cocktail and I turn to look at her.

"That anger of yours can burn me alive, sweetheart, but I'm still going to be here and I'm still not going to let you go."

Chapter Twenty-Nine

Nick

THANKFULLY, THE DRIVE HOME IS SHORT. TEN MINUTES and I pull us into the garage and kill the engine. I'm out before it even dies, walking around the car to get Faith. She's out of the Audi by the time I'm there, facing off with me. "I should go back to Sonoma."

She just burned me all right, scorched me inside and out. I'm pissed. One hundred percent certifiably pissed. I don't say a word. I walk toward her, pick her up and throw her over my shoulder, just like I did the last time she tried to leave. "Damn it, Nick," she hisses. "You can't throw me over your shoulder every time I want to leave."

I don't respond. I'm already walking, opening the garage door and stepping inside the house, my hand on her pretty little ass, my path straight through the living room and up the stairs.

"Nick, damn it."

"You already said that," I say, entering our bedroom and walking through the bathroom to the closet that used to feel too big and is now just right with Faith in the house. I flip on the light and then set her down in the center of the room. "What do you see, Faith?" I don't give her time to respond. "Look around. Your clothes and my clothes. This is two people sharing a life and when you share a life, you don't just leave because you're upset." Realization slices through me. "And if you really want to leave, then maybe you aren't in this the way I am in this."

"That's not true."

"Words versus actions, Faith. I can't keep picking you up every time you want to leave? Stop trying to fucking leave. Or don't. I told you. In or out. You said you were in."

"You *should* have told me, Nick."

"I took a nearly four hundred thousand dollar hit to give that damn place away, Faith. For you. I did it for you. Because after I heard what a club and Macom equaled for you, I wanted you to know the minute I told you that buying it was a *favor*, not some defining piece of my character. Not an indication of who I am or who we are. I waited to tell you. That was a judgment call, but I did it for the right reasons."

"You *gave* it away?" I confirm in disbelief.

I close the space between us and cup her face. "Yes. I did. Because you mean that much to me."

"Please tell me you have a way to get the money back."

"I don't care about the money, Faith. I care about you." My mouth closes down on hers, and I kiss her, deeply, passionately, drinking her in, so damn in need of her right now, and that need claws at me. "Get undressed," I order. "We need to be naked together."

"Yes," she whispers. "We do. I do."

I brush my lips over hers and shrug out of my jacket, and we watch each other undress, the anger between us shifting to something just as dark, just as intense and demanding. Lust. Love. Need. And when we are naked, both of us, we stand there in the fucking closet, but neither of us are looking at the other's body. Our eyes connect, that mask she'd had on and that I'd stuck in my pocket is in my hand, and to her it was a weapon against me and us. A way she made the sex nameless, faceless. To me, it's a way to show her that that will never be possible. Not for us.

"Do you trust me?"

"I trust you."

I walk to her, stopping a lean away from touching her. "*Do you trust me?*"

"*Yes.* I trust you."

"You didn't react like you trust me."

"I obviously have triggers. I realize that now. It's about me, not you."

"It's about us, Faith. Everything is us now."

"I know."

She doesn't, but I decide right then, that I just have to accept the challenge. I'm not a patient man, but I am in love with this woman, and I will help her, not force her, to see how devoted I am to her. I snag the fingers of her hand and walk her into the dressing room connecting to the closet—a small room with one oversize blue and brown plaid chair, a dresser, a standing mirror, and a full wall that is all windows, the view the ocean, the city.

I lead Faith to the chair in front of the ottoman, which is large enough that it might as well be another chair. I then hold up the mask. "Trust," I say softly.

She reaches for it and in the process presses to her toes,

leaning into me, her hand on my shoulder, her nipples brushing my chest. Her lips are a breath from mine. "Because it's different here."

"Is that a question or a statement."

"A statement. It feels different. I'm glad you made me leave."

I cup her head and kiss her, savoring the sweetness of those words on my tongue, before I say, "Me too. But I'm glad we went, Faith. You needed to know. I just don't want us in a place like that."

"I felt that. I needed to feel that." She pushes away from me just enough to slip that mask on her face.

My hands settle at her waist, my lips near her ear. "You know I like control."

My fingers tease her nipple and she arches into the touch, and gives a choked laugh. "You love control."

"Can I have it now, Faith?"

"I love that you ask," she whispers.

"I don't have control that you don't give me. You know that. I know that. And I wouldn't want the lie that is any other form of control. Do you know what I want right now?" I don't give her time to reply. "I want you to feel me so completely that you know, absolutely know, that if there is one person on this earth you can be free with, it's me."

"I do."

"No. But we're a work in progress, sweetheart. You will. I promise, I will make you not just feel those things. You'll know them."

My hands fall away from her and I take a step backward. She reaches for me and I am just a finger out of reach. Her hands fall to her sides, and for nearly a full minute, I just stand there, letting her feel the absence of my touch, letting her wonder what will come next. What will I do to her. I step closer to her again, letting her feel my nearness, and she does. She inhales my scent, on her instincts that tell her I'm in front of her. I lower myself to my knees, but still I don't touch her. I hold my hands at her ankles, but still I don't touch her. I move my hands upward. But still I don't touch her.

"Nick," she breathes out and when she reaches for me, my lips curve, and I allow her fingers to tunnel into my hair.

It's what I wanted. I wanted her to reach for me, to need me. And now that she has, then, and only then, do my hands come down on her hips, my lips to her belly. I cup her backside, and lower my mouth until I'm a breath above her sex. Her fingers tighten in my hair, and I give her a tiny lick. She rewards me with a sexy, sweet moan. I suckle her nub, then swirl my tongue around it, and already she is trembling and can feel how on edge she is, how easily she will shatter for me, but it's not enough. I want more. So much more. An explosion. A connection. More than an orgasm.

And suddenly I know I need to test the waters. I need to know that we are not only moving forward, but that we haven't gone backward.

I stand up, and she breathes out, "Nick," and my name is a plea.

I answer by cupping her face and kissing her, letting her taste *her* on my lips. "I'm going to spank you, Faith," I say, needing to know she won't hesitate. "I am not going to give you any other warning unless you tell me otherwise. Answer now. Trust me or not. Yes or no?"

"Yes."

I sit down and take her with me, pulling her across my lap so that the cushion cradles her body, my hand on her backside. I start rubbing her cheeks, warming her backside, when I feel the punch of ignorance overwhelm me. Of course, she said yes.

I spanked her the first night. She knows how to shut down. She knows how to escape, and *hell*. I'm letting her escape me. I'm hurting the level of trust between us, not creating trust.

I inhale and lean over her, kissing her back, her shoulder, one of my hands sliding under her to her sex, fingers stroking the silky wet heat. I slip fingers inside her, my thumb still working her clit and she was already so damn close that she stiffens and trembles into that orgasm I denied her. I don't let her ride it all the way out, though. I want her to finish with me inside her. I shift our entire bodies, pulling her backside to my front, and I press inside her, my hand covering her breasts.

Her hand is immediately on my hand, and I thrust into her, pleasure radiating through. "God. You feel good," I murmur next to her ear. "So damn good."

She arches into me. "Nick, you...I..."

I pull out of her and turn her to face me, pulling away her blindfold. Pressing inside her again, and cupping her backside to pull her down onto my cock, before I repeat her words, "You and I is exactly right," and then kiss her, a deep, drugging kiss, even as I do a slow thrust followed by another and when I pull back to look at her, to breathe with her, there is a shift between us, an expanding need.

Our mouths come back together, our bodies grinding, pumping, thrusting. It's dirty, it's sexy, it's fiercely addictive, and yet it is sultry, intimate. She tugs my hair free, her fingers tangling in it, tugging at it. Her teeth scraping my shoulder, mine scraping her nipple. The rise of our orgasms are slow, it seems until they're not. Until they're upon us and I am cupping her breast, pinching her nipple, thrusting my cock and she is panting out my name in such a fierce demanding way that I am helpless to stop the explosion. I shudder and she trembles, and we cling to each other until we collapse against each other.

Seconds, maybe minutes pass and we lay there like that until she says, "Why didn't you spank me?"

I pull back to look at her, stroking hair from her face. "I wanted to, but for the wrong reasons."

"I don't understand."

"A spanking is a power play. We both enjoy the give and take that it represents. But it is about power, my power and control, and that has no place between us with a fight in the air and that damn club playing with our heads."

Her hand settles on my face. "The club isn't between us. It's gone. It's done. And Nick Rogers. If I wasn't in love with you before this moment, I would be now."

She presses her lips to mine, and I slant my mouth over hers. In the depths of that kiss is what I have craved, what I have needed: A new level of trust, a willingness to risk it all with me. But hours later as I lay in bed, holding Faith close, I am not reveling in the mountain we've climbed today. I'm too busy looking for a way to battle the sea of sharks that are my lies.

Chapter Thirty

Faith

A NEW DAY DAWNS FOR ME WITH THE EMOTIONAL HIGH of conquering "the club incident" as I call it in my mind, and with Nick and I a little stronger and a lot closer.

And with my car still at Nick's office, I hitch a ride with him, with a Starbucks drive-thru detour a few blocks from our destination. "That Chinese food we left on your conference table is going to reek this morning," I say, as we wait at the window for our drinks.

"Rita is going to give me absolute hell about it, too."

"What are you going to say to explain it?"

"Absolutely nothing."

I laugh. "That sounds like you." I inhale and let it out, dreading the nagging concern that sparks my next question. "Did you ask Beck to confirm my art was bought by legitimate buyers?"

And as if waiting for his answer isn't torture enough, a woman appears at the drive-thru window to take our money. Seeming to sense my nerves though, Nick ignores her and looks at me, and says, "Your sales are one hundred percent legitimate," before he turns to her and offers her his credit card. A minute later, he hands me my white mocha and sets his double shot espresso in the drink holder, rolling the window back up, which is my cue to press for more information.

"Did Beck check out my sales then? Or rather, the buyers?"

He places the car into gear and glances over at me. "This is going to make you doubt yourself, isn't it? You do remember you got into the L.A. show for a reason, right?"

"I do," I say, as he pulls us onto the road. "But I'd like a firm grip on how well I'm doing. And the bottom line here is that if those sales weren't real sales, they might track back to my uncle. That could be the link we need between him and this hell we've been through with the winery. If he was behind those broken water pipes, Nick, I want him to pay."

"And he will. I'll make sure of it."

"We need to buy some time for you and Beck to make those connections. I'd say we could place the winery up for sale, just for show of course, but it would freak out Kasey and the staff. But it might bring our enemy out of hiding."

"And perhaps not in a good way," he says. "Whoever is behind this could see that as my negative reaction as a new investor to the vineyard water damage. They'll also see me as someone who will try to push the price upward, despite that loss. In which case, they might try to further drive the price down by creating another problem."

"But they had to suspect that could be your reaction to the financial blow," I say, as he pulls us into the parking garage and parks next to the BMW. "Maybe that's what they wanted."

"I'm leaning more toward them thinking I'd bow out, and leave it to you, while you would end up just wanting out."

"Which brings me back to my recent sales. To someone trying to give me motivation to get out."

"Your sales are legitimate, Faith, and as for the rest, we can speculate all day, but I'm not ready to take calculated risks just yet. Let's give Beck a little more room to do his job. And the reality here is that now that we've bought out your note, this might fizzle out."

"The water damage says it won't."

"Or it was unrelated, or one last blow delivered by a bad loser." He reaches for his door. "I'll come around to get you."

I don't give him time to help me out of the car. I slip my tan purse, which I've paired with my favorite faded jeans and a matching pair of brown ankle boots, over my shoulder, and open my door. By the time I'm standing, Nick has arrived, and is now towering over me, his navy blue eyes a perfect match for his suit and the dots in his black tie. And really truly, I could stand here and take a deep blue swim in those eyes for a few minutes, or even hours, and be perfectly happy.

"Let's talk cars," he says.

My deep blue spell is broken. "What about cars?"

"Let's buy you something you want and love and not because I care if you drive the BMW or the Audi. Because you need to pick what you love."

"I like the BMW."

"Then we'll custom order you one with the specs you like."

"I can just drive this one."

"What color do you want?"

"Blue like your eyes."

"Interior?"

"Black like my uncle's soul."

"Black like your uncle's soul," he repeats dryly. "There's no question what's still on your mind. You, my beautiful woman, need to let go of the stress. Get your butt to Allure and paint that wall you're supposed to start painting today. And pick a remodeler, if you aren't going to pick a realtor. Let's get your studio up to standard."

"The studio you made me is fine."

"It's not fine. In fact, it's well known that the male population, at least the smart ones, realize that when a woman says 'fine' it's never fine."

I'd answer that claim, but a shout from the distance interrupts. "You have a meeting in ten minutes!"

At the sound of the female voice delivering that message, I turn to find a redhead rushing in our direction, her black high heels, which she's paired with a black dress, clicking on the pavement. "That would be Rita," Nick says, leaning in to kiss me. "I'll call you in a few hours." He takes off, but calls over his shoulder, "Call the realtor. Any realtor."

Rita steps in front of me. "Faith. I've been dying to meet you and I can't even chat. I have to go deal with a million things. Let's have lunch soon."

"I'd love that."

She starts to turn away and I stop her. "Wait. He has a meeting?"

"Yes. Why?"

"Chinese food on his conference table."

"Oh my God. It's the CEO of a bank. It's going to smell to high heaven up there."

She takes off for the elevator and I laugh, walking to the BMW and climbing inside. Happy. I feel happy. Nick and I moved mountains last night and I feel that success between us. But I also feel the heavy weight of knowing that I have an enemy that has now become Nick's. And I really need a paintbrush in my hand before I start thinking about all the ways that enemy might strike next.

By mid-morning, Sara and I have made our final artist picks for opening week and I've been sketching ideas for the wall, which isn't my normal method of working, but this isn't my normal canvas. It's also a really big canvas to mess up. I'm on what must be sketch number one hundred when Chris appears in my doorway, looking his normal, jean-clad, tattooed, cool artist self. "Nick called me."

I set my pencil down. "About?"

"Every customer that bought your work has bought from the gallery on numerous occasions. And every painting was purchased by an individual. He didn't give me details on why you wanted to know this information, but I'll use my imagination. No one bought your success. You made it." He motions behind me. "You going to paint that thing or think about it?"

"Paint it," I say, and that seems to satisfy him, because he disappears into the hallway.

I smile on a sigh with the realization that despite his meeting, Nick made me a priority again. He gave away that club because he made me a priority. He reaches for me constantly in so many ways. It's time for me to reach for him. I need to show how committed I am to him and I open my drawer where I stashed the piece of paper with the realtor choices listed. I'm reaching for it when I pause with a thought. Nick *is* reaching for me. Helping me. Protecting me. I need to protect him. I need to make sure that my enemy doesn't turn on him, and hurt him in some way. I need to buy him and Beck some time to investigate further.

I pick up my cellphone, and assuming that my enemy is my uncle, I dial his number. Unsurprisingly, he answers on the first ring. "Faith," he greets. "I'm shocked you called. Happy, but shocked."

"Yes well, I keep thinking about those photos. I really miss my father and I'd like to see them."

"I'll bring them to you. I'm in New York on business, but I can head that way this weekend."

"I actually moved to San Francisco and I have craziness going on getting ready for the L.A. Art Forum in two weeks. And…I'd rather start with the pictures."

He's silent a beat. "Understood. What's your email? I'll shoot you over a few of them and bring you the box when we meet after your show."

He's teasing me with the photos and setting me up for the meeting. It irritates me, but it also buys me that time. "FWinter@gmail.com. Thank you. I'm looking forward to seeing the photos."

"Of course. Shoot me back an email and let me know what you think of them."

"I will. Goodbye." I end the call knowing the twig I've given him is enough to buy some time for Nick and Beck to figure out what's really going on. Assuming of course that my enemy is my uncle.

It might not be him. In which case, I've bought no time at all.

Chapter Thirty-One

Faith

Two weeks later...

"**G**OOD LUCK TONIGHT AND TOMORROW."

I look up from my desk to find Sara in the doorway. "Thank you. I was nervous two weeks ago when I shipped my work and then I just put it aside. I didn't think about it. But right now, my stomach is at my feet, and I think it's pretty clear that I saved all the nerves for now."

"Nerves are good," she says, walking to my visitor's chair and perching on the arm. "They mean you're experiencing life, not just going through the motions. And I went through the motions for too many years myself. I wish I could be there for you. Chris and I both wish we could be there, but it's just too close to the grand opening here. When are you leaving?"

"Now, actually," I say, standing up, still in jeans, boots, and a royal blue silk blouse, that I will trade in for something fancier tonight in L.A for the Forum launch party. "Nick had a meeting this morning or I wouldn't have come in at all. He's picking me up in a few and we're actually looking at a house on the way to the airport that the realtor swears we have to see and could lose if we wait."

"Oh really? Where is it?"

"It's a penthouse in some new high rise, which I wasn't keen on being in a building, but the views are supposed to be stunning. Nick really wants to look."

"We're in a high rise and it's pretty lovely to have the service and security as well as the views. We love it." She motions to the wall behind me. "It's beautiful, Faith."

"Thank you. I'm so happy you like it."

"Our opening day guests are going to love it, too. We're going to allow only those who attend opening night to visit your room and Chris's. And we'll display a collection of your art on the walls here as well as in your display area. If you think you can spare a few more pieces? I know it's short notice, but—"

"Yes. Yes of course, I can. Thank you. So much, Sara."

"Thank you, Faith, for all you've done. And I know it's a pipe dream, but I'd love for you to take the job I offered you and stay here full time. And since I really just threw it at you without explanation, let me share a little backstory. When Mark owned this place, it was a normal, public gallery. We had full time hours and full time staff. He was going to close it. He shuttered it for a while but was going to re-open it with us."

"Shuttered because it wasn't making a profit?"

"No. Aside from Rebecca's situation, which affected Mark deeply, his family owns the Riptide Auction house in New York. He took over the management of that operation sooner than he'd expected. Chris and I didn't want to take this place on as a full time job so we paid the staff big bonuses and considered closing it down."

"What changed?"

"We started talking and got excited in a new way. We're going to develop new talent and do so mostly with special events, with a healthy portion of the profits going to charity. And because I still travel with Chris, we need someone who understands art and can become passionate with us, while also running the place in my absence. My point here is that if the money is an issue—"

"Yes. Yes, I want to stay, this sounds wonderful and the charity focus is inspiring. I'm really not worried about the money."

"Holy fuck," Nick says, stepping into the doorway, looking delicious in a navy suit that matches his eyes almost perfectly. "What am I going to do with you, woman? Of course, you care about the money."

Sara laughs and stands up, placing us both in profile. "Should I negotiate the salary with you?"

"No," I say. "Nick does not get to negotiate my salary." I look at him. "You do not get to negotiate my salary."

"Technically you're my client and—"

"Stop while you're ahead, Tiger," I warn, "because you won't like the hotel sofa."

His lips curve ever so slightly but he manages a stern look at Sara. "Do right by her."

"Yes sir, Tiger," she laughs, and then glances at me. "We shouldn't let our two men spend too much time together without some rules. Their shared tendencies to control everything around them will have them feeding off each other, and we'll be forced to check them."

"Check me, sweetheart," Nick says. "Just make sure it hurts."

"On that note," Sara says. "I'll leave. Text me pictures from the show. And I'm talking to both of you."

She darts past Nick and she's barely left the office when he's crossed the room to stand next to me, but facing my wall. "The gardens," he says, studying my work before looking at me. "You painted your mother's gardens and you did it in color."

"It felt like a way to make peace with the past."

"Did it work?"

"It helped," I say. "And I think it opened me up to variations of color in my art."

"With good reason," he says. "The details alone are exceptional but the way you used color to create that detail is astounding."

"Thank you, Nick. You are always so supportive."

"Sweetheart, this isn't me being supportive. That sounds like you have a hobby, not a career I admire." He snags my fingers and pulls me to him. "We're going to have an amazing weekend, starting with tonight's welcome party." He kisses me. "Correction. Starting with this penthouse we're about to look at." He glances at his watch. "We better get moving. It's noon now. I want to be in the air by three thirty, so you have plenty of time to relax and dress for tonight. I'm parked out front."

"High places make me nervous," I say as we walk through the gallery toward the front door.

"Since when do high places make you nervous?"

"Since I considered living in the penthouse of a high rise."

"If you don't like it," he says, opening the door and holding it for me. "We'll keep looking but I saw pictures. I think you're going to love it." He motions to the Audi, sitting a few spaces down at the curb. We hurry in that direction and right as I've settled into my seat, and Nick's shut me inside, my phone buzzes with a text. It's one of the many random photos of my parents my uncle has been sending me the past two weeks.

"Why are you scowling?" Nick asks, when he joins me.

"Bill sent me another photo."

"And?"

"They're about thirty years old and standing in front of a Welcome to Las Vegas sign, both laughing." I show him the photo. "His caption: *They were happy. I know there are a lot of things you feel and think about them, but I really think once we chat, you may change your mind.*"

Nick studies it for several beats and looks at me. "How do you feel about what he said?"

"Part of me really craves whatever information he has to give me."

"I assumed you would, but you started down this path to hold him at bay while Beck did his thing. And since nothing else has gone wrong, we can speculate that if he's our enemy, your plan is working. The timing of that particular photo and message, considering you told him you'd meet him after this show is suspect."

"It does seem rather curious."

"In other words," he says, "you're playing him, sweetheart." He starts the car. "Make sure he doesn't start playing you."

"What do you think about the Vegas photo?" I ask as he pulls us onto the road.

"I think he's going to tell you she had a gambling problem. And I'll be interested in where that goes, considering he supposedly didn't talk to her or your father for almost a decade."

"And Beck has nothing for us?"

"Beck makes me want to return to my childhood and play pin the tail on the donkey again where he's the damn ass. He's dry. And I pay him way too fucking well for him to be dry."

"Could it just be over, Nick? I mean, maybe it really was just the bank trying to take advantage of me?"

"It could be."

"But you don't think so," I say reading into his tone. "If Bill was up to something you'd think Beck would find something on him."

He turns the corner. "I hate that he sent you that picture tonight of all nights, and got your brain wrapping around this again. Set it aside." He pulls us into the parking lot of a shiny glass high rise. "We're here and only a few blocks from your job, because we both know you're going to take that job at Allure."

I smile. "Yes. I am."

He stops at the front of the building, and two valets are instantly at our sides. A few seconds later, he palms both of the men money, and joins me at the sliding glass doors. "The key," he says, holding it up. "I told the realtor we didn't have time for conversation."

We enter the lobby, a beautiful pale gray wood covering the floors, with thick cream and gray curtains on the walls, and gray furnishings. The elevator is all glass and as it starts to move, I face Nick. "What do people do if they forget stuff in the car in one of these buildings?"

"The staff will get it for you, or you get it yourself."

"The staff will do that?"

"It's a full-service building and if you tip enough, the staff will know you and be happy to help."

"That sounds expensive."

"Most people living in the penthouse aren't worried about money."

The elevator dings, and we exit, turning left to be greeted by two massive arched wooden doors. Nick opens the doors and I enter, finding myself skipping quickly past the dark wooden floors and balcony to the curved room, and floor-to-ceiling windows with a view of the ocean everywhere I look. "The ceilings are eighteen feet high," Nick says, shutting us inside. "And there's electronic shading for the windows."

"It's incredible." I look over at him as he steps to my side. "What do you think?"

"The same. Incredible."

"Do I even want to know how much?"

"I don't want to tell you."

"Tell me anyway."

"Fifteen million." I gasp and he snags my hand, walking me to him. "It's just a number."

"A huge number."

"Forget the number," he says. "We've been instructed to go upstairs for your possible studio but let's walk the rest of the place first."

"Nick, that price—"

He cups my face and kisses me. "I've wanted to do that since the moment I saw you in your office. You do know the place we have now is almost as expensive, right? And that I'll sell it?"

"Yes but-"

"Money doesn't matter," Faith.. A place we love does." He strokes my hair. "Okay?"

"I can't say okay."

"I will then. I've worked my ass off to be in a position to pick a home with the woman I love, and not worry about how much it costs." He kisses my forehead and then joins our hands again. "Let's explore."

A few minutes later, we've seen five bedrooms, a den, an indoor pool, and an incredible kitchen with a white marbled island with black finished cabinets. And finally, an outdoor space that stretches far and wide, with ivy covered walls and brick steps. We finally head upstairs and I step into a room with arched stained-glass windows at each end, and the same floor-to-ceiling windows lining the entire front wall. And above me is a skylight, a view certain to be moon and stars at night.

Nick steps behind me, his hand on my belly, lips at my ear. "What do you think?" he asks. "Could this be your studio?"

"Oh yes. I love this place. I love it so much. There's inspiration everywhere. The sky and the ocean."

"And an office already built in. I can work while you paint."

I rotate to look at him. "Have I told you that I can't paint when I'm being watched?"

"I watch you all the time."

"You're the only one that I can let watch me, Nick."

"Why?"

"Because you're you. It's the only answer I have."

"Do you want to live here with me, Faith?"

"Yes," I say. "I do, but the impact of this is hitting me. This is big. Buying a new place to be with me is big. Are you—"

"In love with you? Yes. Obsessed with you? Yes. I am. Shamelessly."

"Obsession is—"

"Dangerous. Yeah. I know. Sign me up for more." He kisses me. "Let's go drink champagne on the plane and celebrate our new home and your show."

"We don't have a new home yet, and I'm feeling really nervous about my show. Let's celebrate after it's done."

"You're going to shine sweetheart. And we'll have a home by the time we get to the airport. I'm pulling this place off the market."

He drapes his arm around my shoulder, and we start walking, but I twist around to look at the space one more time. "I really love it."

His hand settles at my back. "We could get that cat you've wanted."

I turn to face him. "Do you like cats?"

"I had a cat growing up."

I blanch, surprised at this news. "Really? What was his name?"

"Asshole most of the time. Jerry the rest of the time. He hated my father. I loved him."

I laugh but sober quickly with a thought that seems important, considering the steps we're taking. "Do you want kids, Nick?"

His eyes meet mine, sharp, dark edges in his. "Kids break," he says. "Parents break them. I decided a long time ago I wasn't going to break any of my own."

Relief washes over me. "You know my family history. I feel the same."

He strokes a lock of hair behind my ear, those blue eyes of his softening, warming. "Possibilities, sweetheart. We'll start with a cat. We'll see where it, and life, lead us."

Thirty minutes later, we're in the lounge area of the plane, champagne-filled flutes in our hands, when the realtor finally calls Nick back. I listen as Nick negotiates, his hand on my leg, touching me—he's always touching me, as if he is truly obsessed. And I like it.

Five minutes later, he ends the connection and leans over to kiss me. "I made sure it's ours. We just need to line up a remodeling expert and decide what we want to do with it before we move in."

"How long will that take, do you think?"

"If I push them, I'd say we can be in the place in eight weeks."

My cellphone rings, and I grab it from the table built into the floor in front of us, glancing at the caller ID. "Josh," I greet, answering the line.

"I got your email about your arrival," he says. "I'll pick you up at the airport. Five o'clock, right?"

"I don't need a ride, but thank you."

"I'm your agent. I'll give you a ride."

"I'm not your only client at the show."

"If you mean Macom, he can drive himself. He lives here."

I firm my tone. "Thank you, but I don't need a ride."

There is a heavy pause. "Nick's with you."

"Yes," I say, my eyes meeting Nick's. "Nick is with me."

Nick's lips curve in amusement and he refills his glass.

Josh is silent for several beats before he replies with, "You need to make some time with me, without him, to meet the people I want you to meet tonight. And we're having breakfast in the morning to talk about those meetings, without him. Don't push back on this, Faith. I can't get you the thirty thousand a painting I want to get you if you don't let me agent."

"I know that," I say, wishing he'd been this eager to sell my work before Chris aided my career. "And I understand."

"You better." He hangs up.

Nick arches a brow.

I sigh and set my phone on the table. "How much did you hear?"

"Enough to know that he has his panties in a wad," he says dryly, "because my very existence guarantees he can't get your panties in a wad."

"Stop saying things like that. It's all I will be able to think about when I am with him."

"Good. You need to be aware of his intentions."

My brow furrows. "You're in a mood. Should we talk about Macom before we get there?"

"Haven't we talked the shit out of Macom as it is?" he asks.

"Yes. And you made reference to—"

"Wanting to beat the shit out of him?" He doesn't give me time to answer. "I do, but I'm really good at fantasizing. Like right now, I'm thinking about you naked, straddling me at about thirty thousand feet, but despite how fucking hard I am just thinking about that, I'll most likely refrain from making it happen until the ride home. And likewise, I'll most likely refrain with Macom."

"Nick—"

"Faith. Are we doing this again?"

My cellphone buzzes with a text this time. I glance at it in my hand to find Bill has messaged me. I read it to Nick. "From Bill: *Just making sure you got the picture and my message?* He's giving me an uneasy feeling tonight. Maybe I'm just nervous that my paintings will be mocked or the man I love will punch the man I never loved, but he is. What should I say?"

"Fuck you, you lying, cheating, lowdown bastard." He downs his champagne. "Another fantasy. Stick to reality. Keep playing him, sweetheart. Soft and sweet. It's your magic and I love the fuck out it."

I inhale and think a moment before I type: *Yes sorry. That topic is emotional and I have my big show this weekend that I'm nervous over.* I show it to Nick.

"Magic," he says. "He'll eat that up."

My phone buzzes again with a new message I read to Nick again. "His reply: *Yes honey. Sorry. I didn't even think about this upsetting you. Go. Make your mark. Make the Winter family proud and I promise you, your father would have been proud.*

He's hit a nerve, and my stomach knots with the very

thought of my father's thoughts on my art. But there is more. Something nagging in the back of my mind that I just can't put a finger on.

"You played the player," Nick says. "Now come play me." He cups my neck and pulls my mouth near his mouth. "Forget Bill, Josh, and Macom. They're making you nervous. Think of me. Think of us." His kisses me, and he makes me forget, but the minute his lips part mine, that nagging feeling returns.

Chapter Thirty-Two

Faith

WE ARRIVE AT THE L.A. HOTEL WHERE THE ART show is being hosted with just enough time to shower and change. The doorman leads us into the fancy suite, that is of course, glamorous; my first view is of a large outdoor area framing a living area, with a connected dining room and a grand piano. Hallways lead to additional rooms and to my left and right are fancy, winding stairwells.

The bellman delivers our bags to the master suite, which is apparently down the right hallway. The minute he disappears into the room, I turn to Nick and softly say, "This is not a hotel room. It's the size of a house."

"You never know when you might want to invite a few gallery owners over or whoever else might help your career," he says, snagging my hips and walking me to him. "And I think you should consider doing just that before we leave."

"That's an incredible idea, but I will be too nervous to do that this time."

"Well keep your possibilities open," he urges. "Bring it up with Josh. See what he thinks."

I soften with those words. "You hate Josh, but you really are willing to support him as my agent, aren't you?"

"As long as he keeps his hands to himself," he says, the light catching on a hard glint in his blue eyes.

The doorman reappears and Nick tips him. I follow the path I now believe to lead to the bedroom, finding it is indeed at the end of the hallway. It has thick gray curtains, a cream colored fluffy rug, a bed so high I need a step stool, and a sitting area. Our bags are nowhere in sight and I walk to the bathroom to seek them out. It is, of course, as luxurious as the rest of the suite, with an egg-shaped tub, shiny white and gray tiles and a massive tile-encased shower.

My hunt for the bags leads me to the walk-in closet, where they sit on suitcase stands, but there is more. There is a collection of dresses, still with the tags on them. Six dresses. My heart starts to race, confusing emotions rushing through me. Nick's footsteps sound and I turn to face him. He appears in the doorway, bigger than life, I swear, and so good looking, so damn dominant in every situation. "You're very overwhelming," I blurt. "Everything you do is big, bold, and extravagant."

"Agreed."

I smile. "That's it? You agree?"

"Yes. Do you like the dresses?"

"I haven't looked at them yet."

"Why not?"

I walk to him and push to my toes to kiss him. "I know you want me to enjoy your money. I know that I can't be with you, and not experience your money. I see that."

"But?"

"No buts other than me suddenly really needing to say something to you."

"Okay. You have my full attention. As I often say, you always have my full attention."

"You will never be the sum of a fancy hotel room or fancy dresses to me. I'm going to tell you that a lot because I don't want you to forget. And on that note. The dresses are exciting. The room is wonderful. Thank you for working so hard to make this weekend special." I give him a quick kiss and when I would turn away, he pulls me to him. His fingers tangle in my hair, and his mouth closes down on mine, and in the depths of that kiss I taste torment that I do not understand. But there is love, and hunger, and need, too.

He pulls back stroking my cheek. "I'd better stop or we'll be late. Look at the dresses. And if you don't like any of them, we'll trade them in."

"What is it that I'm sensing?" I ask. "What's wrong?"

"Nothing you in one of those dresses can't solve." He brushes his lips over mine and releases me, and before I can press him for more, he turns and disappears into the bathroom.

I stare after him and I have no idea what it was about that exchange, but every instinct I own now says that the club wasn't the big reveal I'd thought it to be. That secret that he fears I won't accept, that I've tried to reveal with my paintbrush, has yet to be exposed.

Chapter Thirty-Three

Faith

I'M STILL STRUGGLING TO DECIDE ON A DRESS WHEN THE shower comes on. I step into the bathroom and find Nick's already inside. Still bothered by the exchange we've just had, and the idea that we might go into this night, and an encounter with Macom, with something I don't even understand brewing between us, I strip my clothes away, and step around the tiled wall.

Nick is under the water, eyes shut, head tilted upward, suds pouring over every naked, ripped, perfect inch of him. He must sense my presence, suddenly lowering his chin, his eyes finding me. His gaze skims my naked body. His cock now thick, hard. I walk toward him, and he doesn't move, a dark edginess about him that confirms what I'd sensed in the closet. There is a still a wall between us—a secret. I stop a lean away from touching him, but he doesn't reach for me. I lift my hand and press it over his heart, and that touch is all it takes. He is suddenly kissing me, his hand closing around a chunk of my hair, the taste of him wild hunger with a big dose of that torment I'd sensed. His hands are all over me, his mouth on my nipple one moment, fingers tugging it the next.

Before I know it, I'm pressed into the corner, and he is lifting me, his cock pressing inside me, stretching me, filling me. That wild hunger dominates, and it consumes me right along with him. I want him deeper. I want him harder. I want his mouth on my mouth. We don't last long, though. Both of us are too aroused, too urgent. I shatter, my sex clenching the thick width of his shaft. He shudders in response and soon we are holding onto each other, breathing together—fast and then slow.

He eases me to the ground. "That wasn't supposed to happen."

I tangle fingers into his wet hair. "We needed that."

He inches back to look at me. "Why do you say that?"

"I don't know. I just felt it. I needed it."

He studies me for several beats, his expression unreadable. He kisses me again, a deep stroke of tongue followed by another before he says, "I love you. Finish your shower."

And then he is gone and for reasons I can't even explain that have nothing to do with how hot and naked he is, or how much I love him too, I want to pull him back. So much that it hurts to deny that need.

I finish my shower, slip on a robe, and step to the sink next to Nick, who is in a towel only, with shaving cream on his face and a razor in his hand. I slip in front of him. "I'll do it."

"You need to get ready. It's late."

"I have time."

He gives me a heavy lidded look and hands me the razor. "Goatee or no goatee?" I ask.

"You tell me."

"I like the goatee," I say stroking the foam from his face. "It gives you a dangerous edge."

"And you like dangerous?"

"Only when it's you."

He takes the razor from me. "This is going to get us naked again. Go get ready." He kisses me and foams up my face. I laugh and move away, the mood decidedly lighter.

I dry and flat iron my hair to a blonde shine, choosing neutral colors for my make-up, except my lips. I choose a deep rose that is almost pink, and it will match the colors in my necklace that I now never take off. I walk to the closet and stand in front of the dresses again. The blue one he got me weeks ago is for tomorrow for sure. Tonight though, hmmmm.

My gaze radiates to a simple elegant dress with a beige underlay and ivory lace overlay. If I want to appear as an artistic type, it's muted and beautiful, but I don't reach for it. My attention rockets to another dress, an evergreen shade with a silk sheen that so perfectly matches one of the stones in my necklace that it can't be an accident. It fits my newfound love of colors, and I smile. This is the dress.

I quickly pull on a pair of thigh high black hose I've packed in my suitcase, and then inspect the shoes Nick also had delivered, choosing a pair of black heels with a sexy double ankle strap. And then I pull on the dress, the deep V managing to show skin, not cleavage. The skirt flares to the knee, while a full sash ties at the left hip. It's stunning. And of course, Nick remembered purses, or the shopper he hired remembered. Four expensive purses that are all Chanel. I choose a small black bag with a sparkly logo and a bit of shine to the rather traditional and perfect style.

And then I inspect myself in the mirror, nerves attacking my belly. Tonight is big. Tonight I am in a world I'd dreamed of not just visiting, but embracing. And I'm there with Nick, who I'm suddenly eager to see. I fill my purse, and slip it over my shoulder before hurrying through the bedroom to the living area. I find Nick in a sharp black suit with a black tie.

His eyes light on me and he ends his call, the two of us walking toward each other, meeting at the back of the couch, a brown contemporary style that matches the two chairs framing it. Nick whistles as we grow near. My cheeks heat, while a smile touches my lips as I realize the dots in his tie are *evergreen.* I run my hand down it. "How did you know that I was going to pick this dress?"

"It matches your necklace perfectly."

"You chose it."

"I did."

"When and how?"

"I sent the shopper photos of your necklace and she sent me back options."

He just made the romantic surprise that was those dresses even more romantic and personal. "I love this dress."

"It's beautiful on you."

There's a knock at the door and he kisses me. "I'll get it."

"Who is it?"

"No idea," he says, leaving me to find out.

Curious, wondering what Nick is up to because this has to be Nick being Nick, and doing something unexpected and wonderful. I inch up a few feet to try and see who is at the door. It opens and I hear, "I have a delivery for Ms. Winter."

"From who?" Nick asks, wiping out the idea that that it's from him with the question.

"I'm sorry, sir. I don't know."

Nick opens the door to allow the bellman to enter and he's holding a giant bouquet of flowers and a box of some sort, but I think it's Godiva chocolates. My stomach clenches with the certainty this is a problem. The bellman sets the delivery on the coffee table, gives me a nod, and a "Good day, ma'am" before departing.

Nick joins me, his expression indiscernible. "You should read the card."

I wait until the door shuts behind the exiting bellman before responding. "It's going to be from Bill. He's laying it on thick now."

Nick rounds the couch and pulls the card from the bouquet, holding it up, an invitation in the action. Dreading what is to come, I join him and take it, tearing it open. And then cringe with what I read:

Faith,
Congratulations, baby. You did it.
See you tonight, FINALLY.
Macom

I hand Nick the card. He takes it and reads it.

"I'm sorry," I say.

He glances up at me. "For what? Godiva is good chocolate. Let's try some." He sits down and opens the box.

I blanch, confused by his reaction. He takes my hand and tugs, urging me to sit. "Chocolate, sweetheart. We missed lunch."

I ease onto the cushion and he sinks his teeth into a piece of chocolate. "Did you know that I have a weakness for chocolate?"

He holds a chocolate to my mouth. "Try this one."

I take a bite. "Well?" he prods.

"It's delicious," I say, and it is but the chocolate is not my focus right now. "You're not upset at all?"

He leans in and kisses me. "Sweetheart, if a box of chocolate and some flowers win you over, then you weren't ever mine to start with. But you *are* mine. He just doesn't know it yet."

There is a promise that he will capture me in those words that makes me nervous, but he pops another piece of chocolate in his mouth, stands up and takes me with him. "Let's go show off that dress and your art." And then he kisses me again, and when his tongue touches mine, the heady taste of sin, satisfaction, and chocolate overwhelms my senses. He overwhelms my senses and I forget to worry about anything and everyone else, Macom included.

But when we reach the elevator and step on the car, me in front of Nick, him holding me from behind, I remember the phone call they'd shared and the obvious realization I've ignored hits me. I turn to face him. "He just issued you a challenge, didn't he?"

Nick arches a brow. "Did he? Because you of all people know that I can't turn away from a challenge. And that could be very bad for him."

The elevator opens to the busy lobby and when I turn, I find myself facing the devil himself: Macom is standing with Josh a few feet away.

Chapter Thirty-Four

Faith

SEEING MACOM AGAIN PUNCHES ME IN THE CHEST, AND A world of dark, jagged emotions slash a path through me. A moment later, Nick's hand settles at my lower back, and all is right in my world, and not because I feel protected. Because he's here. Because he's Nick. That's all my mind has time to process before we're crossing to meet them, both men watching us approach, both in expensive suits. Josh in navy blue, his dark hair as perfectly trimmed as usual. Macom stands out in a tan suit among dark colors, his curly hair is a bit wild. The color choice expected, as is the disarray of his hair, I know that he believes to be sexy. He likes to be different, and I used to see that as artsy and unique. Today it reads as tasteless, as was him sending me those gifts, when I know Josh had to have told him I was with Nick. When both Nick and I had told him that

I was with Nick.

Josh leans in to speak to Macom, clearly telling him to leave. Macom quite obviously snaps back at him, most likely throwing around his power. Macom won't back down. Not here. This is his castle and he's king. He thinks that makes Nick a peasant, but he's wrong.

Nick and I arrive to stand in front of them, me directly in front of Macom. My gaze meets his, and the heat in Macom's stare is awkward and so blatant, so "I want to fuck you again" that there is no way Nick doesn't see it. I look to Josh, who smiles and winks. "Looking gorgeous, darling. We want people to know your work, but it doesn't hurt for them to remember you're as stunning as your work."

"Thank you, Josh."

"You've always been stunning, Faith," Macom dares.

Nick looks at him. "Macom, right?"

"Yes," he says. "Macom Maloy."

Nick arches a brow. "I believe I've heard the name, outside of what Faith has shared in graphic detail, of course. Up and coming, aren't you?"

"Up and coming?" Macom replies tightly. "Not many people call me up and coming."

"Ah well, they will, I'm sure. Hang in there. You'll be a Chris Merit in no time who is a big fan of Faith's by the way."

Macom's lips tighten. "So I hear."

"On another topic," Nick continues. "I should say thank you. Aside from the fact that you lost Faith, which led her to me, I love chocolate. Faith and I ate that shit up." He glances at me. "Didn't we, sweetheart?"

Considering Macom looked at me like he wanted to lift my skirt, clearly baiting Nick, I don't so much as miss a beat. I look from Nick to Macom. "Yes, thank you. The chocolate and the flowers were lovely. And it was unexpected considering our last communication."

Macom's lips twist wryly. "That was interesting, but something tells me this night will be as well." He glances at Josh. "I need you at the stage in forty-five minutes." And on that note, he leaves.

Josh exhales. "Holy hell. Let that be it. Awkward, fucked up, but done." He pins me in a look. "Head to the second level. That entire floor is the party. At eight o'clock there will be a ceremony, at which time they will announce the top new artists of the year. And I'd tell you that might be you, but I won't see your work until I walk up those stairs."

"It's displayed tonight?" I ask, suddenly anxious.

"Some of it. Each year, the show's top two executives pick the top three pieces for each artist. No one is allowed to see those picks in advance."

"Isn't Macom a part of the board in some way?" Nick asks.

"He is," Josh says, "but his role is more public show than anything. He didn't get a vote on entries and he didn't get a vote on the winner that will be announced tonight. He does most likely know the winner, as he's presenting the award. Which unfortunately, means it's not Faith. If it were, he'd have told me."

I didn't even know about the award. I didn't hope to win, but that announcement still cuts.

"Well, as far as I'm concerned, her accepting that award from him would be poetic justice for the way he put himself above her."

Josh declines to comment, which isn't a surprise, since Macom is his biggest client. "You're already a winner tonight," he says to me. "I need to handle a few things. Go upstairs. Drink. Eat. Revel in this night. In half an hour, I'm going to find you and you will come with me. We will meet some powerful people you need to know." He leaves.

Nick turns me toward the lobby, his arm around my shoulder. "You okay?"

"You loved the chocolate?"

"I'd love it better melted and on you, so I could lick it off. Let's decide that's going to happen sometime this weekend."

I laugh. "You're so damn bad, Nick Rogers."

"In case you didn't get the memo, I'm not a nice guy. You think Macom noticed?"

I laugh, and we're about to head up a winding set of stairs when a couple in their late fifties to early sixties, and in casual wear, steps in front of us. "Nick Rogers," the man says. "Holy hell. It is you."

"David," Nick says, shaking his hand before looking at the woman. "Elizabeth." His hand returns to my back. "This is Faith."

"Nice to meet you, Faith," they both murmur.

"What brings you to L.A.?" the man asks. "Playing shark, or what is it, Tiger?"

"Actually, Faith is a gifted artist that's in the L.A. Art Forum." Pride fills his voice and warms my heart. This man supports me. He loves me. Life is good and Macom is a blip on the screen.

"Oh my," Elizabeth says. "You're an artist, Faith? That's why we're here. We're going to the public event tomorrow. I can't wait to see your work. We love to discover new artists."

"Thank you," I say. "I'd love to have you view my work."

"And on that note," Nick says, "we have a party to celebrate her art tonight."

"Understood," David says. "But as a quick side note, we're actually considering taking our company public. We'd like to have you on board."

"That's a conversation for Monday. This weekend is about Faith."

"Of course it is," Elizabeth says. "We will see you tomorrow, Faith." She touches my arm. "Good luck."

And then they are gone and we are walking up the stairs. "Were they important?"

"He's worth about a billion dollars."

"Nick. You just blew him off."

"Tonight isn't about him. If he has a problem with that, fuck him."

"Nick Rogers," I say, giving his sleeve a tiny tug, that earns me the focus of those navy blue eyes.

"Yes, sweetheart?"

"I'm a little too crazy about you."

"Not yet," he says, giving me a wink that does funny things to my belly. "But we're getting there."

We reach the second level and the entire floor is literally the party, clusters of women in fancy dresses and men in sharp suits everywhere. Elegant multi-colored chandeliers dangle at random locations from above. Waiters work the crowd with drinks and there are tables filled with finger foods. "We still haven't eaten," Nick says. "Shall we grab a few snacks?"

"I'll drop it, spill it, and generally make a mess." I glance at him. "I need to know which three pieces they picked."

"I'd like to know, too," he says, motioning me toward a sign that leads to the display room while another, next to it, points to the ceremony's location.

We walk that way. "Why am I suddenly so nervous?"

"Because in your mind you know your top three picks," he says, as we reach the doorway, "and you're about to find out, if the judges agree." He halts us and turns me to face him. "Name your top three."

"You. An Eye for An Eye. An older piece I called Sonoma Sky. What do you think?"

"My picks as well."

"Do you know Sonoma Sky?"

"I studied, and admired it when we packaged it up. Let's go look." He starts to turn and I catch his arm.

"I want you to be there."

"Why, Faith?"

"Because that painting was the first one I painted for me in a very long time. And you're the first thing I've done for me in a very long time."

He reaches up and drags his knuckles down my cheek. "I'll show you how much that means to me later, *alone*." He motions to the door. "Let's go look."

I nod and we enter the room, people milling about displays, and of course, Macom's is the centerpiece. And maybe it's my nerves, but heads turn as we walk the crowd, seeming to land on Nick and then me. Which is quite possible since my heart is racing so fast that I can barely breathe. Finally, we reach my display and I step inside to find exactly what I'd hoped for: Nick, An Eye for an Eye, and Sonoma Sky. Nick's hand settles at my back. "How do you feel?"

I glance up at him. "Validated."

"Good. You need that. You lack confidence you need to find. I should buy the one of me."

"If you buy it, then it looks like I can't sell it. I'm still inspired. I'll be painting you again."

"Is that right?" he asks, heat in his eyes.

"Oh yes. And I'll know every piece of your story, before you tell me your story."

Something flickers in his expression that I can't name, there and then gone, but before I can ask him about it, Josh suddenly appears, standing beside us, and cursing under his breath. "Holy hell. Who painted these?"

I face him. "You hate them."

"I fucking love them. They aren't you."

"They are me. The real me."

"Interesting." He glances over my head at Nick and then back to me. "Come. Let's go meet important people. Alone."

I turn to Nick and his hand settles at my hip. "I'm fine, sweetheart. This is about you, not me."

"I know, but—"

"Go. Meet people."

"What are you doing to do?"

"Drink insanely expensive whiskey, watch people, and find us a spot in the ceremony room."

Josh steps to my side. "Time is ticking."

I push to my toes and kiss Nick. He cups my head and kisses me again, this time with a sexy slide of tongue. We share a smile and I join Josh, who looks more than a little irritated, but any thought that he might voice that irritation is quickly side-tracked. Almost instantly, within a few steps, we're intercepted by one of the show's sponsors who wants me to meet another sponsor out on the party floor. It snowballs from there, though not many of the meetings feel important. I search for Nick, and occasionally find him in the crowd, sharing a small smile with him.

This continues for a full hour before Josh points at a small standing table that is now free. "Let's talk," he says, as we claim our spots across from each other, his fingers thrumming on the wooden table. "I hate to do this here, but it's important, since the rest of the weekend will be open to the public. And it's clearly a challenge to get you away from Nick 'fucking' Rogers."

"Nick 'fucking' Rogers is supportive of me and you. He rented the bungalow in the hotel with the thought that you could invite clients for a private party this weekend."

He ignores the offer. "You painted *him*."

"Yes. And obviously it was a good decision. Every person we met mentioned that painting."

"The painting is good, but as your agent, I see a habit."

"Habit?"

"Things become bigger than your art. Macom. The winery. Nick."

"You and Macom made him bigger than me."

"That's not true," Josh says. "He was my client before you. I was trapped in your own submission to him. And now it's happening with Nick. You didn't want to leave him to meet people."

"He's my guest and inspired me to paint again. He helped me get a grip on the winery."

"And there it is. I told you. He fucks you and uses you. He wants the winery."

"He does not want the winery."

"Make sure before it becomes a devastating realization that shoves you into a corner again. Because we're going to get offers. I don't want either of us to look like fools. Better yet, sell the damn winery, Faith. It's a distraction. You've made eighty thousand dollars in two weeks. More will follow."

"The winery isn't a distraction," I say, though those words might be a bit half-hearted. "Additionally," I add. "I moved to San Francisco and I'm working at the Allure Gallery, with Chris and Sara Merit. The pay and the opportunity are both great."

"Why am I just now finding this out?"

"You knew I was part of the gallery opening."

"Why am I just now finding this out?" he repeats.

"I don't want Chris used to move my career ahead," I say,

only now admitting that very real concern. "Chris and Sara are my friends. Promise me."

"I'll talk to Chris—"

"No. No, you will not. Promise me."

His lips tighten. "I promise." He is silent for several beats before he says, "We're friends. I care about your success. Come to L.A. in a couple of weeks. *Alone.* Let's do some career planning."

Nick's warnings ring in my head, driven home by the way he's kept me far away from him tonight. "Are we too personal, Josh?"

"I care. Most people want an agent that cares."

"But are you too personally involved with me?"

"We're friends."

"Macom is your friend."

"You are too, Faith. And I'm the best damn agent out there. You need me. I deserve you. I've ridden the highs and lows with you. You don't get to leave when you have some success or when I push too hard. We're a team. Agreed?"

He's right. He has stuck it out with me. "Yes. But you need to know that I have moved in with Nick. He's not going away, so please treat him accordingly."

"You moved in with him," he states flatly.

"Yes. Please treat him—"

"Understood," he says, glancing at his watch. "We need to get into the ceremony."

"I am going to go freshen up," I say, not about to let him come up with a reason to separate me from Nick for the ceremony. "I'll see you inside."

He studies me several beats. "Are we okay?"

"Yes. Of course."

He gives a short incline of his head. "You need to be seated in ten minutes." He leaves then and I turn to find a bathroom, and run smack into a hard body, big hands catching my waist. The musky scent of familiar cologne washes over me even before my gaze lifts, and I find myself looking into Macom's green eyes.

Chapter Thirty-Five

Faith

I PUSH AWAY FROM MACOM, BUT HE TIGHTENS HIS GRIP ON my waist. "We need to talk. Let's set a time and place."

"Let go of me, Macom, or I will *make* you let go of me."

"When the ceremony is over. I'm in room—"

"You need to be on stage," Josh says, suddenly by my side. "They're looking for you."

Macom's eyes meet Josh's, anger crackling in their depths. "Now?"

"Now," Josh confirms firmly.

His jaw tenses and he looks down at me. "10:10. After the show." He releases me and fades into the crowd.

I turn to Josh. "Thank you."

"I told him not to pull this shit, but look, Faith. For what it's worth, he talked to me last night. He was torn up. He has regrets. He feels like a shit. He seems to just need to apologize in person and if you don't want him, he'll accept it."

"He doesn't want to apologize. He wants to make me another conquest."

"All I can tell you is my take, and I don't see it that way. But moving on. I'll see you inside." He steps away from me and there is a ceremony announcement. The crowd immediately starts moving and I end up in the crunch of bodies, a sardine in a can, as we slowly ease toward the door. Impatient, I slip my purse across my chest, and then try to find a hole to break free.

More aggressive actions work, and I push through the bustle of people with a good amount of speed. The bodies bottleneck near the door though, and I'm stuck, unable to proceed forward. That's when a hand comes down on my arm and suddenly I'm folded into Nick's arms. "Hey there, sweetheart."

I smile with the realization we're just inside the ceremony room, against the wall and out of the rush. "You saved me again."

"I'll always save you, but I think you know that by now."

"I had a Macom encounter."

"And?"

"I ran into him, literally. He took that opportunity to corner me. Josh intervened and Macom backed off. But I don't think me avoiding him is going to work. I need to just handle him, once and for all."

"How?"

"I need to get through this ceremony and then figure it out. Let's sit at the back so we can escape when it's over."

"You sure you want to do that?"

"Oh yes. I've met everyone and anyone, and that's an entirely different story."

There's another announcement. "Please take your seats

now," someone says over the intercom.

Nick drapes his arm around my shoulder and we quickly scan the rows of seats facing the stage, before locating, and claiming back row seats. Not more than a minute later, one of the event founders that I'd met earlier steps to center stage and begins to speak without wasting time on fluff. She gets right to the point of the event: The artists. A big screen is lowered and it starts rotating with images of this year's artistic participants, as well as the top three picks for each that were on display tonight. The name "Winter" places me at the end of that line up, and when they read out An Eye for an Eye, I cringe with the certainty that it will garner Macom's attention. Nick knows, too. His fingers flex on my leg where his hand rests. But soon, the moment is muted as the speaker launches into an anecdote about the first event held by the organization fifteen years ago.

Finally, it's time for the award to be announced, which means Nick and I can escape, and the real experience, the show, will be only hours away. Macom steps to the podium to announce the winner, thankfully a really long way from myself and Nick. "Each year one blossoming talent is picked from the show's participants," he says. "Tonight is no exception. Tonight I will announce one shining star that will be featured at tomorrow's show at the entryway as all visitors enter the showroom. In the past, we've named such artists as Mallery Michaels, Kat Martin, and Newman Wright. Famous names I know you all recognize. If you're lucky, you own one of their creations. And so tonight, in the tradition of greats, I will announce a new great. I have to tell you, this one is special. I'm close to this person. She has always been a shining star in my eyes."

I suck in air at the "she." Nick leans in even before my name is even called and says, "Poetic justice, sweetheart."

"This year's winner," Macom says dramatically, "is Faith

Winter. Faith, come to the front, please."

Shock rolls through me. "This can't be happening," I whisper, applause clamoring around me.

"It is happening, sweetheart," Nick says. "Go accept your award."

"I'm trembling," I say. "Nick, I'm trembling hard."

"I got you, sweetheart," he says, standing up and taking me with him, guiding me to the center row, which from the back, now looks incredibly long for someone as unsteady as I am right now. Nick seems to know this, hitching my hand to his elbow before taking a step, walking that one, and every one that follows with me. "Deep breath," he murmurs softly.

I nod, and draw in air, holding it before I let it out, while my mind focuses on one coherent thought: *My dream of a career as an artist is becoming real.* I repeat this thought about ten times before we reach the stage. "Congrats, sweetheart," Nick says, as a man in a suit offers me his arm and helps me up the stairs.

In five steps, I am on the stage and completely unprepared for a speech. I'm most certainly unprepared for Macom's greeting, which includes pulling me into a hug. "It was fate that I presented this award," he murmurs in my ear. "We're going to celebrate tonight." He releases me and I'm too overwhelmed right now to do anything but dismiss him immediately and step to the microphone.

Suddenly, lights are shining on me and unknown faces are looking up at me. Seconds tick by before I realize this is where I need to speak. "Hi everyone." Audience voices reply, and smiles abound, which eases my nerves. "To say that I am stunned and appreciative would be a gross understatement," I continue. "It seems I almost forgot how to walk while trying to get to the stage. Which brings me to the person who helped me make that walk and who not only encourages me daily, but inspired one of the paintings on display tonight." I search for Nick and find him at the edge of the stage. "Thank you, Nick. I know that I would not be here without you. And I know you would tell me that I would have found my way no matter what. But it's a better journey with you." He presses two fingers to his lips and then does a little motion toward me before I refocus on the audience. "Thank you specifically as well, to those who saw my entries, and then my work, and offered me this amazing recognition and opportunity. I hope everyone enjoys the show tomorrow."

I step away from the microphone to the clamor of more applause and I fully intend to join Nick at the bottom of the stage, but the man who'd helped me up the stairs stops me. "We need you for a photo op backstage."

I'm then ushered away, and I try to turn to find Nick, but the lights are in my eyes. The next thing I know, Macom is at my elbow and cameras are flashing around us. "Congrats, baby," Macom says, as we shove through a curtain.

I'd tell him not to call me baby, but I have no idea who the other man at my opposite elbow is, and I'm swarmed by people before I can reply anyway. Cameras flash at close range and I'm hurried to stand in front of a photo backdrop. I'm also holding a statue that is a paintbrush and palette that I'm pretty sure I was given on stage, and the fact that I don't remember getting it is a testament to just how consumed by nerves I am.

Suddenly, Macom is sent back to my side for additional photos, along with a show sponsor, both instructed to stand beside me. Both place their hands at my back, but Macom's is low, too low for comfort. I don't want to seem as if I can't support the organization when my ex is involved and I try to be savvy in my avoidance. The minute the shot is done, I step to the opposite side of the sponsor, placing him in the center. And this kind of push and pull with Macom continues until I can take no more.

"Excuse me, please," I say to a man who seems to be in charge. "I need to attend a meeting. Thank you for everything." I hold up my statue. "Really. Thank you." I dash toward an exit sign, and I don't stop. I close the space between me and it, and push the bar on the door beneath it. On the other side, I find myself in some sort of narrow hallway that renders me trapped if Macom tried to follow. Wanting out of this maze, I head down the path, and I'm close to an archway leading to another room when a door opens in front of me and Macom steps in my path.

I start to back up, but he's fast and already he's in front of me, his fists on the wall on either side of me, caging me. And with the statue in my hand, I'm at a disadvantage that reaches beyond his size versus mine. "Please move," I say, not because I want to be civil, but because I know him. If I set him off, this gets worse.

"Baby, please talk to me. Don't put me through seeing you with that man for another minute. I saw the painting. I know what it means. I hurt you. I get it. But you've punished me."

"That painting wasn't about you, but me. *Step aside*, Macom."

"It killed me to hear you thank him tonight. It's you and me. It's always been *you and me*."

"There is no you and me."

"I'll be more supportive in all things, your art especially. Whatever he's doing to help you at the winery, I'll do ten times as much."

I laugh without humor. "Priceless. Josh took all of thirty minutes to run his mouth to you. And you can't do ten times what Nick does because Nick is a hundred times richer than you. *Move.*"

"Faith—"

"Move or I will put a knee in your groin so hard that your

balls will retract and disappear."

He reaches for my face and leans in, intending to kiss me, and I don't hesitate. I raise my knee and I don't hold back. He grunts and doubles over. "Fuck, Faith. You fucking bitch." He sucks in air and straightens, leaning close again, his breath warm on my cheek. "You will pay for that. You will not get into another gallery in L.A., ever." He turns away from me and starts walking, or rather hobbling in obvious pain.

I sink against the wall, aware that I've provoked the vicious monster I was trying not to provoke right up until the moment I stuck my knee in his balls. But I also know him well enough to know that he's gone. He's not coming back.

"What the fuck," he growls and I look right to discover Nick is standing under the archway, his shoulder pressed against the wooden frame. "Move out of my way," Macom orders, trapped the way I was just trapped.

"Here's the thing, *Macom*," Nick says. "No. Not until I'm ready."

"You don't want to fuck with me."

"I have compromising *naked* photos of you," Nick says. "I have IRS documents, bank records, and the list continues, all of which have your name on them. And if you don't believe that I will use those things fifty ways to Sunday, you haven't re-searched me the way I have researched you. Touch Faith or her career again, and I *will* come for you."

They stare at each other for all of two beats, before Nick steps aside and Macom quickly leaves. I walk to Nick and he im-mediately folds me into his arms. "How long were you there?"

"The entire time," he says. "And I let you handle him as you wanted to handle him, certain that he'd give me a reason to punch him. But then you went off and retracted his balls before I got the chance."

I laugh. "I can't believe I said that." I cringe. "I can't believe I told him that you're a hundred times richer than him."

"Why? I am." He softens his voice. "You okay, sweetheart?"

"Yes. I am. Really okay, actually. And ready to go upstairs."

He slides his arm around my shoulder and we start walking through what looks like an empty banquet room. Thankfully we make it to the elevator without being stopped, and we wait on a car. The doors open quickly and Josh steps out. "Faith. Holy hell. I've been looking for you. You rocked it tonight."

"You're fired," I say.

He blanches. "What?"

"You told Macom about our conversation. We're done. I won't change my mind."

Nick catches the door as it tries to shut, and I step around Josh. Nick and I enter the car and when we face forward, Josh has turned and is staring into the car. Nick punches in the code to our floor and the doors shut us inside. "That was unexpected," Nick says.

"But necessary. I'll deal with a new agent hunt next week."

I rotate to face the window, the stars and city lights flickering in the night sky. Nick steps behind me, holding me close. "I thought you didn't like heights."

"I changed my mind," I say. "I'm not going to be afraid of anything."

And as Nick murmurs, "Congratulations, Faith," I feel as if the past is now behind me, and a new beginning, before me. Everything that was once wrong is now right.

Chapter Thirty-Six

Faith

THE MORNING OF THE SHOW, I'M NERVOUS. BY AFTERNOON, I'm so high, I'm flying. Macom and Josh stay away from us and the interest in my work, and invitations to events, overflow. And Nick and I have so much fun together. Sometime around lunch we hear that the apartment is ours, and Nick takes me to an incredible restaurant to celebrate it all. On Sunday morning, we have breakfast in our room and I gift my flowers to the maid. Nick refuses to give up the chocolates and we proceed to eat most of them on the plane home.

Come Monday morning, Nick is scheduled to begin the negotiations on a merger that he warns me will make for an intense few weeks. He leaves the house wearing one of his sharpest suits, and a dark, cutting edge that says he's already in battle mode. I am feeling rather fancy today and since a dress doesn't make much sense for a pre-opening at the gallery, I trade in my jeans for dress pants, boots, and a soft, pink V-neck sweater that pairs with the classical flagship Chanel purse that had been in the items Nick bought me over the weekend.

I arrive at Allure with a smile on my face and a stack of cards in my pocket. I settle behind my desk to find a random list of things Sara needs to accomplish before the gallery opening, and a formal offer of employment.

Oh yes, I think. Life is good.

Sara appears in the doorway, looking adorable in jeans and Keds. "Well?" she asks, claiming the visitor's chair in front of my desk. "How was the show?"

"Amazing. The Forum picks one up-and-comer to watch every year and they chose me."

"Oh my God. Woohoo! I'm so excited for you. You said nothing of this when you sent me photos this weekend."

"It just didn't feel real," I say. "It's a big surreal."

"Of course it is. Are you still riding the high?"

"In a big way and even after I fired my agent."

"You fired your agent?"

"Yes. And it was past due. He's my ex's agent and it just got sticky." I set the stack of cards on my desk. "And I have all these people wanting to buy work or book me for events. I'm going to start a hunt today."

"Let Chris help."

"No. No, I don't want to intrude or seem like I'm using you, or him, for my own benefit."

"I'll call my agent," Chris says, appearing in the doorway in a brown Harley shirt, after clearly hearing our conversation. "If he can't take you on, he'll help you find the right match."

"You don't have to do that," I say quickly.

"Why the hell not?" he asks. "You wouldn't be here if we

didn't believe in you."

Sara twists around in her chair to look at him. "She won the Forum's up-and-comer award."

"Not a surprise to me at all," Chris says, pulling his phone from the pocket of his jeans and punching in a number. "Gabe," he says. "Yeah, man. I have a new artist for you. I'm behind her. We're trying to convince her to work here at Allure with us. She's helping us launch and she's on display here. Yes. Call her here."

Sara holds up a hand and when Chris offers her his attention, she points to the stack of cards. "All offers she needs managed."

Chris gives an incline of his chin. "She comes with offers from an event she just did. A stack of them she needs managed." He listens a moment. "I'll tell her." Chris ends the call. "He's headed into a meeting. He's going to call you this afternoon, but he's on board."

"That's incredible of you," I say. "Thank you. I...hate to seem unappreciative but I've been through Macom being Josh's star. I don't want Gabe to sign me because of you."

"A valid concern," Chris says, "but that's not Gabe's style. He's got a mind of his own and balls the size of Texas. You'll like his balls, I promise."

We all laugh and Chris glances at his watch. "I need to head to a meeting." Sara pushes to her feet and hurries to Chris, kissing him, before he departs. I smile because, I have a lot to smile about, and I sign the offer letter. And when Sara turns to face me again, I hold it up. "I'll get to work on your things-to-do list, boss."

Now Sara is smiling. "You're staying."

"Yes. And I'm thrilled to be here."

We chat a few minutes, and she leaves me to my work. About an hour later, I receive a call from Gabe. Fifteen minutes later, I send him samples of my work. Another fifteen minutes later, and I have a new agent. I'm dying to call Nick, but he's in those intense negotiations. I could text, but that is a distraction he doesn't need as well. Sara and I celebrate by walking to the coffee shop, and we return with white mochas and chocolate chip bagels. Nick sends me a text at noon: *Hell here. I'm going to be silent and late tonight. You okay?*

My reply is simple: *I'm great. You focus on your negotiations.*

He doesn't respond which tells me hell is real for him right now. I consider all the ways I can ease the stress when he gets home tonight.

Home.

Our home.

I revel in those words.

It's nearly six and Sara has just left the gallery. I'm finishing some paperwork before I leave as well. I file away the documents I've just finished before I reach for my purse, when my phone buzzes with a text. I glance at the message to find Bill is the sender.

I need to speak to you urgently. I'm at the coffee shop next door.

My heart starts to thunder in my chest. He's here? I text him back: *What coffee shop?*

Rebecca's, he replies.

How does he know I work here? Did I tell him? Did Kasey?

My fingers hover over the call button for Nick, but I think better. I dial Rita. "How busy is he?"

"At the moment, he has ten people sitting at a conference table and they all want to kill each other."

"All right then," I say, and because I don't want to freak her out and have her freak him out, I add, "now is not the time to talk dinner."

She laughs. "No. Not right now. He could be a while. Or not. Sometime these things end abruptly."

"Okay. Thanks, Rita."

"Congrats on your show, Faith. Nick came in this morning bragging up a storm."

"He did?"

"Yes. He did. He's incredibly proud of you."

"Thanks, Rita. He says it to me but it's pretty special to hear it from other people."

My phone buzzes again. "Talk to you soon," I say, and end the call to read the new message: *It's an emergency, Faith.*

He's going to press me about the winery. I know it. And I'd decline the meeting if I wasn't afraid he'd go after the winery in some way again, and hurt the employees. Or Nick. He could go after Nick, and while Nick can take care of himself, he doesn't need to fight a war I create, when he has his own he's fighting right now, in this moment.

I stand up and slip my purse over my shoulder, dread in my belly, but I can do this. I'll navigate whatever he throws at me, milk him for information and missteps, and then hand it to Nick. Ready to get this over with, I hurry through the gallery, lock the doors, and make the quick walk to the coffee shop. I step inside and wave to the regular girl, June, behind the counter before my gaze lands on Bill sitting in a booth.

I cross the space between us and sit down. "What's the emergency?"

"Look, honey. You're the closest thing to a daughter I have. I know you don't believe I care, but I do. And it killed me to be shut off from you."

"And yet you slept with my mother."

"That's a complicated story that I still believe is not my story to tell. But I need you to set that aside, just for now. Because I need to tell you a story that ends right back here, in the present, with you."

"I'm listening."

"I heard rumors that you were struggling to pay the bills and I called the bank. They told me you bought out the note."

"I did buy it out."

"You mean Nick Rogers bought it out. He's an owner now, right?"

"Emergency," I say. "You said there was an emergency."

"We need to go back in time. Way back. Your mother had a gambling problem and they were in a lot of debt. You father contained it the best that he could. Back before he and I had our falling out. Some men came to him. They offered him a hundred million to sell out."

I blanch. "A hundred million? Why so much?"

"They were bad men *and* there's mercury on the property, a fact that I had buried way back then. No one else knew."

"Mercury? I assume it's valuable, then."

"It's used for weapons and these men were the kind of men who knew all about weapons."

"How do you know this?"

"Your father came to me in dire straits because they're also the kind of men that don't take no for an answer. They'll pay you, but you take what they offer."

"But they did take no for answer."

"Only because I hired an ex-CIA agent to help us. He tipped off the right people and they handled it."

My brow furrows. "Why would they pay my father at all if they were that bad?"

"They couldn't just take it without question, not with the

way your father loved that place. And they knew that. They ran everything through a legit investment operation and the truth is, that mercury might not be worth much to you and me, but to them it would net billions."

"Obviously there's more," I say, not liking where this emergency is leading.

"Your mother started gambling again when your father died and this time she went off the deep end. She came to me for money. I helped her and tried to get her into rehab, but she pushed back. She wanted to sell. She wanted to find the men who wanted the mercury."

"Oh no."

"I'm afraid so. She told me you wouldn't sell and that I had to find a way to get around you having to sign off on the deal, and that if I did, she'd split the profits. I won't lie to you. Your father and I had disagreements, but I agreed with him on the mercury. Selling to those people would be blood on his hands he didn't want, and neither do I. I told your mother I'd look into pushing you out of the deal, but eventually told her there was no way around it. I urged her to go to you and confess the gambling issues. I told her I'd even buy the winery and give you both a profit."

"She said no."

"She said no and I told her I was going to you. That's when she showed me a video of the two of us together and threatened to take it to my wife. I was out then, but I kept tabs on things, waiting to see if you needed me. And that brings me to where this is headed. I knew when you sued her for the property and I wanted you to win. I would have offered to fund your legal fees, but you hated me and wouldn't even speak to me, and if your mother found out, I was at risk with my wife."

"Why would my father want me to inherit the winery if it

put me in danger?"

"This was ten years ago, Faith. I buried the mercury. The CIA buried the mercury. And you were not going to sell, which means no one who wants the mercury could get it."

"I still don't see where this is going. What is the emergency? Are those men back? Did my mother contact them?"

"If those men are back on the radar, they're working smarter this time."

My heart starts to race. "What do you know? Just tell me."

"I followed the legal case between you and your mother. I know who your attorney was and I know who her attorney was."

"And?"

He sets a folder in front of me. "Look inside."

I flip it open and I'm staring at a birth certificate for a Nick Marks. Mother: Melanie Marks. Father: Nathan Marks. The attorney who represented my mother. My heart is now skipping beats. I flip the document to find a court document changing the name of Nick Marks to Nick Rogers.

I swallow and I almost choke. I can't catch my breath. I can't breathe. "I need to go," I say, but he catches my arm.

"Easy, honey. Let me help you."

"No. No. I—"

"Listen to me," he says firmly. "If he's involved with the mercury hunters, this is bad news. We need to come up with a plan together."

"I need *to go*," I say, pulling away from him. "I'll call you. I just...not now." I all but run for the door, and barely remember the moment I get in the car. Nick's car. Oh God. My entire life is wrapped around a man conning me. So many things don't add up, but the bottom line is that Nick is Nathan Mark's son. He never told me that. I start the engine and I don't even know where I'm headed. I end up parked in the parking lot of the high rise that is supposed to be our new home.

I sit there thirty seconds, or maybe thirty minutes. I have no concept of time. My phone rings and I reach for it, my hand shaking as I find Nick calling. I answer it.

"Hey sweetheart," he says.

His voice, rich and masculine and beautiful and deceitful tears holes in my heart. "I know," I say.

"What?"

"Nick Marks. I know who you are."

Chapter Thirty-Seven

Nick

NICK MARKS.

That name is a blade in my heart. The connection to my father that brought me to Faith. It's also the connection I've always known could rip her out of my reach. "Faith, sweetheart—"

"Don't speak," she orders, her voice breathless. "It won't help you. And it just hurts me."

"I don't want to hurt you. I would never hurt you."

"And yet you did."

"Where are you? I'll come to you and explain."

"You made me trust again and now you made sure that I will never trust anyone again."

Rita and North walk into my office. "Get the fuck out," I snap.

Rita's eyes go wide and North is already tucking tail and running. Rita backs out and shuts the door. "Where are you?"

"Was it the mercury? Were you after a big payoff? Of course you were. Money loves money."

"What mercury? Faith, talk to me."

"So you can lie again. And again. And again."

"We have to talk. *Where* are you?"

"I don't want to see you, Nick. Not now or ever."

"I love you, Faith. I love you so much it hurts."

"Liar," she says, her voice quaking.

"Faith—"

"Don't find me. Don't call me. And let me be clear. If you show up at my work, at the winery, at my home, I will call the police. Don't test me. You think you're a badass, but liars aren't badasses. They're just bad people. I left your BMW in the parking lot of your new apartment."

She ends the call. I try to call her back and it goes directly to voice mail. "Fuck." I call again. And again. "Fuck. Fuck. Fuck." I face the window and press my hand on the glass, my head tilted downwards. "Fuck. I cannot lose her."

I straighten and dial Beck. "Mercury. This is about mercury. I don't know how or any details except that. Connect the fucking dots. I need answers. And hack the autopsy report. I need that now, too."

"Faith knows."

"Yes, she fucking knows."

"Then Bill is behind this. He showed up near her office and I couldn't get through to you to tell you."

"So he told her who I am and that there is mercury on the property."

"He made her believe you want the property for the mercury."

"Obviously. He turned his intentions into mine and my damn lie allowed it to happen. Where is she now?"

"She went to Sara and Chris Merit's apartment."

"Of course. The one place I can't get to her at and she knows it." I scrub my jaw. "At least she's safe. Get me answers. I can't go to her and make my case without answers."

"I hack that report daily. It hasn't been input yet."

"You have mercury now. Connect the dots."

"If he believed that connected the dots, he wouldn't have given it to her."

"Connect the fucking dots." I hang up and dial Abel.

"Hey hoe, what the fuck is up?"

"I don't care whose house you have to go to, or what you have to do, but you get me those autopsy reports."

"She knows."

"Yes. She knows. Get me the reports." I hang up.

My phone rings and it's Chris Merit. "What the hell did you do, man?"

"It's not what it seems and I'm not going to explain that to you. All I will say is that I love her. I love her the way you love Sara. I ordered her a ring. I bought an apartment to customize a studio for her."

"Well, I'm not an advice kind of guy, and she's not saying anything other than you betrayed her in an unforgivable way."

"I didn't cheat. I knew who she was before I met her and didn't tell her. At the time I didn't plan on fucking her, let alone falling in love with her. And that's all I'm saying."

"Fair enough. What's your move?"

"What I want to do is pick her up, tie her to my bed, and make her stay until she listens."

"You do that and you had better have a way to justify lying to her because this cuts deep. She's not good, Nick. You hurt her.

You hurt her bad."

"I know. And that guts me."

"Get your ducks in a row and give her some time to process."

"Right. Time. A barbaric form of torture."

We end the call and I say "fuck you" to time and waiting. I text Faith: *Your uncle set me up. It's not what it seems. I love you. I want to marry you, Faith. Please talk to me.*

I get an error message. She's blocked me.

Chapter Thirty-Eight

Faith

The first night without Nick...

I LAY IN CHRIS AND SARA'S SPARE BEDROOM, STARING AT the ceiling, an invisible knife carving holes in my heart. I replay the conversation I had with Bill, and the implications. And then I replay the conversation with Nick, how sincere he sounded. God. I'm a fool. And he's such a good liar. Everything he did felt real. We felt real.

I have no place to live. I need an apartment and clothes. I have no clothes. I don't have a car. At Nick's recommendation, I gave both of the cars to Kasey. Nick made me dependent on our life together. I roll to my side and tell myself not to cry. He's not worth it. I don't cry. I won't cry for him. But somehow my cheeks are wet.

The first Monday and my first morning without Nick...

I wake up to coffee and Chris and Sara. Watching them together is both beautiful and salt in an open wound. An hour later, I arrive at Allure with Sara and wearing Sara's jeans, my own boots, and her Allure t-shirt. We have interviews today for several staff members, and that means no time for self-pity. I dive in and get to work. By mid-morning, my new agent has sold every piece I had in the L.A. Forum for thirty thousand apiece. Even the painting of Nick, which kind of guts me, but it's probably for the best. I have this instinctive urge to call and tell Nick, and that guts me. And so I don't tell anyone, not even Sara. I refocus on what's important. I have a great agent, a great job, and money, which is suddenly important, since I need new everything. It's a relief. I call a realtor.

Come lunchtime, we've hired a receptionist to start on Monday and I already have two apartments to look at after work. At nearly four, Sara pokes her head into my office. "Delivery," Sara says, setting a large envelope on my desk.

I stare at the handwriting on the front that is clearly Nick's, and let out a breath. "Thank you." I look up at her. "I'm looking at apartments tonight and going to buy some clothes."

"Don't feel rushed. I have clothes and we have the space."

"I know you mean that, but I think I'm going to rent a hotel room until I find a place."

"That's not necessary. You know that."

"I do. I really do but honestly, you and Chris are so damn wonderful together, I can't take it. That sounds horrible. I'm sorry."

"It sounds honest. Do you want me to go shopping with you?"

"No. Last night I needed you badly and you were there for

me and I can't thank you enough. Tonight, I need to be alone."

"I can fully understand that, but if you change your mind, our door is open."

"Thank you."

She disappears in the hallway, and I stare at that envelope, my throat constricting. I throw it in the trash. I pull it back out. I throw it in the trash. Damn it, I pull it out and open it. Inside I find my favorite paintbrush with a note.

Faith:

I came to you looking for answers to questions I didn't even know I needed to ask. I found those answers in you. Paint me. You'll get your answers too because there is only one answer: Us.

I'm coming for you and I'm doing it with proof that I don't want anything but you.

I love you,

Nick

I read that note over and over: *I'm coming for you.* And he will, and I'm going to send him away, no matter how much I hurt all over again.

My first Tuesday without Nick...

I wake in a hotel room and order room service. When my coffee and omelet arrive, I eat it alone. Alone is safe. I forgot that. I won't forget again.

Bill tries to call me about a dozen times. I ignore him. It's probably not fair, but I feel angry at him for telling me what I needed to hear.

My first Wednesday without Nick...

I don't order room service, but I walk to work and stop in at

Rebecca's and get coffee. I carry it with me to my desk at Allure. I drink it.

Alone.

I end the day with a text from Josh. He's wiring me my twenty thousand dollars minus his fee. I don't reply. Bill calls me. I don't reply. When he sends me a text, I *do* reply: *I need time.*

I say nothing more.

My first Thursday without Nick....

I have settled into my hotel, bought a frugal wardrobe and found an apartment a few blocks from the gallery that has an upstairs perfect for a studio. It's an expensive rental, but I need a space that I can make mine.

I'm about to leave for the day, when I get a strange phone call. "Faith Winter?"

"Yes."

"Names Ned. I'm your broker."

"I don't have a broker."

"You do. You invested sixty thousand in a hot stock. I want to cash you out."

"Nick did this, didn't he?"

"Yes. He did. Good fucking news for you, too. You're up a hundred and fifty thousand but you need to get out while you're on top. Do it?"

I'm stunned. Blown away. Confused.

"Do it? Snap. Snap. This is time sensitive."

"Yes. And send the money to Nick."

"Can't do that. He put it in your name. You have to send it to him yourself. Gotta go. Toodaloo and all that shit." He hangs up.

My first Friday without Nick…

I start the day feeling Nick's silence. I don't want to feel it, but I do. I comfort myself by putting the down payment on my apartment, but by evening the idea of a weekend alone is pretty much gutting me. I need things to fill my apartment. And when Bill calls, I answer. I agree that we need to meet. And I decide to rent a car and head to Sonoma for the weekend, talk to him, check on my house, the winery, Kasey, and gather some of the leftover personal stuff I still have there.

Because being alone is not better, even if it is safer.

Chapter Thirty-Nine

Nick

My first night without Faith...

Hell.

My second night without Faith...

Hell.

Every night without Faith...

Hell.
If she's going to Sonoma, so am I.

The minute I hear Faith has rented a car, I know she's driving to Sonoma. And I don't want her there with Bill. I don't want her there, or anywhere, without me. And I'm done waiting on the autopsy report and answers. All fucking week I've waited without Faith. And so, I hit the road in the BMW, for Sonoma, with a ring in my pocket and my heart shamelessly on my sleeve.

Because being alone is fine, as long as long as being alone is with Faith. Otherwise, *alone is hell.*

Chapter Forty

Faith

MY NEW LANDLORD CALLS ABOUT THE TIME I AM ON the road to Sonoma, confirming I can move in next weekend. I tell her how excited I am and I try to sound convincing, but reality is setting in. I'm leaving Nick behind. I use my Siri feature to call Kasey.

"Hey, Faith," he answers. "Good to hear from you, stranger. I guess you meant it when you said you were going to let me run the show."

"I did. I do. I am coming into town just to get some of my things this weekend. You want to have dinner?"

"Of course. When?"

"Saturday night?"

"Perfect. I'll come to you after we close up."

I have Siri dial Bill next. "Faith. Are you on your way here?"

"I am. I think I'm ready to talk. How about coffee tomorrow morning?"

"That works. When and where?"

"Do you just want to come by the house? I'm afraid I might get emotional about my parents and I really don't want to be around people if that happens."

"Eight?"

"Eight."

"And I understand you getting emotional, but we'll get through this."

"Thanks," I breathe out and when I hang up, I'm pretty sure I've misjudged him for a really long time.

I reach for the radio, but it starts to rain and I listen to the thrum of droplets on the windows. I love the rain but tonight, it feels like I'm in an empty hole. *Alone.*

And it doesn't ease up. In fact, the rain is heavier, and the night pitch dark when I pull up to my house, and I am hollow inside except for a stabbing pain. I don't belong here anymore. I don't know why I wanted to come here. I almost turn around and leave, but I set up meetings. And I have random things in there. And I really need things that feel familiar.

I walk up the steps, key in my security code, miraculously getting it right the first time, and enter the house.

The rain is making me crazy. It taunts me. It repeats Faith's words: *Liar. You hurt me. You made sure I will never trust again.*

I dial Beck, desperate for anything I can share with Faith. "I'm going to see her. Your time is up."

"I'm onto something," he says. "One of my CIA contacts has a ping on that mercury, and flag boy got a hit. There's a connection there."

"Where is he now?"

"Hanging out in a cabin on the outskirts of Sonoma. He tells locals he is having a Zen retreat."

"The autopsy report."

"Nothing yet but I'm working on it. I'll be in touch." He hangs up.

Fifteen minutes later, in an absolute downpour, with adrenaline surging through me, I pull into the driveway of Faith's house. Our house. I'm going to fix us. I park behind her car, and shrug out of my jacket and tie. The rain doesn't ease up and I toss them in the back seat, and just say screw it. I exit the car and take off running, stomping a path up the stairs, and I am literally so drenched I might as well have stood in the shower. But I'm here. She's here.

I ring the doorbell and nothing happens. I ring it over and over, and then start pounding on the door. "Faith! I know you're here. Talk to me. Faith!" Still nothing. I stomp back down the stairs and into the rain, the real storm raging inside me. I face the house and look for a light in her studio that I don't find. "Faith! I'm not leaving until you talk to me. Open a window. Anything. Faith!"

The front door opens and I run up the stairs to find her standing in the doorway, behind the screen. I reach for it, but it's locked. "Open the door sweetheart."

"I need you to leave."

"I'm not going to leave. I need to touch you again, Faith. I need to kiss you."

"You will never touch me again. Leave or I'll call the police."

"Nothing your uncle told you about me is the truth."

"Nathan Marks isn't your father?"

"He is, but it's complicated. I'll explain everything. Let me come in."

"No. You're still you. You still affect me and that just makes me angry. I am not as stupid as you made me. And I'm not ever going to be stupid again. *Leave,* Nick." She shuts the door.

I press my hands to the door frame, and lower my chin. "Damn it." I sit down next to the door. Eventually she will figure out that I'm not leaving.

Fifteen minutes later, it's clear that she gets that point when a police car pulls into the driveway.

I stand up and walk to meet the officer, and after some smooth talking, I get in my car and drive to my rental house down the road. I don't dry off. I walk in the door, skip the lights, and head to the huge brown leather chair in the living room, where I sit down to think through what comes next.

Because I'm still not leaving. Because *I have* to touch her again. *I have* to hold her close to me in *our bed.* I have to put that ring on her finger and call her my wife. And I want to watch her paint every day for the rest of my life. I need to think. I can figure this out. I know I can figure this out.

Time ticks by: seconds, minutes, an hour. I've been in this damn chair *an hour* with no good plan when my cellphone rings. Hoping like hell it's Faith, I yank it from my soaking wet pocket to find Abel's number. "The autopsy report," he says immediately.

I sit up straight. "Tell me."

"It's not logged yet, but my insider says it's being sent to the DA. It wouldn't be sent to the DA if they didn't come to the same conclusion we did."

"My father was murdered. I need to call Beck."

I end the connection and knowing I can't get close to Faith right now, I auto-dial Beck, with one thing in mind. Making sure Faith is not next.

Chapter Forty-One

Faith

I wake Saturday morning with the same thought I fell asleep thinking, and the same thing I'm thinking now standing at the kitchen island: I can't believe I called the police on Nick. Just seeing him made me weak in the knees, and he stood in the rain for me. I wanted to believe that meant we had something real, but he lied to me. Over and over, he lied to me. That is not the kind of "real" I want in my life. But Lord help me, I wanted to open the door and feel him, taste him one last time.

The sound of rain pattering on the windows sends a chill down my spine as I walk to the bedroom to pull a V-neck black sweater over my black tank that I'm wearing with black jeans. Apparently, I'm back in funeral mode. The doorbell rings and I race down the hallway and inhale on a rush of nerves before reaching for the door. I open it to find Bill standing there in khakis and a button down, a jacket over the top that has rain droplets all over it.

"Come in," I say, backing up, but he shrugs out of his jacket and leaves it on the porch rail.

He joins me inside and I motion toward the kitchen, hurrying that way. He shuts the door and follows, his footsteps heavy behind me. I round the island and he claims the spot across from me, and his tall frame and broad shoulders, paired with his blue eyes, which are so like my father's that it hurts my already broken heart.

"Coffee?"

"I'd love some, but you stay where you are. I can see your supplies here. I'll mix me up a cup." He rounds the island and I have this odd sense of claustrophobia, but maybe it's not odd. I have spent a lot of years distrusting him, hating him. That won't go away overnight.

It's not long and we are sitting on stools across from each other. "What have you done about Nick?"

"I left him."

"What about the winery?"

"It's mine," I say. "It's handled." But as I assure him of this, I realize I've not thought about this at all myself. Nick doesn't own the winery, but maybe he just did that to seem honorable and planned to convince me to sell?

"Really?" Bill says, pulling me back into the moment. "It was that easy?"

"Yes. It's handled."

"Well, I don't know how you managed that, but I'm damn glad. I'm concerned about his connections on this mercury though. I have some people looking into it." He gives me a level stare. "It's okay to want to focus on your art and just sell. You know that, right?"

"I don't want to sell," I say, making that decision as I speak the words. This place is stability for me. I need it, but what I say to him is also true. "I will protect this place, just like my father wanted to protect it. And I have a good team. I'm okay."

"Are you sure? Because I could buy it and protect it for you. And heck, I'll do some improvements and get a tax write off."

He says it so lightheartedly that it feels innocent, but I don't know. He does like money and he too might find a hundred million dollars appealing. "I'm not selling. More now than ever, I know that's the right decision." A thought hits me. "You know, you sent me that Vegas photo with a note."

"I just wanted you to know that yes, your father did some things with, and for, your mother that went against his grain, but he loved her deeply. And she loved him, too. She just had issues. And as much as I hated to see him hurt, I often thought that few people love like he loved." He knocks on the counter. "I forgot a meeting I have this morning, but I wanted to see you. I am going to leave you to enjoy your Saturday on your own. If you need me, I'm here. I'll show myself out." I stare at his spot for several moments, remembering a conversation with my father. It had been just him and me at the kitchen table:

"I want to go to Vegas for my twenty-first birthday and I want you to come," I'd said.

"Honey, I hate that place. I went once when I was twenty-five and bad stuff we won't talk about happened. It's bad luck. I won't go back. Ever."

"But Mom loves Vegas."

"Yeah," he'd said tightly. "I know."

He'd gotten up and given me his back as he walked to the sink.

I grab my cellphone and tab through the photos Bill sent

me and there is only one of my mother and my father, and that's the Vegas shot. I study it now, and I can't be sure that's my father and not Bill. Did Bill send me a photo of him and my mother, cheating on my father, as a way to lure me into meeting him?

Nick's words come back to me: *Nothing your uncle told you about me is the truth.* Was Nick telling the truth? I shut my eyes in frustration. He's Nathan Mark's son. That is the absolute truth and Bill told me that truth. I shove a hand through my hair. "Stop, Faith. Stop looking for a reason to forgive Nick." No matter what, I add silently, I remind myself that Nick lied to me. I know he knew that his father was my enemy. So the bottom line is that Nick feels right and good while Bill still feels bad and even a little scary. But Nick is the one whose carved out my heart.

Chapter Forty-Two

Faith

NICK HAUNTS ME THE REST OF THE DAY.

I can't get him out of my head, but I try. I spend most of the day packing up the house even though there really isn't much of what I pack that I want to take with me. I don't go to my studio, but once I've thrown on dressy jeans and a sweater for dinner with Kasey, I am ready early. I walk upstairs and stand in my studio. And I see Nick everywhere. I painted him here. I got naked with him here. I fought with him here. God, I love him. This is gutting me. I need to understand. Maybe then I can move on.

I sit down against the wall and unblock Nick's number on my phone. I sit there, trying to decide if I really want to do this, and the answer is yes. I'm ready now to do this. I dial Nick. "Faith. Sweetheart."

I love his deep, rich voice and I love when he calls me sweetheart. "I need to understand."

"Let me to come to you."

"No. Because when you touch me I forget everything else and don't tell me that's a good thing. It's not. Not right now."

"I need you to look into my eyes and see the truth."

"Please just tell me."

"My father was giving your mother large sums of money. It made no sense. And then he was dead, and he'd never had a heart problem in his life. It didn't add up. I thought your mother killed my father, but then she was dead of the same cause."

"Oh God. You thought I did it and yet you fucked me?"

"I knew you didn't do it as soon as I met you."

"Did you?"

"Yes. I felt it. I didn't want to admit it at first, but I know now that I felt it from the beginning."

"You *thought* I was a killer," I press, still stunned by this news.

"For a hiccup of a moment, Faith. But no more lies. I didn't come to you with good intentions and I damn sure didn't come to you planning to fall in love. But I did. I love you, Faith Winter. So fucking much. Which is why I couldn't tell you."

"Lies are not love," I say, unable to even try and mask the anger and pain in those words.

"If there was a murderer on the loose, I was afraid they'd turn to you. I needed you close. I needed to keep you safe. I knew you'd react like you did this week. I know you. And I don't blame you, but, Faith…I had an autopsy done on my father."

"And?"

"It's being referred to the DA."

"He *was* murdered."

"Yes. Which means so was your mother."

"I don't know how to digest that fact. My mother was *murdered*."

"I know. I feel the same way about my father. I wasn't close to him, but nobody was supposed to take down that bastard but me. And full disclosure. Beck has men watching you. To protect you."

"I'm suddenly comforted by that news. You should have told me. I would have been angry but I would have understood. Finding out how I found out was pretty horrible. It cut me."

"I know. I don't know if I'd do it differently though, Faith. Protecting you was everything in my decisions."

"The mercury?"

"I knew nothing about that until you said something about it. And Beck thinks there's a connection to a man I saw with a flag tattoo that afternoon we went to lunch."

"Flag? There was a flag on the money clip I found."

"Yes. We believe that was his."

"Which means he was at my house." I don't give him time to reply. "Who is he? What is he?"

"Jess Wild is his name and he's ex-CIA."

Alarms go off in my head. "Bill said he hired someone that was ex-CIA to help him with the men who wanted to buy the winery for the mercury. He came here today. He tried to buy the winery."

"As I predicted, he would."

"Do you think he wants to sell it for the mercury?"

"Yes. I do. And sweetheart, he would have a strong claim to inherit if you were dead."

I shiver. "He gave me the creeps today. Are you sure Beck has someone watching me?"

"Yes. He does. And Faith, before we move on. I can prove everything I'm telling you."

"I don't need proof. I should have listened sooner, but you hurt me. You hurt me so badly. There was the club thing and people around me are never what they seem to be. You know this. I thought my heart was going to explode with the idea that you were one of those people."

"I know I hurt you, but if you give me the chance I will spend the rest of my life making it up to you. Let me come over."

The doorbell rings. "Oh God. I'm having dinner with Kasey. He was supposed to call first. I can't cancel. Or maybe I can. No. We were just supposed to bond. I wanted to see how the winery is doing. But I feel nervous now."

"Talk him into ordering in. I'll come over the minute he leaves."

"Yes. Come over."

The doorbell rings again. "I'll text you when I head back here or when he's gone if we stay in."

"Don't have dessert."

His voice is raspy and affected. It affects me. "No dessert," I promise and hang up.

For a moment I stand there, and I can breathe again. The doorbell rings a third time and I hurry across the room and downstairs. I reach the door and peek out of the window. Sure enough, it's Kasey. I open the door and motion him inside. "I thought you were going to call?"

"My cell went dead and I didn't have a charger on me. Are you hungry?"

"I am. Where do you want to go?"

"Freda's?"

"Oh yes. I love that place. What do you think about ordering in so we have more time to talk?"

"That sounds good."

We head to the kitchen and I find Freda's number. Once our

order is placed, Kasey comments on the décor. "I love the place. And don't you have an amazing studio here? I'd love to see it. I watched you grow up. This stuff makes me proud."

"Of course. Come on." I motion him forward and we head up the stairs.

I am the luckiest fucking man on the planet. I hang up from Faith, relieved, and relieved. I'm so damn relieved, and considering I'd been jogging when she called, trying to calm my fucking mind, I head to the shower. I make it fast and dress in the closest pair of jeans I can find and t-shirt from the Art Forum. I open the nightstand drawer and pull out the velvet box there, opening it to display the ring: Classic, round, elegant and one of a kind, just like Faith. The important item, the ring, goes in my pocket. I'm proposing now, tonight.

I've just pulled on my boots when Beck calls. "Listen and listen carefully. I just pulled my man off Faith's house. I had no option. Jess Wild is in play. He's a bad dude and while my men are good, they don't have his skill or nastiness. I can't risk one of them without the other, with this guy. But he's the dangerous one. We have him in our sights. Faith will be fine."

"Jess Wild, meaning, the ex-CIA flag guy?"

"Yes."

I'm already walking toward my car. "Tell me what the hell

you've been working on."

"My CIA pal connected us to the right people. Turns out the agency has had eyes on Jess and Bill for a while now but Jess went off radar several months ago. Jess disappeared after you saw him that day again but we have eyes on him tonight and they want us to detain him."

"Fuck me," I say, climbing into my car and starting the engine. "I don't like how this sounds. I'm going to Faith's house just to be safe."

"And just so you know, there's another player."

"Who?"

"The guy who runs the winery. Kasey. But there is reason to believe he's being blackmailed."

"Holy fuck he's at Faith's house." I back out the drive, and disconnect Beck, dialing Faith. She doesn't answer. "Fuck. Fuck. Fuck." I dial again. And again.

I round the corner and there are flames coming from the direction of Faith's house. Everything goes into slow motion from there. I call 911 and the minute I turn onto Faith's long drive, it's clear the house is engulfed. I end the call and gun my engine, screeching to a halt in front of her house, and out of the door the minute I'm in park. I launch myself forward and up the stairs but I can't get the door to open. I try the code. Still nothing. It's jammed. Wasting no more time, I kick the window over and over, until it cracks. I yank the pieces away, my hands bleeding but I don't care. I enter the house and holy hell the entire downstairs is on fire. "Faith!" I shout. "Faith!"

"Nick! Nick, help! I'm upstairs."

I jump flames left, right, left, covering my mouth as I reach the stairwell that is all but consumed by flames. "Go to the window!" I shout.

"It doesn't open!"

This is not good news and I study the top half of the steps that are not yet engulfed. I don't think. I act. I jump over the flames and grab the railing, launching myself over the top, flames scorching my jeans and my fucking hair and neck. I pat it out, or I hope I do, but keep moving. The minute I see Faith, I breathe out, relieved but I stay focused. "We have to break the window," I say, the sound of sirens lifting in the air.

"I tried," she says, coughing, using one of her smocks to cover her face. "It won't break."

"Call 911 and tell them we're trying to break the glass." I use my shirt to cover my mouth and run into the office and dig around, finding a tool kit, and grabbing a hammer. The flames are now at the door. I find the spot near the tree I know climbs her house and start pounding the glass over and over, harder and harder, and finally it cracks but not enough. And smoke is everywhere, the thick air, challenging my lungs, but I keep moving. I kick the glass again and repeat, and then go at it with the hammer again. Another crack follows. Then another.

Finally, there's a hole.

That's when there is movement and noise outside, shouts lifting in the air. A firefighter sticks his head through the hole I've created. "Stand back!" he shouts and I don't miss how he looks ominously at the flames quickly encroaching on us.

I pull Faith with me to the wall, flames a few feet from us. An axe hits the hole I've created and in a matter of seconds, I have Faith at that window handing her off to a firefighter. I follow immediately, and the minute my feet hit the ground, I grab Faith and we're ushered away from the building. We collapse under another tree, and almost immediately, she's grabbing my face. "You're burned. Nick you're burned. Your hair is scorched."

"I don't care about my hair," I say, pulling her forehead to mine, cupping her head. "God woman. I almost lost you. I can't believe I almost lost you."

"I can't believe you came after me. You could have died."

A paramedic squats beside us, quickly checking our vitals and then focused on me. He bandages my hand and neck. "Your neck needs to be treated at the hospital," the EMT says. "And that hair of yours is going to smell to high heaven. Cut it off."

"It's fine. I'm fine."

The man gives my neck a concerned look. "Really you should—"

Beck appears and squats beside us. "He's fine man. Move on." The EMT gives him a scowl but obeys, standing up and leaving. Beck eyes me. "Did I mention I was on my way here?" He looks at Faith. "I'm Beck. Glad you lived. Sorry your house didn't." He looks at me again. "Kasey, Bill, and Jess are in custody. Kasey and Bill are singing like birds. Jess is not. But the bottom line here per Kasey is that Bill threatened Kasey's sister or so he says. He agreed to set this fire and take a payout a little too quickly for me to buy into that."

"Kasey set the fire?" Faith gasps.

"You didn't know?" I ask.

"He said he had a surprise for me and ran downstairs. He told me to wait in the art studio." The next thing I knew, the place was on fire. I don't know how it didn't get to me sooner. The stairs were on fire from the beginning." She covers her face. "I can't believe this." She drops her hands. "Did he kill my mother?"

"Bill says Nick's father was controlling your mother. He wanted the winery, too, and I assume he knew about the mercury. Per Bill, they both became a problem. Like you did, Faith. And that's all for now. I need to go hand off Jess to those who shall not be named." In typical Beck form, he just stands and leaves, without another word.

I turn to Faith. "Your house—"

"Doesn't matter."

I cup her face. "I can't lose you."

Her lips curve. "Then you won't."

I reach in my pocket and retrieve the ring. "Marry me. Be my wife."

She breathes a heavy breath. "Your hair and skin are scorched and you're proposing?"

"I'd propose if my entire body was scorched. Marry me. The ring is—"

"Gorgeous. Stunning. Huge. I'll need a bodyguard."

"Does that mean you'll marry me?"

"Yes. Yes, I will marry you."

I pull her lips to mine and kiss her, like I might never kiss her again. And I plan to kiss her that way every day for the rest of her life.

Epilogue

Faith

Three months later...

IT'S OUR FIRST MORNING AT OUR NEW APARTMENT, NICK and I sit down at a table on the patio with plates of pancakes in front of us, made of course from a mix, because that's my specialty. I'm still in his t-shirt I slept in last night, while he's in his pajama bottoms and another t-shirt that fits nice and snug across his chest. That snug fit is exactly why I haven't stolen that particular shirt just yet. His hair is loose, longer now again, though he tested out the shorter style for all of about a month. Nick just doesn't do conventional.

He fills our glasses with fresh Mimosas. "How does the new place feel?" he asks.

"Exciting," I say. "I'm dying for the studio to be done next week. I have orders and shows, and painting to do."

His phone buzzes with a text and he glances down at it. "Rita made it down to the winery to help Carrie this morning. Rita says that she is impressed. And we both know that Rita is not easy to impress."

Carrie being Kasey's long time second-in-charge who is now running the winery. "I like Carrie, too," I say. "I always liked her but she was just overshadowed by Kasey. And now that the government came in and claimed the mercury we don't have to fear another problem. I can't believe Bill and Kasey went to jail and so quickly."

"A plea deal works that way but he's still going to be inside a long time while Kasey will be out in a year."

"I still can't believe he was involved. And Jess Wild. We'll never know what happened to him, right?"

"The CIA deal with their own." He changes the subject. "Back to the winery. No regrets over keeping it?"

"No regrets at all. You know how the fire affected me. I gave myself the freedom to live and to let it go."

"But you didn't let it go.

"No. We've made it possible to maintain my father's legacy, while I'm creating my own, at least I hope that I am."

He holds up the card from my father. "Then you're ready for this."

I swallow hard. "Oh."

"No?"

"Yes." I firm my voice. "Yes I am." I stand up and take it from him, walking to a small sofa seat a few feet away. Nick joins me and I slowly peel open the seal and remove the handwritten note. Just seeing my father's script steals my breath. I start reading out loud:

Faith:

If you aren't painting right now, it never really mattered to you. It wasn't your passion. Because when something is your passion, you can't let it go. You can't walk away. The winery was that for me and so was your mother. Both had flaws but it's the imperfection in things that are often perfection. I always assumed that one day I'd tell you how proud I am of you for fighting for what matters to you, for embracing your passion. I just needed it to be the right time. If you're reading this, I never got the chance to pick that time and the moral of the story, is that life is short. It could end tomorrow. All or nothing, Faith.

I love you forever,

Dad

Tears are streaming down my cheeks and Nick is on his knee beside me. I lean forward and press my hand to his cheek. "All or nothing."

He kisses my hand and says, "Let's set the wedding date. We were waiting until things calmed down. That's now."

"Let's elope. Now. Right away. All or nothing."

Nick smiles. "All or nothing. Name the place.

THE END

BUT I HAVE TWO BONUSES FOR YOU IN THIS BOOK, SO KEEP READING!

Have you read Chris and Sara's story yet? Start with book one in the Inside Out series, IF I WERE YOU, which is now in development for film/TV—BIG ANNOUNCEMENT COMING IN THE NEXT 30 DAYS!!

SIGN UP FOR MY NEWSLETTER TO BE THE FIRST TO KNOW!

lisareneejones.com/newsletter-sign-up

And just for a teaser, I've included Chris and Sara's infamous, and oh-so-sexy Window Scene—turn the page to read it!

The Window Scene from *If I Were You*

THE ELEVATOR IS RIGHT OFF OF THE FANCY LOBBY AND past a security booth. Chris punches the button and the doors open immediately. I follow him inside, and watch as he keys in a code. The doors shut and he pulls me hard against him.

My hands settle on his hard chest, inside the line of his jacket, and warmth spreads through me. "What just happened?" His hand brands my hip.

My breasts are heavy, my nipples aching. "I don't know what you mean?"

"Yes. You do. Second thoughts, Sara?"

I scold myself for being so transparent. "Do you want me to have second thoughts?"

"No. What I want is to take you to my apartment and make you come and then do it all over again."

Oh…yes please. "Okay," I whisper, "but I think you should feed me first."

His lips curve into a smile, his eyes dancing with gold specks of pure fire. "Then you can feed me."

The bell dings and the doors begin to open. Chris wastes no time pulling me to the edge of the elevator, and I watch in surprise as a gorgeous living room appears before me, rather than a hallway. Chris has a private elevator and I am entering his private world, a world very unlike my own.

Chris releases my hand, our eyes lock, and I read the silent message in his. Enter by choice, without pressure. On some level I sense that once I enter his apartment, the decision to do so is going to change me. *He* is going to change me in some profound way I cannot begin to comprehend fully. I think he might know this and I wonder why he would be so certain, what is etched with such clarity to him beneath the surface.

He has misplaced doubts of me in this moment, as he'd doubted me at the gallery. I can see it in his eyes, sense it in the air. I refuse to allow his lack of confidence in me, or anyone else's for that matter, to dictate what I can or cannot do ever again. I've been there and I ended up on the sharp edge of a cliff, about to crash and burn. I'd recovered, and I am beginning to see that locking myself in a shell of an existence isn't healing. It's hiding. Regardless of what happens at the gallery, I'm done hiding.

My chin lifts and I cut my gaze from Chris's and exit the elevator.

My heels touch the pale, perfection of glossy hardwood floors and I stop and stare at the breathtaking sight before me. Beyond the expensive leather furniture adorning a sunken living room with a massive fireplace in the left corner is a spectacular sight. There is a ceiling to floor window, a live pictorial of our city, spanning the entire length of the room.

Spellbound, I walk forward, enchanted by the twinkling night lights and the haze surrounding the distant Golden Gate Bridge. I barely remember going down the few steps to the living area, or what the furniture I pass looks like. I drop my purse on the coffee table and stop at the window, resting my hands on the cool surface.

We are above the city, untouchable, in a palace in the sky. How amazing it must be to live here, and wake up to this view every day. Lights twinkling, almost as if they are talking to each other, laughing at me as they creep open a door to the hollow place inside me I've rejected only moments before in the elevator.

I swallow hard as the song 'Broken' from the band Lifehouse fills the room because Chris doesn't know how personal it is to me. *I'm falling apart. I'm falling to pieces, barely hanging on.*

This song, this place with the words, and I am raw and exposed, as if cut and bleeding. Who was I kidding with the refusal to hide anymore? This is why I've hidden. The past begins to pulse to life within me and I am seconds from remembering why I feel this way. I refuse to process the lyrics and shove them aside. I don't want to remember. I can't go there. I squeeze my eyes shut, trying to seal those old wounds, desperate to feel anything but their presence.

Suddenly, Chris is behind me, caressing my jacket from my shoulders. His touch is a welcome sensation and when his arm slides around me, his body framing mine from behind, I am desperate to feel anything but what this song, no doubt aided by the wine, stirs inside me.

I lean into him and hard muscle absorbs me. There is a strength to Chris, a silent confidence I envy, and it calls to the woman in me.

His fingers, those talented, famous fingers, brush my hair away from my nape and his lips press to the delicate area beneath, creating goosebumps on my skin. And still, I barely block out the words to the song, and their meaning to me.

As if he senses my need for more—more something, anything, *just more* - he turns me around to face him and his fingers tangle almost roughly into my hair. The tight pull is sweet, dragging me from other feelings, giving me a new focus.

"I am not the guy you take home to mom and dad, Sara."

369

His mouth is next to mine, his clean male scent all around me. "You need to know that right now. You need to know that won't change."

But the song does change and this time to another track on what must be a Lifehouse CD. 'Nerve damage' begins to play. *I see through your clothes, your nerve damage shows. Trying not to feel...anything that's real.*

I laugh bitterly at the words and Chris pulls back to study me. And I am not blind to what I see in the depths of his green eyes, what I've missed until now, but sensed. He is as damaged as I am. We have too many of the wrong things in common to be more than sex, and the realization is freedom to me.

I curve my fingers on the light stubble of his jaw, the rasp on my skin welcome, and I have no idea why I admit what I have never said out loud. "My mother is dead and I hate my father so don't worry. You're safe from family day and so am I. All I want is here and now, this piece of time. And please save the pillow talk for someone who wants it. Contrary to what you seem to think, I'm no delicate rose."

A stunned look flashes on his face an instant before I press my lips to his. The answering moan I am rewarded with is white-hot fire in my blood that he answers with a deep, sizzling stroke of his tongue. He slants his mouth over mine, deepening the connection, kissing me with a fierceness no other man ever has, but then, Chris is like no other man I've ever known.

His tongue plays wickedly with mine, and I meet him stroke for stroke, arching into him, telling him I am here and present, and I'm going nowhere. In reply to my silent declaration, his hand cups my ass and he pulls me solidly against his erection. Arching into him, I welcome the intimate connection, burn for the moment he will be inside me. My hand presses between us and I stroke the hard line of his shaft.

Chris tears his mouth from mine, pressing me hard against the window, and I know I've threatened his control. Me. Little school teacher Sara McMillan. Our eyes lock, hot flames dancing between us and some unidentifiable challenge.

Some part of me realizes the window behind me is glass, and all things glass can break. He knows this too, it's in the dark glint of his eyes, and he wants me to worry about it. He's pushing me, testing me, trying to get me to break. Because I slid beneath his composure? Because he really believes I am out of my league? And maybe I am, but not tonight. Tonight, as the song has said, I am broken and for the first time perhaps ever, I am not denying the truth of all of my cracks. I am living them.

I lift my chin and let him see my answering rebellion. His fingers curl at the top of my silk blouse and in a sharp pull, material rips and the buttons all the way down pop and clamor in all directions. I gasp, in unfamiliar territory, and burning alive with the ache I have for this man.

He turns me to the window, and my hands flatten on the glass. Wasting no time, Chris unhooks my bra, and it and my blouse, are off my shoulders in moments. He is behind me again, his thick erection fitted snugly to my backside.

"Hands over your head," he orders, pressing my palms to the glass above me, his body shadowing mine. "Stay like that."

My pulse jumps wildly and adrenaline surges. I've been ordered around during sex, but in a clinical, bend over and give me what I want kind of way I tried to convince myself was hot. It wasn't. I hated every second, every instance, and I'd endured it. This is different though, erotic in a way I've never experienced, enticingly full of promise. My body is sensitized, pulsing with arousal. I am hot where Chris is touching me and cold where he isn't.

When he seems satisfied I'll comply with his orders, Chris

slowly caresses a path down my arms, and then up and down my sides, brushing the curves of my breasts. He's in no hurry, but I am. I am literally quivering by the time his hands cover my breasts, welcoming the way he squeezes them roughly, before tugging on my nipples. I gasp with the pinching sensation he repeats over and over, creating waves of pleasure verging on pain, and the music is fading away, and so is the past. *There is pleasure in pain.* The words come back to me, and this time they resonate.

His hands are suddenly gone, and I pant in desperation, trying to pull them back.

Chris captures my hands and forces them back to the glass above me, his breath warm by my ear, his hard body framing mine. "Move them again and I'll stop what I'm doing, no matter how good it might feel."

I quiver inside at the erotic command, surprised again by how enticed I am by this game we are playing. "Just remember," I warn, still panting, still burning for his touch. "Payback is Hell."

His teeth scrape my shoulder. "Looking forward to it, baby," he rasped. "*More than you can possibly know.*"

CHECK OUT THE COMPLETE INSIDE OUT SERIES NOW!

lisareneejones.com/connected-books/inside-out-series

DIRTY MONEY

Don't miss my DIRTY MONEY SERIES featuring the super sexy, alpha SHANE BRANDON! Books one and two, HARD RULES and DAMAGE CONTROL are available now. And book three, BAD DEEDS, is out on August 8, 2017, and book four, END GAME, is out on January 2, 2018.

Check out all the titles here: lisareneejones.com/dirty

ABOUT THE SERIES

Wall Street meets the Sons of Anarchy in HardRules, the smoldering, scorching first novel in the explosively sexy new Dirty Money series from *New York Times* bestselling author Lisa Renee Jones.

How bad do you want it?

The only man within the Brandon empire with a moral compass, Shane Brandon is ready to take his family's business dealings legitimate. His reckless and ruthless brother, Derek wants to keep Brandon Enterprises cemented in lies, deceit, and corruption. But the harder Shane fights to pull the company back into the light, the darker he has to become. Then he meets Emily Stevens, a woman who not only stirs a voracious sexual need in him, but becomes the only thing anchoring him between good and evil.

Emily is consumed by Shane, pushed sexually in ways she never dreamed of, falling deeper into the all-encompassing passion that is this man. She trusts him. He trusts her, but therein lies the danger. Emily has a secret, the very thing that brought her to him in the first place, and that secret could destroy them both.

EXCERPT

His hand curls around mine and he drags it to his knee, and the way he's looking at me, like the rest of the room, no, the rest of the world, doesn't exist, steals my breath. I haven't allowed anyone to really look at me in a very long time.

"Emily," he says, doing whatever he does to turn my name into a sin that seduces rather than destroys me.

"Shane," I manage, but just barely.

"Did you say yes to dinner because you didn't want to be alone?"

I am not sure where he is going with this, if it's about reading me or if he needs validation that I am here for him, so I give him both. "I like being alone," I say, and on some level, it really is true. "I said yes to dinner because you are the one who asked." My lips curve. "Actually you barely asked. You mostly ordered."

"I couldn't let you say no."

"I'm actually really glad you didn't."

"And yet you say you like being alone?"

"It's simple and without complication."

"Spoken like someone who's lived the opposite side of the coin."

"Haven't we all?"

"Who burned you, Emily?"

I blanch but recover with a quick, "Who says anyone burned me?"

"I see it in your eyes."

"Back to my eyes," I say.

"Yes. Back to your eyes."

"Stop looking."

"I can't."

Those two words sizzle, matching the heat in his eyes, and my throat goes dry. "Then stop asking so many questions."

He reaches up, brushing hair behind my ear, his fingers grazing my cheek, and suddenly he is closer, his breath a tease on my cheek, his fingers settling on my jaw. "What if I want to know more about you?"

"What if I don't want to talk?"

"Are you suggesting I shut up and kiss you?"

Yes, I think. Please. But instead I say, "I don't know. I haven't interviewed you as you have me. I know nothing about you. I want to know if you—"

He leans in, and then his lips are on mine, a caress, a tease, that is there and gone, and yet I am rocked to the core, a wave of warmth sliding down my neck and over my breasts. He lingers, his breath fanning my lips, promising another touch I both need and want, as he asks, "You want to know if I what?"

Everything. "Nothing."

Also by
LISA RENEE JONES

THE INSIDE OUT SERIES
If I Were You
Being Me
Revealing Us
*His Secrets**
Rebecca's Lost Journals
*The Master Undone**
*My Hunger**
No In Between
*My Control**
I Belong to You
*All of Me**

THE SECRET LIFE OF AMY BENSEN
Escaping Reality
Infinite Possibilities
Forsaken
*Unbroken**

CARELESS WHISPERS
Denial
Demand
Surrender

DIRTY MONEY
Hard Rules
Damage Control
Bad Deeds (coming August 2017)
End Game (coming January 2018)

WHITE LIES
Provocative
Shameless

*eBook only

About the Author

New York Times and *USA Today* bestselling author Lisa Renee Jones is the author of the highly acclaimed INSIDE OUT series. Suzanne Todd (producer of *Alice in Wonderland)* on the INSIDE OUT series: Lisa has created a beautiful, complicated, and sensual world that is filled with intrigue and suspense. Sara's character is strong, flawed, complex, and sexy - a modern girl we all can identify with.

In addition to the success of Lisa's INSIDE OUT series, she has published many successful titles. The TALL, DARK AND DEADLY series and THE SECRET LIFE OF AMY BENSEN series, both spent several months on a combination of the New York Times and USA Today bestselling lists. Lisa is also the author of the bestselling DIRTY MONEY and WHITE LIES series.

Prior to publishing Lisa owned multi-state staffing agency that was recognized many times by The Austin Business Journal and also praised by the Dallas Women's Magazine. In 1998 Lisa was listed as the #7 growing women owned business in Entrepreneur Magazine.

Lisa loves to hear from her readers. You can reach her at www. lisareneejones.com and she is active on Twitter and Facebook daily.